ROOM FOR IMPROVEMENT

A Billionaire Romantic Comedy

ROYAL RESORTS
BOOK 1

JESSICA GREGORY

Copyright © 2023 by Jessica Gregory

Cover design by Qamber Designs & Media

Cottman Data Services Pty Ltd

All rights reserved.

No part of this book may be reproduced in any form or by any electronic or mechanical means, including information storage and retrieval systems, without written permission from the author, except for the use of brief quotations in a book review.

The characters and events portrayed in this book are fictitious or are used fictitiously. Any similarity to real persons, living or dead, is purely coincidental and not intended by the author.

All brand names and product names used in this book are trademarks, registered trademarks, or trade names of their respective holders. Cottman Data Services Pty Ltd and Jessica Gregory are not associated with any product or vendor in this book.

PROLOGUE

*JFK Airport, New York
Late Monday night*

The British Airways flight from London's Heathrow airport slowly taxied to the stand and came to a gentle stop. Rising from his seat, Bryce carefully packed his laptop and papers.

The passenger who had been seated across the aisle from him stepped out as Bryce opened the door to his private suite. The plane had just landed, but the guy was already on his cell phone. "Of course you can get the matching wallet, honey. What's the point of having a YSL handbag if you don't get the other pieces. I love you. See you soon, sweetheart."

The two men exchanged a brief nod in greeting, before Bryce motioned for the other passenger to go ahead of him, toward the exit.

You're in more of a hurry than me, buddy. I hope the girlfriend and the money both last.

His younger brother Matthew jokingly liked to call these

sorts of guys, *baby millionaires*. Like all newborns, they had bright eyes and were attention seeking.

A pang of jealousy had Bryce forcing a tight smile to his lips. At least the other guy had someone who was waiting for him at home. It had been many years since a friendly female had greeted him as he walked through the front door.

A senior flight attendant tapped Bryce on the arm. "Mister Royal, I've just checked with guest services in the Concorde Suite, and they have advised me your driver will be waiting for you once you have fast tracked through customs. Your VIP personal assistant is already on standby at the gate with your immigration documents ready."

"Thank you."

Bryce would normally have arranged to make use of one of the House of Royal private jets for such a trip, but his father's email had been clear. He was booked on a commercial flight out of London that afternoon and he was to tell no one where he was going. As far as his team in Edinburgh were concerned, their boss had gone back to London to conduct negotiations for a new resort acquisition. Only a small number of trusted House of Royal staff members were aware that Bryce was in fact headed home to the US.

Without the use of one of the company private jets, flying First Class on British Airways was the closest thing to roughing it that a billionaire like Bryce Royal ever got. He breezed through immigration, and his luggage was already being loaded into the trunk of the understated black limousine when he walked through the doors of the VIP lounge a short while later. It had been ten long months since he had last set foot on US soil.

He stopped and sucked in a lungful of air, then slowly let it out. *Calm. Calm.* His stomach was in knots. He'd been summoned home at short notice, but he still had no idea as to what awaited him when he arrived at the Manhattan offices of Royal Resorts. Whatever it was, it had his father rattled.

"Welcome to New York, Mister Royal," said the driver.

Bryce stirred from his faltering attempt to settle his nerves.

"Thank you, it's good to be home."

I just wish this was a personal trip to see family and friends.

The last time he had seen a member of his immediate family was when his brother Jordan had made a brief, unexpected stopover in London on his way home from Europe some six or so months earlier.

Climbing into the back of the limo, Bryce turned on his cellphone, and hit the *Recent* list. He called the number at the top. He wasn't the least bit surprised when it went straight to voicemail.

"Hi Dad, I'm here. Flight was good. I'll email you over some preliminary thoughts on the French and Italian quarterly hotel occupancy numbers." He hung up and ran his hand roughly over his face. "Damn," he muttered, before calling the same number again. "Dad, if you get this message, please call me back tonight."

He has to know I won't get any sleep if I don't know what's going on.

He'd been instructed to keep his travel movements a closely guarded secret. He was not to call any members of the family to let them know he was coming. The only person he was allowed to talk to was Edward Royal. But during the brief call he'd had with the head of Royal Resorts USA earlier that morning, his father had simply told him to keep his mouth shut and get himself onboard the next flight to New York.

His cell beeped and a message appeared.

> Good to hear you. Talk in the morning. Don't unpack.

Something big was going down at Royal Resorts, and Bryce had a horrible feeling he was about to be thrust right into the middle of it.

Maybe I should have had a glass or two of the French red on the flight, it would have taken the edge off my nerves. This not knowing is killing me.

Glancing out the window of the limousine, he caught a final glimpse of the baby millionaire standing on the sidewalk. A long legged, blonde bombshell was wrapped up in his arms, and the guy was grinning from ear to ear.

Bryce Royal existed in a world where wealth and power went far beyond money, yet he envied the other guy. Tomorrow morning, Bryce would be the one waking up alone.

That's if I get any sleep.

CHAPTER ONE

New York City
 East 93rd Street
 Tuesday morning

"Spike. Here kitty, kitty." Vivian Holte leaned out the window, beckoning to her housemate's cat. There were times when having the fire escape located at the front of your apartment was a godsend. Those hot August nights when you just needed to sit outside and try to catch a breeze rather than attempt to sleep in your sweat soaked sheets was one. She'd given up counting the number of times the building's superintendent had sworn he had ordered them a new AC unit. But like the sparkly unicorn she'd been promised on her ninth birthday, the air conditioner was yet to materialize.

At five am, on a chilly October morning, Vivian fervently wished her apartment didn't have any form of balcony, because if it didn't then the gray tabby which belonged to her friend Grace wouldn't be happily sitting outside. The cat slowly blinked at Vivian, taunting her.

"Come on Spike, you precious girl. I have a plane to catch," she pleaded.

Spike sniffed her disinterest at hearing Vivian's predicament. Vivian couldn't blame her. The pampered kitty wasn't the one with travel plans. Nor would she be going into the office to meet with her boss before enduring a hair raising taxi ride to JFK airport, not to mention the joy of the soul-sucking check-in queue. The prize for making it through to the departure gate was a six hour flight to LA, seated in coach while sharing stale air with several hundred other passengers.

No, Spike could sit out here all day long and please herself. The life of a cat was one Vivian envied.

Rising up on her toes, Vivian swung a leg out the open window, ducking her head as she hoisted herself onto the ledge. Her left foot hovered above the wrought iron grate. She didn't want to climb out as it would mean having to climb back in. She had a horrible habit of misjudging the gap between the floor and the bottom of her foot. Falling, and ending up a tangled mess on the carpet wasn't in her morning plans.

Reaching into her jean pocket, Vivian produced her secret weapon. The one which no cat could ever resist. A sachet of adult tender tuna dinner.

She ripped the top open and held out the pack, waving it in Spike's direction. "Look what Vivian has got for you, Spiky girl. Yummy. Come on. Come and eat."

When it came to this princess of a feline, Vivian had learned long ago that all human pride must be set aside, and the cat worshipped as a god.

The window of the room next door slid up and a familiar face appeared. Grace was Spike's human mother. A twenty-five-year-old Black woman who dominated the investment banking scene by day and enjoyed hot and heavy dates on the other side of their shared bedroom wall by night. Grace leaned out, took one look at Vivian's offering, and huffed. "You're not giving her the fancy wet stuff, are you? I told you she was on a diet until she saw the vet at the end of the week."

Vivian glared at her friend. "I am giving her whatever it takes to get her back inside before I have to leave. I'm meant to be at the office in less than an hour. Feel free to come and wrangle your fur baby yourself. That's if you can spare the time."

Grace had had a date last night, and if the noises which had drifted through the wall from her housemate's bedroom had been any sort of indication, it had been a very successful one.

"What about your date? Don't tell me he fled before the sun rose. You have to stop hooking up with vampires."

Grace grinned. "It was fabulous. And it's still going."

A second head now appeared. This one male; and from the look of his dark cloud-like hair which sat in a halo around his ebony face, he was thoroughly sex and sleep messed. Vivian privately envied her friend the hook up.

"Let me get dressed and come in to help you. I am very good with cats," offered Grace's date.

The second he disappeared, Grace shot Vivian another wicked grin. "Believe me, Marlon is a master of pussy."

That remark sent a provocative image of a man burying his face between Vivian's legs straight to her half-awake brain. The sachet of cat food crushed between her fingers, and gravy squirted all over her hand.

I need to get back on the dating scene and soon.

Her housemate's raucous laughter was still ringing in her ears when the door of her bedroom opened. She turned to see Grace's date of last evening enter the room. He was wearing boxers, but they did little to hide his assets.

Oh great. Now what I am supposed to say to him without it coming out as super creepy. Thanks, Grace.

He held his hand out. "Here, let me. I'm Marlon. You must be Vivian."

A relieved Vivian immediately took him up on his offer and climbed carefully back inside. She had just handed Marlon the cat food when a robe clad Grace wandered into the room. Was there nothing more awkward than making polite conversation with the two people who had kept you awake for most of the previous night while they went hard at it in the room next door?

I'm not a prude, I'm just a bit jealous.

Catching a glimpse of her bright red cheeks in the mirror, Vivian died a little.

Grace confiscated the pouch from Marlon. "You'll have to rely on your charm, honey. Spike is not meant to be having any sort of fatty food this week. Knowing her, she's already been out begging the neighbors for secret snacks."

One of the local Italian grocers loved to feed tidbits to Spike when Grace wasn't looking. When it came to food, the cat had no shame.

Vivian's gaze dropped to her suitcase and carry-on back pack. "If it's alright with the two of you, I'll leave you to deal with Spike. I have a flight to catch later this morning, and a billion things to do before then."

"I wish I was getting on a plane. I miss travelling. You meet the best of people on the road," lamented Grace.

The two women had met on the platform of a train station in Denmark some three years earlier and been a firm part of each other's lives ever since.

On her way to the window, Grace stopped and dropped a peck on Vivian's cheek. "Safe travels hon. See you later in the week. Bring me back some of that Californian sun."

"SPF 50 sunscreen says otherwise. You know how quickly my pale skin burns," replied Vivian.

New York in October was actually Vivian's favorite time of the year. The weather was perfect. The heat of the summer was gone, and the horrid tourist crowds had dropped back to their usual level. Her job as a reviewer for a luxury resort and hotel magazine meant travel, but right now, Vivian would much rather be staying in New York and enjoying the last days of Fall than getting on a plane for the West Coast.

Then again there are those cocktails and warm breezes.

When Grace's hand settled on Marlon's firm rounded ass, Vivian took that as her final cue to leave. It didn't take a genius to figure out that the two of them would be heading back to bed, and another round of noisy lovemaking, as soon as Spike had been retrieved.

"I'll see you soon. Oh, and nice to meet you, Marlon."

She hoisted her backpack onto her back and drew up the handle of her rolling suitcase. It was an easy four minute walk from their building to the 96th Street Station, but at the other end there was a painful ten minute trudge to the company offices which were located in Greenwich Village.

Travel light was Vivian's personal mantra, but with changes in weather, and a brand new luxury resort to review, she was stuck with having to take check in baggage this trip. Delicate evening wear had a nasty habit of getting crushed when shoved into a backpack along with a laptop, keyboard, and a power strip. Rolling clothes into a pack looked great on Instagram when you were heading off on a hike into the mountains but in reality, it plain sucked. The last thing she wished to be doing at the end of a long day of cross country traveling was to be steaming the creases out of her clothes.

Vivian headed down the stairs and out into the chill of the New York pre-dawn. She had a long day ahead of her.

CHAPTER TWO

Reaching the offices of Luxury Hotels and Resorts Worldwide in Christopher Street, Greenwich Village, Vivian stopped outside on the sidewalk and took a minute to catch her breath. A lick of sweat slid uncomfortably down her back.

I've got to exercise more. I'm twenty seven and that short walk shouldn't have me huffing like I've climbed Mount Everest.

She lived a half mile from Central Park, so had no valid excuse for not going for a run or a brisk walk every day. Finding the time in her busy daily schedule to stop and put on her trainers was Vivian's current pathetic logic for exercise procrastination. The dark truth was somewhat less glamorous.

Who am I kidding, I'm the problem. I hate all that huffing and puffing.

Trying to keep up with all those lithe runners and power walkers left Vivian with the feeling she was an abject failure. Whenever she measured herself up against the other women of the upper east side, in their two hundred dollar color block leggings, she couldn't help but come up short.

I'll get back into yoga. I promise.

With a six-hour flight plus transfer time to California ahead of her, it was going to be a long, exhausting day. First things first. Her morning ritual had to be observed.

Get to Starbucks and down a Frappuccino.

The bright light of sunrise peeked between the tall glass towers of Lower Manhattan. New York might be a jungle, but nothing made her heart happier than watching the golden glow of the morning as the city stirred to life.

See you Friday NYC. LA here I come.

CHAPTER THREE

Meanwhile in Lower Manhattan

Draining the last drop of his precious morning espresso from its tiny cup, Bryce Royal grabbed his suit jacket and headed for the door of his serviced apartment. He was almost out into the hall when he stopped and quickly dashed back inside. From the dining table he snatched up a small silver bag.

"Disaster narrowly avoided," he whispered.

Inside the bag were gourmet Jamaican coffee beans. Before Bryce had obeyed his father's urgent command to come home, he'd ordered two bags to be brought up to his suite at the Royal Resort in Edinburgh. The coffee in America was improving, but he wasn't taking any chances.

Living in Europe for the past four years, he'd developed a good nose for great coffee beans. New York coffee was nothing like the beautiful espressos they served in Italy. Bryce showed no mercy to anyone who thought that a Caramel

Brulée Latte was a beverage suitable for a fully grown adult to drink. He was an unashamed coffee snob.

By the time he made his way from the Forty Second floor of the glittering tower on Eleventh Avenue, to the offices of Royal Resorts on the Eighty Fifth floor, the sun had just crept above the horizon. The whisper-quiet elevator took him to the executive floor in a matter of seconds. As he stepped out, Bryce stopped and took in the view which the floor to ceiling windows afforded.

A billion dollar view for a billion dollar company.

The city and the Hudson River lay before him. Europe with all its history was superb, but the US and New York in particular would always be home. Nothing on earth could come close to the power and energy of this town. The singer, Frank Sinatra had it right when he'd said he wanted to wake up in a city that doesn't sleep.

"It's good to be home. I just wonder for how long, and under what sort of circumstances," he muttered.

During Bryce's previous trips home to the States, it hadn't occurred to him that he might actually be homesick, but this morning the pangs of missing family and friends were sharp in his chest. The fear of why his father had ordered him home in such a hurry only added to his already frayed nerves.

I wish Dad had called me back last night.

His father's long-time personal assistant greeted Bryce at the door of the executive suite. The immaculately dressed Janice had worked for Edward Royal for as long as Bryce could remember, and from what he understood, many years before that. She had even been a bridesmaid at his parents' wedding.

"Good morning, Janice. How are you this fine day?" he said, dipping into a bow. He would do anything to lighten the dark mood.

Janice gave him a tight smile in return. "It's lovely to see you, young Bryce. We miss you here. I'm sorry you didn't get much notice about this trip."

Young? I'm thirty four. And I'm feeling every day of it this morning.

He bent and brushed the lightest of kisses on her flawlessly powdered cheek. Janice was the epitome of a highly paid Manhattan executive assistant. She arrived at the office each morning in her own chauffer driven town car.

"I miss being here too. It's good to be back. Has my father arrived?"

"Yes. Edward is waiting for you in his office. Is there anything I can get you?"

Bryce slipped her the bag of coffee beans. "If you could find a home for these and perhaps someone in the catering team to make me an espresso, I would be eternally grateful."

She took the bag and placed it on her desk. "Leave it to me. Now let's go and find your father."

He followed Janice across the executive reception area and through the open door of his father's office. Edward Royal, who was standing at the window, turned as his eldest son entered the room.

When his father beamed at him in the only way that a proud father could, Bryce was suddenly transformed back to being a ten year old boy who had just won at Little League. There was something special about the connection that he shared with his dad, one that made him both proud and uncomfortable, for it didn't seem to exist for his two younger siblings. He was his father's first-born son; Edward held onto the traditions which meant that the order of birth of the Royal children still somehow mattered.

Bryce accepted his father's hug.

"So good to see you, son. I'm sorry about the short notice. How was your flight?"

"Fine. I got plenty of work done on the plane, and I'll

catch up on more today. I emailed you those occupancy reports and my review. Let me know when you've had the chance to read them."

"Is there anything else you require, Edward?" asked Janice.

"No, thank you, Janice. I think we have everything. But I would ask for you to please lock off access to this floor for the next hour. I don't want anyone wandering in here and disturbing us."

Janice headed for the door. "Very good. If anyone calls, you are working from home this morning. I will be back in a little while with Bryce's coffee."

As soon as she was gone, Bryce met his father's gaze. "What's with all the cloak and dagger? I haven't even been game to call Mom. What gives?"

"Have you eaten?" asked Edward.

Bryce nodded. He'd enjoyed a leisurely breakfast of a fresh omelet and fruit just after four o'clock. His body was still on UK time, and his troubled mind meant he'd barely slept. Normally he would have gone for a walk or hit the Royal Resorts office gym, but his father had been strict with his instructions that he keep his visit home a tightly held secret.

Royal Resorts was a branch of the House of Royal international luxury conglomerate. The worldwide Royal family company included business dealings in high end travel and leisure, beauty and cosmetics, fashion, watches, and jewelry, as well as selective retailing. While Edward Royal headed up the US operations of Royal Resorts, he also had board oversight of all the other global hotel and resorts in the House of Royal collection. Bryce's father was a powerful and at times intimidating man.

His father gestured to the coffee and plates of food on the office sideboard. "It's the good resort coffee."

Bryce shook his head. "Thank you, no. And while I can't

believe I'm actually saying this, there are more important things concerning me right this minute than a second cup of coffee. So I have to ask, why am I here? You have me worried sick."

His father took a seat on the long leather couch which sat in the open space between his desk and the sideboard. Bryce dropped into one of the matching arm chairs opposite. He unbuttoned his immaculately tailored fine wool jacket, making himself as comfortable as his concern would allow. His father wouldn't summon him home like this unless something was terribly wrong.

Edward sat forward, clasping his hands together. Bryce's breath caught.

Please god, don't let it be an illness in the family.

With the immense wealth at the Royal family's disposal, they could handle most things. But money didn't always buy happiness or health. There were some challenges in life which couldn't be cured, no matter how big the balance in a person's bank account.

Edward cleared his throat. "The Laguna Beach resort is a ruddy disaster. The early reviews are scathing. We are losing money hand over fist. And your brother seems to have just washed his hands of the whole thing entirely. Jordan's not even in California, he's back here in New York hiding away in his apartment. I have the board of Royal Resorts on my back, demanding answers and at the moment I have none to give."

Bryce was ready to weep. No one was dying. On the long flight from London, he'd imagined all manner of disasters which might be waiting for him at home. A poor resort launch hadn't figured in his concerns.

What a relief.

Laguna Beach was the brand new, billion-dollar resort in California. And it was in trouble. He'd heard whispers that things weren't going well on the West Coast but hadn't honestly been too concerned. Resorts were notorious for having false starts. Even for a company such as Royal Resorts, minor teething problems were nothing new. With hard work and application they were usually dealt with quickly.

Bryce wisely kept those thoughts to himself. He was acutely aware as to how important this new resort was to the Royal Resorts brand and just as importantly his father. Edward Royal had long held ambitions for the family company to become the preeminent resort provider in the US. The global brand already held many top rankings in Europe and the Far East, but the American market was where the future growth lay. A major misstep now could see the House of Royal plans falter. Edward would never allow that to happen.

"Has Jordan said anything about what is happening at Laguna Beach?" asked Bryce, suddenly hoping Janice had managed to find someone able to master the coffee beans. His father's words had changed his mind, he was now in desperate need of that second cup of coffee.

Jordan Royal had been tasked with bringing the California resort to life and making it a success. And while the middle Royal brother had made some serious errors of judgement when he was younger, most of which had fortunately ended after he'd had a long stint in rehab, the past few years had seen him rise through the ranks of the company to become one of its most trusted executives. Laguna Beach should have signaled his arrival as a future board member of Royal Resorts.

Edward shook his salt and pepper haired head. " I want this situation dealt with and fast. But in order to do that, I need a full understanding of the magnitude of the problem. I've tried, but I can't get a sensible answer out of Jordan. He is actively avoiding my phone calls, communicating only via email. Your brother is the reason why I sent for you."

Understanding now settled heavily on Bryce's shoulders. Jordan had matured significantly over the past few years, but when he felt under threat, his old bad habits had a tendency to resurface. He resorted to ducking and weaving his way out of a straight answer. *Not to mention ass covering.* Bryce loved his brother, but the truth was Jordan's wild younger years had gifted him with some sharply honed but not admirable skills.

Jordan. You had been doing so well. What on earth could have happened?

"So this is why you've brought me all the way from the UK? I mean I can take a look at the figures, talk to some people, if you like? Maybe even sit Jordan down and pose the hard questions to him. He might be more open if I'm the one asking."

And pigs might fly.

His father righted himself and got to his feet. He paced back and forth in front of the window, his hands resting on his slim hips. The morning light glinted off his gold and silver cufflinks. For a moment Bryce wondered if his own dark brown hair would look the same at that age.

He carries the distinguished English gentleman look so well.

"The Laguna Beach resort is the first of our Platinum Collection properties. It's meant to be our premium brand. The one which sees Royal Resorts feature in the top one hundred global awards for travel and leisure. At the moment that seems an impossibility," sighed Edward.

Bryce bit his bottom lip. He was sorely tempted to mention that one of the resorts he had managed in Italy had been placed at number fifty nine in the previous year's list. Not a mean feat in any one's terms, but he kept it to himself.

This was the US, the biggest leisure market in the world. And the home turf of some of their major rivals in the hotel and resort market. If Royal Resorts could win here, they would be unassailable.

The words of his father's short email received yesterday morning now shone bright in his mind. It had been more than a few bullet points of instruction, it had been a cry for help. Bryce had printed it out and repeatedly studied it during the flight home hoping it might give him a clue.

Come to New York. Urgent. Tell no one where you are going. Can't risk company jet. British Airways 6pm flight booked. Heathrow Airport, Windsor VIP Suite. Concorde VIP service at JFK. Serviced apartment ready for you. Talk tomorrow, Dad.

There were few people within the business that Edward Royal fully trusted, and Bryce was privately proud that he was one of them.

Whatever his father asked of him, he would deliver. "What do you need me to do? As always, I am at your disposal."

Edward's head dropped forward, and his shoulders lifted as he took in a deep breath. When he looked up at Bryce, his face was a study in deep conflict. "I need you to take the jet and go to California and undertake a full investigation. In secret. Find out first-hand how, and why this resort is failing. We have to get it up to being a six star resort and fast. Janice, has you booked in under a false name. I'm really sorry son, but you'll have to leave this morning. The board members held a brief tele-conference last night while you were en route, and they want answers. I am begging you Bryce, get this mess fixed."

His feet had barely touched US soil and he was dog tired, but the job had to be done. Bryce slowly rose from his chair, but a niggle of unease sat heavy in his stomach. If he did this, it would mean going behind his brother's back.

Jordan will be gutted when he finds out. And he will. This is going to cause real damage between us. How do we come back from that?

Things must be dire in California for his father to go to

the extreme length of bringing him all the way back from Edinburgh. A billion dollar asset was on the line. Along with his brother's future in the company if Bryce was reading correctly between the lines.

Please god, don't let what I find in California be the reason for Jordan losing his future at Royal Resorts. He's, my brother. He would see that as an unforgiveable betrayal.

No matter his private reservations, Bryce had a job to do. His father was counting on him. "I'll go back down to the apartment and get my things."

There was a knock at the door, and Janice poked her head inside. "Edward, the car is waiting downstairs. Bryce, I've been to your apartment and repacked your suitcase. It's in the car, ready for when you leave. I put your coffee beans in an airtight container, and they will be waiting for you when you return."

He would bet fifty bucks Janice hadn't done anything about getting him a coffee, rather she had been operating under his father's prearranged instructions and gone straight to Bryce's serviced apartment the moment she left Edward's office.

You don't need to manipulate me like that Dad.

Bryce's brows knitted together. He hated the idea of someone else packing his things. There wasn't anything untoward in his luggage, but he guarded his privacy. He glanced at his father, but Edward's mood was hard to read. Now was not the time to raise the issue of Janice knowing which fragrance of cologne Bryce preferred or that he still carried in his luggage the stuffed pink pig he'd had since a small child.

"Thank you, Janice. Call and let the driver know Bryce will be with him shortly," replied Edward.

If he wasn't so certain that this problem was keeping his father awake at night, Bryce would have suggested he spend a day or two in New York getting acclimatized—as well as undertaking a private attempt to speak to Jordan. The worry lines on Edward's brow told him all he needed to know. This was a major company crisis and it had to be dealt with as a matter of urgency.

He is relying on me. I can't let him down. I just wish he was more open about things.

"Alright I will go, and report back as soon as I can. Depending on how things look when I arrive, I might even be able to give you an update tonight." Bryce took two steps toward the door, then stopped. He was prepared to accommodate his father's demands, but his unease was growing. Pitting son against son like this wasn't something he would have done if he was in his father's position. This had to be said.

"I just want it noted that I am not comfortable with having to lie to Jordan. He isn't a little boy, and if he has screwed up, then I think he needs to understand the depths of his mistake. Give him the opportunity to prove that this was a temporary lapse in judgement. Jordan has his pride. With the right support he will fix the resort. I have faith in him."

Edward shook his head. "I'm sorry if this puts you in a difficult position with your brother. I'm not sure what is wrong with him, but his head is clearly not in the game. I can indulge him so far as a father, but as a major shareholder and board member of the House of Royal, I can't be seen to be giving him special treatment. His coming back to New York leaving the job unfinished in California has put me in an impossible situation. If a senior executive is not up to the task, then he has to go. I will fire anyone who I deem as being incompetent, and that includes family."

Bryce swallowed his objections. His job was clear. Go out to California, see what the devil was going on, and report back. If things were as bad as the expression on his father's face, then Bryce was about to cut the ground out from under his younger brother.

"Jordan is family, but you can't allow that to cloud your judgement or your reading of the situation. If this resort fails, it puts the entire Royal Resorts US operations at risk. That means not just our money, but thousands of people's jobs and livelihoods."

Bryce nodded. His father's message had been received, loud and clear.

I must be fair and impartial. People are going to make decisions based on what I report back to Dad and the board.

He had to hope Jordan didn't try and call him. It wasn't all that often that he did; but since Bryce wasn't a master of the art of lying, if Jordan did reach out, it wouldn't take much for him to figure that his older brother was up to something.

I'm going to have to avoid his calls and ignore his emails for as long as I can.

Bryce would keep pretending he was in London. He didn't want to guess as to how long his flimsy ruse would hold. In the hotel business everyone knew everyone. It wouldn't be long before someone from the Royal Resort Edinburgh let slip that Bryce was supposed to be in London. And if Jordan happened to call the London office, he would quickly discover that no one in the London office knew where Bryce was either. His brother would become more curious. Then he would start asking questions.

When Jordan finds out the truth—that I lied to him—there will be hell to pay.

The Royal brothers valued loyalty above all else. In this case, betrayal even came with a pretty swinging price tag. A failing resort worth a billion dollars. As for their father's trust, that was priceless.

He was going to California. With a five and a half hour flight across country ahead of him, Bryce's day had transformed into another unexpectedly long one. "I had better get going then. I'll talk to you tonight."

His father quickly crossed the floor and wrapped him up in a hug. Unlike their first embrace, Bryce was reluctant to accept this affection. He felt dirty at what he was being tasked to do, going behind his brother's back went against the bonds of family.

Edward's arms held the embrace of not only his love for his eldest son, but also his trust. The unspoken plea that he was relying on Bryce to come through for him.

"When you return, we should organize a family dinner. I will make sure Matthew is back in town. Your mother will like that, and it will put me back in the good books with her."

Matthew Royal, the youngest of Bryce's siblings, was currently in Colorado working on another pending Royal Resort purchase. Over the past few months, Bryce and Matthew had talked at length via Zoom over the proposal to buy a run down, abandoned resort in Aspen. Unlike Jordan, Matthew was more than happy to ask for Bryce's advice.

Releasing Bryce from his embrace, Edward took a step back. He shook his head. "Your mother is annoyed that I am sending you to California without telling anyone that you are back here in the States. She understands my reasoning, but she is still not happy that I have placed you in the middle of this disaster. She is also angry at me for putting you and your brother at possible odds."

Understatement of the year. Thanks for the vote of support, Mom.

Bryce was glad to hear his mother understood the impact that today might have on the family. It could well cause a rift that may never heal.

The sooner he went out to the West Coast, saw the resort for himself, got a first-hand understanding of things, the better. After that he would take the time to sit down with Jordan and try to talk things out. He could only pray that his brother would understand the impossible situation Bryce had been put in by their father.

He dreaded having that conversation with Jordan. Knowing his younger brother, it wouldn't be a sweet little tète-a-tète, more like a knock down, rough as hell bar fight. Patience had never been one of Jordan's virtues. Bryce had a horrible suspicion that his hot headed nature was part of the reason why the California venture was running off the rails. Reformed bad boys still had a tendency to walk away from their problems rather than deal with them.

That has to be the reason.

"I have to go, Dad. Give Mom my love. I'll report back on my findings as soon as I can."

"I will. And thank you."

Bryce headed for the door. California and a billion dollar problem awaited him.

CHAPTER FOUR

JFK Airport
Tuesday 8am

At least it's not the holidays or spring break. The queue could be worse.

Vivian pushed her suitcase forward a half foot, then stopped. The check in line was moving, slowly, but she was making progress.

"I bet Vogue doesn't make their people fly coach," she muttered. She'd seen the movies, the people who worked for the glamorous magazines were always seated in First Class and got use of the business lounges at airports. They were also immaculately dressed and arrived at their destination looking nothing short of fabulous. The food stain on the front of her hoodie had only caught her eye a few minutes ago. No one would ever have her marked as a reviewer for a glossy travel magazine.

Hollywood had its idea of how magazine reviewers and contributors dressed and travelled. It was a pity that the truth was a lot less fancy. It was also a good deal more smelly, cramped, and uncomfortable. There were bags and people everywhere in the crowded terminal at JFK.

The man behind her clearly didn't understand the meaning of the word personal space. But if he got any closer, she was going to invoke her citizen's right to bear arms. Her sharp elbow would be moving back at a fast rate, and there would be but a scant apology when she connected with his stomach.

All I want is to offload my suitcase and go find a sweet beverage. And a bagel.

The thought of cream cheese and lox had her stomach rumbling. She could deal with jam-packed airports and cheap flights, but Vivian drew the line at airline food. She didn't need to read all the clickbait posts on social media about how terrible the catering was on planes, or how long the coffee sat in the pots. Years of flying had taught her the undeniable truth.

And whoever thought a piece of plastic cheese and a thin slice of oversalted ham slapped between two hard crusty slices of bread constituted a toasted sandwich should go and hang their head in shame. She could never understand why the inflight menu paid more attention to its weird Spotify playlist and origins of this month's guest chef rather than the actual food it intended to serve the paying customer. A pleasant smile and an accompanying 'no, thank you' was always her response to the flight attendant whenever they stopped the meal trolley at her row.

The line moved forward to the accompanying tune of the shuffle of bags and frustrated sighs from her fellow travellers. Vivian quietly smiled to herself. There was a game she liked to play at the airport. It involved spotting the passenger who was attempting to carry the strangest thing on board a plane with them. This year's current front runner for the gold medal was a lady who not only brought a bread making machine with her, but successfully argued that the TSA permitted such items. After a good deal of to and fro at the check in counter, she won. Vivian had quietly applauded both the audacity and the sheer lunacy of deciding that taking a bread maker on holiday was a good idea.

Her all-time favorite. The G.O.A.T. of all travellers was the guy who talked a major airline into letting him bring a disassembled trampoline into the plane's cabin. This legend wasn't just hauling one of those new round ones either, no, he had gone for the old school rectangular model with the long enclosure poles. Vivian still chuckled recalling the stupefied looks on the faces of the flight crew as the passenger slid the poles along the floor. Then taking his First Class seat, promptly asked for a glass of wine and a charcuterie platter. Vivian hadn't had the opportunity to see what was on the fancy cheese and cold meats plate the gentleman ordered, rather she had kept on heading down to the back of the plane, to her seat in coach.

That was the day when she realized First Class came with more than just early boarding privileges. It wasn't just a better seat, it was a better life.

One day I will have enough money to be able to afford all those things. One day.

By the time she finally made it to the head of the line, Vivian's stomach was rumbling. Its demands for a bagel were becoming louder by the minute. The sooner she could offload her suitcase and get through security, the better. With Starbucks in another terminal, and Vivian not interested in hiking for a hot drink, this morning she would have to go with beverage plan B. A super sweet hazelnut americano.

Vivian pumped her fist as she finally walked away from the check in counter. She was under the weight limit and her scheduled flight was still on time. After the messy and expensive break up with Pete, she was overdue for some good luck.

California here I come. A business trip with no complications.

She was still smiling by the time she made it through security screening and into the air side of the terminal. Her love life might well be a smoldering mess and her personal credit card close to being maxed out, but no one could take this moment of joy away from her.

Vivian Holte, resort reviewer was going on assignment. Tonight she would be resting on magnificent linen in a private room of a brand new billion dollar resort with the gentle waves of the Pacific Ocean singing their lullaby to her as she fell asleep. Flying First Class was one thing, experiencing two whole days of pampered resort luxury was even better. Her smiled widened. *Life's tough.*

CHAPTER FIVE

New York
Hudson Yards, Lower Manhattan

Bryce slid into the soft leather seat of the limousine which was waiting for him downstairs. The driver closed the door, and in less than a minute they were headed into the early morning New York city traffic. It was a six minute trip from the Royal Resorts offices at Hudson Yards to the VIP helipad at West 30th Street. Bryce barely had time to answer three emails from his assistant, before the car had come to a smooth as silk stop. Flipping the case of his iPad closed, Bryce tucked it into his slimline briefcase and as soon as the driver had opened the door, he climbed out.

"The helicopter should have you at Teterboro airport in twenty minutes, Mister Royal. The jet is already on stand by and waiting for your arrival."

"Thank you."

Janice would no doubt have made all the arrangements herself, and in doing so managed to keep everyone in the

New York office in the dark as to who was using the company plane today and where they were going.

After making his way through the gates of the VIP helipad, Bryce was greeted by a neatly dressed attendant in a black suit and tie. "Good morning, sir. If you would please follow me, the pilot is ready for takeoff."

Everything was a rush this morning. New York pace. He had forgotten how fast this city moved. Life in Europe and the UK always had an unhurried start to the day. In London or Edinburgh he would be leisurely finishing his second cup of coffee while quietly tossing up whether to have a third when his scrambled eggs eventually arrived.

The helicopter was humming, its blades chopping through the air as Bryce followed the ramp attendant along the red carpet and boarded. In line with the secrecy of his mission, he wasn't surprised that he was the only passenger. Janice would have made that a firm stipulation when she arranged the booking. His luggage was loaded into the seat behind. Slipping out of his jacket, he put his life vest on then reached for the safety harness, and buckled himself in. The attendant checked Bryce's harness, smiled, then gave him the thumbs up. After a small adjustment to his headset and mouthpiece, he was good to go.

This isn't my first helicopter ride.

As the blue and white Bell helicopter rose over the Hudson River, Bryce indulged in the view. The morning sun glistened on the water. He had just turned to take in the view of the city skyline when his phone rang. Retrieving his cell from his briefcase, he checked the screen. *Jordan* appeared. Bryce let it go to voicemail. If he was still in London as he was meant to be, it would be early afternoon, and he would more than likely be out and about in the city, or in a meeting. He wouldn't be trying to talk over the sound of a helicopter.

He couldn't talk to Jordan. The lie had to hold.

"Sorry buddy, but Dad needs me to do this," he whispered. He put the phone away before his brother's name could taunt him any further. Guilt sat heavy in his heart.

If Jordan did happen to suspect something was amiss, Bryce had a pretty good idea as to whom his brother would call next. Bryce's UK personal assistant, Heather, who was currently based in Edinburgh had been given clear instructions as to what to say if Jordan did happen to ring.

A notification appeared on his cell. His brother had left a message. He was tempted to retrieve it, but the noise volume inside the chopper would make it hard to hear whatever Jordan had to say. Bryce wanted to be in the quiet privacy of the Royal Resorts jet when he listened. If his brother had caught wind of his arrival in New York, he didn't want to be within earshot of anyone else when he listened to the voicemail. The leisure market was a hot bed of gossip and rumors.

"It's a beautiful morning, where are you off to today, sir?" asked the pilot through his headset.

Bryce forced a tight smile to his lips, then replied into the mike. "Yes, it is a magnificent day. Pity I have to leave town. I'm heading to California for a couple of days. San Francisco. I might see if I can squeeze in a trip up to Napa for a spot of wine tasting."

It was a calculated lie, and Bryce had a strong suspicion he would be telling quite a few more tall tales before the day was over.

CHAPTER SIX

Bryce's phone rang twice more before he crossed the tarmac at Teterboro private airport and boarded the Royal Resorts Gulfstream G650er. He didn't answer either of them or bother to check who they were from. There wasn't any point. His gut told him they would both be from Jordan.

Stepping onboard the plane, he was greeted by the male flight attendant. "Good morning, Mister Royal. We will be ready to taxi shortly. Is there anything I can get you once we are in the air?"

Bryce was half way to handing over his jacket when he locked eyes with the attendant. "Patrick? Don't tell me your mother made you get out of bed at some ungodly hour and do this run."

Patrick raised his eyebrows. "Mom and Dad said I needed to earn my keep this year, if I am going to take a break from my studies. Your father said he had the perfect job for me."

Bryce could just imagine Janice and Edward coming up with a plan to make sure her son worked every day that he kept himself out of grad school. Patrick's career path would likely see him work his way up through one of the House of

Royal companies, so it made sense that he got first-hand experience in dealing with billionaires and their travel habits. A million other young people would give their all to get a chance to experience working for someone like Edward Royal. To be privy to some of the House of Royal's business dealings.

I bet his mom stood over him as he signed the NDA.

"A strong coffee would be great, Patrick. Espresso, dash of milk. Please."

"Yes, Mister Royal."

Bryce winced. *Mister Royal?* This was the same Patrick with whom he'd shared a fireside whisky on Christmas morning at the Royal family retreat in Turks and Caicos last year. It was odd to have a friend address him in such a formal manner.

"Did Janice insist that you must call me that?"

Patrick nodded. "Yes, she did, Mister Royal. She was most insistent."

They exchanged a knowing grin, then Patrick took Bryce's jacket and carefully hung it up. "As soon as we level out, I will prepare your beverage, Mister Royal. Your father has said he appreciates my inflight coffee making skills."

Chuckling, Bryce checked his watch. It was a few minutes before ten thirty. He had a long flight ahead of him, but the jet was configured in such a way that he would be able to set his laptop up with a large screen and get some serious work done. This unexpected trip home to the US didn't stop him from having to meet his responsibilities for the European Royal Resorts operations. It just added to his workload.

Settling into his seat and clipping his seatbelt closed, he muted his grin as Patrick ran through the safety demonstration for him. As expected, it was word perfect and smoothly presented. Other jet owners might ignore those sorts of details and demand that the plane leave, but the House of

Royal had strict policies when it came to members of the family adhering to all safety protocols. Everyone knew the adage about there being old billionaires, and reckless billionaires. It was rare to find an old, reckless one.

"Thank you, Patrick. Could you please inform the pilot I am happy for wheels up when he is ready to depart?"

Bryce retrieved his phone from his briefcase and sat it on the table in front of him. He couldn't avoid Jordan's calls forever. But he couldn't talk to him right now. The shit would eventually hit the fan, but before it did, he would simply have to stall for time.

If Jordan had the slightest inkling as to what was going on, at least Bryce would be on the other side of the country when his younger sibling stormed into their father's office and started demanding answers.

But he's avoiding Dad, none of this makes sense.

Most of the time Bryce was honored to be a big brother, but there were other times, like this, when it was a complete pain in the ass.

CHAPTER SEVEN

LAX
Later that afternoon

Vivian hummed 'the wheels on the bus go round and round' as she stood beside the baggage carousel. It was the only way to keep her temper under control. Forty five minutes after landing in LA and she still hadn't caught a glimpse of her black and white checkered suitcase.

She fired off a quick message to her mom.

> Safely arrived in LA, waiting on bags. love u.

If she had the choice, she would love to be able to travel with a bright green and pink trimmed suitcase. Unusual luggage tended to stand out amongst the never ending sea of plain black bags. But while distinctive suitcases might work well at the airport, they looked out of place in the lobbies of expensive hotels and resorts.

The job of a resort reviewer was to be seen but not

remembered. If word got out that one of the reviewers carried a unique suitcase, hotels would soon take note. Which would mean that whenever she checked into a resort, staff would be sent to fawn all over her and Vivian would never be able to write a balanced review again.

Her thoughts of bold luggage evaporated as a cheer went up among the gathering. She leaned forward catching sight of the pile of new cases which had just dropped off the delivery belt and onto the carousel. Vivian took a step back as the masses descended to claim their luggage. When the milling crowd eventually disbursed, she was left with the disappointing discovery that her suitcase was not among the remaining bags.

Damn. I want to get to the resort and grab a shower.

The plane had been clean, but all that time spent sharing the same air as several hundred other people always left her skin with a greasy feel to it. As soon as she checked in to a resort or hotel post flight, she always hit the shower and scrubbed herself clean.

I hope the spa at the Royal Resorts Laguna Beach is top notch. I could do with a mini facial. My poor skin has suffered enough lately. I hope they have some opening specials.

One of the major perks of travel writing was that as a reviewer she often got to test the extra service offerings at the various hotels at which she stayed. Spa treatments were the ultimate bonus. And if there was one place on earth where Vivian felt truly at home, it was lying face down on a massage table, while a professional masseuse used their magic fingers to work out the knots and kinks in her back.

When her finances were in their usual more healthy state, Vivian would top up her travel per diem and really indulge. For this trip she would have to see just how far Lionel's extra two hundred dollars could be stretched. She had a sinking feeling that it wouldn't be all that much.

"Oh finally," she muttered as her suitcase came into view. She had begun to worry that her luggage had missed the flight, and she was going to have to get about in jeans and her stained hoodie.

Relieved, Vivian made her way over to the carousel and scooped up her luggage. Bags safely in hand, she headed for the exit, her destination—the green and black rideshare shuttle bus service which would take her to the LAX, Uber pick up zone.

With another hour of travel down to Laguna Beach still ahead of her, Vivian hoped she would experience a quick and smooth check in when she reached the resort.

Dear god, don't let there be a CPA or financial planning convention at the resort this week. I couldn't handle all those pasty-faced accountants hogging the pool.

Barring long lines of people all wanting itemized expenses and complimentary drink coupons, Vivian's calculations now had her sitting by the pool sipping a cocktail by 6pm PST at the latest.

She could almost taste the first sip of her pink paloma cocktail.

"Mister Royal, we will be landing at John Wayne Airport, in Los Angeles in the next hour."

Bryce glanced up from his laptop. The people who worked for the House of Royal would never be so crass as to simply call it LA. Even NYC was New York City. Edward Royal had a thing about maintaining standards, claiming it set them apart from the mainstream. Bryce secretly thought it was just being anal and pretentious.

"Excellent, thank you Patrick."

An hour, perfect. He had enough time to have a wash and change into resort suitable attire. Arriving fresh to the hotel would mean he would be mentally and physically ready to spot the immediate signs of trouble. A tired guest checking in was only focused on one thing, getting to their room.

Bryce finished the email he'd been working on and hit send. As far as the rest of the Royal Resorts executive team were concerned, he was still in the UK. He was most certainly not in the US let alone anywhere near their troubled Californian resort. The longer he could maintain the façade, the better.

The unopened email from his brother was a concern. How long was Bryce going to be able to stay undercover? The subject line of WHERE ARE YOU? CALL ME was a dead giveaway as to Jordan's current state of mind.

Midafternoon West Coast time, Bryce stepped onto the tarmac of John Wayne Airport. He was dressed in a sandy brown off-the-rack, Canali linen suit. On his feet were the obligatory Gucci loafers. After changing on the plane, he had checked himself in the mirror.

Sorry Dad, but I really liked this suit, and I couldn't be bothered going all the way to see cousin Nico in Milan just to get one tailor made.

A pair of silver framed sunglasses from the Pelle d'estate range, a House of Royal private brand, completed Bryce's California look. He wanted to look like he had money but not appear filthy rich. Millionaire vs. billionaire. Experienced and clever resort staff could tell the difference long before they caught a glimpse of the level of credit card their guest used to check in.

Bryce headed toward the sleek black Mercedes sedan which stood waiting for him.

Patrick hurried alongside. "I trust the car is to your satisfaction, Mister Royal."

"Yes, thank you, Patrick. Nicely understated. Can you make sure I have use of the car for the entire duration of my stay? Hopefully, I will only be here for a few days, but you never know."

"Of course, Mister Royal. The car is yours until you are ready to return it." The young man handed Bryce an envelope and smiled. "Tip money. Mom, I mean Janice said since you had just arrived back in the States you likely wouldn't have many bank notes on you. She asked me to arrange these."

Grateful, Bryce took the money and went to tuck it into the pocket of his pants. Patrick's eyes grew wide with dismay. "Mister Royal, I beg of you, please, don't ruin the line of the linen." He took the money out of the envelope, and patiently waited while Bryce placed it into his own bill fold and then inside the pocket of his jacket. Bryce got a nod of approval for his efforts.

"Will you be taking the jet back to New York tonight?"

Patrick shook his head. "No, Mister Royal. Your father didn't want it returning to town just yet. He was very clear in his instructions that both the jet and the crew remain here in California until you are ready to return to the East Coast."

That was good news. If the Royal Resorts plane was quietly tucked away in a hangar at John Wayne Airport, it would help keep his visit to the Laguna Beach resort a secret. He nodded. "Thank you, Patrick, I appreciate your efforts in making sure that news of this trip remains on a need to know basis. I will see you in a day or two."

He didn't have to say more. If this young man had plans to make a successful career within the House of Royal, his parents would have pressed upon him the first and most important lesson of all. When it came to matters of business, keep your lips shut.

"I will call you if I need anything. In the meantime, find yourself a nice hotel, and go check out the sights."

It went without saying that Patrick couldn't check into the Royal Resort. Bryce had no concerns that with all the other fine establishments which Laguna Beach had to offer a young man, Janice's son would have little trouble finding ways to amuse himself.

"Good luck, Mister Royal."

He bade Patrick goodbye with a cheery word of caution. "Laguna Beach has some great bars, just don't go too hard on the corporate card. Remember your mom is the one who approves them."

With a soft smile on his face Bryce turned and headed toward the hire car. It wasn't all that long ago that he had been a young man with partying on his mind. His role as a senior executive of Royal Resorts had seen those days growing ever smaller in the rear view mirror.

Focus on the job at hand, Bryce.

From now, until the moment he set foot back on board the private jet, he wasn't Bryce Royal, billionaire, he was simply Bryce Jones, another well-dressed guest who was about to check in to the Royal Resorts Laguna Beach for a few days of sun and relaxation.

He would maintain the business traveler façade, but all the while he would be keeping his eyes and ears open, looking for signs of trouble. He had a horrible feeling that if Jordan had indeed let standards slip, it wouldn't take long for the resort's shortcomings to make themselves known.

CHAPTER EIGHT

From behind the steering wheel of his car Bryce snatched glimpses of the front gardens either side of the main road which led into the Royal Resorts Platinum Collection, Laguna Beach. Everything seemed well maintained. The newly laid and painted road immaculate. He made a mental note to come back later and make a closer inspection of the grand sweeping driveway.

After a short drive from the airport he pulled up in front of the entrance a little after 2pm. A valet greeted him and took his car keys. Bryce tipped the valet just the right amount. Not too much that the guy would go talking to his friends about the guest in the designer suit, and not too little that he was branded a cheapskate by the resort team. Word about the big tippers tended to get about quickly. The last thing he wanted was for a small retinue of tip seeking resort staff to be haunting his every step.

Bryce stood with his luggage, watching as his hire car disappeared into the underground parking garage. He turned, expecting to find a luggage valet, ready to assist, but was disappointed to discover there was no one around to help. He was on his own with his bags.

Not a good start. Jeez Jordan, where are your people?

He hauled his own suitcase and bags through the front door of the resort. When he reached the check in desk, Bryce glanced at his watch. His Vacheron Constantin informed him he was a little early. *Perfect.* Here was a golden opportunity to put the resort reception team to the test. Would they let him into his suite, or would they hold fast to the three o'clock rule and make him wait? For the sort of money the resort charged for such a room, they shouldn't so much as blink at his arrival time.

Janice had booked Mister Bryce Jones into a sea view private suite for three nights. Jones was actually his mother's maiden name, and Bryce used it whenever he wished to travel incognito. Jones was the perfect surname. It was easy to remember, but common enough that no one paid it any mind.

The front desk clerk ignored him for a moment. He was making an intent study of his computer screen. He should have at least acknowledged a guest. Bryce's temper spiked, hot. This was not how Royal Resorts operated. *Guests are our lifeblood.*

That refrain was tattooed into his brain. From day one of working in the family business, his father had pressed on all his sons the golden rule, the guest experience was everything.

Make the guest feel special. First impressions, people. Come on, greet me properly.

He cleared his throat, and the clerk finally lifted his head. It took only a second or two for the man's gaze to take in Bryce's expensive suit and the limited designer sunglasses hanging leisurely from the front of his pristine cream linen shirt. Were those dollar signs in the clerk's eyes?

Bryce slid his black credit card across the counter. "I have a booking for three nights. I would like to check into my room now please."

He was following the valet and his luggage to his suite within a matter of minutes.

CHAPTER NINE

Vivian was seated in the back of the Uber when her phone rang. She grabbed it out of the side pocket of her bag, took one look at the name on the screen and quietly swore.

What could Pete possibly want to say to me after every shitty thing he's done?

She blamed curiosity for giving into temptation and answered the call. "What do you want, Pete? Please don't say more money because you have already taken enough. I don't have anything left."

The seductive voice of the man who had smashed her heart to pieces drifted down the line. "Oh come on babe, I thought you would enjoy my parting gift."

His parting gift. I'm the one whose credit card got charged.

She focused her gaze on the floor, not daring to check if the driver was eavesdropping in on the conversation. Of course he was, if she was driving a car and her passenger took a call like this one, she would be listening.

"I can't afford a thousand dollars of dental work, so why would you think I'd be happy to waste my money on a dating app for millionaires? Sorry, the super wealthy," she snapped. The home screen of the app had made it clear that the word millionaire was beneath the kind of people who had no issue with handing over a thousand dollar a year annual subscription fee. Vivian couldn't begin to imagine what having that sort of money would even look like.

Pete's smooth voice transformed into a dirty chuckle. "Aww, Vivian. Honey. I was only trying to help. Guys like me are hard to get over. I'm sure there are plenty of men with nice fat wallets just waiting to find a girl like you."

The word sucker was implied. Vivian sighed. "You do know I can't get the money back. *Asshole*. As soon as you completed the profile information using my name, and agreed to their terms, the contract was binding. And what about the rest of my money, when am I going to see that again?"

Silence hung on the other end of the line, and for the briefest of moments she held out hope that Pete might feel bad enough about what he had done and actually offer to pay her the money back.

"Yeah, the money is all gone, and I'm a bit short on cash at the moment. I sent you the login and password for the dating app. I did you a favor. You should be thanking me. But look at it this way babe, you now have a whole year to find a guy who can give you the money. Though you might have to earn the cash through services..." A rough laugh floated down the line.

"You fucking asshole. Do you have any idea...Pete? Pete?" The bastard had hung up on her.

Breathe. Breathe. He's gone. Next time don't pick up his call. Better still, block his number.

Her fingers moved carefully over the screen. Pete was now blocked from calling her from his cell. Her hand was shaking as she put the phone away.

It's done. You're over him. He is no longer a part of your life.

At least Pete had shown his true colors before their relationship went one step further. Before she gave up her room in the apartment she shared with Grace and actually moved in with him. Grace no doubt would have let Vivian move back in with her, but the humiliation would have been awful.

She turned and glanced out the window. Anything rather than meeting the gaze of the driver, whom she sensed was eager to impart his own words of relationship wisdom. Vivian had received enough of them from Grace and various other well-meaning friends. She didn't need a stranger putting his two cents worth in as well.

The Uber swept down the long winding drive. Green lawns, edged with beautifully trimmed garden beds, spread out on either side. Vivian gently smiled. *Stunning.* If there was one thing that Royal Resorts excelled in above all other resort companies, it was the grand entrance effect. Most of their guests may not be among the super wealthy, but they certainly made them feel like they were, even if it was just for a little while.

Her bank account was in a battered state, along with her heart, but at least she would be sleeping in a luxury resort tonight. Nothing soothed a torn opinion of yourself better than the soft weave of percale sheets.

But first I am going to have a cocktail and then a long walk on the beach.

Thank heavens sampling the resort food and drink was included in her job description. You couldn't wax lyrically about a hotel's wine selection without having first tried it.

While the driver grabbed her suitcase from out of the car's trunk, Vivian sat in the back and carefully touched up her matte lipstick. Remaining in the car was a deliberate act. Only peasants hung around the trunk of a car waiting to retrieve their luggage, and the last thing she wanted to do was to stamp herself as being someone who didn't belong at the Royal Resorts Platinum Collection, Laguna Beach.

"I am officially on the clock. Time to get my business woman in need of a holiday vibe on," she whispered, slipping her Mac lipstick case back into her bag. Two hours out from LA she had changed into a blue and white polka dot blouse, matching it with a black A-line skirt and plain heels.

The door of the car opened, and a uniformed valet bowed his greeting. Vivian swung her legs out in true movie star style and rose to her feet. She gave the little sigh she had perfected from watching the *Devil Wears Prada* too many times. One day she would treat herself to a copy of the black blazer the lead actress wore after her fashion makeover.

"Welcome to the Royal Resorts Platinum Collection, Laguna Beach," announced the valet.

Royal Resorts had clearly moved with the times and dropped the archaic madam and sir routine. Thank heavens. Being called madam or ma'am made her feel old.

"Thank you." Vivian nodded to her luggage. "Just the one case, I'm traveling light."

She'd heard it from someone on a plane as they made their way into First Class last year and the smooth tone of the line had stuck with her ever since. A bubble of excitement bounced in her belly every time she used it.

I'm in LA, the city of faking it until you make it. I may as well play the role of a wealthy resort guest.

She followed the valet through the ornate sandstone entrance and into the airconditioned resort lobby. Her gaze slid left and right as she walked, taking it all in. Only a real tourist would stop to rubberneck at the ceiling, and the Italian marble floor. No, she was far too world weary to do such a tiresome thing. Later she would come back and sneak some photos for the magazine.

She tipped the valet, then joined the surprisingly lengthy queue to check in.

A queue? Not good. I hope it's not a sign of things to come.

From where she stood, she was able to see the front desk. There were three staff bustling about the place, busily processing guests. Her gaze drifted to the two empty computer stations. It was 3.30pm, prime check in time. Every single counter should be staffed at this hour of the day. Even management should be on hand to make sure that every guest only had to wait the bare minimum before being handed their key cards.

A wave of exhaustion washed over her. It might be midafternoon in California, but her body was still on New York time, which meant it was 6.30pm. After an early start followed by a long day of travelling, she was well past the point of being ready to be shown to her room. Her mind was already mentally peeling off her clothes and stepping under a hot shower.

This lack of service was not like her usual experience of Royal Resorts. They prided themselves on a quick and smooth guest experience. A small cross went against the Laguna Beach resort report card.

I don't normally get to mark their book this early. Those rumors about the resort having teething issues might be right.

When she finally made it to the head of the line, Vivian offered her corporate credit card, the plain one which said Lionel Investments Inc on it. Lionel somehow thought it was funny to have his name on all the business cards. Vivian suspected it made him feel important, so she just went along with it. She didn't care either way, as long as it was accepted.

Her own personal card would have sent up a red flag as even the smallest of charges would have smashed through her credit limit. According to her monthly credit card statement, at the current rate she was paying it off, it would be one hundred and nine years before she cleared the debt.

Her thoughts shifted to settle on what was happening in front of her. The clerk who was supposed to be checking Vivian into the resort was busily tapping away at her computer. Then she tapped some more. A crease appeared on the woman's brow.

Vivian's heart sank as the clerk's fingers came to an abrupt halt. From her long experience of dealing with the front desks of hotels and resorts, this was never a good sign.

Please don't let the card have been declined.

Any minute now she would have to call the office and ask that the accounts team made a quick payment. Hopefully someone was working late. If not, she would be put in the embarrassing situation of having to sit in the lobby until the card could be sorted.

The woman finally cleared her throat. "I'm sorry madam, but your room isn't yet ready. I am informed by housekeeping that it may be a thirty minute wait."

Madam. She had obviously missed that bit of training.

Her social *faux pas* was instantly forgiven as she handed Vivian a small card. "Please enjoy a complimentary cocktail in the Sunview Bar while you wait." She motioned in the direction of a nearby doorway.

Vivian smiled and took the card. "Thank you." A short delay was always made better by a free drink. They might have been trying to bribe their way out of trouble, but at least the front desk was making an effort.

She left her luggage with the valet team and headed for the bar.

Not long after he arrived in his suite Bryce dashed off a quick email to his father. The news wasn't encouraging. While the front desk had allowed him to check in early, he suspected it was based purely on the clerk having judged his manner of attire.

The valet who had accompanied him to his room had left without giving Bryce the Royal Resorts personal welcome speech. The young man knew enough to hang around for his tip, but he clearly hadn't been trained in how to show a newly arrived guest the features of their room.

He wondered whether it had been a mistake for him to book a private suite, but if the resort was going to make the global awards, Bryce was well aware that it wouldn't be on the basis of their standard room offerings. Accolades were handed out to those hotels and resorts which stood head and shoulders above the others. The award winners were those that made their high paying guests feel their money had been well spent.

Closing his laptop, Bryce placed it and all his papers into his suitcase and locked it. If housekeeping happened to visit his room while he was out, he didn't want them finding evidence of who he really was or what he was doing at the resort.

There was one more new email from Jordan in his inbox, but Bryce didn't open it. The longer he left things, the less he would have to lie about his whereabouts.

Dad, do you have any idea of the predicament you have placed me in?

When he did finally speak to his brother, he wanted it to be after he'd gained a full understanding of how things at

Laguna Beach were going. His experience so far wasn't setting his world on fire.

He was still operating on the eastern time zone, and since it was now well past five o'clock in New York, a drink was in order. Grabbing his room keycard, Bryce headed out, making a beeline for the bar.

Let's see what the catering team has in store for Mister Jones. It had better be outstanding.

CHAPTER TEN

The bartender had been heavy handed with the ice. Vivian's complimentary cocktail was nothing short of a soggy mess. Summer sangria was meant to be a refreshing mix of fruit, wine, vodka, sprite, with a sprig of mint. The ice was the finishing touch, not the bed on which the whole drink rested and then died.

At least it's not going on my room tab.

Paying twenty five bucks a glass as it was listed on the bar's menu would have left her furious. Resorts were notorious for their over inflated prices, but that was because the drinks were supposed to be fabulous.

This icy sludge is a far cry from fabulous. Watery and weary.

She tapped her hand lightly on surface of the table in front of her. There was something not quite right about the place, but unlike the top of the table, she couldn't quite put her finger on it. The Sunview Bar definitely lacked the feel of a welcoming and vibrant drinking spot.

This place should be pumping, not giving off the silent vibes of the reading rooms in the New York Public Library. Where are all the other guests?

It was heading into the late afternoon, and the room was almost empty. A couple of suited businessmen hanging out closer to the bar were onto what Vivian guessed was their third bottle of a liquid lunch. A honeymoon couple was sitting out on the balcony staring lovingly into one another's eyes. Apart from those guests, the place was bare.

She sipped a little more of her drink, then deciding it was a lost cause, set it aside and rose from the table. Hopefully things would pick up later when people started to arrive for evening drinks. With luck by then, the barman might have found his game and eased off on the ice.

Right now I don't particularly care. I just want to get my room card and then have a long hot shower.

On her way out to reception, Vivian passed another guest who was heading into the bar. It was a tall, dark haired man in a stone colored suit with contrasting cream linen shirt. Clearly wealthy if the cut of his jacket and the expensive watch on his wrist were any indication. She recognized the private brand of the understated sunglasses which sat on his face. Her well-trained reviewer eye picked up those small but important details in an instant.

He gave her a cheerful smile in greeting, and Vivian caught her own reflection in his sunglasses as she smiled back. Hers however was a tighter grin, courtesy of her jet-lagged state and disappointing cocktail. She could only hope his first drink was more of a success.

Give it twenty minutes buddy and one lifeless drink. You might be heading out of here without that sexy, happy grin. What a shame.

They passed within a few feet of each other, and from the sound of his footsteps the other guest kept on walking. Vivian's own pace however slowed. She could blame it on the impeccably cut suit, as she turned to take one more look at the stranger. That particular shade of fabric wouldn't work on most other men, but then again, his ass did fit his pants to perfection.

Well-cut designer wear. Nice. Ooh, and super expensive shoes.

Vivian indulged her appreciative gaze before taking in a slow deep breath. Oh yes, he was a fine male specimen. Everything was handsomely put together. Even the way he walked spoke of calm confidence. And she could admit to being a sucker for a pair of designer sun glasses.

The object of her close study stopped to look out the window toward the sea. He must have been enjoying the view, as the smile was still on his face.

When was the last time she had stopped and really ogled a guy? Vivian couldn't remember. Her tongue found its way to her lips, brushing gently over them. If her first drink hadn't been such a disappointment, she might have been tempted to linger in the Sunview Bar, perhaps even strike up a conversation with the newcomer. She was single, and there was nothing to stop her talking to a stranger and sharing a laugh or two over a cocktail.

Vivian let out a long slow breath. A pulse gently throbbed between her legs as a hunger awakened.

God, I hope my room is ready.

She was in sudden need of some private alone time with her battery operated friend and some lube. Two showers might well be in order. One steamy, the other stone cold.

CHAPTER ELEVEN

Talk about the land of the dead. There was barely anyone in the bar. Bryce shuddered to think how the sales receipts for the day would look. *Dismal.* On his way in he'd passed a young woman on her way out of the bar. He'd been tempted to turn and give her long brown hair, and that tight black skirt which hugged her hips a second look, but the dearth of customers in the Sunview Bar had caught his immediate attention.

Glancing around the near empty room, Bryce spied a half finished drink on a nearby table. He quickly put two and two together. The woman in the polka dot blouse had clearly decided her expensive cocktail wasn't worth finishing.

Little wonder she barely managed a polite smile in response to mine.

After checking the sea view, he ordered a drink and took a seat in a booth. For the next hour, Bryce sat and watched the door. During that time only a handful of people wandered in. Most stayed for one drink, then left. The Laguna Beach resort was a brand new luxury resort. It should have been packed with people eager to test its offerings. His father's concerns about this major company investment were fast becoming his own.

Jordan, I think you've missed something in doing a soft opening. Do people even know about this place? Or if they do, are they actively avoiding it?

The big formal public launch scheduled for early December had better set this town on its ear or they were in serious trouble. A resort hemorrhaging cash could pose a real risk to Edward's US expansion plans.

Bryce finished his glass of Australian shiraz and headed back to the bar. It was time to put the barman to the test.

"A gin and tonic please."

The barman blinked slowly, then set about making the requested drink. The last of Bryce's faint hopes that the bar might hold the secret to the resort's success died. He wasn't much of a gin and tonic drinker, but it was one of the best ways he knew how to test the merits of a bartender. You didn't judge a guest by their choice of food or drink. A blink or a raised eyebrow was enough to tell him that the man didn't approve of his choice of spirits.

It's not your role to pass judgement buddy, you should be more concerned with making me, a paying guest, feel welcome while at the same time creating an excellent drink. One which I will enjoy so much that I will come back for another. And tip you generously.

Damn. All the things that should have presented the Royal Resorts brand in its finest light were sadly lacking. Grabbing his drink, Bryce headed out to the balcony. His father's dreams of winning an award for this resort were a long way from coming true.

"Bryce?"

At the mention of his name, he stopped mid stride. His gaze landed on a former team member from one of the Spanish resorts. As the man moved forward, Bryce briefly shook his head. *Not here.*

He let out a sigh of relief as the man turned on his heel and retreated back into the kitchen. Bryce set his untouched drink down on a nearby table and quickly left the bar.

Back in his room, he waited. It wasn't long before there was a knock at the door. Tony had obviously found his old boss among the new guest check-ins and noted the number of Bryce's suite.

"Bryce, it's good to see you. I'm sorry if I caused any problems in the bar. I was just a little taken aback to see you. I thought this was Jordan's gig."

Bryce stepped forward and offered his hand. "No damage done, Tony. There wasn't anyone in the bar to see me. Which to be honest is a real worry."

Tony nodded. "Are you here to check things out while Jordan is back in New York? If you are then I have to say that's a huge worry off my mind. This place is not getting off to a good start."

He refused to give voice to the truth that he was betraying his brother. Bryce decided a little white lie would be the lesser of two evils. "I hadn't realized Jordan was home on the East Coast until after I had checked in. Talk about the two of us having poor timing. I just happen to be passing through LA, so I thought it would be a good idea to come and see the place."

His fingers settled nervously on the back of his neck. He'd worked with Tony long enough to sense that he wasn't buying the bullshit story for one single minute. "Look. I can't really discuss anything, but I'd appreciate it if you didn't use my name around the resort. I need to receive a proper guest experience if you get my meaning."

Tony had been in charge of a large catering team at the Royal Resort in Barcelona, so if anyone had a good inkling of what Bryce was asking for, it was him.

"Of course. If there is anything I can help you with, you only have to ask."

His father had sent him out to California, leaving him with no real time to review who was on the staff roster at Laguna Beach. Without knowing the team list or where loyalties might currently reside, Bryce feared he'd made a major misstep.

"What role are you performing here, Tony?"

Please don't call Jordan. If you do, he'll be on the first plane out of New York. If there is any chance of my brother forgiving me for this, he has to hear the truth of my deception from me.

"I'm actually in charge of the food and beverage teams. I hadn't planned to be working this job at all. I was going to take some time off now that I'm back in the States, but your brother Matthew gave the resort manager my phone number. He called and begged me to come on board until they could find a permanent head."

Matthew knows this place has issues. Why am I just finding out?

They had opened the resort without a proper team in place. Things were going from bad to worse. He was certain his father was not aware of this, and when he did find out, Edward would hit the roof.

"When you say resort manager don't you mean Jordan?"

Tony shook his head. "No, Jordan put a manager in place six weeks before we were due to open. He was supposed to be the assistant manager, but Austin has basically been in charge since then. I don't where he came from, and while I would say he's not entirely clueless, it's pretty clear he's in well over his head."

Who the devil is Austin? And what has Jordan been doing all this this time?

"What happened with the original head of catering?"

"Apparently Jordan insulted the guy's partner, who was

head of special events or something. From what I heard, they both quit on the spot."

That explains the soft opening and lack of vibe about the place. Does anyone even know about the resort?

Bryce's heart began to race. Adrenaline pumping through his body at an unhealthy rate. If what Tony was saying was true, Jordan had put some unknown guy in charge and then walked away from overseeing the launch of a billion dollar resort.

Bryce had dealt with resort disasters before. He wasn't ever going to forget the night he'd had to manage the evacuation of a hotel full of guests in the face of a fast approaching hurricane.

Slow down your breathing and take stock. It's just a shitshow, no one is in danger. Lives are not at stake.

Something had to have happened for his brother to suddenly up and leave the resort in such a poorly managed state. In the five years since Jordan had got clean and sober, he'd never once let the family down in such an obvious way.

I almost wish you would get on a plane and come back to California, then I could talk to you. Man to man, without Dad interfering.

Bryce let out a slow, calming breath. It didn't pay to appear too frazzled in front of the staff. That's how wildfire rumors started. And when the gossip got traction, people had a nasty tendency to call in sick or simply quit.

Tony knows I am worried, the guy's not an idiot.

"Thanks Tony. Let me get a better idea as to how things really are around here. I might look to catch up with you again if I have any further questions. When are you next back on shift?"

"Tomorrow afternoon, unfortunately. After having worked the past thirty days straight, I was meant to be finally taking a day off. But since we are so short on staff, and there is a lunchtime BBQ and buffet for a wedding party, I'm going to be overseeing the poolside team instead of catching up on my sleep. The catering team is very green, and so I fully expect to be hands on with the cooking."

Bryce finally let his hand drop, his neck was starting to ache. "I will find you. And I think you might be right about the quality of the staff. The bartender in the Sunview Bar just silently judged me for ordering a gin and tonic."

Tony winced.

After Tony left, Bryce paced the room for a time. He needed to burn off some nervous energy. His initial thoughts had been that Edward was overreacting to the resort's teething problems, but if Jordan had put some unknown manager in charge, and even a seasoned operator like Tony was voicing his concerns, then things didn't look good.

He flipped open his laptop and logged into the company employee database. It might have been a long day, and he was in dire need of food, but before he ventured out again, he wanted to find out as much as he could about this Austin guy. Bryce Royal didn't base his decisions on rumors and opinions, he worked with hard indisputable facts.

It was close to eight by the time Bryce finally closed his computer. He had spent long hours checking the personnel records of several dozen Royal Resorts Laguna Beach employees, all of them Jordan's hires. He knew as much of Austin Brown's life story as the man's own mother probably did.

Austin's record in the resort business was reassuringly solid, but in Bryce's opinion he was nowhere near ready to head up a three hundred bed luxury resort. Jordan had left a major Royal Resorts company investment in the hands of a young buck, only a couple of years out of grad school. Little wonder things were looking more than a bit shaky.

He picked up his phone. His father answered on the second ring. "How bad?"

Bryce's teeth grazed his bottom lip. *Just spit it out.* Having to deliver this first report on Jordan's failing project was making his gut churn.

"I'll need a few more days Dad, but my impression is that your star quarterback might have just thrown a hospital pass to the team's receiver."

"Hmm. I'm not entirely sure I understood what you just said, could you perhaps rephrase it, but in the King's English?"

Edward Royal might have lived in the US for the past thirty odd years, but he had never taken to American football, preferring the English Premier League to the NFL. He was a die-hard Chelsea FC fan. Only the foolhardy dared to call the world game 'soccer' to Edward's face.

"Earlier this evening I ran into another team member, Tony, who used to work for me in Spain. We had a private chat during which he mentioned that Jordan had hired an assistant manager, but instead of taking him under his wing, he effectively left this new employee to run the place."

"Bloody hell." Edward's polished English accent couldn't hide his annoyance. There was a moment of silence, and Bryce could only guess what his father was thinking. None of it would be good news for Jordan. Fatherly love aside, Edward expected the same from his sons as he did any other executive. Mistakes were eventually forgiven. Deliberate dereliction of duty was not.

"This is what I want you to do for me, Bryce. Stay for as long as you need to in California. Use the resort like a full paying guest. Swim in the pool. Eat breakfast in the café. Order room service. All the works. In the meantime, I will keep going through the operational and financial reports. If I am going to tear your brother a new ass, I want to have plenty of ammunition on hand when I do it. Can the chap you spoke to be relied upon to keep quiet about who you are?"

"I think so," Bryce answered, with both eyes tightly shut

as he took in his father's threat to inflict bodily harm on the middle Royal son.

Jordan. I'm doing my best, but you haven't given me much that I can defend you with.

"Tony isn't a fool, and he knows if anything gets back to New York, he'll be the first person we would suspect. He's not going to risk his career to help Jordan." Bryce thought for a moment, carefully considering his next words. He hated having to ask, but he had to know. "Speaking of Jordan, has he reappeared at the offices yet? Have you spoken to him? He's sent me several emails, and I have been dodging his calls all day. I shouldn't have to hide from my own brother."

For another long minute, silence sat heavy on the other end of the line. Finally, Edward let out a tired sigh. "I know, and I am sorry, son. I promise I will make it up to you when you get back to New York." Bryce caught the sound of his mother's voice in the background. Alice Royal didn't approve of late night business calls. If she knew it was her eldest son on the line, she would be yanking the phone out of her husband's hand.

"I'd better let you go, Dad."

"Thanks. I have meetings in the morning from seven o'clock. Call me tomorrow, when you have time for an update. Good night, Bryce. And thank you. I love you."

"I love you too, Dad."

His mother's voice became louder. "Is that Bryce?"

The line went dead. Bryce winced. He had no doubt that right this minute Alice would be giving Edward a hard time about not allowing her to speak to their son.

He fired off a quick text.

> Sorry Mom. Had to go. Catch up soon. Love you. B.

Bryce pushed back from the table and got to his feet. He

was tired, but at that stupid point of almost being over tired. He had traveled across the Atlantic, snatched a few hours' sleep, then come all the way out to LA. He glanced at the bed and gave a brief shake of his head.

If he went to bed now, he was certain he wouldn't be able to sleep. Hours of tossing and turning would likely follow.

His father had said he needed to use the resort facilities to their fullest. Bryce couldn't get to the day spa at this hour, which left no other option. It was time to go and sweat out some of his frustration in the twenty four hour gym. After that, he would see how the restaurants were doing, and for his brother's sake, hopefully find them busy with happy, paying customers.

After returning to reception from the bar and her disappointing cocktail, it was another long and testing forty minutes before Vivian was finally able to strip off her clothes and hop into the shower. The valet who had delivered her luggage had given her a quick run-down of the room, including how to use the TV remote, but he could only offer up a blank look when she enquired about the dining options for the evening. She tipped him and let him go.

It seemed that whoever was in charge of training the staff was only getting through to a certain number of them. The service levels were patchy at best. Nowhere near the standard that a resort such as the Royal Resorts Platinum Collection, Laguna Beach, should be delivering to its guests.

After drying off and brushing her hair, Vivian picked up the remote. She was pleased to see they had at least managed to get her name on the welcome screen.

The online menu of offerings for guests was impressive.

She had to hand it to them, any hotel that offered a near round the clock room service knew its market. A quick check of the spa menu had her opening her laptop and googling *myofascial release therapy*.

"Impressive. That's more than most resorts offer."

But her heart was set on a pedicure, she clicked on the link and searched for available time slots. *Damn*. They were fully booked for tomorrow, and she would have to call to be placed on a wait list.

"Oh, well. Let's see if we can find somewhere good to eat for tonight."

The first night in a resort was always an odd experience. She would seek a nice dinner, maybe have a glass or two of wine, then make it an early night. Tomorrow would be a big day, she would have to be up with the sun and putting the resort through its paces. Taking magazine worthy photos on the sly involved a particular skill set, and she was keen to be able to send plenty of good shots for her boss to have his pick for the next issue.

From her suitcase she took out a green cotton dress dotted with tiny white flowers. It was super girly, and Vivian loved it. The green went perfectly with her blue-green eyes. If one frock in her whole wardrobe spoke of long walks on the beach and soft kisses, it was her fifteen dollar JC Penney bargain. She could still recall the moment her mother had spotted it during the sales at the department store near their family home in Queens. Vivian snapped off a quick selfie and sent it to her mom.

She slipped her feet into the only summer sandals she owned. A tan low-heeled cross-strapped pair that went with every outfit. They made packing for review trips an effortless affair.

Her long light brown hair was held off her face by a thin silver hair clip. Simple little touches like this helped to turn her look from every day to evening stylish. A matching clutch purse was big enough to hold her cell and room key card.

It was time to go out and do some people watching. Her job tonight: observe how the bar and dinner service went, while keeping a keen eye on the other guests. People might not say what they thought of their meals or the wait staff, but few could keep their faces from telling the true story. Vivian loved to read people.

CHAPTER TWELVE

Supper in the main dining room was an uneventful and uninspiring event. Vivian could have counted the guests seated at the nearby tables on one hand. In the end she put it down to her six thirty booking being a little too early. She hated eating late.

If there was one thing she could never get her head around, it was people who thought it perfectly acceptable to eat their evening meal at nine o'clock. Most nights, especially post-Pete breakup, Vivian was already in her PJs and reading in bed or else lying on the couch mindlessly scrolling through Netflix's menu at that hour of the night. If she did eat at such a late hour, it was usually a salty snack from the kitchen cupboards.

Her forty dollar pasta had been nice, but nothing to write home about. The twenty dollar sticky toffee pudding fortunately lived up to its hype, and she was still running her finger around the inside of the bowl when the waiter came to clear it away.

Her plans for tomorrow included joining one of the mid-morning get-to-know-the-resort tours of the grounds. Vivian had always found them to be a great way to get her bearings. And to snap off loads of pictures.

If Lionel wants pics, he will have them.

Later she planned to indulge in a few hours lazing beside one of the sparkling pools while soaking up the sun. A well balanced review took creative time.

Hopefully the staff at the pool knew how to make better cocktails than the bartender in the Sunview bar. If they did, then one or two icy Laguna Beach Sunset cocktails would be downed in order to aid Vivian's muse.

By midafternoon she'd be ready to head back to her room, to knuckle down and write the first draft of her resort review. That would give her time to enjoy the resort over the next day or two, add some sparkle and polish to the final article, before emailing it to Lionel before she stepped onto the plane bound for home on Friday.

But all of that was for tomorrow. *What about tonight?* Vivian considered her next move for the evening. Bar, bed, or beach?

Her hand settled over her belly. Pasta and dessert had filled every corner of her stomach, leaving her feeling a little uncomfortable.

I need to haul my lazy ass down to the beach. A good walk and some fresh air, and then I might find it a bit easier to sleep.

She signed for her room charge, adding a generous tip. The friendly and efficient restaurant staff seemed to have the hang of things. Why the rest of the resort services seemed to run so hot and cold in their delivery she couldn't understand.

After making her way out of the restaurant and past the pool, Vivian started down the short set of steps which led to the beach path. There were a few other guests making their way toward the small private beach cove.

The evening sun was just dipping into the ocean, leaving a sky of gold and red, as Vivian stepped onto the sand. She stopped and took off her sandals, holding them by the ankle strap as she walked along the beach.

Look at that view. Stunning. Gorgeous. Vivian was New York born and bred, but few things could compare to a Californian sunset. With the sand between her toes and the warm Pacific night air, the stress and worry of the past few months drifted away with the tide. It had been a long day, but she had won some significant victories.

I've blocked Pete's number. That's a big step. I should be proud of myself.

Vivian smiled recalling Grace's response to the news that her housemate would no longer be accepting calls from her ex.

"Never again will I let a man dictate my sense of self-worth," she muttered.

The next man whom she let into her life would be someone who made it his business to value her. She would make it clear; the first time he tried to lie to her, they would be history. Once burned, now twice shy.

And it didn't matter how good any man was in bed, her credit card would remain securely under lock and key. Holding down a decent job and being able to pay his own way was going straight to the top of her 'must have' list.

Standing facing the ocean, Vivian pulled back her shoulders and proudly whispered to the waves. "Let it be known from here and across all the seven seas, I am officially declaring tomorrow as being Day One of my post-Pete life."

When she got back to New York, she and Grace would hold a wine-fueled parade around the living room of their apartment. Spike would be appointed grand marshal. She grinned at the thought. Her heart was already feeling lighter for having made the decision to move on. Her overstretched credit card balance would follow in time.

The thought of money had Vivian's mind drifting to the

expensive dating app. The one designed for millionaires to find love. Somewhere among the future titans of New York there had to be a decent guy.

I might as well use the subscription. I've paid for it.

When she found a spare minute, she would download the app and log in. Knowing Pete, he would have set up some stupid details in her profile, such as her having an extensive collection of other people's toe nail clippings. As soon as she was logged in, she would change her password to one that no one would be able to guess, along with two-factor authentication.

She was determined to wrestle back control of her life and set it on an even course. "I am in control of my destiny once more. The next man who wants my heart had better make sure he deserves it."

Bryce was half way to the poolside gym when he caught sight of the sun heading down the sky. Sunsets in London, where he was usually based were nothing compared to the glow which sat over the Pacific coast.

"Wow. That's amazing."

A gaggle of other guests was making its way along the beach path, the sand no doubt the best place to enjoy the evening spectacle.

Bryce went to continue on his way to the gym, but his feet slowed once more. He was far from a gym junkie. As far as he was concerned, working out was a necessary evil. A six pack wasn't one of his life's goals. He could confess to wanting to look good in his suits, and what a healthy body could do to attract the female eye, but he would never be one of those men who worked out to reach the adrenaline high.

Forget the gym, I need the sand and the sunset.

Quickly toeing off his sneakers, and slipping out of his sports socks, Bryce headed toward the nearby beach steps.

From the main resort a long, well-sealed, wide path ran down to the shore. From the way it had been built, it was clear the design had taken into account guests with prams and strollers, and those in need of supported access.

As he drew closer, Bryce spotted the special matting which had been installed on the beach. The matting connected to the path and allowed guests with wheelchairs or mobility aids to reach the water. Royal Resorts prided itself in having a global design team who worked hard to ensure that all guests were able to access and enjoy facilities.

At the end of the path Bryce stopped and took in the view. He hadn't been out to the site before, but he had seen plenty of photos. This was a prime location, one which Edward had privately coveted for a number of years.

"Giving this resort to Jordan is a great idea. I think he is ready to handle the job of bringing a project to life. He can do this. I believe in him."

His own words of some two years prior now came back to haunt him. He was still at a loss as to where things had gone wrong. Yes, Jordan had been a bit of a wild child. Things had only come to an end when their frantically worried mother had admitted her middle son to a private rehab center in Pennsylvania. As far as Bryce knew, Jordan was still clean and sober these past four almost five years.

Oh, god what if he has relapsed. Or if he's got into something that won't show up on his regular drug tests. No. No. He wouldn't. He wouldn't risk losing it all.

Bryce caught his negative thoughts before he spiraled down into them, but it took a great deal of effort to push them away. His therapist had called it catastrophizing. Seeing something and imagining the worst of outcomes. The problem was not only recognizing when he was doing it, but having the patience to be kind with himself as he steered his thoughts to a calmer place.

Pick up the puppy and move it gently away. If it comes back, you keep doing the same thing. Gentle reinforcing of positive behavior. When you get back to New York, talk to Jordan. Face to face.

He was still busy with his self-talk as his bare feet touched the sand. He was tired. Frustrated.

And exceedingly lonely.

No amount of pep talks, or therapy, could alter the fact that his bed was empty at night. It had been for a long time. To someone looking in on his life, traveling the world First Class might appear glamorous, the truth however was a horrendous amount of work hours, with little time for himself. Or for social opportunities where he might seek to find a life partner.

The memory of the baby millionaire and his girlfriend wrapped in each other's arms at the airport popped into Bryce's mind. As he pushed the unwelcome thought away, his gaze settled on the silhouette of a young woman, framed by the fading light.

She was standing on the water's edge, doing exactly what Bryce had planned to do. Dipping her toes in the bubbling surf, but not getting anything else wet. She had a pair of sandals in her hands.

"You and I look like twins," he said, glancing down at his sneakers which dangled from his left hand.

She turned, took in his shoes, and gently laughed. "We do. I hadn't planned to come down here, but the colors of this sunset are just out of this world. I had to come and see."

Bryce recognized her. It was the woman he had seen on his way into the bar. Her long light brown hair once more caught his eye.

He saw an opening. "You and I passed one another in the

Sunview Bar earlier this afternoon. I couldn't help but notice you didn't finish your cocktail. Not to your liking?"

She shook her head. "It was more ice than cocktail unfortunately. I had a long wait to check into my hotel room, and they gave me a drink voucher, so I shouldn't complain."

Bryce winced in sympathy. What was the point of handing out a complimentary voucher if it only served to lessen the guest experience. "I haven't eaten yet. I don't suppose you've had the chance to try the main resort restaurant, have you?"

"Actually I did have dinner there. I was going to order room service but changed my mind. I flew in this afternoon, and after spending the better part of the day on a stuffy plane, I felt the need to get out and find some fresh air."

He caught the distinctive note of a New York accent in her voice. His first instinct was to ask where she was from and add in his own provenance, but he bit his tongue.

Don't. You're meant to be undercover. Let her think you are just another guest.

Seeing the resort through a guest's eyes and getting an unguarded review of things was gold to any good hotelier. Experiencing things for himself was one thing, but it would always come through the filter of who he was and his company background. Once a resort manager, always a resort manager.

"What did you have from the menu? Can you recommend something for me?"

Her gaze drifted slowly over his gym gear. The hint of an appreciative smile tugged at the corner of her mouth. She was liking what she saw.

Bryce took a step closer.

CHAPTER THIRTEEN

Mister designer suit hottie from the bar was standing a few feet away casually asking her about food. For a minute she was too busy taking in his solid thighs and muscular arms to answer. It took every ounce of Vivian's self-restraint not to lick her lips when her gaze drifted slowly over his package.

Thank you, gods of Lycra.

She released a tight breath. If someone were to ask if she had a favorite build in a male, he was standing right in front of her. Decent muscles, not overly built. This was a man who took care of his body, but didn't worship at the altar of high reps.

Food. He was asking about the food.

"I had the crab pasta and that was nice. The dessert was good."

That was the second time she had used the word nice to describe the food. Perhaps they were going with a safe menu while they bedded the resort down, and when it officially launched in another month or so, they would announce their star studded food and beverage offerings.

For their sake, she hoped they did. If not, the Royal

Resorts Laguna Beach was going to be no different to any of the other beachside hotels in this part of the country. And with the caliber of their nearby competition, they would soon be crushed.

Mister Hottie moved another step closer. "So would you recommend the restaurant?"

Normally when a man did this Vivian's sense of danger rose a notch or two, but not with him. Something about this stranger spoke of a good heart. Protector. Loyal.

Stop it. I can't trust my instincts. I thought Pete was a good guy, too.

Vivian shook her head. Fatigue must be making her mind fuzzy. It had been an extra-long day beginning with an early start and a fussy cat. Bed was what she needed.

Her touch starved body whispered its desires. Man. Bed.

I have got to get laid soon or I will go mad.

She had a thousand dollar subscription to a millionaire dating app. There had to be one or two lonely millionaires in New York City, ones who might be willing to overlook the fact that she had a low paying job and only managed to live on the Upper East Side due to the charity of her trust fund best friend.

"I take that as a no."

Vivian blinked hard, back to the now. She had been staring at this poor guy who was trying to ask about the resort food, and she had been away dancing with the fairies, her thoughts on silk sheets and hot nights with rich men.

"Sorry. I'm just tired. The food was nice, but to be honest, I've half-forgotten it already. I do plan to linger over the breakfast offerings at the Beachside Café in the morning and see if they have anything more appealing."

"That sounds like a good way to start the day. I might come down and see what the café has to offer in the way of coffee. I'm sorry to have disturbed your evening. I hope you get a good night's rest."

She turned to face the water just as the sun dipped below the horizon. A red fireball lit the sea.

The stranger whispered, "Absolutely magnificent. It was worth coming a long way just to see that sunset. My day is complete."

Vivian's heart stirred, and she found herself suddenly close to tears. When she turned back, he had moved and was making his way along the beach toward the path. She'd lost the chance to make any further small talk.

Come on Vivian, that was rude of you. The poor man was simply trying to make polite conversation and you blew him off.

She made herself a small promise. If she and the nice man with excellent taste in suits and gym gear did happen to meet again in the morning, she would make the effort to be more friendly toward him. Life had taught Vivian that most men were decent and trustworthy. Not all were lying assholes like her ex.

The waves beckoned once more, and she moved closer to the water. "Ooh, that's cold." She waited for a moment letting her feet get used to the temperature, before taking another step. Before she knew it, the water was lapping at the hem of her dress, but she didn't mind. The sea called to her, whispering that she should toss away her cares and just keep going.

She did. Another step had Vivian laughing as the water rose over her knees and kissed her thighs. The gentle touch reminding her of a lovers caress. She took another step into deeper water.

A strong arm wrapped about her waist and pulled her back. A deep male voice cautioned. "It's forty miles to Catalina Island if you intend to swim out to sea."

The nice man from a minute earlier held her firmly in his

embrace. She'd been lured by the siren's call of the Pacific Ocean.

If he hadn't stopped me, I probably would've kept going.

He steered her back to the safety of the water's edge, where an embarrassed Vivian took in the state of her clothes. And his. She'd waded out into waist deep water, and he'd come in to save her. From herself.

"Oh god, I am so sorry. Look at your gym gear. The salt water will destroy your sneakers."

He glanced at his clothes and gave a disinterested shrug. "It's ok, I was only half interested in going to the gym anyway, so you probably saved me the hassle. Now I have a perfectly good excuse not to go for the rest of my stay. Thanks."

She'd been distant and rude to him, and he'd come out into the water to stop her from doing heaven's know what. Swimming all the way to Catalina?

"I'm really sorry…"

"Bryce, Bryce Jones." He held out a hand.

"Vivian." After shifting her sandals she took his hand, and they shook. "Nice to meet you, Bryce. And thank you for stopping me from diving under the next wave and heading out to sea."

His answering smile set her heart tap dancing. *He was being a hero. Squee, they really do exist.* "You're welcome, Vivian, I'm just glad I'd turned back to look at the sunset one last time and caught you before you went full mermaid." Those words set heat racing to her cheeks. She really had been about to transform into a mermaid.

Her gaze took in his shorts and t-shirt. Bryce was soaking wet, and everything clung perfectly to his body. *Oh boy.* Even in the fading light, there was no mistaking how toned he was, nor what seeing him like this did to her hormones. *And I thought he looked hot in a designer suit.*

"Are you alright?"

An embarrassed, Vivian nodded. "Yes, I'm fine. It's been a long day of travelling, I guess my brain must have flipped a switch. I'm going to head back to my room in a minute and try to get some sleep."

"I can walk you back to the main resort building if you like. It's no trouble," he offered.

He'd rescued her from the waves. A damsel was obliged to let a hero bask in his rescue glory for a little while. Vivian glanced at her sea soaked dress. "I think I've spent too much time at the beach already tonight and I'll need to rinse this out before the salt dries. Thanks for the offer, but you don't need to walk me home Mister Jones, you've already done more than enough."

The look of concern on Bryce's face was enough for her to sense he wouldn't leave until she did. "Honestly, it's no trouble. I'll need to go and change so I'm heading the same way."

She couldn't refuse him. "Ok, but only if you let me thank you one more time for stopping me from going full Ariel mode."

Bryce chuckled. "It's a deal. And I'll keep an eye out for singing and dancing crabs as we head up the beach."

As they moved off the sand and toward the path, Vivian fell in beside Bryce. She couldn't help but notice the spring in her step. He was nice. Could her run of bad luck with men finally be coming to an end?

CHAPTER FOURTEEN

The sun was still a good hour from rising when Bryce climbed out of bed the following morning. He had slept, but it had been a fitful, restless mess. He had dreamed of receiving a hundred emails from Jordan in the space of an hour and then his phone had melted down from ringing nonstop. Guilt sat heavy in his chest.

He really ought to call his brother but lying was not one of Bryce's strengths. If they spoke, it wouldn't take long for Jordan to get the truth out of him.

I could call Matthew. Bryce was tempted to hear the friendly voice of his youngest brother. But no. He was meant to be in London. Calling Matthew would only make this already awkward situation that more complicated.

That's the last thing I need right now. Jordan thinking I am playing the two of them off against each other.

There were barely two years between Jordan and Matthew. To say they saw one another as competition would have been a gross understatement. And if Matthew had the slightest inkling that there might be a way for him to get one up on Jordan, Bryce had no doubt he would take it.

This stays between Dad and me, until it doesn't.

An hour later, freshly shaved and wearing his favorite Italian resort wear look, Bryce strolled into the Beachside Café. He took in the layout. Muted sandy beige tiles met sea blue and white. The expansive clear windows which opened onto a breathtaking view of the Pacific Ocean gave the space all the decoration it required. Bryce gave the designers a tick of approval. Only a fool would try to compete with mother nature.

He took a few more steps into the café then stopped. A deep intake of breath confirmed what his eyes were telling him was sadly lacking. There was no enticing aroma of eggs or freshly cooked bacon. No hint of herbed mushrooms.

"Where is the breakfast buffet?" he muttered under his breath.

Everyone knew that holidays and hotel retreats meant a large plate and several trips to the various tables and bain-maries with their warm and delicious delights. Every single resort he had ever managed had prided itself on offering an extensive breakfast menu. If guests didn't go home having put on a pound or two, he was failing at his job as a hotelier.

Bryce caught the attention of a passing waiter. "Excuse me, is this where I come for breakfast?"

Perhaps he had it wrong and the main dining room was where crispy hashbrowns and roasted tomatoes could be found. Where mountains of freshly baked muffins rose high into the sky.

"Yes sir." The harried looking waiter pointed at a chalk board pinned high on the wall. "That's the breakfast menu. If you join the queue at the counter, you should be able to order, then find yourself a seat."

"What about table service?"

The waiter half snorted, half laughed in response. "There is no table service, sir. We only have three staff rostered for breakfast each morning, and I'm barely keeping up with clearing away plates."

Bryce's fingers itched to grab his phone, hit speed dial, and call his brother. What the devil did Jordan think he was doing having guests lining up to order breakfast? And why were only three people working?

What part of luxury resorts did Jordan not understand?

Getting angry on an empty stomach wasn't a good idea. He joined the end of the queue. The café was busy. Bryce dreaded to think what this place would look like on a long weekend or during the holiday season. It would be chaos.

Just add it to the report for the board.

A tap on his shoulder had Bryce turning round. His gaze landed on the top of a mop of light brown hair. The owner of the golden locks lifted her face, and his heart gave a happy leap of joy. "Vivian!"

My little mermaid.

"Good morning," she said, offering him a cheery greeting. Her bright face spoke of someone who had slept well. Whose life wasn't beset with half the troubles he had to contend with today.

Maybe her subdued mood last night really was just fatigue.

"Good morning to you, too. Did you manage to get down to the beach and see the sunrise, or are you resisting the waves this morning?"

She laughed. "You've got to be kidding. I watched the sunrise from the comfort of my bed. I only volunteer to do super early starts if there is a vacation flight involved or I have partied through to the dawn."

He drank in her delight. "And how often do you party through to the morning?"

Vivian slowly shook her head. "Not in a long time. Once you hit twenty seven, your body starts punishing you for alcohol and sleep deprived transgressions."

A smile found its way to his lips. It wasn't just her khaki shorts and pale pink t-shirt which were cute.

This woman is lovely. The day is looking up.

CHAPTER FIFTEEN

Vivian wasn't about to admit to anyone, least of all a stranger, that the last time she had pulled an all-nighter was for an old job at a gaming magazine who needed someone to cover the New York Comic Con. Mister Hottie in his couture resort wear didn't seem the type to appreciate the attention to detail which went into the fine art of cosplay.

She nodded toward the chalkboard menu. "I'm thinking the breakfast burrito, what about you?"

His brows knitted in confusion, then he softly chuckled. "A burrito for breakfast. Tell me we are in America without telling me we are in America."

The gentle throb which had pulsed in her sex when she first spotted this handsome man, returned. She had encountered this friendly stranger only a couple of times, but he certainly had an effect on her. The memory of what she had done with her little battery operated friend just thinking about Bryce late last night had heat burning on her cheeks.

I think I might be about to test the theory as to whether you can actually die of embarrassment.

He held out his hand. "Bryce Jones, it's a pleasure to meet you…again."

Vivian shyly took his hand. "Vivian Holte. Again."

"And what brings you to sunny California Ms. Holte?"

She grinned up at him. It was best to avoid openly telling people she was a resort reviewer, lest they try to 'help' her write the review. Other people's impressions could well cloud her own. "The launch of the Royal Resorts Platinum Collection brand in the US, are you kidding me? I had to come and take a look." She leaned in and whispered. "And I got a good deal on my room."

There. Not a lie.

If Bryce went to the trouble to look her up online, he would see she was a reviewer. She wasn't hiding who she was, just not making a thing of it.

Bryce Jones. I really like that name. It suits him.

She especially liked the way it slipped easily from his lips. And the way it sent a shiver down her back. For the third time in less than a day, she found herself privately ogling this man.

"May I help you?"

Bryce's gaze shifted from her to the server at the front counter. Her new gentleman friend was at the head of the line. Vivian went to take a step aside, but a warm hand took hold of hers and drew her gently back. "As a reward for you resisting the lure of the ocean, let me treat you to breakfast."

His deep brown eyes rendered her powerless to refuse his generous offer. *I don't know if I can say no to this guy ever.* It took a great deal of effort for her to tear her gaze away. She glanced at his hand, to his ring finger. It was bare, and there was no tell-tale sign of a wedding ring tan.

Please lord don't let this guy be a serial away cheater. Don't let him be lying to me or anyone else. I've had enough of liars and cheats.

She lifted her face and found him staring at her. His gaze

informing her he had watched her furtive move. "Rest assured, Vivian, there are no social obligations which would preclude me from sharing breakfast with a lovely young woman." Bryce had read her mind.

There was something about the way he talked that had her figuring her breakfast companion had received a quality education. More than likely an expensive one. And the rounding of some of his words reminded her of Grace. They both spoke like someone who had either lived overseas or regularly mixed with the sort of people who owned houses in the wealthy enclave of the Hamptons.

"Sorry," she replied. Her trust issues were not going to go away any time soon.

Bryce turned to the counter staff. "Good morning. We would like to order two of the breakfast burritos. I'll have a medium café latte, with a triple shot of espresso. And my friend…" He glanced back at Vivian over his shoulder and playfully raised his eyebrows.

She couldn't help but smile at him. Bryce made her feel like a giddy miss from the eleventh grade. "A caramel latte, please."

His brows rose ever higher. "And I had such hopes for our friendship. Flavored coffee…you crush me, Vivian."

He was still shaking his head in mock disgust when they finally made their way over to a nearby table and sat down. When their coffees arrived, Vivian took a sip of her sweet drink. She did her best to suppress a shudder as the first mouthful went down. The kitchen had been heavy handed with the syrup, and it bordered on sickly. But she drank it. Her new friend might well sit in judgment of her beverage taste, but it was a hill she was prepared to die on. Or at least lose a tooth over.

"And what brings you to the resort, Bryce? Don't tell me it is just their triple espresso," she teased.

"I deserved that. I must apologize, I am known as a bit of a caffeine snob. I've lived overseas for a few years and the coffee here in the States still has some way to catch up with Europe. I arrived in town earlier in the week for a home trade show and I heard about this place and thought it would be nice to take a couple of days off to get some R&R. Home shows are long nights and lots of talking to people."

The little bubble of hope thinned in her chest. It wasn't as if she wanted to date this man, but the notion that he didn't even live in the same country came as somewhat of a disappointment.

"So you don't live in the US?"

Shoot. He had slipped up on the lie. Now Vivian was intrigued about where he lived. He really ought to get better at lying, but Bryce struggled at duplicity.

"I...I have recently moved back. I'm currently based in San Diego."

Leave it at that, she doesn't need to know any more of your backstory. The less bullshit you try to wade through, the better.

His relief when Vivian simply nodded and let the matter go was palpable. She didn't offer any information about her own career, and he got the impression she wasn't all that interested in discussing it. The food arrived and Vivian's eyes lit up. "This looks good, let's eat."

They tucked into their breakfast. The first mouthful of his burrito had Bryce quickly forgetting about his eggs and bacon. He might privately frown at them but when it came to the combined might of eggs, potato, and cheese all wrapped up in a fresh tortilla, he was powerless. His stomach grumbled its avid approval. Even the coffee was good. Bryce was however still undecided as to whether this minimalist menu was the right way to go. Only time, and guest feedback would tell the true story.

But we definitely need more staff during the breakfast shift.

The food was delicious, and so was the company. He couldn't help but notice the furtive glances which Vivian shot his way every so often. She seemed as interested in him as he was in her.

His life lacked the simple joy which came from sharing moments of pleasure. It had been far too long since he'd taken time for himself to stop and smell the roses. He was at a holiday resort, where people came to relax and recharge.

Bryce was a firm believer in manifesting your own future. Maybe the universe had been listening to his heart's deep desire.

Why couldn't I spend the day with this woman? She seems to like me.

Dare he take a chance?

CHAPTER SIXTEEN

Breakfast together became a morning walk along the beach, then a stroll through the resort grounds, which finally ended at the beach front coffee nook for another drink. As they made their way around the resort, Vivian stopped every so often to take pictures with her phone.

When he and Vivian parted later that morning, it was with the understanding that they would try and catch up later by the main resort pool.

Bryce headed back to his suite in a happier mood than he could recall feeling for quite some time. There was something about Vivian. She had a zest for life he was sadly lacking. The old proverb about all work and no play making Jack a dull boy kept rolling around in his mind.

You really need to carve out some time for yourself, Bryce Royal.

It was impossible for him to have a work life balance when he didn't have a life outside of work.

When Bryce rang his father, Edward was in a meeting, and Janice took the call. "Your father wants you to know that the board is asking questions about how things are going in California. He has promised them a detailed report by the end of the week at the very latest and requested that I press upon you the imperative need to see the job is done properly."

"I understand. Could you please let my father know I am doing my best. Thank you, Janice."

As soon as the call ended, Bryce set his cell on the table with more force than was necessary. There was a reason why they made impact-proof phone covers.

Thanks for nothing, Dad. Seriously. I'm not the one who has screwed up here. Why aren't you taking it out on Jordan, he's the one still in New York?

His good mood of the morning evaporated. He was angry, and more than a little resentful. He could understand his father's position and the need to get to the bottom of things, but the way that the message had been delivered struck Bryce as insensitive. Not of the pressing situation at the resort, but of him personally. This wasn't his problem, it belonged to Jordan. He was doing everything he could to give his father, and through him the board, a clear picture of what was happening here at Laguna Beach. Edward should show a bit more appreciation.

The therapist he had been seeing in London over the past year would no doubt tell Bryce to let it go. To not fall victim to his childhood jealousy over the way his parents had always let Jordan get away with things. As the eldest child, he had been the one to toe the line, to set the example. Jordan had done what he damn well pleased, and everyone had paid the price.

Yes. Including Jordan. No one has paid higher for his actions than him.

"Breathe in. Hold for a count of three. Breathe out. Repeat." Deep breathing exercises were the bane of his life. It annoyed him further when he was left to confess that they worked.

"Think happy thoughts."

Now was not the time to give in to his emotions. He'd spent an hour or so with a lovely girl this morning, at the end of which they'd agreed to meet up later at the pool.

"Ok, Dad. You want a full report of how things are here. I will do just that."

What better way could there be to show the board and his father what their paying guests thought of the resort than to observe Vivian's impressions of the service and offerings as she spent a relaxing afternoon at the main swimming pool, while enjoying all that a private cabana could offer?

I just happen to be the lucky guy who gets to share that time with her.

CHAPTER SEVENTEEN

Thank heavens for Macy's and the July sales. Vivian had treated herself to a cute red two piece swimsuit. The shirred top held her generous bust in place, and the high waisted bottoms gave her the right amount of modesty. Grace might feel comfortable in getting around in a cheeky bottom bikini during the summer, but not Vivian.

Vivian's black beach wrap stayed securely tied until she had made it all the way from her room to the pool. She wasn't one for lugging all her things down to the poolside change rooms and then bringing them all back. And she had no intention of attracting unwanted attention by wandering through the hotel in a bikini. As a solo female traveler, her sleezy guy radar was well-tuned.

Arriving at the adults only pool, she immediately began searching for Bryce. This was where he had said they would meet. The pool was, like much else at the resort, pretty empty.

A smattering of honeymooning couples were seated in the private cabanas which were situated a little further back from the poolside chairs and tables. When she caught sight of a cabana host carrying a tray with bottles of sparkling water and a large bottle of champagne on top, Vivian quietly sighed.

If my personal credit card wasn't such a disaster, I might have treated myself to a cabana day. Oh, well.

While scrolling through the resort guest menu last night she had seen the poolside services and they looked amazing. But Lionel's expense budget only went so far.

"There you are."

A now familiar voice reached her ears. Vivian did a quick check of her beach wrap making sure it was still securely tied before turning.

All thoughts of her own modesty fled the second she clapped eyes on Bryce. On the fine dusting of dark hair on his naked chest. And on the low slung swim shorts he was barely wearing.

Oh boy. And I thought he looked hot in that designer suit.

She blinked slowly taking in the sight of his happy trail. It led down to a place which her imagination was well past making mental pictures of, and which also had her wondering if she had packed the recharge unit for her little battery operated friend. Vivian regretted having worn the breast hugging bikini top. Once she removed the wrap, there would be no hiding her hardened nipples.

I hope the water is warm, because that's the first place I'm going.

Her gaze remained locked on his designer made swim trunks. They had to be couture because only a skilled pair of hands could craft such fabric magnificence. A maestro of the machine. A legend of the loom.

They hung so invitingly low, it would only take a gentle tug...

"Hey. Eyes up here."

Oh shit.

He had caught her checking him out. There were no two ways about it. "Those are...um." That was the extent of Vivian's vocabulary. She was too busy wrangling her traitorous tongue, doing her all to stop it licking her lips once more, to say anything else.

When Bryce's hands settled on his hips she didn't know where to look. If her credit card wasn't already maxed out, she would have offered him serious money to give the top of his trunks a little push...down. It would have been worth every cent.

"Oh god, I am so sorry. I was shamelessly ogling you," she stammered.

And enjoying every second.

She was certain that wearing those trunks would have gotten Bryce arrested in several states. Visions of him being handcuffed and helpless sprang to mind. In her fast evolving wicked fantasy she would be the corrupt small town cop and he would have to offer his naked body to her in order to secure bail.

You have the right to remain naked. My body will be used against you.

And when she was done with him, he would forget all about his one phone call or the need for legal representation.

Vivian was doing her best to push away her lustful thoughts, but she was losing the battle. Bryce glanced down at the waistline of his shorts and grinned. "I suppose from where you stand, they look a touch indecent. I can put a shirt on if you like."

"No." The word came out of her mouth at an all too hasty rate. From where she stood, Bryce's swim attire was perfect. "A shirt would ruin the look."

He raised an eyebrow at her words. "To be honest, I've lost a little weight since I bought them. I've usually only worn them on the continent. In countries like Spain, they wouldn't even get a second look on the beach. The Europeans have the skimpy swimwear look mastered."

I really have to dust off my passport. And then demand a Mediterranean assignment.

"I don't expect they will get me into much trouble here, I'm not planning on straying too far from the pool and our cabana for the next few hours."

Our cabana? Vivian's gaze followed to where Bryce pointed. At a nearby cabana, a resort attendant was setting a tray of sparkly drinks on a table.

Vivian broke free of her lust-filled imagination and took in the cabana. There were two loungers topped with yellow and cream striped cushions, positioned side by side. It wouldn't take much to push them together and create a makeshift bed. The cream curtains which framed the cabana were tied back by a bright yellow sash. The décor had California sunshine vibes stamped all over it. The resort might be lacking in some aspects but around the pool they seemed to have got things right.

"You hired a cabana. For us?" He had said 'our cabana', not his, and for some reason that made it all the more special.

"Yes. I was kind of hoping you might want to spend some more time with me. But if you don't, I will understand. Mermaid duties and all."

Vivian brushed her teeth over her bottom lip. She was sorely tempted by the idea of spending the rest of the day with Bryce. There was no doubt that he was hot. And those swim trunks of his had her lady parts begging for some intimate attention.

But she barely knew this man, and after her recent run of shitty male encounters she was wary. Could she take a chance on this stranger?

"No obligation. No pressure. If we spend the afternoon here together at the pool, when the sun sets you can simply say a polite thank you and then take your leave. I won't be offended, Vivian. Women shouldn't be made to feel they have to offer anything when it comes to sharing time with a man."

Wow. What Vivian would give to be able to clone Bryce Jones. She had met plenty of guys who thought that by paying for an espresso martini, they had a golden ticket to a quick blowjob in the back of a nightclub.

"That would be lovely, thank you Bryce," she replied.

They were in a public space, with people around them. If her host did transpire to be a creep, she could simply head back to her room. Her instincts told her that he wasn't that sort of man. It still took a moment for Vivian to silence the little voice in the back of her mind, the one which tried to patiently remind her that she had thought her ex was a decent guy, and Pete had eventually shown himself to be anything but.

What did Grace call spending time with a man like Bryce? Oh, yes, a palate cleanser. Something to refresh your heart and mind after a bad breakup. Her friend usually included a night of hot sweaty sex, Grace's words, as part of the deal, but today Vivian was simply content to let things play out. Bryce had made it clear he wasn't expecting anything other than companionship from her, and with that in mind she decided it would be a mistake to create any further preconceptions about how the day might end.

The cabana was gorgeous. The enormous plump cushions on the loungers were divine, and the roof cover was perfect. A little California sun was a blessing, but sunburnt skin was not. After taking a few photos of the stylish poolside shelter, Vivian sat on one of the loungers. She placed her small tote bag which contained a few personal items, and her cell under the nearby table.

Bryce dropped onto the chair on the other side of her and motioned to the drinks. "Would you like a sparkling water, or could I temp you with a glass of Prosecco? I didn't order champagne because I find the lighter bubbles are a better poolside drink."

She couldn't help herself, she grinned from ear to ear. It was unusual to meet a man who understood his bubbles. And the way he said bubbles had her mouth running dry. That thing with his accent was there again. It reminded her of the men she occasionally encountered at the expensive resorts, the ones whose families were regularly featured in the social pages. The private tennis club and golf set.

For heaven's sake don't ask him if he has a holiday home in the Hamptons.

"Prosecco please, thank you Bryce. I must confess I am a girl who loves a drink in a long, tall glass."

A bit like her men. Standing behind Bryce in the café line earlier, Vivian had hazarded a guess that Bryce was close to six foot three. Tall, nicely built, and surprisingly single.

While he worked the cork gently out of the bottle, she posed the question which had been on her mind since breakfast. "If you don't mind me asking, how is it that you're still single? There must be laws of nature that prohibit such a thing when it comes to a man like you, Bryce."

There I said it. Please don't let him suddenly decide to mention a fiancée or a boyfriend.

The chances of anything possibly happening between them might currently be remote, but she still wanted to be able to play out the fantasy. Even if it was only in her head.

"A man like me, hmm?" Bryce arched a playful brow at her as the cork came free with a gentle pop. He picked up a glass, tilting it slightly as he poured the sparkling wine. This was a man who knew his way around a champagne flute.

What else does his know his way around? Don't. Look. At. His. Tongue.

Flustered, Vivian brushed back a stray lock of hair which

had fallen in front of her eyes. "Well, yes. You have to know you are gorgeous. I stopped and checked you out after we passed in the bar yesterday. And yeah, I did like what I saw on the beach last night too."

He smiled. "I'm single because I spent a number of years working overseas. I travel a lot and trying to maintain any sort of relationship is difficult when I'm always moving from one place to the next. I did try the long distance thing for a year, but it was impossible. Whenever I was in town, she was away working. In the end, we decided to be friends. Some might say we both gave up."

He handed her a drink. And another warm smile. "What about you? I'm surprised that a beautiful woman like yourself is holidaying solo. Or is there a special someone somewhere who couldn't take the time off work to come with you, Prince Eric perhaps?"

Vivian took a sip of her prosecco. She stared at the glass, unable to meet Bryce's eyes. It was hard to answer this question without reliving the pain. "I was in a relationship. It ended three months ago. Turns out my prince was actually a lying wart faced frog. He not only cheated on me, but just before we split, he went on a spending spree using my credit card. He put me in a five-thousand-dollar hole, complete with a thousand bucks a year membership for a millionaire dating app. You could say that at the moment I have some real trust issues when it comes to relationships. I have always thought that loved mattered, but I'm beginning to think that for some people it doesn't."

It sounded funny putting it that way but laughing in the face of heartbreak was a bitter lesson she had been forced to learn. It was either that or spending every day in tears. And as much as she would like to have stayed in bed and wallow under the covers, bills had to be paid.

After the breakup with Pete, Grace had given Vivian an

entire weekend to cry herself out. But first thing Monday morning, her best friend had dragged her out of bed and made Vivian get dressed and go to work. Grace's tough love had been just what she needed.

"That's a really rotten thing for your ex to have done. I take it you can't cancel the subscription."

"No. They have a no refunds policy. I expect millionaires don't give a damn about that sort of money." Unfortunately she did.

Vivian caught herself before she started down the spiral of self-pity. She had today to spend time with a charming, handsome man. Her ex was not going to spoil it.

Bryce held his now full glass up to hers, and they clinked. "To those of us doomed to be crossed in love, and the hope that our special someone is just around the corner."

"As long as they are not hanging around that corner, armed with a baseball bat, waiting to mug us."

When her cabana companion roared with laughter, Vivian found herself chuckling at her own tasteless joke. Bryce wasn't just super sexy, he was adorable. A small sigh of disappointment escaped her lips. Why did he have to live on the other side of the country?

The more she looked at him, the hotter he became. By the end of the first bottle of wine, Vivian was convinced Bryce Jones might just become the one who got away. The one she would never have.

But what if I took the chance and at least claimed today...and tonight?

She mightn't ever get this moment again. And if she didn't seize it, regret would surely follow. After working free the ties on the front of her wrap, Vivian let it fall open. There was no mistaking the appreciative gaze which Bryce roamed over her bikini clad body.

"I am looking forward to our afternoon, Bryce, thank you for inviting me."

Vivian was done with regrets. If they were still together when the sun set, and Bryce Jones asked her to share a night of sweaty, hot sex with him, she knew what she would say.

Yes.

CHAPTER EIGHTEEN

Bryce broke through the water, and into the bright sunshine. He sucked in a lungful of air. After three glasses of prosecco he needed to clear his head. A dip in the generous sized pool was perfect. It was made all that more perfect by the woman in the red bikini whose legs he deliberately brushed past on his way to the surface.

"You have a strong stroke Bryce," said Vivian.

At those words, his sorely neglected manhood pricked to attention. It liked what it heard.

Down boy. She means my freestyle.

Coming to stand alongside Vivian, Bryce brushed back his hair. "My mother had me and my brothers take swimming lessons from an early age. She was desperate to make sure we were all drown proof. There was no mucking about with junior life preservers or floatation devices, you learned to swim."

Alice Royal had lost a relative to a water accident at a young age and had made it her mission to make sure that none of her offspring ever suffered the same fate. If he was ever blessed with his own brood, Bryce intended to do the same and have them learn as soon as they were able.

"You are no slouch in the pool, Vivian. I can't believe you almost beat me in that underwater race."

He had thought to go easy and possibly let her win, but Vivian had quickly shown him that she could cut through the water like an Olympic champion. It had been a close run battle by the time they reached the other end of the pool, with Bryce just managing to touch the tiles ahead of her.

He was enjoying today. Work had kept him busy over the past couple of years, with Bryce often putting in eighty hour weeks. The Europeans all said he was mad, but mostly they put it down to his American background. What they didn't realize was that his running of the resorts on the Continent and the UK were a test to see if he had what it took to eventually succeed his father, to become CEO of Royal Resorts USA.

"Do you fancy a spot of lunch? I saw one of their wood-fired pizzas coming out earlier and it looked delicious," he offered.

"Pizza sounds perfect. I did check out their menu last night, and the four mushroom pizza caught my eye. Of course being a New Yorker, I reserve the right to judge any pizza these West Coast people serve up," replied Vivian.

Bryce shook his head. "I've lived and worked a lot in Italy, so I think I should be the one to decide whether the pizza is worthy of its name."

Vivian's haughty glare had him grinning. "Are you really prepared to take me on over pizza when I have almost twenty four million people in the tri-state area at my back?"

He threw up his hands in mock defeat. "Alright. Let's hop out and get dried, then I'll get the cabana host to order us some food. I could do with an espresso, I've only had one so far today.

"How many do you usually drink?"

"By this time, I'm usually onto my fourth."

Vivian waited, hanging back in the water while Bryce headed for the ladder. It was a deliberate ploy on her part. If she delayed things, it would give her the opportunity to observe him as he climbed out. It was like watching one of those male cologne ads in real life. She appreciated the way the water beaded and dripped off Bryce's broad shoulders and down his back. The only thing missing was a hot music soundtrack.

She moved closer taking in his toned ass. The way those swim trunks hung so low on his hips was criminal. Her mind was still playing out the fantasy of her being a cop and subjecting Bryce to a full body search. When it came to her sexy imagination, she knew exactly where to pat him down in the search for his concealed weapon.

Gee, Vivian, you are acting like a bitch on heat. What is wrong with you?

Bryce had no idea the danger he was in. If he kept on giving her these porny wet dreams, she would fall on him like a ravenous sexy beast the second he made any sort of move.

Whoa girl; he said this was a no obligations day. And that works both ways. Don't go assuming just because he is a man that he will want sex.

She already had Plan B figured out. On the way back to her room, she would call in at the gift shop and pick up some batteries. There would be no need for lube. Her imagination had all her lady parts well and truly hydrated. Her nipples were still on high beam, but they had been that way all morning.

When she reached the ladder, Bryce was waiting. In true

gentleman style, he offered her his hand as Vivian stepped onto the pool deck. Her heart gave a little flutter as they exchanged a soft smile. She couldn't remember a time when a man had made her feel this way. Horny and gooey all at once.

They made their way over to the cabana and a search for towels began. Vivian checked the little cupboard behind the sunbeds, the obvious place where she would expect to find them. It was empty. *Another mark against Royal Resorts Laguna Beach. They really have made a slip-up with this new Platinum Collection.*

"We might have to go and ask at the pool desk," she suggested.

Bryce disappeared. When he returned his cheerful mood had darkened. "You wouldn't believe it, but they are out of towels. How can a resort charge for cabanas and not provide towels?"

According to the attendant, whose story was backed up by their cabana host when he returned from ordering their lunch, the pool area often ran out of towels midafternoon. The next load of dry ones wouldn't arrive from the laundry service until close to six o'clock.

Vivian stood shaking her arms doing her best to air dry before the food arrived. "They seem to have a bit of a linen problem. Last night it took me two phone calls and a visit down to the front desk before I managed to get a duvet."

"What? Your room should have had proper bedding when you checked in."

"Well, it didn't. It looks to me like someone scrimped on the linen budget. And considering the fact I had to wait forty minutes for my room yesterday afternoon, I think it's not a good sign for the future success of this resort. There is clearly room for improvement."

A thoughtful look appeared on Bryce's face, and for a moment she thought he was going to say something. Instead he seemed to grit his teeth. The smile he gave her was a forced one. She respected him for making the effort to keep his temper under control. The lack of towels wasn't the fault of the pool staff. If anyone was to blame it was the senior management.

But whatever was going on at the Laguna Beach resort, the staff seemed to be well aware of it. Vivian had seen this sort of situation before at other hotels. Operators would make the decision to open early in order to get some badly needed cash after having used up all their development money. Could Royal Resorts be running that low on funds?

She pretty much had her review already written in her head. Checking out the rumors online likely wouldn't change it. They would only serve to confirm Vivian's growing suspicions.

See what the rumor mill has to say. This place must have cost a bomb to build, and they wouldn't be the first people in the leisure industry to find themselves facing money problems.

She knew exactly where to look. If there were real issues here, the folks at *Leisure Line* were sure to know. Once she got back to her room later this afternoon, she would check out the gossip blog. Even if it was as a postscript to her main review, she owed it to future guests to let them know if their vacation was going to be less than six star. If they should be looking and booking elsewhere.

Was one of America's biggest resort companies in serious financial trouble? That was the billion-dollar question.

CHAPTER NINETEEN

"Thank you for a lovely afternoon, Bryce. And as much as it pains me, I must concur with your official pronouncement that the pizza was delicious. I would struggle to find one better in New York. Someday I will make it to Italy and be able to taste the food for myself."

Well fed, Vivian tied her beach wrap at her waist and picked up her tote bag. Whatever the resorts issues with linen, at least they seemed to be ironing out the food and beverage situation. Bryce had ordered them both an after lunch cocktail and it had been delicious. Her prayers that someone would have a word with the bar staff and told them to go easy on the ice had been answered.

Vivian was torn. She would love to stay by the pool with Bryce, but it was getting close to four o'clock, and she had work to do. This might be a holiday for him, but she was on assignment. Lionel was depending on her to deliver the review by the end of the week.

"Are you sure you can't stay longer?" The plea in Bryce's voice had her wishing that by some form of miracle Jerry had remembered he had a ski resort review to pen and had actually managed to deliver it to Lionel.

As grandpa used to say, if wishes were horses, beggars would ride.

"Unfortunately not. As lucky as I am to be on vacation at this resort, I do have a little bit of work I need to finish. My boss is expecting a business report from me tonight. It's almost seven on the east coast and I promised I would get this work done."

It was lovely that Bryce seemed genuinely sad at her leaving. Guilt stirred within. The thought of disappointing him nagged at her conscience. Finishing the full draft of the review would only take her at best two hours, and then her evening would be free.

"I feel really bad about leaving you, would you be available for a late dinner tonight? How does eight o'clock sound? My treat," she offered.

I hate eating late, but I want to see him again.

Bryce rose from his lounger and came to Vivian's side. He had done the same thing a couple of times already, and she liked it when he stood this close. It had her feeling something that she worried had died after discovering her boyfriend had not only been cheating on her, but he had been racking up debts on her credit card.

That feeling was hope.

His fingertips brushed against her arm and a shiver of lust coursed through her body. Bryce made her feel many things. Most of them salacious and wicked.

Does he feel the same? Will he ask me to sleep with him? God, I hope so.

The longer they spent together, the more Vivian wanted Bryce.

"Go and do your work, Vivian. In the meantime I will book us a table at the hilltop restaurant for eight. And don't you dare think of picking up the check. I was raised a gentleman and that means dinner is on me. I insist."

Vivian offered him a soft smile. "Alright, but if we are both still here tomorrow, I am picking up the tab for the beach club fish and chips at lunch. No arguments."

Her breath caught as he leaned in. Her gaze settled on his mouth. On those perfect lips. "I will see you at the restaurant at eight, Vivian. Don't be late."

As Bryce placed a soft kiss on Vivian's cheek, she silently chastised herself for not having turned her head. The heat of his breath on her skin had her heart doing a happy dance.

I want him to kiss me. Everywhere.

Her heart, and other pertinent parts of her body, were all thrumming their demands as Vivian headed back to her room. The message they were sending was loud and clear. Her body ached for a night with Bryce, and to wake up in his arms.

Back in her room, Vivian opened up her laptop, and checked her emails. One was from Lionel. The subject line read, CALL ME.

She picked up her phone and dialed.

"Ah Vivian. Good. I was hoping you would call before it got too late on that side of the country. It's about your review. I need it tonight."

Oh no. The little lie she had told Bryce about sending a report to her boss tonight had now become truth.

She'd planned to spend the next day going over the piece and polishing it to a submittable standard. "But I haven't visited the day spa. And there are other places I haven't eaten. Can't this wait? I thought I had a couple more days."

Lionel huffed down the phone. "Yeah, sorry kid, but Phoebe is struggling to get her piece on the new resort in Tahiti loaded. Something about their internet connection continually going down. I need your review to take up her space. If you can push another five hundred words on top of the normal brief and some extra photos, we might be ok."

Unlike Jerry's crock excuse, Vivian could believe Phoebe's story. If her fellow correspondent said she had internet issues, she was telling the truth.

The pressure was now on for Vivian to come through for everyone at LHRW magazine.

Ok, you can do this, you know enough about Royal Resorts Laguna Beach to produce a balanced and well written article.

"Give me a couple of hours and I will have it to you. I took some photos around the resort and at the poolside earlier today, and I think they came out really well. I'll send them through now, and you can take a look."

She could swear the sound of Lionel's brain clicking over that problem drifted down the phone line. "Thanks Vivian. I'm sure they will be great. I wish I had more contributors who were as reliable as you."

This wasn't the first nor the last time that Lionel would put her in such a position. Whenever someone had to come through for him, it was her.

The afternoon with Bryce had set her in a reflective mood, one where she wasn't just going to do yet another favor for Lionel because someone else had let him down. She worked hard for the magazine, it was time her boss showed her a little more appreciation.

"I will get the review to you this evening, on one condition. You have to give me an international feature. I've worked hard on the US ones, so I think I have earned the opportunity to file something from further afield."

She could do better than Jerry with his cavalier attitude and last minute rushed pieces. Another sigh, followed by a huff of annoyance. "Ok, how about something in Cancun, Mexico?"

"No. Italy. I want something in Italy. One of the boutique

chains is doing an upgrade of their Lake Como resort. I want in on that assignment." A gorgeous old resort situated on the shores of the famous Lake Como was undergoing a major refurb. That's what she wanted.

Bryce's mention of how amazing the food was in Italy had triggered something in the recesses of her memory. Her own brief travel experience in Europe a few years earlier had been cut short due to Vivian running out of money.

Your other option is to get back on the phone or email or whatever and try to convince Jerry to get on a train and quickly file his Japanese ski resort piece. Good luck with that.

"Full review in my inbox by midnight New York time. And it had better have something captivating to say. I need a headline which grabs."

"Deal."

She hung up the call. The words of the article were already half written in her head, including the eye catching headline.

By the time she met with Bryce for dinner at eight, Lionel would have his review along with some Instagram worthy photos. Soon she would be making plans to eat authentic pizza in Italy.

Tonight however, she had plans to feast on a hot American male.

CHAPTER TWENTY

Bryce had a few hours to kill. After Vivian left, he'd returned to his own suite and changed into a casual pair of shorts and collared linen shirt. His Italian resort look felt a little out of place in the late California afternoon. Once dressed he went for a long walk around the grounds of the resort.

Two things focused his mind. The first—the resort and his need for a detailed understanding of all the ways it was falling short of expectations. That was why he was here. It was the job he'd been tasked with by his father and the board.

The second, and infinitely more compelling, was what he was going to do about the sexy, sassy girl from New York. Bryce wasn't normally one for resort romances, or secret trysts, but Vivian had him thinking he might dare to break his own rule.

It's not set in stone. Mixing business with pleasure is just something I've tried to avoid. But Vivian is different from other women, she is a breath of fresh air.

When he was working at the European resorts and in New York high society, people knew he was Bryce Royal, he didn't hide his identity. His family name meant having to deal with women who were not only attracted to him, but to his bank account. At times he wondered what they saw first, the man or large dollar signs. Some of the husband-seeking females made no secret of the fact that they were prepared to go to great lengths in order to get hold of his money. The gold diggers left Bryce wary of romantic entanglements.

Ms. Vivian Holte, however, didn't have a clue as to who he was, and that made all the difference. She liked him just for him.

By the time he had returned from his stroll around the grounds, Bryce had come to some important decisions. First, he was going to pull the resort's finance reports, and do a deep dive into the development expenditure, focusing on guest fronting items such as linen. No guest should ever have to deal with a lack of towels or bedding. Then he was going to review the staffing costs.

That should only take him a couple of hours, after which he would email his initial findings to his father, along with some recommendations. The board could mull over those and decide what they felt had to be done.

After that he was going to take some time for himself. Put on his best Italian linen suit, have a close shave, and then head out to meet Vivian. Over drinks and dinner at the hilltop bar, he would do his best to read her mood and see if the connection he had sensed had grown between them this afternoon was still there. If it was, he would look to take things further.

It had been a long time since he had seduced a woman. Well over a year since he had last shared his bed with a warm, willing female. Pleasured his partner. His body thrummed with barely restrained need.

Vivian was single, and so was he. They were adults. No strings. No attachments. If they wished to end the evening in one another's arms, there was nothing stopping them.

At the door to his suite, Bryce came to a halt. He smacked his key card to his forehead.

I am getting ahead of myself. I told her this morning there was no obligation. And what if Vivian doesn't see me in a romantic or sexual way, if she only wants companionship? A friend to share a meal and a pleasant evening.

The words of advice Edward had passed down to all his sons sat front and center in Bryce's mind. When it came to the delicate matter of sexual relations, consent was everything. There was nothing more attractive than hearing a woman say yes, and then being able to deliver a night filled with meeting her every sexual desire. A gentleman always asked the lady what she wanted.

Where and how this evening ended would be Vivian's choice. He hoped she would choose him and this hotel suite.

CHAPTER TWENTY-ONE

Vivian was having second thoughts—about herself and whether she could allow a stranger to seduce her. She and Bryce had shared a fun afternoon, splashing about in the pool, and lazing around sipping drinks. By the time she left the cabana, she had been certain about what she wanted. Now, she wasn't sure if she could do this. If this was what she did want.

She grabbed her cell, took a deep breath, and fired off a quick message.

> I've met a guy.

She picked up Grace's call on the second ring.

"You don't send that sort of message, Vivian Holte, and not expect me to hit dial. So spill, young lady."

Vivian propped herself up on the pile of pillows she had stacked against the bed head. She was due to meet Bryce for dinner in just over an hour. Her prosecco bravery had long dissipated and now she was wondering what to do. Grace was far more self-assured when it came to men.

"He's in homewares. Has lived overseas but is now back in San Diego. Not married. And yes, I did look for the tan lines of a wedding ring." Grace would have slapped Vivian around the head if she had failed to do that minimal check.

"Out of ten?"

Hmmm. She'd never been able to get a grip of the whole 'he's a Wisconsin seven which means he is a New York five' thing. "He's good looking. Well spoken. Ah. Um." Bryce was much more than that, and she knew it.

Watching him climb out of the pool this afternoon had seen her tongue threaten to hang out of her mouth like a cartoon character. "I would say he is close to a New York eight. Maybe a nine."

"Hot damn," squealed Grace as her polished private school accent disappeared momentarily.

Vivian put a hand over her eyes and softly chuckled. A continent might separate them, but she could still imagine the look on Grace's face right this minute. It would be one of wicked glee.

"A New York eight, and you are calling me for what? Advice on how to get a seriously hot guy into bed? Don't you dare undersell yourself."

Grace knew her only too well. She had undersold herself far too many times. Even Pete had said that about her, and he was a solid New York six.

"I'm just a little unsure about getting back on the horse."

A roar of laughter had her pulling the phone away to save her hearing. For a minute Vivian sat and stared at her cell, waiting until the snorting and guffaws died down.

"You get back on that horse, my girl, and you ride it until your world explodes in a fiery orgasm."

Vivian's gaze slipped to her vibrator. She had got it back out of its red silk bag but unlike yesterday, she hadn't used it. An electric buzz would be a satisfactory way to take the edge off her cravings, but nothing compared to the sensation of skin on skin sex. The only thing she wanted touching her in a sexual way tonight was Bryce. So why couldn't she stop the worry that he wasn't what he seemed?

Because Pete broke my ability to trust. Vivian covered her face with a hand. *Grrrr. I have to stop thinking about him.*

"But seriously, Vivian. You need this. It's the best way to draw a line under the past. You sleep with this guy and Pete the ass is no longer the last man you had sex with, done and dusted." There was a long moment of silence after which, Vivian did a quick check to make sure Grace was still on the other end of the line. "You say he lives in San Diego. This is your perfect chance to have a no strings attached affair. He goes back down the coast, and you get on a plane home. No one gets hurt."

Trust Grace to put a logical spin on the situation. But she was right. If she did sleep with Bryce, it could be with the full knowledge that she wouldn't ever see him again. There wouldn't be the remotest chance that one day she would bump into him as she stepped off a subway train. And if he wasn't what he seemed, would it even matter?

She glanced at her battery operated friend. *Sorry honey, you are going back in my suitcase. I'm getting some real action tonight.*

"Alright. If the opportunity presents itself, I will spend the night with him. He has an ocean view suite. And before you ask, yes, I did pack my blue cocktail dress."

She wasn't ready to become a cat lady just yet. Besides Grace was Spike's cat mom, not her.

A year ago Grace had pressured Vivian into buying the dress. It had cost her a serious amount of cash at Saks Fifth Avenue, but if there was any garment in her wardrobe guaranteed to have men checking her out, it was the halter neck treasure which she took with her whenever she was staying at a high end resort.

"That's my girl. I told you that dress was a wise investment. They should have it listed on the New York stock exchange. Its trading code would be SEX, and I'd make a killing shorting the stock."

Grace worked for one of the big investment and trading houses on Wall Street. She liked to make up finance and sex analogy jokes. Vivian didn't have the heart to tell her friend that most of them went over her head.

Ok, if Bryce asks, I am in.

Decision made, Vivian nodded to herself. Her little blue devil dress was going out to shine in a California sunset. And if things went well tonight, she would be wearing it again tomorrow morning as she stole back into her room.

"I've got to go Vivian, Marlon will be here soon, and we are heading out for drinks and dinner. I hope tonight goes off like an orgasmic rocket. If you are ready to get back in the game, then when you're home, I think we should look at that dating app *he who shall not be named* signed you up to and see what sort of talent it attracts. And yes, I am going to utter the magic words—use this guy as a palate cleanser. Now go and get some."

Grace was gone before Vivian could make her protests. She wondered what sort of guy would willingly sign up for a thousand dollar a year dating site. No doubt many of them would be ambitious, driven, and determined. Men who saw themselves going places. But somewhere in the middle of all the finance brokers and C grade celebrities there might just be a special man, one brave enough to swipe right for a poorly paid travel writer who couldn't afford to renew her subscription.

"Even money mavens need love."

She tossed her cell onto the mattress and went to take a long, hot shower.

CHAPTER TWENTY-TWO

Nerves had Vivian pacing her room long before she was due to meet Bryce for dinner. She'd checked her emails and Lionel had confirmed he'd received her review. He was happy with both the magazine copy and the photos. Vivian sent a brief reply, noting their agreement for her to do the Como piece. Lionel was a good boss, but it paid to have those sorts of things in writing.

Review done and dusted. Well done, Vivian.

Her mind wouldn't settle. *Time to venture out and have a calming cocktail.* If she didn't, there was every chance she would wear a hole in the carpet of her room.

The restaurant was exactly how she hoped it would be, mood lighting and an unobtrusive sound track playing low in the background. Whoever had designed this part of the resort had read the memo about letting the Pacific Ocean be the star. As Vivian took a seat at the bar, she gave it a tick of approval.

I expect it was the same member of the design team who insisted on the glass windows in the breakfast space. I am glad I mentioned them and the view in my review.

Lionel had always impressed upon her the ideal that resorts were meant to be in tune with the landscape. The guest experience should be one of taking home memories of food and the wonderful locale. Soft sheets, and excellent service was merely a side dish. He might be right about stunning locations, but then again, she doubted he'd ever had to go to a hotel reception desk late at night and beg for a duvet.

As the bartender sat her tall glass of Royal Mimosa gently in front of her, Vivian wondered if somewhere deep inside, Lionel didn't really understand resorts. They were meant to be a whole. A complete experience. And in the case of the expensive ones offered by groups such as Royal Resorts, they were supposed to leave their guests with an incredible and lasting memory of their stay. Unfortunately, the Royal Resorts Platinum Collection, Laguna Beach, had missed the mark. There was so much room for improvement.

The review is done, now it's time for me.

The warm air kissed her skin. Tender fingers of breeze threaded their way through her long tresses. It felt like an imaginary lover was touching her body. Vivian took a sip of her cocktail as the sensuous night air had her sex clenching with need. The heady beat of desire drummed through her body.

She shivered as a warm fingertip traced its way down the skin of her naked back. When Bryce leaned in and whispered, "You look stunning," she was ready to call for the check and drag him back to her room.

"May I join you?" he murmured.

She swallowed deep and replied in a voice thick with anticipation. "Yes, please."

He took the stool next to hers and held his hand up to catch the bartender's attention. Vivian was just about ready to melt when Bryce ordered a drink in fluent Spanish. She wasn't the least surprised that he could speak another language.

She smiled as he exchanged a few friendly words with one of the resort staff. Some people had a way with others and Bryce Jones seemed to be one of those men who was not only comfortable in his own skin but happy to make others feel good.

Why some woman hadn't already snapped him up Vivian couldn't for the life of her fathom. If he was as good at everything as she suspected he was, Bryce was the kind of man who many women would have had no qualms about throwing away their own life plans in order to follow him around the world.

Maybe that's not what he wants. He might be looking for a woman whose destiny is as important to her as his is to him. Then again, he couldn't make a long distance relationship work.

She studied her drink. This man lived on the other side of the country. Any future with him would be impossible. Her family was in New York, and she couldn't imagine a life where she was thousands of miles away from them.

A glass of red wine soon appeared next to her cocktail glass. Yet another sign to show that Bryce was definitely not the sort of guy she usually encountered on her resort assignments. Most American men tended to go for a craft beer, or if they were trying to impress her, a Scottish whisky. Her dinner companion this evening broke all the rules.

And she liked him for that, for drinking what he wanted rather than trying to make a statement.

That short blue dress and those sky high heels made him weak at the knees. The moment he laid eyes on Vivian from across the sandstone tiled bar entrance, Bryce had slowed his steps. He took in the halter neck and bare back. The way her long light brown hair hung over her shoulder had him sucking in a deep breath. There was something about long straight hair that did it for him. The symmetry of its lines coupled with her soft womanly curves had Bryce wanting to worship every inch of Vivian with his mouth. And that was just for starters.

She was statement dressing tonight. Her intentions clear. Or at least he hoped that was what was happening, because if he was reading the blue silk dress and the way it clung to Vivian's body wrong, then he was in for a long evening of discomfort.

If only his cousin Camille could see her little blue rebel dress and how it had caught the eye of every man in the room, she would be thrilled.

He was tempted to tell Vivian that he had been there the day that dress had first come to life on Camille's sketchbook. Next to the sketch, she had written the words *on the prowl,* and they had both laughed about it. A woman wearing that dress was definitely hunting for either a man or a handful of compliments. Or both.

At that time, no one else knew Camille Royal was secretly designing a ready to wear collection for one of the major New York department stores. A bold career move which would eventually see her thrown out of her father's haute couture workroom and banished from the family estate just outside of Paris. Bryce had immediately offered her sanctuary at his London home.

Camille, your little blue rebel dress is perfect.

He couldn't help himself. As soon as he drew close, his fingers reached out and touched Vivian's naked skin. When she let her head drop back and took in a deep breath, he sensed she was as tightly wound as him. If he asked, there was every chance she would let him take her by the hand and escort her from the bar. Their evening would begin and end in his hotel suite. But he wanted to wait. All good things took time. And Vivian Holte was exceptional.

Sliding into the seat next to hers, he paused, letting the subtle hint of her perfume wash over him. Warm botanicals sat softly on her lightly tanned skin. He'd noted that when they had been together at the poolside, Vivian had spent much of her time staying out of the sun. Her skin spoke of a woman who was serious about protecting it from harmful UV rays. Smart girl.

He took in the barman's name tag and hazarded a quick guess that in a city where almost half the population was of a Latino background, Santiago might well speak Spanish. Bryce's Spanish wasn't flawless, but as he chatted with Santiago it soon became apparent that his efforts to speak in the man's mother tongue were greatly appreciated.

Wine glass in hand, Bryce turned his attention back to where he planned it would remain for the rest of the evening.

"How many languages do you speak?" she asked.

He grinned at her. "I'm fluent in French, as I learned it at school. I can hold a decent conversation in Italian, and of course you just heard me talk to the barman in Spanish. I do however draw the line at German, it's beyond my capabilities. Fortunately for me, English is widely spoken in business in Germany."

It sounded like he was bragging, but his command of several other languages had just been something which came from being part of a global family. He doubted there was anyone within the Royal family who didn't speak at least one other language outside of their native tongue. Even his French cousins had learned to speak English albeit reluctantly.

"So what do you actually do for a living, Bryce? I know

you said you were in homewares, but what does that really mean?"

He could tell what she was doing. Trying to find out a little more about him. Put her finger on what sort of man spoke many different languages and traveled a lot for work. His cover story was a variation on the one used by many members of his family when they were trying to remain incognito.

"I work for a homewares distributor. Europe has been my base, but I also deal with Mexican and South American suppliers. Which is why I am currently based in San Diego. It's a quick, cheap flight to Mexico City from just over the border in Tijuana."

Vivian nodded and sipped her drink. She looked as if she had bought the dull story and was ready to move on with spending time with him. Bryce was more than happy to accommodate her wishes.

"Would you like to move to our reserved table? I expect we'd both be more comfortable in a chair, these bar stools are not the best," he suggested.

If they were tucked away in a corner, they could talk in private. The bar was too public a place for any real conversation. He wasn't lying about the bar stools being uncomfortable. The padding on them was almost nonexistent. They were hard on the back and hips. Someone had gone for look rather than function when they ordered them. And the guests were the ones who would be paying the price for such an obvious oversight.

It was yet another resort failing Bryce would be adding to the growing list of problems he intended to include in his report to his father and the Royal Resorts board.

I wonder if Jordan has even sat at this bar. He surely couldn't have thought this was the sort of comfort we should be offering to our high paying guests.

As Vivian stepped down from the bar stool, Bryce offered her his hand. His gaze settled briefly on her thigh as the dress rose higher. An involuntary gasp escaped his lips.

Their eyes met and Bryce could have sworn that Vivian's bluish green ones shone with more than a hint of challenge. She was daring him to say something. And as much as he would love to have made a comment about the blue silk and her skin, he sensed it was too early in the evening to let their growing lustful attraction take full command.

"Let's eat. I have a feeling we are both going to need our energy later."

Her soft approving smile as she accepted his hand went straight to his loins.

CHAPTER TWENTY-THREE

This dress was her greatest weapon, but it was also her weakness. Where the silk touched her breasts, there could be no hiding the fact that her nipples were peaked and hard. Achingly so. The thin fabric of her strapless bra did nothing to keep her obvious state of arousal from view. When Bryce led Vivian to an out of the way table, she was relieved.

More than one other male guest checked her out as they walked across the small restaurant space. Bryce glared at one man who made a not too subtle attempt to ogle her. She might well be a twenty first century independent woman, but she secretly relished his sign of possessiveness. He sat next to her in the curved booth. The touch of his leg against her bare knee sent a jolt of lust rushing through her body.

How fast can we eat, and then get out of here?

As if reading her thoughts, a waiter appeared and handed them both menus. Vivian ran her gaze quickly over the dinner offerings. It was the usual Californian fare. Fancy burgers, tacos, and prime New York steak. Every single one of them were the natural enemy of her slinky, silk dress.

The last time she had paid to get this particular little

number professionally dry cleaned, it had cost her sixty five bucks. At the moment, with her credit card balance in its current precarious state, she would do anything not to have to spend that sort of cash. She'd learned that if she kept the dress free from any stains, and then washed the under arms in cold water, she could hang it up to dry. Gravity tended to deal with smoothing out the wrinkles.

Grace of course would be mortified to discover that this was how Vivian dealt with an expensive designer dress, but then again, her friend had never had to worry about money or where it came from. Not that she resented Grace's good fortune in the least; Vivian had been on the receiving end of her friend's generosity from the very first day they'd met while backpacking in Europe.

"Thoughts?" asked Bryce.

"The pan roasted king salmon looks good," replied Vivian, her gaze fixed firmly on the menu. Going straight to the mains was a bold move, but she really didn't want to waste time on entrees. And in this outfit, only a fool would brave soup and salad.

The curved high back of the dining booth was generously padded. The sensation of the cool fabric against her skin had little goosebumps forming on her arms and legs. When Bryce shifted even closer, and the leg of his linen pants brushed against her thigh, Vivian bit down on her bottom lip.

Another wild porny fantasy dropped into her mind. This one involved Bryce slipping his hand up her skirt and toying with the lace edge of her panties. She hadn't realized how sex starved she was until tonight. Grace's words ordering Vivian to ride the horse until she reached orgasm rose ever higher in volume.

Bryce leaned in. "An excellent choice. I think I might go with the good old sea bass. Of course if either of us gets hungry later on, they do have an in-room dining service that goes until 6am."

Vivian's teeth crushed into her bottom lip. If she didn't get her lust under control and soon, there was every chance both the salmon and the sea bass would go to waste.

Those two little words, *later on*, dripped with sensual promise.

CHAPTER TWENTY-FOUR

They barely made it through dinner. The constant sideway glances coupled with the occasional brush of fingers saw Bryce asking for the check as soon as their plates had been cleared away.

Vivian slipped her hand into his as they walked from the restaurant. While this move eliminated the need for Bryce to growl at any other male guest, hungry gazes still tracked her progress.

Once they were outside, Bryce slowed his steps. Vivian sensed a moment of hesitation on his part. A question perhaps.

Maybe he is worried we're rushing this, or that it's not what I want. I hoped the dress spoke volumes, but who knows? He might just be having second thoughts.

How did she tell him that she desired him, without appearing too desperate? That the careful way she had dressed and put on her makeup tonight had been to send a clear message? She might well view tonight as a holiday fling, but she had chosen her look especially for him. Vivian had chosen Bryce.

"Would you like to take a walk on the beach or…" he asked.

Vivian swallowed deep, then summoned her courage. "Do you have a view of the ocean from your suite?"

His grip on her hand tightened just enough to let her know what he thought of her question. Of how it affected him.

"I have a balcony from which you can see the entire resort's private cove. I would be more than happy to show it to you."

It was a short walk to his suite, and the whole time Vivian's heart was thumping hard in her chest. Anticipation, lust, and a heady dose of adrenaline coursed through her veins. There was no doubt in her mind that she wanted Bryce, craved what this man might offer her. A night of pleasure. One without any expectations of tomorrow. Or disappointment.

Men had let her down enough in the past for her to have developed a certain degree of wariness when it came to the male sex. Her once-too-many-times broken heart had learned to deeply mistrust.

At the door of his room, Bryce let go of Vivian's hand. He took a step back, leaving a foot or two distance between them.

"Today has been an unexpected delight with you Vivian. And dinner was especially lovely."

Her brows furrowed. He sounded like an English gentleman. One of those characters you saw in a movie who was rich, posh, and inevitably turned out to be the villain.

You are not a villain Bryce. I can feel it in my bones. You are one of the good ones.

He cleared his throat. "What I am trying to say, without sounding crass, is that I really like you. Where things go from this point is entirely up to you, Vivian. If you would like to join me in a glass of champagne while viewing the Pacific Ocean from the balcony of my suite, that would be a pleasant way to end the evening. Or you could stay and see the sunrise from my bed. In my arms."

Her heart gave a nervous flip. This man could give lessons on the perfect way to ask a woman to sleep with him. From the way Bryce's warm words kissed her skin, Vivian sensed he knew exactly what her answer would be.

She reached out and plucked the room key card from his fingers, then tapped it against the door. The gentle click of the door unlocking spoke of her decision.

Summoning her bravery once more, Vivian stepped through the door, tugging a grinning Bryce with her.

No sooner had the door closed behind them, all pretense at polite manners fell away. Bryce backed Vivian up against the door, his hands were in her hair and their lips were locked in a fierce embrace. She sent a prayer to heaven, grateful that she had worn her super insanely high heels. It gave her valuable inches in meeting Bryce's lofty height. Making it easier to capture and hold his lips to her sensual ransom.

His right hand pulled free of her tresses and gripped her ass tight, drawing her against him. There was no mistaking the state of his arousal. His hard cock pressed into her belly, and Vivian sighed. She couldn't wait until this man was on top of her, between her legs and thrusting deep into her sex.

Oh yes, I am going to let you ride me like a starter in the Kentucky Derby.

Her own fingers were not idle; they set to work on the buckle of his belt, then the button of his pants. The moment the zipper reached the bottom, she slipped her hand inside and took a firm hold, seizing her prize. Bryce broke the kiss and in a gruff voice which went straight to Vivian's sex, gently scolded, "Greedy girl, don't be in too much of a hurry. We have all night." He shrugged out of his jacket and threw it onto a nearby chair.

I am in so much trouble. If he calls me a bad girl, I might just explode on the spot.

She didn't release him, rather settled into a rhythm which had him groaning against her mouth. His tongue delved deep between her lips, thrusting in time with her stroking of his cock. It was wonderful to have a hot and hard male at her mercy. Especially a guy like Bryce. There was something about him that spoke of a man who rarely let others take the lead. Who liked to be in control.

He drew back from the kiss, settling his strong, firm hand over hers. "Let's take our time. Your pleasure also needs to be attended to Ms. Vivian."

She was ready to melt. There was nothing left of her brain, just an urgent craving for his hands to roam all over her body. To claim what he wanted. To take what she was willing to give.

Claim me. Take me. I want it all.

Bryce's arms settled on Vivian's waist and he lifted her up. She wrapped her legs around him, hooking her ankles together behind his back. The gods of strappy sandals had known exactly what they were doing when they created these heels. Locked together, he carried her over to a huge California king bed.

To Vivian's surprise he didn't toss her on the bed, rather sat her gently, almost reverently down on the edge of the mattress. He knelt before her. "I want to make love to you Vivian. To show you a night of sexual pleasure. But first I need to hear you say that is what you want."

Her heart swelled at his words, knowing that he acknowledged the importance of consent. There had been times at college where Vivian had found herself engaged in intimate situations that later she had come to realize had not been fully consensual on her part. She had let guys pressure her into sex, and then regretted it. Fortunately, time and experience had granted her the wisdom of knowing when to clearly articulate yes or no. To be the one who decided if, when, and with whom she had sexual relations.

With Bryce, it was a yes.

"I want you, Bryce. Skin on skin, hot and heavy."

Their gazes met and in the depth of his dark brown eyes she could have sworn she saw flames. They were ablaze with lust. He was going to take her to the highest of heights.

His fingers settled on the straps of her evening gown, loosening them from around her neck. "This looks like an expensive dress, so I think I should remove it with care."

Bryce got to his feet and held out his hand. Vivian eagerly accepted it, gasping as he first pulled her upright, then spun her about so she was facing away from him. If she hadn't already been near giddy with lust, this would have done the job.

His hands settled lightly on her waist. She closed her eyes as his lips traced the same path down her spine which his fingers had done earlier. Then all the way back up. Touching. Teasing. Setting her heart racing.

"These little hook things are always a challenge," he murmured in her ear.

She hummed. "Try doing them with your arms behind your back. It took me five minutes to get the clasp to close when I was dressing for dinner."

The hook released. Slowly the zipper on the little blue number went all the way down. Bryce tugged the ties at Vivian's neck free. There was nothing left to hold the dress to her body. The fabric fell with a hush and pooled at her feet. Whoever had designed this dress knew a good deal about the practicalities of being able to step out of it while wearing high heels.

Bryce, gentlemanly as ever, picked up the silk confection and laid next to his jacket on the chair. "We can't have your pretty dress all crumpled now, can we?"

Vivian stood before him, clad only in the matching panties and strapless bra that Grace had forced her to buy when she splashed out on the dress. They were a ridiculous barely-there lace and satin set. The sort of frivolous thing a bride wore on her wedding night. Totally impractical but designed with a wicked purpose in mind.

They were a weapon of seduction.

She stifled a grin as Bryce's gaze roamed hungrily over her body. From the way he was looking at her, she sensed he wasn't sure where to begin the sexual feast.

"You do know you are still fully dressed," she teased.

He nodded. "I'm aware of that fact, Vivian. Give me a minute here. It's a tough choice between both of us getting naked straight away, or you agreeing to a spot of roleplay."

Vivian sucked in a shaky breath. His plans had better not involve any form of restraint. Sure, she'd fantasized about cuffing Bryce earlier, and she wasn't entirely against it, but those sorts of things only came when trust had been fully established. Fancy hotel suite and all, but she wasn't going to let a man who was barely past being a stranger tie her up.

Bryce must have read the expression of worry on her face. He came to her placing soft reassuring kisses on her lips. "I wasn't thinking anything too kinky. You must feel safe with me at all times. I was going to suggest you might like to be serviced by me while I am still dressed. You would be naked on the bed, and my face would be between your legs."

She let out the breath she had been holding. If he only knew that this was one of her favorite stories, the sort of sensual encounter she fantasized about while she pleasured herself at night. A fully dressed man between her thighs. *Yes, please.* And with a gorgeous hunk of a man like Bryce, it would be a million times hotter than anything her imagination could create. Her sex throbbed its approval.

"I would like that very much, Bryce." When she added a breathy, "Please," he licked his lips.

"Take off your bra and panties, Vivian, but leave the heels on. I want to feel them digging into my back when I fuck you."

Holy mother...oh god. Whatever I did to deserve tonight, let me do it again.

His lust filled gaze never left hers as she unhooked the strapless bra, and then stepped out of her underwear. Vivian dared not look at the panties, knowing full well they were a sodden mess. No man had ever made her feel this wanton, this powerful.

Not until Bryce Jones.

He lay her back on the bed and gently spread her bare legs.

Yes. Yes. Yes.

She closed her eyes, clutching at the soft bamboo sheets as Bryce's tongue delved deep into her sex. He parted her soft folds then paused to blow cool air on her exposed bud. Vivian whimpered. Her back arched off the bed. A firm hand settled on her stomach, holding her down.

Oh my god.

She'd had sex plenty of times before, but nothing like this. The man kneeling on the floor in front of her was a master of the art of pleasuring a woman. His tongue work had her seeing stars. When he sucked hard on her clit, Vivian's grip on the bedsheets tightened. Her hands balled into fists as he slipped two fingers deep into her sex and began to stroke.

Any minute now, she was going to explode.

Her fingers grasped at his hair. "Slow down, please Bryce." As much as her body screamed for release, she wanted more. They had all night.

His lips left her body and from somewhere his voice drifted to her ears. "Is this how you want to come Vivian, or would like me inside you?"

Ride that horse hard.

He had better have a huge cache of condoms or she was going to be in serious trouble. "Protection," she whispered.

"Of course."

He rose to his feet, produced a condom from his pants pocket, and smoothed it over his hardened cock, still exposed from when Vivian had unzipped him earlier.

"Consider tonight as a long banquet, one with many courses. This is but the first time I will have you, Vivian. I want you to come in every way possible."

And with those words, he flipped her over onto her stomach. Vivian barely had time to gather her thoughts before Bryce drew her roughly to her knees. He slipped three fingers into her sex, the stretch giving her a pleasurable burn. Vivian shuddered as he worked her tight clasp deeply once more, bringing her closer to climax. "Please, Bryce," she begged.

I'm not sure how much more of this I can take.

"Please. Such perfect manners," murmured Bryce, continuing to stroke her sex. He blazed a heated trail of desire down her spine; it was a mix of hot kisses and teasing nips with his teeth. She would bear the marks of his sexual conquest in the morning.

His last bite was a sharp one on the flesh of her ass. Vivian gasped. "Bryce!" He might well behave as a gentleman outside of bed, but there was a wild side to him. And she loved it.

"Are you ready to be claimed, or would like more of my teeth? Your fine ass could definitely take a few more bites." His laugh was deep, dirty, and spoke of a wicked mind.

"I need to be fucked."

"As you wish. Prepare yourself."

Vivian barely had time to steady herself before Bryce sheathed himself deep in her body. Her greedy sex took every inch of his cock. The muscles of her inner walls clenched, and he groaned. "You do need to be fucked. Now, how will we proceed for this first encounter, slow and steady or hard and fast?"

There was no doubt in her mind how she wanted this, how she wanted him.

"Hard and fast. Don't hold back. No mercy. I want it all."

His hands gripped the side of her hips. "That's what I was hoping you would say." He drew back, then slammed hard into her sex.

"Yes. Yes," she urged him on.

The thrusts became strong and unyielding. His grip firmed. There would be bruises to go with the bite marks. She didn't care. Her whole body was focused on finding her release.

The rough abrasion of Bryce's linen pants was heaven against her naked skin. When she finally felt the sharp edge of her climax, Vivian cried out, begging him. "Please. Harder. Punish me."

She came in a blinding rush, crying out as her orgasm swept over her in a great wave of pleasure. Her fingers clenched the bedsheets. The walls of her pussy throbbed. She was utterly boneless, ready to collapse onto the mattress.

But he showed her no post climax mercy, continuing to pound his cock hard against her sensitive flesh. Slap. Slap. Vivian saw stars. Bryce's arm came around her, holding her to him. She loved it when a man took her like this, deep and hard. When he mastered her body for his pleasure.

His hold firmed. One. Two. Three deep, glorious strokes. At the end of the third, he swore under his breath, then stilled. Their chests rose and fell as they both sucked in air.

In the quiet of the room, Bryce whispered. "Vivian, you are the most amazing woman I have ever met."

From another man, that might have just sounded like a post-sex thank you line, but from Bryce she felt its weight. This moment of intimacy with her actually meant something to him.

Vivian blinked back a sudden tear. No matter what the morning brought, she would never forget this night. Every man from now on would be benchmarked against Bryce Jones.

CHAPTER TWENTY-FIVE

The morning sun was streaming through the windows when Vivian woke. She reached across the bed, searching for a warm male body, but found only cooled sheets. Bryce was gone.

She rose up on her elbow, peering through the veil of her tangled hair. Across the room, the glass door which led out onto the balcony was closed. Bryce stood outside with his back to her. He was on his cell. And from his stance and body language, the conversation he was having wasn't a pleasant one.

Throwing back the bedsheets, Vivian struggled out of bed. As she moved, every muscle in her body protested. And well they should. Last night and well into the early hours of this morning, Bryce had shown her what a real man could do. What sexual pleasure meant.

A smile tugged at her lips. He had been magnificent. Talk about getting back on the horse. Her body felt like she had ridden not only the Kentucky Derby, but also the Belmont Stakes. She had been hoping to have Bryce again this morning, and complete the triple crown of racing, but he seemed distracted. To her added disappointment, he was also half-dressed.

Vivian was part way to reaching for the dressing gown which she had earlier abandoned on the floor, when she caught sight of Bryce's left hand as it shot out to the side. Whatever he was saying to the caller, his body was adding its own emphasis to his words. Her lover of the evening was not a happy man this morning.

Morning regrets? I hope not. Please don't let that be a woman he's talking to.

Last night had been a life defining experience. From the dinner in the restaurant, to the hours of heated sex, right through to the super cheesy nachos she and Bryce had shamelessly indulged in at 3am. Every moment had been magical. She had fallen asleep in Bryce's arms with his soft kiss on her lips.

The day had clearly brought with it some problems for Bryce. She was torn. Should she leave him a note on the beautiful stationery pad which sat by the bedside and quietly leave? Or should she go and hit the shower, pretending she hadn't witnessed the terse phone call he was conducting out on the balcony? Hopefully Bryce would have finished his call by the time she was done.

I should go.

She had just hooked up her bra when Bryce turned and walked back into the room.

One minute Bryce was laying on his back, with a sleeping sated Vivian sprawled across his chest, the next he was prizing her off him and reaching for his cell. Upon seeing *Heather* on the screen, he climbed out of bed, shoved on a pair of boxer briefs, and headed for the door which led out to the balcony.

"Hi Heather. What's happening?" Bryce's assistant knew he was at the Laguna Beach resort and would not have called him unless it was urgent.

"Morning Bryce. Just ringing to give you a heads up. Jordan knows you are in the States. Apparently, he's been calling everyone in New York this morning, your time, and someone let slip that the company jet is in California."

Fuck.

Jordan wasn't stupid. It wouldn't take long for him to put two and two together and figure that Bryce had gone behind his back.

He glanced back at the bed to where the gorgeous Vivian lay fast asleep. This couldn't have come at a more inopportune time. "Thanks, Heather. I'll call you back later."

Reaching the glass door, he opened it. Bryce stepped out into the bright Californian morning sunshine, then slid the door closed behind him. His lover didn't need to wake to whatever was about to go down with his wayward sibling.

The time had come, he couldn't avoid Jordan any longer. Bryce hit dial then put the phone to his ear. Jordan answered on the third ring. "You've been dodging my calls. You don't answer my emails. I couldn't figure out why. I thought you must have been super busy— in London. So tell me Bryce, how's the weather on the West Coast this morning?"

There was no mistaking the accusatory tone in his brother's voice. Jordan had figured out that Bryce wasn't in England. The game was up.

It was bound to happen. But I just wish you had let me have this morning with Vivian.

There was no point in lying. Jordan knew he was in LA. Bryce focused his gaze on the blue waters of the Pacific

Ocean, bracing himself for whatever storm was about to come.

"The weather is fine here in California, Jordan, thank you for asking. I'm at the Laguna Beach resort on behalf of Edward and the board."

He only ever used his father's first name when he was discussing business. It was a warning sign to his brother: he wasn't here on vacation, and this went beyond family.

The angry huff on the other end of the line spoke volumes. Jordan was taking Bryce's words in, and he was far from happy.

Bryce wanted to add that he wasn't here by choice, but he sensed that wouldn't help Jordan feel any better about his brother's betrayal. *I'm sorry, but there was nothing else I could do.*

"If it's any sort of comfort I am staying here incognito, and no, I haven't yet spoken to your assistant manager Austin, though it is on my, to-do-list."

"Thank you. Can I ask how things are going?"

Jordan shouldn't be the one asking him that question. His brother should know exactly how things were going in California. He shouldn't be in New York, he should be here.

Bryce pinched the bridge of his nose. "It's bad, Jordan. Staff are run off their feet during breakfast service. There are not enough towels at the pool. In fact, not enough linen in many places. I spoke to a guest who said it had taken her two phone calls and a visit to the front desk simply to get a duvet for her bed." He raised his left hand and punched the air in frustration.

He wasn't about to tell Jordan that it had been Vivian, the woman who was still curled up in his bed, who had shared the full details of that particularly embarrassing story over corn chips and salsa in the early hours of this morning. When she'd first mentioned it at the poolside, he'd thought she was joking. She wasn't, and heads were going to roll.

"Oh. I was kinda hoping things might have settled down, I did the best I could," replied Jordan in a distracted tone.

Lord give me strength.

Bryce puffed out his cheeks, frustrated that he was being forced to state the obvious. "Hope is not a plan."

"You could have told me you were back in the States, and that Dad had sent you on a secret mission to LA. I didn't think you would ever put business ahead of your own brother. I wouldn't do that to you," chided Jordan. His voice now had a definite edge to it.

"And you could have told Dad that you left a rookie in charge of a billion dollar investment while you got on a plane and went home. Did work get in the way of your social life?"

"Ah, there you go again, Bryce. Hiding behind Dad. Don't you have your own voice or are you just a fucking Muppet who only speaks when his hand is up your ass?"

Bryce clenched his fist as Jordan's words struck home.

Don't let his anger drag you into saying something you later regret. Something is wrong in Jordan's life, don't add fuel to the fire.

"You could have told me you were having trouble with this place. I would've helped you, and no one, not even Dad would have ever needed to know. The only thing left to do now is to sort out the mess. We still have a billion dollar resort to launch. Not to mention salvaging the Platinum Collection brand."

And I am out of time.

If Jordan and others in the New York office had gotten wind of his being here, it wouldn't be long before someone at Laguna Beach received a whisper as to the true identity of Mister Jones in ocean view suite seven. There would be little point in him staying on after that, the staff would no doubt be tasked with the job of fawning all over him.

He turned from staring out to sea, his heart sinking as he caught sight of a tussled haired Vivian standing in the middle of the room. She was awake, and if she had seen him on the phone, would know he was in the middle of an argument with someone.

I wanted one more day with her, or at least tonight. Was that too much to ask of the universe? To spend a few hours with a sexy, intelligent woman?

If people started acting strange around him, she would think it odd. And then she would discover that Bryce Jones didn't exist.

I lied to her about where I am from, what I do for a living. I even gave her a false name.

How could he tell this amazing woman, who had shared her body so generously with him, who had trusted him, the truth? He'd lied to her, and not just about minor things. Vivian was trying to recover from the end of a terrible relationship which had left her with deep-seated trust issues. Finding out that he too was a barefaced liar would crush her. There had to be a way for him to keep his identity a secret from Vivian.

"Jordan, I have to go. I'm going to take the car and go up to LA this morning to meet with the linen company. If there is one thing I can do before I leave here, it's to put in a priority order for more towels and bedding."

"I didn't mean for this to happen, Bryce. And I'm sorry about the Muppet quip, I know you are your own man. I've messed up, again."

The thing which both frustrated and concerned Bryce was that until the past day he had been certain Jordan had got his life sorted. If Bryce hadn't fully believed that he wouldn't have even considered, let alone backed his brother to manage this important resort launch.

"Look, I'll be back in New York in a couple of days. We can talk then. In the meantime, I would suggest going through the online travel review sites and seeing what our guests have said about this place. There is likely to be other things that I have missed, which the board needs to know are being addressed."

"Thanks Bryce. Talking would be good. Bye."

He punched the red end-call button a little too firmly. Cell clutched tightly in his hand, Bryce reached for the door. His hopes of sharing a peaceful morning with Vivian in his embrace had just evaporated.

The situation with Jordan would take some resolving, but he was confident that when he was back in New York they could sit down and try to sort things out.

Back in New York. Vivian is from New York. This could become more than a one night stand. I have to figure out how I can tell her and get her to trust me.

It was taking the coward's way out, but he only had capacity to navigate his way through one tricky issue this morning. Going up to LA and begging the linen company for a priority order had to unfortunately come first. That was why he was here.

Last night with Vivian had been special. It was more than just sex. Talking and laughing with her over sour cream and salsa had tugged at his heart. Had his soul whispering to him once more. *I am lonely.*

He'd lied to her, but Bryce would do whatever it took to convince Vivian to give them a chance at a real relationship. She was a rare woman and only a fool would let a woman like her walk out of his life. Telling her the truth of his identity, was only the beginning.

How do I get her to believe in me? If she can't trust me, she will never love me.

CHAPTER TWENTY-SIX

"Bad news?" asked Vivian. There was no point in pretending that she hadn't watched a clearly rattled Bryce talking on the phone.

"No, just a team member who doesn't seem to get the team part. We have a supply problem with an order, and I am going to have to go into the city and sort it out." He slowly shook his head, disappointment evident on his face. "I was hoping to spend the morning with you. In fact the entire day if given half the chance. But the work issue can't wait. I'm really sorry, Vivian."

Vivian's heart did a little dance of joy at hearing Bryce's words. He wanted to see her again, share another night of passion. But if anyone understood sudden changes in work plans, it was her.

"I was looking forward to us taking a walk on the beach, after we'd had..."

She left the rest unsaid, tugging at the loose ties of the dressing gown. Bryce only had to offer, and she would happily be naked and beneath him once more.

Instead, he raked his fingers through his hair, and sighed.

"That was my plan as well. Will you still be here tonight? I thought maybe we could try dinner again and see if we can make it through entrée as well as main course this time. Or not."

The promise in Bryce's words, sent heat pooling between her legs. No sane woman would think to pass up the opportunity to spend another night with this amazing man. To reach the heights of pleasure once again with him.

The review article had been submitted, her work was done. Lionel hadn't said anything about needing her to cut short her stay and return to New York. The room had been paid for, and she had pulled her boss out of a tight jam. As far as she was concerned, she was owed this time, to spend it doing something just for her, to live a little.

"Yes, I'll be here. I'm going to head back to my room and let you get your work done. Can we meet at the bar at say six?"

He crossed the room in an instant and swept her up into his arms. Her body melted in anticipation of more bone deep pleasure as Bryce's lips brushed over hers. The kiss was tender, full of promise, but it ended all too soon.

"I really should take you back to bed and have my wicked way, but you deserve my full attention, and I can't avoid this meeting."

She kissed him, then drew out of his embrace. The sooner Bryce went to see his supplier, the quicker he would be back at the resort. "Go and sort things out. In the meantime, I'm going to steal this robe and head to my room. I might even try to get some more sleep. You are a demanding lover, Bryce."

He grinned at her. "I'll see you tonight?"

"That's a promise."

With her dress slung over her arm and her killer heels dangling from her fingers, Vivian did a hurried walk of shame back to her room. When she passed another guest in the hallway, she did her best to avoid their gaze. There could be no mistaking what she had been up to last night. Or how amazing it had been. She didn't care what people thought, she couldn't stop smiling.

At least the robe covers the bite marks and small bruises. Best night of sex ever.

Following a long hot shower, she changed into a pair of leisure pants and a comfy cotton sweater. If Bryce was going to be out for most of the morning, and she no longer had to worry about a deadline, today was the perfect day for lounging around. And if she couldn't get an appointment at the spa, then she would have to settle for another swim. There would be other review assignments where she could spend Lionel's two hundred bucks.

If I do go for a swim, it won't be the same without Bryce and those low slung swim trunks.

She flipped open her laptop. A few minutes to catch up on social media then head down for a spot of breakfast. While the early morning nachos had indeed been filling, Bryce had made many demands of her body. Vivian was in dire need of refueling.

I might order a Starbucks delivery. I'm sure the resort won't mind if I get a Frappuccino sent in.

Vivian had spied the green siren sign of her favorite coffee shop on the road close to the resort. A less exhausted person might actually pull on their sneakers and go for a walk, but today she was simply going to hang out.

"You never know, Lionel might call and ask me to expand

further on my piece. I can't be too far away if it's an emergency," she lied to herself.

Knowing her boss he would have given her review a quick check, chosen some of Vivian's more appealing photos and already have sent it to be formatted and added to the next issue of Luxury Hotels and Resorts Worldwide.

She scrolled absentmindedly through the usual social media sites, but none of them yielded anything of note. It was midweek and no one's life had blown up in the past twenty four hours. Her friends tended to leave the drama for the weekend.

Her finger tapped on the link to *Leisure Line*, and her gaze immediately focused on the whispers column. "Come on give me some juicy gossip this morning."

Royal Rumbles?

The headline caught Vivian's interest. The Royal family was not known for making the press in any negative way. A family conglomerate which spanned across the globe, with interests in not only hotels and resorts, but high end fashion, homewares, and beauty. And while Royal was the name behind many famous brands, it was rare to actually see a picture of any members of the family.

Rumor has it that the US board of Royal Resorts are looking to make some changes at the top. Jordan Royal who was a potential candidate to eventually take over from his father, Edward, as CEO of the group's US resort operations, is reported to be getting pushed out of the way by his older brother Bryce. Bryce Royal who has been heading up the group's European operations for the past four years, is rumored to have slipped back into New York earlier this week.

Vivian didn't take in the rest of the article. Her gaze was

locked on the accompanying photo. It was of the three Royal brothers. Bryce, Jordan, and Matthew. They looked to be at some sort of black-tie charity event. She didn't need to read the caption which noted who was who.

She already knew Bryce.

The brown eyes which smiled out from the picture were the same ones which had stared into hers, as Bryce had made slow, masterful love to her only a matter of hours ago.

Bryce Jones was Bryce Royal.

Nausea rolled over her as cold realization hit.

"He lied to me."

The man she had spent last night with wasn't in homewares, and he certainly didn't live in San Diego. He was Bryce Royal, the New York billionaire.

This is his resort.

Abandoning her laptop Vivian shot to her feet. She began to pace the floor, panic rising with every step. Wearing a hole in the carpet seemed a really good idea right now. Hell, she'd happily pay for it.

"I have to get out of here."

A strangled laugh escaped her lips. "Well at least I can tick that off my bucket list. Slept with a billionaire." And if anyone ever asked, she could confirm, that super rich people were hot as fuck in bed. They probably went to a super-secret and fabulously expensive sex finishing school in the French Alps.

But no matter how wonderful he'd been between the sheets, the warm and charming Bryce had still lied to her.

Oh god, was he laughing at me behind my back the whole time?

She'd been a fool to think she could have a fling with a handsome guy and for it not to come back to bite her soundly on the ass. *I even have the marks on my skin to prove it.* For some unknown reason, the universe seemed determined to spite her.

Her restless feet finally came to a halt. Hands fisted by her sides, Vivian took in a slow deep breath. It was times like this she wished she hadn't given up on her daily yoga and meditations. Her mind was a whirl of indecision.

Shit. Shit. Shit.

"I have to get out of here."

She headed for the bathroom and quickly packed her toiletries. Her dress went into its silk bag, then joined the rest of her stuff in her suitcase. A hurried check under the bed, and in the wardrobe revealed no stray items.

Five minutes later, dressed in her most comfortable travel clothes, Vivian used the online checkout service to settle her bill, and left a tip for housekeeping on the table. Under any other circumstances she would have waited for the luggage service, but she was desperate to leave. The way her luck was currently running, she would probably bump into Bryce in the lobby. She couldn't bear the thought of what he would say if he discovered she was attempting to make a fast getaway. What lies he would offer up.

No. I've had my fill of bullshit excuses from men. I'm going home.

Dropping her room keycard into the box in the foyer, she headed straight to the concierge. "I need a ride to LAX as soon as possible please. Uber. Cab. Whatever. This is urgent."

She didn't care how she left the resort, just as long as she was gone. The day which had started out so full of promise had gone downhill at a rapid rate.

Climbing into the back of the cab, she gave one final glance at the hotel entrance. As she did, a flurry of thoughts dropped into her mind. Bryce had slipped back into the US on the quiet and then come out to California. He'd checked into his own resort under a false name. There were rumors of issues at Laguna Beach.

He didn't care about me, so why should I care about his stupid resort.

He hadn't trusted her enough to feel he could share his identity. Hadn't thought her worthy of the truth of who he was.

Vivian angrily brushed away a tear. She was not going to cry over a guy who had clearly decided right from the outset that she meant nothing more to him than a plate of nachos and a night of fun.

When will I ever learn, if a guy seems too good to be true, it's because he's full of it.

CHAPTER TWENTY-SEVEN

The Royal family estate
 Armonk, New York
 Saturday evening, two days later

"As I said on the phone, you should have told me. What happened to brotherly loyalty?"

Bryce gritted his teeth. He didn't need this, especially not from Jordan. He was back in New York, suffering through a tense family dinner. These things were normally enjoyable occasions. Rare moments of Royal family togetherness when he was able to make it home to the US. But not tonight.

Jordan, seated on the other side of the brown and gold bespoke tamarind wood table, bristled with fury. Bryce was under no illusion that it was all for show. To get back at their father for having asked him to go out to California.

Bryce wasn't going to give Jordan the argument he was clearly seeking. He'd done what had been asked of him at Laguna Beach, given the board the full report, then got back on the plane and returned to New York. Jordan could complain about being undermined all he liked.

Edward had made it clear that he considered Bryce's mission as having been a success. The executives of Royal Resorts now had a clear understanding of the situation in California. A plan to bring the resort back on track was no doubt being formulated. But Bryce didn't welcome his father's praise. He had nothing to celebrate.

He'd been ghosted by Vivian.

The meeting with the LA linen contractor had been one of the most deeply embarrassing in his entire career. Standing in the middle of the warehouse, he'd been informed that Austin had cut the original linen order by half. A red faced Bryce had been forced to plea for the rest of the order to be urgently backfilled. Whatever money Austin might have thought he had saved was now gone. The fast-tracked order had come at a premium price.

By the time he finally got back to the resort, Bryce had been aching to see Vivian. To find a moment's peace in her embrace. He couldn't share all his troubles with her, but he'd been hoping her smile and tender touch would take the edge off his frustrations.

On the traffic snarled drive back from LA, he'd decided to come clean. To tell Vivian who he really was and give her a full explanation as to his reasons for the subterfuge. The connection he had felt between them was something he'd hoped would allow Vivian to see her way to forgiving him. He didn't want her to think he was the same as her ex, the one who had charged all that money to her credit card.

And if things had gone according to his hastily put together plan, they would've had more time to spend together at the resort. They could have shared more passionate moments in his suite while at the same time nurturing the buds of their deepening relationship. At the end of their stay, lifted a rock in either Italy or France, they uncovered an ancient Roman ruin. Working within local laws while also winning over nearby residents took a degree of delicate finesse. He was grateful that Jordan wasn't running the Aspen operation.

"Did you get to spend any time for yourself while you were in California, Bryce? You work so hard. I wish you would take a day or two off," asked Alice.

Bryce turned and gave his mother a tight smile. He ignored his brother's huff from across the other side of the table.

His mind drifted back to that glorious sun-drenched afternoon he'd spent by the pool with Vivian. And the long night of passion which they had shared. But he wasn't about to mention that he had seduced a resort guest while he was on business. Especially not when his father was within earshot.

"No Mom, I didn't. And yes, you are right, I do need to make some time for myself at some point."

He didn't add further to his comment. Alice Royal had made it plain that she was eager for grandchildren. All three of her sons were of an age where, according to her, they should be actively looking for their future life partners.

This was not the time nor the place to tell his mother that she was right. That over recent months he'd been thinking a great deal about his future. Of finding a woman to share not only his bed, but his name. He didn't want to be a bachelor, he wanted to be a husband, and a father.

Vivian might have blown him off, but she had been right in stating that she believed love mattered. Perhaps he should sign up for the dating app that she had mentioned. He couldn't be the only lonely billionaire in New York City.

I wonder if she is using the app?

It could potentially be a way to reach out and connect

with her. Worst case, he could get to the bottom of why she had checked out the resort without telling him.

Forget it. Vivian clearly just wanted a night of sex. She got what she wanted and then left.

If only he could stop thinking about her.

CHAPTER TWENTY-EIGHT

*The Holte family home
 Fresh Meadows, Queens
 Saturday evening*

"You could sue Pete, I'm sure that he has broken some credit card or finance law," offered Brenda.

Vivian shook her head. She'd already been down that road with Grace. The money it would cost for her to take her ex to court would be greater than the amount she already owed the bank.

"I've cut my losses and moved on, Mom. Can you please pass me the towels?"

They were standing side by side in her mother's laundry room, folding Vivian's clean clothes and linen. Apart from the obvious difference in their ages, mother and daughter were the spitting image of one another. Both had straight, light brown hair, and greenish blue eyes. The family had a running joke about Vivian being her mom's time travelling sister.

It was a weekly tradition for Vivian to make the trip out

to Fresh Meadows, Queens to wash her things. The apartment she shared with Grace on the upper east side was in an older building and as much as things had been updated over time, the plumbing couldn't handle the demands of modern washing machines.

The time involved in sitting in a public laundromat was beyond Vivian's limits of patience. It was much simpler to get on a train and go out to the burbs and see her family. Her dad cooked a mean spaghetti sauce, and he always sent her home with a container of leftovers, so there was that as well.

Her mother passed over the towels and Vivian spent the next few minutes slowly folding them, before stuffing them into the rucksack she had brought with her.

"Your brother offered to go and see Pete, but your dad warned him against it."

The Holte family was the best. Vivian's birth father had died in a car accident when she was five. Her mother had eventually remarried, and that union had resulted in Vivian gaining two half-brothers. Fortunately her family was not into half anything. If you were family, you were fully in.

"It's ok, Mom. I'm serious. Pete is a done deal. Firmly in my past. In fact..." She hesitated for a moment, unsure as to how much to tell her mother. They were both adults, but like all parents, Brenda still viewed Vivian through the lens of a parent.

"In fact what?"

Here goes. "I met a guy while I was on assignment in California. While it was a short lived thing, it helped to draw a line under Pete and me."

Bryce Royal was just another liar who I will have to get over. Another line to draw.

She hoped that was enough. Grace had been eager for details when Vivian got home, and had insisted nothing was beyond her, but this was different, it was her mom.

Brenda handed her the last of the laundry, and before leaving the room gave Vivian a pat on the shoulder, saying, "Well done, sweetheart. Let me know if you want to talk further."

Yeah, well done me. I've gone from thieves to billionaires. And both turned out to be douchebags. The only difference was that Bryce didn't need to steal my credit card.

"Thanks, Mom."

Back at the apartment in the city, Vivian lay on the couch in full sloth-mode. Grace and Marlon had gone out for the evening. That particular romance was still going strong. Marlon who also worked in finance, apparently ticked quite a few of the suitable life partner boxes. Vivian quietly wondered how long it would be before Grace took him to meet her parents.

And how long until she and her friend had a conversation about living arrangements? If Marlon moved in here, or Grace went to take up residence at his swanky Manhattan address, Vivian would likely have to find a new place to live. She certainly couldn't afford this one on her own, and any new housemate would want her to pay more than her current base level rent.

If she moved back home, the commute to Greenwich Village from Queens would be an hour and a half both ways. She felt ill just thinking about the hours she would waste on catching trains.

Doing her best to forget about possible impending doom, and with Spike curled up at her feet, Vivian was spending her evening quietly scrolling through her phone.

A message from Grace popped up.

> If you are sitting on the couch, drinking wine while mindlessly scrolling, then at least log on to the dating app and fix your profile so you can snap up a millionaire.

"I wasn't just scrolling. I was researching. People need to know the truth about what that famous actor from ten years ago really looks like now," she whispered at the screen.

There wasn't any wine in the apartment and she couldn't be bothered getting dressed and walking down to the grocery store on Second Avenue.

The mention of the dating app sent her mind racing back to California. To the night she had spent with Bryce Royal. He had been so unlike her previous boyfriend—until he'd been almost exactly like him.

"It's a pity that Bryce Jones wasn't a real man. I could have been happy with a guy like him. But he wasn't real, was he Spike?"

The cat moved from her position slowly making her way up to settle on Vivian's thighs. Vivian idly scratched the spot on the top of Spike's head between her ears. She earned an appreciative purr for her efforts.

"How about we do what your human mom says and take a look at this millionaire dating app."

Vivian's thumb pressed on the app icon. She popped in the login and password her ex had sent. The app instantly opened to her profile, and Vivian's heart sank. Pete, bless his cheating little heart, had done a real number on it. From the way he had Vivian describing herself, she sounded more like a hungry mountain troll than a person.

He's lucky I blocked and deleted his number.

Sending death threats via phone was a federal offense, and Pete was just the sort of guy who would probably call the cops.

If the lack of activity on her profile was anything to go by there weren't any other love seeking mountain trolls in the tri-state area.

Vivian fixed her profile, made it as honest as possible, then hit save. She also changed her password.

Well, I have spent good money on this app, it's time I tried to get a couple of bucks worth of value out of it.

She clicked the location to New York City and got to swiping. Forty minutes later, Vivian closed the app in disappointment and placed her cell on the floor. Surprise surprise, every single millionaire, male and female alike, had tagged themselves as being powerful alpha highflyers and in the market for a partner who was nothing less than a New York ten.

"Even millionaire mountain trolls don't stand a chance," she muttered.

Shifting the cat off her legs, Vivian went to find some shoes. She'd changed her mind about going to the grocery store. Losing a thousand bucks on a pointless dating app was something which had to be celebrated. The occasion called for nothing less than a three dollar bottle of white wine.

CHAPTER TWENTY-NINE

Hudson Yards, New York City
Late Saturday night

The Mercedes luxury SUV cruised to a smooth halt in the underground parking garage of the House of Royal building on Eleventh Avenue. Jordan turned off the engine, and there followed a moment of silence.

On the drive back to the city, all three Royal brothers had stuck to safe topics such as football. Bryce, who was a Giants fan, put up with an hour of crap talk from Jordan and Matthew who both followed the Jets. Considering how tense things had been at their parents' home, it made sense for him to let them have their fun and simply suck it up.

"Does anyone fancy a late night cup of cocoa?" offered Matthew who was seated in the back seat.

Up front, Bryce and Jordan exchanged a look, and both nodded. "Yeah, that would be good."

They headed for the private elevator which serviced the Royal family apartments. When they got inside, Jordan pressed the button. "How about you both come up to my place. I have a good selection of water."

Bryce and Matthew both nodded. As a recovering addict Jordan found it hard to go to places where the only non-alcoholic drinks on offer were usually either coke or plain bottled water. In his apartment, he had an impressive range of alcohol free drinks and Fiji Water on tap.

"Bryce and I are sorted," said Matthew. He magically produced a bottle of wine from under his jacket.

"Where did you get that?" asked Bryce.

Matthew grinned. "Dad's wine cellar. Thought we might end up having a late night drink, so I stole it before we left." He held it up to the light and Bryce caught sight of the label.

"Wow. That's a five hundred dollar bottle of Chateau Mouton Rothschild. Dad will kill you if he finds out you've taken it."

"Make that eight hundred bucks, and he won't know if we all keep our mouths shut," replied Matthew.

"Yeah. We have got to start teaming up with each other," added Jordan.

The elevator came to a stop, and they all piled out. Jordan tapped his keycard on the security pad and pushed the door of his apartment open. Matthew followed, leaving a contemplative Bryce to trail in their wake.

While his brothers set about sorting out bottles and glasses, Bryce pondered his next words. It was time. If tonight's dinner had shown him anything it was that the gap which divided the three of them was widening. Their father, whether he meant it or not, was driving a wedge between his sons.

I have to say something and now.

Bryce cleared his throat. "We three need to work out what to do about Dad and the business. It looks like I am going to be staying in the US for at least awhile and after what happened with me being sent to Laguna Beach, I'm worried that he is playing us off against one another."

Jordan nodded. "Tell me something I don't know."

"Yeah," added Matthew.

"I know the whole first born thing stems from his own family, with his grandfather being a duke. The English nobility with it's *the son gets the title and the land* while the rest of the kids get nothing has shaped his worldview. But this is the US, and that mindset has to stop. And it stops with us."

Bryce hated being made to go behind his brother's back, and if he didn't call a halt to this sort of thing now, he feared it would only get worse. His brothers both nodded their agreement.

"Good."

Drinks in hand they ambled into the living room. Jordan swiped his hand over a lamp and the room was immediately bathed in a pale light.

"You do know they have invented dimmers for the main lights in these places," offered Matthew.

Jordan turned to the window. The lights of New York were the perfect backdrop. "Yeah, but the old school lamp just gives the right ambiance."

"Ooooooh, ambiance." Bryce and Matthew, both gave him their teasing response. It had all three of them laughing.

Matthew took up a spot in the corner of the couch, leaving Bryce to move some cushions out of the way at the other end. As he lifted the pile, something fell out and onto the floor. He bent and picked it up.

It was a large red and white t-shirt. Emblazoned on the front was the word.

Chloe

On the back were the words.

The World is my Lover Tour

"Didn't figure you for a Chloe fan, Jordan." The words had barely left his lips before the t-shirt was snatched out of Bryce's fingers. Jordan quickly tucked it under his arm, but Bryce noticed his brother's hands were shaking. Were those tears in his eyes?

"Are you alright, Jordan? What's wrong?"

"Nothing. The shirt was just a mistake from the laundry service. I meant to get them to come and collect it. Someone in the building must be wondering where it went. It was a mistake. A mistake." Jordan hurriedly left the room, taking the shirt with him.

When Bryce gaze Matthew a questioning look, his brother shook his head. "I'm not at liberty to discuss anything, but I think you might want to cut Jordan some slack when this is all over. Things are not what they seem."

Things must be bad if Matthew is defending Jordan.

He raised his glass. "Drink up, Bryce. We need to finish this wine, and then you are going to hide the evidence."

"Why am I covering up the crime?"

"Because Dad would never suspect you of doing anything wrong. He knows you are far too honest."

Bryce sipped his expensive French wine. If the price he had to pay to get back in good with his brothers was to share in the spoils of a wine heist, then it was worth paying. Just being with them, being home, was such a priceless thing.

I miss these two. I think it's time I started making plans to come home, permanently. If there is something wrong in Jordan's life, I can't help him if I'm three and a half thousand miles away.

CHAPTER THIRTY

Royal Resorts Offices
  New York City
  A wet and cold Monday, nine days later

Bryce's fingers hit the delete button. Click by click, Vivian Holte slowly disappeared from his computer screen. He was not going to search for her. She must have had her reasons for ghosting him, and only a schmuck would go chasing after a woman who clearly didn't want to be found.

I was interested in her, but not desperate.

As much as he tried to stop thinking about her, his thoughts kept returning to the warm, smiling girl he had met in California. To the wonderful night they had shared. He couldn't recall the last time a woman had got under his skin. But Vivian certainly had.

You have to move on and get over her. Stop trying to figure out why she left.

Vivian hadn't tried to rob him, none of his stuff had been touched. Granted, his valuables had been locked away in his suitcase the whole time she had been in his room, but she'd not even attempted to charge a coffee to his bill after he had left for his meeting with the linen company.

He'd been sure she wasn't married, or if she was, she'd been a player long before he had met her. It would have taken a special talent to be so open and honest, while at the same time a liar and a cheat. His gut told him that wasn't Vivian. And yet...

None of it made sense.

What a shame. I think she and I could have had a real connection. A future.

Pushing back from his desk he spun his chair to face the window. "I lied to her." Maybe this was fate punishing him for being false.

Bryce shook his head. Why did Vivian have to come from New York? Eight and a half million people lived in the city. She'd picked the perfect place to hide.

She didn't want to know you. Get it through your thick skull. Vivian is gone.

He'd just made the decision to put Vivian firmly in the past and move on with his life when there was a loud rap on his door. Bryce turned as his father stormed into his office.

Edward tossed a bound stack of papers onto the desk and swore. "This is a bloody shit of a disaster."

Bryce's gaze landed on the pile. It was Luxury Hotels and Resorts Worldwide. While he didn't have time to normally read it, he still knew the publication. It was one of the major international and US hotel and resort rags, as his father liked to call them.

He picked it up and quickly scanned the cover blurbs. On the right, in prime position, written in bold yellow letters were the words:

Royal Resorts Platinum Collection, Laguna Beach:

'Room for Improvement'

His heart sank to his designer shoes. *Oh, no.* Bryce lifted his gaze and took in the expression on his father's face. It was clear that Edward's hopes for a global top 100 ranking for the billion dollar resort had been crushed by whatever had been printed in the magazine.

"What rating did they give us?"

Edward closed his eyes, then let out a sigh. "Three stars. And I think they might have given us one of those out of pity. Laguna Beach was meant to be the one that all others measured themselves up against. Our shining beacon. Fuck."

As Bryce opened the magazine his father headed for the door. "I need some air. I'm going to get my driver to drop me off so I can go for a long walk in Central Park. I will talk to you later, son."

"Don't you want to wait until I've read it?"

"No. I have to get out of the office, because if I see Jordan, there is a very good chance that I will murder him. After that, well...let's just say, I've seen enough TV shows to be certain that I don't ever plan to set foot inside Rikers prison."

Under other circumstances, Bryce would have brushed off his father's remark. However, the look of broken hope which sat on his face spoke volumes for Edward's mental state.

Bryce wisely let his father go. A long walk would hopefully do Edward's mind and mood some good. Rising from his chair, he followed Edward to the door and closed it after him. He was tempted to ask one of the office assistants to go and ask in-house catering to grind up some of his Jamaican coffee beans and brew him a fresh espresso.

I have a feeling I might need something stronger before this afternoon is over.

Bryce dropped back into his chair and flipped open the

magazine. Thumbing through it, he stopped when he caught sight of a double page spread of the golf course and beach at the Royal Resorts California resort. He pushed away the memory of the morning when he and Vivian had walked the grounds. Of her happy smile as she snapped pictures with her cellphone.

The accompanying article was titled *Room for Improvement*.

It sounded like a school report. Could do better in class. Lacks attention. The usual things he had overheard his parents arguing about during Jordan's days at high school. A poor school rating was one thing, this was… "A bloody shit of a disaster," he muttered, echoing his father's words.

Watered down cocktails. Lack of towels by the pool. Tick. Tick. Then something caught his eye. A comment about the reviewer's efforts to get a duvet struck a nerve. The more he read, the closer to boiling point his blood rapidly grew.

Whoever the reviewer for the magazine was, they too had eaten in the restaurant and found it to be adequate. They had also spent time at the poolside cabana. At least they had thoroughly enjoyed the woodfired pizzas. The mention of a long delay in checking in and then time wasted in the soulless Sunview Bar, drove Bryce to the verge of dashing the magazine against the window.

He simmered with a slow burning rage as he finally turned to the page which listed the magazine's contributors and staff writers. Among the names, one stood out.

Vivian Holte. Vivian.

He had slept with a resort reviewer while she was on assignment.

His hand went to his mouth as the truth of the situation crashed down on him. She had to have known who he was. Was that what she meant when she said she'd taken a second look at him when they passed each other in the bar?

She was a resort reviewer for one of the biggest travel

magazines in America, she had to have known who he was. *And that means, oh.* It went both ways. While Vivian hadn't specifically mentioned her occupation, she had given him her real name. Had she assumed he was a regular reader of the magazine, and would therefore have known who she was?

She gave you her name. Oh, no.

Bryce's pulse raced. Had this all been a game to her? Was Vivian that corrupt a reviewer that she would willingly let him seduce her? A night of amazing sex for a rave review. Had that been her plan all along?

Anger coursed through his veins. Vivian. Sweet. Sexy. Devil between the sheets Vivian had given the Laguna Beach resort a three star review.

No.

She gave me a three star review.

I put my soul into the hours we spent together making love, and she gave me...a three.

He swayed as he got back to his feet. Shock and the bright burning flame of humiliation was all too real. "What the actual fuck?" Bryce raked his fingers through his hair.

Everyone in the hotel and leisure business knew that when a magazine gave you a three star review, they really meant it was a two, but they were trying to be kind. No one wanted hotels or resorts to fail.

At the window, Bryce rested his face against the cool glass. It didn't help. He was beyond feeling anything other than flat out rage.

Vivian had slept in his bed. They had shared a night of intimacy that would forever remain in his memories. She was the woman against which all others he seduced would now be judged.

And she gave me a three. Bumped up from a two.

He'd really liked her. Had even been trying to figure out how to explain his false name and ask for a chance to see her again in New York. But she'd known. And she'd been exploiting it. Her story about the lying ex-boyfriend was probably just that —another lie.

His hands clenched into tight fists. The dreadful review wasn't just a trifling thing in a magazine with a few thousand subscribers. Luxury Hotels and Resorts Worldwide carried real weight in the industry. Vivian's scathing review presented an existential threat to the House of Royal's US based resort business. The Platinum Collection's light was already dimming, this review might well see it go out.

But for Bryce, it was also deeply personal. Vivian had not only abused his trust, but she'd also openly mocked him. But in writing that review, she had made a mistake, she had made a powerful enemy.

I know where to find you, Vivian Holte.

Revenge came next.

CHAPTER THIRTY-ONE

New York City
Tuesday night

"I've mixed with millionaires all my life, but I never knew that so many of them were such creeps," huffed Grace. "I thought this dating app was supposed to send you recommendations of potential partners, not the lineup of villains from an episode of NCIS."

It was almost two weeks after Vivian had returned home early from her trip to California, and she and Grace were spending the evening at home half-watching a series on Netflix. Grace's now official boyfriend, Marlon, was out of town at a finance conference in Chicago.

The truth was, neither Vivian nor Grace was actually watching any of the TV show. A little while earlier, Grace had commandeered her housemate's cellphone and was checking out the millionaire dating app.

For the past day or so, Vivian had been swiping left. There hadn't been one guy whose profile pic or bio had

Hindsight was a bitch. "I told him about Pete. And then, yada yada." Vivian waved her hand about. "I gave the resort a less than stellar review. Bryce must have read it, seen my name, then signed up for the dating site. He thought to put little old me firmly in my place."

Which he had most certainly done. Her chances of getting any sort of date from the millionaire dating site now lay in ashes. She might as well have flushed a thousand dollars down the drain.

Grace climbed off the sofa and got to her feet. She looked ready to punch something or someone. "Sheesh, Viv he puts the bilious in billionaire."

Vivian snorted at the wry joke. It was either that or crying. And she was well past the point of sobbing her heart out over men.

"So what are we going to do about it?" asked Grace. Her friend was not the kind of girl who took this sort of thing lying down. Grace's father had broken through many glass ceilings on his way to becoming one of the East Coast's richest African Americans, and he had instilled in his daughter a strong fighting spirit.

If this had happened to Grace, she would've been on the phone to her lawyer and Bryce Royal would have had a stack of legal papers in his hands well before the next morning. But Vivian didn't have access to those sorts of resources, and truth be told she didn't want to fight Bryce. She simply wanted to go on with her quiet life and continue to travel the country writing balanced stories about the hotel industry, penning reviews which people could trust. She didn't want to get tangled up in a fight with a billionaire.

I gave his resort a fair review.

Bryce clearly hadn't seen it that way.

She rose from the sofa. "I'm going to bed, that's what I

am going to do. I have an early flight to Galveston in the morning. Lionel wants my next review by mid-week."

"So you are just going to let this millionaire douchebag treat you like that?"

Vivian nodded. "Actually, I'm pretty sure he is a billionaire." She had checked Bryce out online while sitting at LAX waiting for her flight home. "Then again, it's all just numbers."

Grace slowly shook her head. Her housemate wasn't foolish enough to try and convince Vivian to do anything further about Bryce. "Behind those numbers lies power."

"And private jets."

Her secret dream, one she had never shared with anyone was to ride in a private jet. Just once in her life, she wanted to see how the super-rich lived.

"My dad says they are overrated," offered Grace.

Vivian headed for the door of her bedroom. She was tired. Now was not the time to mention to her best friend that at least her father could draw on real life experience for his opinion.

"Night, Grace. I'll shoot you a text once I land in Texas."

"Night, sweetie."

She would stand by her review of the Laguna Beach resort, and Bryce Royal could go to the devil.

CHAPTER THIRTY-TWO

There were few spare seats around the boardroom table at the Royal Resorts office. Bryce took a copy of the agenda from Janice with a wry smile. Farther down from him sat Jordan. His brother's eyes were cast down, studying his pile of papers with far too much interest. And while sympathy stabbed at Bryce's heart, in the current situation he was powerless to do or say anything to help.

The other night in his brother's apartment Jordan's odd behavior had hinted at something being seriously wrong in his life. And while they had reaffirmed their brotherly pact to support one another, Bryce was finding it difficult. He was torn between duty and loyalty.

Why didn't you reach out to me Jordan?

Edward swept into the room and headed straight to the top of the table. He was followed by several other people, a couple whom Bryce didn't recognize. He wasn't surprised. He hadn't been back in the New York office long enough to learn the names of all the new hires.

I should introduce myself to those people. They are obviously keeping their distance since they don't know me.

Bryce's thoughts of hosting a small in-house meet and greet disappeared the second he spotted what was tucked under his father's arm. It seemed that wherever Edward went so did the now crumpled travel magazine. The agenda had many other items on it, but he had a horrid suspicion that Janice's carefully crafted agenda was about to become meaningless.

All heads turned as the magazine landed on the table with a loud slap. "Laguna Beach is an unmitigated disaster," announced Edward.

"I would agree that it has its problems, but it's not a complete write off," suggested Bryce. His father did have a tendency to let his temper take over at times. He had clearly been stewing over the review and decided this executive meeting was where he was going to vent his rage.

Jordan glanced up and momentarily caught Bryce's gaze. His slow blink an unmistakable 'thank you' for his show of support.

Bryce turned and looked back at his father, and as he did Edward's eyes locked on him. He took in a deep breath. For the briefest of moments, Bryce imagined that his father was going to accept his calming words. But when Janice placed a pile of papers on the table next to Edward, Bryce's heart sank.

"I wish I could concur with you Bryce, but unfortunately the reviews say otherwise."

His father pulled a piece of paper from the top of the pile.

Edward held the document high in the air, waving it around. All eyes were glued to his every move. "I've also spoken to our mystery guest team. Three of them have stayed at the resort in the past month. They all say the same thing. There are not enough staff on shift at any time. The assistant manager is cutting corners at every opportunity. The only thing he hasn't managed to completely stuff up is the food and beverage, and that's because Tony is in charge, and he won't let anyone touch his budget."

Bryce glanced at his brother. To his credit, Jordan was paying full attention to their father.

When Edward reached for another piece of paper, Bryce silently chided himself for not having grabbed his third coffee of the morning when he'd had the chance.

Sitting quietly while his father read aloud from scathing reviews of the Laguna Beach resort was one of the longest half hours of Bryce's life. Long check in lines. Overcharging on the bills. The list went on and on. The lack of towels. Guests having to go to the front desk in order to source bedding.

At least I've fixed that problem. Housekeeping have confirmed they received the extra linen order.

Edward's fingers tapped on the creased glossy cover of Luxury Hotels and Resorts Worldwide. "I thought they were taking things a little too far with this 'Room for Improvement' review, but to be honest I think we might have gotten off lightly. The more I have read this piece, the more I have come to realize that it was a fair summation of the clusterfuck that is our newest resort."

An audible gasp rippled around the table. Edward Royal was a man who used foul oaths sparingly. Bloody was about the worst the well-spoken Englishman lowered himself to using in meetings. Clusterfuck was like listening to an atomic bomb going off.

Bryce gritted his teeth. He hadn't seen the reports from the mystery guest team. They were saying the exact same things that Vivian had done in her review. The review which he'd taken as a personal insult and then gone online to publicly attack her credibility and character over. According to his father, Vivian hadn't been spiteful in her review of the Laguna Beach resort, she had been refreshingly honest.

What if her review was just about the resort, not me?

It didn't explain why she'd ghosted him, but maybe Vivian had just been doing her job. Which meant he had overreacted. And badly.

His father's fist pounding on the table stirred Bryce from his scattered thoughts. "When did Royal Resorts require guests to bring their own linen? If there has been a policy change, no one bothered to inform me. Ladies and gentlemen, we are the purveyors of luxury resorts, not summer camps."

He nodded toward Janice, who to Bryce's relief removed the pile of papers from in front of her boss. The message had been delivered. Edward was not a happy man. And when Edward Royal was displeased, heads tended to roll.

"Jordan."

The middle Royal son snapped to attention. Bryce's gaze darted around the room. No one dared to look at Jordan, every pair of eyes was cast down. It was like being back in school and the principal was dishing out a punishment that everyone was keen to avoid.

"Go to your apartment and pack a couple of large suitcases. You are leaving for Los Angeles today. When you get to Laguna Beach you will take over the day to day running of the resort. I don't care whether that means you have to clear plates from tables or make beds. You will stay put in California until I can find a suitable replacement. I've spoken to your assistant manager, and Austin Brown is going to report to me each day on the efforts you are undertaking to dig us out of this gargantuan hole which you have thrown us all in. Am I clear?"

"Yes, sir."

"And before you think of getting on a plane and coming back here, I want a full report from you as to why things got to the state they have. I want details of every single point where you have failed, and what you should have done in the first place."

Bryce's heart went out to his brother. A public dressing down was never a nice thing, and he could just imagine that this meeting had set Jordan's hopes to be seen as a capable Royal Resorts executive back at least a year or two. "How about we accept that what's done is done, Edward, and let Jordan worry about fixing it. When he is eventually back in New York, he and I can sit down and do a full debrief together."

Edward took in a slow breath. It was rare for anyone in the Royal Resorts office to question him, but Bryce was prepared to stand his ground.

"Alright. Let's get the resort back on track, and then the two of you can prepare a report to the board explaining how this will never happen again."

The rest of the meeting's agenda was dealt with in short time. It was obvious that the only thing Edward Royal had really been interested in dealing with this morning was the situation in California. When he finally closed the meeting, Edward motioned for both Jordan and Bryce to remain behind.

As soon as the boardroom door was closed, Edward rose from his chair and gathered his sons around. "Now, gentlemen, I know that was a rather unfortunate meeting, and one which will no doubt have tongues wagging for the rest of the day."

Bryce and Jordan nodded.

"But it had to be done. We can't have a billion dollar investment become the laughing stock of the leisure market. Jordan, you are booked on the 2pm American Airlines flight out of JFK. Bryce can deal with any other matters you might have outstanding here in New York. Call me when you arrive at the resort."

Their father was sending Jordan on a commercial flight to LA. If that didn't send a powerful message of parental disappointment, nothing did.

To Bryce's relief, his brother had the good sense to simply reply. "Yes, sir," before leaving the room. As soon as the door closed, Bryce turned to his father. "I wasn't seeking to undermine you in the main meeting, Dad." He didn't want to be another problem his father felt he had to fix. "Just tell me what you need me to do."

"Actually nothing, son. Take a few days off. Your mother is right, you work too hard. It wasn't fair of me to drag you all the way back from Scotland and drop you into this mess. But now that you are here, I think you should take some time for yourself. Go relax."

His father was telling him to relax, while at the same time sending one of his brothers out to California with the proverbial flea in his ear. The notion didn't sit all that well with Bryce.

"You didn't have to defend your brother, Bryce. He's not fifteen. He needs to be the one to deal with this, no one else. You went to California, you did what you had to do, and now you need to step back. Let me close this out."

"Alright. I will stay out of the way. But are you sure about me taking time off?"

Edward nodded. "Yes. The next year or two is going to be very busy for you. I've been discussing things with the board, and we are seriously considering moving the timeline up."

Bryce's brows furrowed. Timelines were always moving. "I don't quite understand."

"I know you were planning on spending another year in Europe, but I think it's time you returned permanently to New York. I am standing down early in the new year, and the CEO position is going to be offered to you."

They had talked about Bryce maybe one day taking over

from his father, but in his mind that was years away. Edward was in his mid-fifties, a long way from retirement.

Bryce's stomach dropped. He had been toying with the idea of coming back to the States, but he hadn't seen this career change happening anytime soon. He searched his father's face for answers. "Are you well? Oh, god, please don't tell me you are ill."

Edward shook his head. "As we say in England, fit as a fiddle. No, I just want to focus on other projects. I can't do that if I am in charge of the US operations. And to be honest your mother wants us to travel a bit more, to be guests of our resorts, not have me working in them."

Bryce let out a sigh of relief. In his mind his father would live to one hundred. While coming home had always been in his long term plans, he had hoped to complete his secondment to the European branch. "What about the Paris acquisition?"

Edward winced. "I was wondering when you would mention that little project. I'm sorry but it's no longer yours."

Royal Resorts had been in private negotiations to buy a mansion in the middle of the French capital for close on four years. The current owners, two elderly sisters, seemed to be enjoying making a major luxury house jump through the hoops.

"I know you wanted so badly to be in charge of the Paris project, but the company needs you here in America. And while you might see it as a bit of a loss, I want you to think about how this change fits in with your future. If you are based here, then you could look to other aspects of your life. To finding a wife."

He gave a nod to his father, then headed for the door. If he let Edward get started in on one of his long fatherly chats about family and life balance, he wouldn't get the chance to catch Jordan before his brother left.

"Let's talk again about the CEO role. And yes, I will take a couple of days off...soon."

If he was going to be a success as head of US operations, one of the first things Bryce was going to have to focus on was finding a way to help his brother find his place within the company. He couldn't begin to do that while Jordan was on the other side of the country.

And what about those other relationships?

The little voice had started up again. Guilt over what he had written about Vivian on the dating app had been tapping a steady beat in his brain for the past hour. He pushed it away. Right this minute, he only had the energy to deal with one troubled relationship.

I have to speak to Jordan before he leaves.

CHAPTER THIRTY-THREE

His brother was waiting for Bryce when he returned to his office. Jordan was perched on the edge of the desk, arms folded, and huffing with frustrated disgust.

Jordan pushed off the desk and began to protest. "I can't believe the old man is sending me commercial. The jet is available, but I have to go and sit with the great unwashed on an airline."

I thought we were past all this, for fuck's sake. Come on Jordan, give me a break.

"You will be flying business class, which is better than most other people ever get to experience. In the spirit of our brotherly pact, can I offer you some advice?"

It took all of Bryce's willpower not to reach out and give his younger sibling a clip over the ear, as he met Jordan's hardened eyes.

I can't believe you are giving me this bratty attitude.

This wasn't a backyard game of football where you tried to stare your opponent down as you came for him, this was business. At stake was a billion dollar resort.

"What?"

Bryce gritted his teeth. He'd take a bullet for his brother, but damn, he was a pain in the ass. "Try and move past your personal issues or at least work around them as best you can. When you are at the resort, take the time to go back to the basics. Customer service. Guest experience."

Jordan rolled his eyes. "You think I don't know all that? I didn't start with this company last week."

Bryce's sound advice wasn't being taken the least bit graciously. "Fine. Well then, let me give you this other piece of advice. Get your head out of your ass. If you don't, Dad is going fire you. And if he doesn't then I will, the second I take over as CEO."

He hated seeing the shock which registered on his brother's face. The US Royal Resorts board was yet to ratify his father's choice of Bryce as the new head, but Edward had made his position clear. He wanted to step back and focus on other areas of the business. Jordan may once have been a possible candidate for the role, but after the disaster in California no one would risk it. Bryce was the clear and obvious best choice.

"When... when were you going to tell me?" stammered Jordan.

"I just did. The board is meeting soon, Edward is going to table his transition plan." Guilt dropped onto his shoulders. Bryce had always been at pains to make sure his younger siblings didn't feel as if he always came first. They might be Royal in name, but this was no formal line of succession. "I didn't know he planned to move things up, not until he told me just a few minutes ago."

Bryce would've much preferred to have sat on the news, but once again Jordan had pressed his buttons. He secretly hoped that in telling Jordan what was soon to happen, he would come to the realization that if he didn't lift his game, he wouldn't be able to call upon brotherly connections to save himself.

Jordan closed his eyes. This was clearly a difficult moment for him. While Bryce had been in Europe running that side of the business, Jordan must have figured he had an inside run on the American CEO role. But only someone who wasn't paying careful attention would miss seeing Edward's shadow as it loomed over the business.

His brother's shoulder sagged the instant Bryce's hand settled on it. Something was wrong. The worry over what it could be had kept gnawing away at him since the day he'd gotten the call from Edward to return to the states.

He was shaking that night at his apartment. What could be so wrong?

"You were killing this gig for the past few years, and then this…I don't understand. And yes, I expect you don't want to share whatever it is with me right now, but when you are ready, I will be here for you." He'd genuinely believed Jordan had finally put his wild billionaire bad boy ways behind him. His troubles were all in the past. If he hadn't, there was no way Bryce would have backed his brother for the Laguna Beach project.

I went out on a limb for you Jordan. The least you could do is tell me why you have dropped the ball so badly.

"Thanks, Bryce. I have to go pack. I've a plane to catch, and a resort to fix." Jordan stepped away, leaving Bryce's hand to drop limply to his side. "I'll see you when I get back to New York, whenever that is."

Bryce gave up the battle and let his brother go. The office staff already had more than enough gossip to mull over for when they hit one of the local bars later tonight, he didn't need to add a screaming row to the mix.

As he watched his brother disappear through the doorway, Bryce was left to wonder what had transpired in the months since he had last been home at Christmas. All the self-assured sassiness so characteristic of Jordan was gone, and in its place stood a sad, broken man.

I will be here for you, but you have to trust me.

CHAPTER THIRTY-FOUR

Bryce spent the rest of the morning wading through emails from the European desk. His second in command and distant cousin Marcel was holding down the fort. And he was doing a solid job. There was every chance that he would be considered to take over managing the European and British resorts permanently. The House of Royal had an unwritten policy that family members held senior roles within the company. Sometimes Bryce wondered if that was such a good idea.

The knowledge that Marcel would probably get to handle the Paris project made him jealous. The US based CEO role was a huge step up, but Bryce had long held a private ambition to create the ultimate luxury hotel in the French capital. The House of Royal had started in Europe and as one of the few American members he was keen to show the world that a New York born and bred hotelier had what it took when it came to delivering an opulent guest experience.

He had just finished his fourth coffee for the day when his head dropped, and he closed his eyes. Something else apart from Jordan and the hotel in Paris had been nagging at him all morning. The thought of Vivian Holte and the spiteful way he had struck out at her, refused to go away.

Bryce had come to bitterly regret what he'd done. He was nothing more than a rich spiteful bully. Giving her a terrible review on the millionaire dating app had been a nasty, underhanded, and shameful act on his part.

Just because you did it on the sly doesn't make it any less of a crime. You still lashed out. Still sought to cause Vivian real pain.

His conscience continued to bother him. Who was the bigger ass, him, or her ex— right now it was a close call. He knew she couldn't afford the subscription, and in the ultimate act of cowardice had decided to take something she had confided in him and use it against her. He'd burned any chance she might have had of finding a decent guy through the millionaire love app.

And then like a weak assed villain, you went and made your profile private.

There was something to be said about revenge being a dish best served cold. He was its poster boy. He'd been angry the afternoon he'd posted the payback review on Vivian's profile, believing that she had used her rating to judge him personally, so he'd judged her right back.

Bryce was now having to face his own cold, hard truth. He had been the only person handing out false names and lies in California. Vivian had just been doing her job.

"I have to fix this," he muttered.

Picking up his cell, he opened the app, and immediately searched for Vivian's profile.

If I can at least delete the review, then message her, she will know that I am sorry.

It was easy enough to find Vivian, her name was the only one in his search history. It came up, but it was grayed out. His thumb clicked on the link which should have taken him to her bio, but it wouldn't work.

Was the site down? He didn't have any experience when it came to dating apps, so why Vivian's profile wouldn't load had him utterly perplexed. Bryce searched the FAQs, then quietly swore. She had deleted her profile. Vivian Holte was no longer a member of the millionaire dating community.

"Damn. Now what am I am going to do?"

He dropped the phone onto his desk. A quick search online had him dialing the main phone number of the travel and leisure magazines' office. If he could talk to her, perhaps even arrange to meet, he might be able to resolve this misunderstanding.

Misunderstanding. Is that what you are going with? Really? Gutless prick.

His conscience was riding his ass hard today.

"Good morning, Luxury Hotels and Resorts Worldwide." The voice down the line was friendly and actually human. Bryce had gotten so used to dealing with bots and recorded messages, having a real person on the other end of the line had him faltering with his opening words.

"Um, yes. Ah. Good morning. Um." *Come on!* "Yes. I am a friend of Vivian Holte and was wondering if I could speak to her, please?"

Gee you made a meal of that.

Apart from a stammering mess, his request had come across as all too formal. Bryce had been hoping to go with him being a friend of Vivian's to allay any suspicions, but now realized that a friend wouldn't call at work using the official office number. He would have her private cell.

"I'm sorry but Vivian is away on assignment. Would you like to leave a message?" came the polite reply.

So she was out of town. There went his hopes for a deep, groveling apology over drinks and tapas. "Could you perhaps give me her cell number and I can call her myself, save you the trouble?" he offered.

"I'm sorry, but we don't give out the personal contact details of our staff contributors. You could leave a message on our contact form, which is on the main website. I can give you the details."

"Perhaps you could give me her email address?"

"No, I can't. Please look up our website for further information. Goodbye."

Click. Bryce stared at the screen of his cell for a moment. He was tempted to call back and tell them that he was Bryce Royal, and people didn't put the receiver down on him. His saner self had him setting the phone aside.

A knock at the door stirred him from his irrational thoughts of getting in a cab and going down to the offices of LHRW magazine. The universe was finally taking pity on him.

Jordan's assistant, Sheila, stood in the doorway. Bryce beckoned her in. "Hi Sheila."

"Hi Bryce, do you have a spare minute?" All the Royal Resorts office staff was on a first name basis with the executive team. Even Edward had reluctantly dropped his insistence on the Mister Royal routine a little while ago. Janice was the last one holding onto it when it came to the company plane.

"Yes, come in, have a seat." He had a sudden and urgent need to be nice to someone. To confirm to himself that he wasn't a complete monster.

Sheila, who owned a pale complexion and bright red hair, took the chair opposite to Bryce's desk. She was a tall mid twenty something woman, who from all reports had grand plans to one day join the management program. Edward had mentioned that the board were paying for some of her college tuition fees, as Sheila's family didn't have the money. Bryce liked that about the Royal Resorts team; when they saw talent and potential, they were prepared to back it.

She sat stiff backed in the chair, one hand resting over the other in her lap. Bryce caught a glimpse of Sheila's lilac painted fingernails as they dug into the back of her bottom hand. "Since Jordan is likely to be in California for an extended period, I was hoping I could come and work for you. I've worked on and off for your brother for close to three years, and I'm across a lot of things in the business. And I am a fast learner." The lilt of a Scottish accent was unmistakable in her voice.

Bryce nodded. He liked that Sheila was taking the initiative, not waiting for someone to find her something to do while her boss was gone. Jordan had enough on his plate without having to manage his staff as he scurried out the door. Sheila's self-confidence spoke of a future senior manager.

His UK based assistant Heather had elderly parents and they were rightly her priority. She wasn't in a position to move to the US. Having a ready-made assistant here in New York would help him greatly.

If Sheila has worked for Jordan for three years, she might know what is bugging him. Though her role with him being 'on and off' is a bit of a worry. Has he been trying to do things for himself, and coming up short?

"Let me clear things with Human Resources, I wouldn't want to step on any toes. But yes, having someone who can help get me get up to speed on things in the office would be great. Thank you, Sheila, I appreciate it." Clasping his hands softly together, Bryce offered her a comforting smile. "Speaking of Jordan, are you and my brother close? I mean, does he talk to you?"

Her posture changed in an instant. Sheila sat back in her chair and crossed her legs. She was a wearing a navy blue and white pinstriped pant suit, the ultimate New York power outfit. The added raised eyebrows said all that was needed to tell Bryce what she thought of his ham-fisted way of asking her to spill his brother's secrets.

"Let me make this plain, Bryce. I know all your brother's dirt. Even the stuff he thinks no one else knows about. Jordan has given me the sort of opportunities within this company that few others would have ever done. So when I say I would not only take a bullet for him, but I wouldn't cry out as I did, you had better believe it."

Bryce suppressed the urge to clap his hands together in gleeful appreciation. Sheila was just what he needed. Smart. Cunning. And above all else...fearlessly loyal. When the time came for him to challenge the House of Royal senior executive policy about non family members, he had a feeling Sheila's name would be one of those he tabled.

"Excellent. So we are agreed that I never asked you to spill the beans on my brother?"

"Correct. Now what else can I help you with?"

Bryce cleared his throat. "You wouldn't happen to know how I could get in contact with someone who works for Leisure Hotels and Resorts Worldwide magazine would you?"

A smile appeared on Sheila's bright red lips. "No, but I know someone who might."

CHAPTER THIRTY-FIVE

A few minutes later a curious Bryce followed Sheila as she marched across to the other side of the building. She stopped at a door and quickly rapped on it. A muffled voice came from within, after which Sheila opened the door and popped her head inside. "Do you have a minute, Mia?" She turned and beckoned for Bryce to follow.

Behind a desk piled high with reports sat a young Black woman. As Bryce stepped through the door, she rose from her seat and offered him a welcoming smile. "I was wondering when you were going to get around to coming to see me."

Mia Allen stepped into his embrace, and they shared a friendly hug. Over Mia's shoulder, Bryce caught the look of surprise on Sheila's face. "Mia did a secondment in Italy a year or so ago, and she worked for me at one of the resorts on the Amalfi coast. I didn't realize it was Mia you were bringing me to meet."

Sheila rolled her eyes. "Of course I should have known you and Mia would have been acquainted. Is there anyone she doesn't know?"

As the two young women grinned at one another, Bryce

recalled that Mia did seem to know everyone. Even in Italy, she was always greeting people like they were long lost friends. She was just one of those people who had connections everywhere.

Including, so Sheila tells me, a connection to Vivian's magazine.

He was at pains that his request for information about the elusive Vivian Holte came off as a mere trifle of interest, rather than the reality of something which was burning a hole in his brain. Bryce took a deep breath and spoke as calmly as he could. "Sheila tells me you used to work at LHRW magazine before you came to work for Royal Resorts."

Mia nodded. "Yes, I worked for them when I first came out of college. Before I joined the Royal Resorts management program. I'm currently working with your brother Matthew, as his assistant manager." She explained it in such a way that it was clear she had expected Bryce to already know that much about her. He caught the *work with*, not *work for* part of the sentence.

This is Mia, remember, the girl with the eye for detail. She never forgets anything.

There was no mistaking the sly look which passed between Mia and Sheila. His discomfort grew as Mia stepped past him and quietly closed her office door. "Why are you interested in the magazine, Bryce?"

It went without saying that his request wasn't a business one. If it was then he would have simply picked up the phone and called the managing editor of Luxury Hotels and Resorts Worldwide. He wouldn't have had to come to some of the other members of the office staff in order to gather information.

They had him in a bind, and if the cunning grin on Mia's face was anything to go by, she knew it. Matthew's assistant manager was the same as Sheila, a quick learner.

Top of the field in the fast track management program.

"Or is there a particular someone you need to talk to? If you were able to give us a name, then perhaps we might be able to help you," offered Sheila.

They were enjoying this, watching one of the Royal brothers squirm would have likely made their day. Their week. Mia and Sheila were going to make him suck it up big time before they offered to help him find Vivian.

"Vivian Holte. She is a writer for the magazine."

Mia let out a snort, and her hands went to her hips. "You mean she is the writer who gave the Laguna Beach resort a three star review. Please don't tell me you are planning to confront her, because that would be most unprofessional of you, Bryce Royal. Let alone suicidal."

He had no intention of causing further harm to Vivian. *I have done enough of that already to my everlasting shame.* His motives were quite the opposite. He wanted nothing more than to hold her, kiss her, and beg for her forgiveness. Still he had to ask. "Why would that be suicidal?"

Sheila crossed her arms, and her eyebrows did their lifting thing again. "Because Mia would kill you, that's why."

Oh.

If he did eventually manage to talk to Vivian, he was going to eat some serious humble pie. So he may as well start practicing now.

"Ok, but this stays within these four walls. Please."

Mia and Sheila both nodded.

"I met Vivian in California. And...um...ah." Bryce pinched the bridge of his nose. For all his wealth and fancy clothes, he was more than a little clueless about how he should handle such a delicate matter. Especially with these two women.

The silence in the room was deafening.

How do I say this and not come off sounding like Mister bloody Darcy?

"I said something horrible to Vivian and I feel the need to apologize."

"And?" replied Sheila.

These two women worked with Jordan and Matthew, they were both fluent in the language of the Royal men. Which meant they were not going to let him get away with such a vague comment.

"Look. We hit it off. After the review came out, I did something that I am not proud of, but which has to stay private between the two of us. But I lashed out, and I'm sure I hurt her. I really need to speak to her, preferably face to face. I tried calling LHRW, but they said they don't give out the private details of their correspondents."

"Why would you do that? Her review was fair. It's not Vivian's fault that Laguna Beach is in trouble," replied Mia.

"I know that now, but at the time I suspected Vivian knew who I was, and she used me. I kinda took the review as a critique of my performance in the bedroom."

Sheila shook her head. "That doesn't make sense. From what Jordan said, you'd checked into the resort under a false name. And let's not forget you've been in Europe for the past four years, so how would Vivian know what you even look like?"

His hot headed theory that Vivian had used sex with him to influence her review was beyond ridiculous. Bryce accepted that now. "Can we skip to the part where we all agree that I am an idiot, but one who is keen to try and remedy this situation."

Vivian, I am so sorry.

Bryce held his breath. Mia would be well within her rights to refuse to help him. He could only hope their friendship from her time in Italy had earned him some points.

"Yes, I think we can all agree that you have stuffed up.

Give me a few minutes and let me see what I can do," replied Mia.

He let out the air. *Phew.* "Thank you."

Mia stood staring at Bryce for a minute, before an exasperated Sheila took a hold of his shirt sleeve and began to steer him toward the door. "She means go for a walk, Bryce, and let her make some calls. We will let you know when we have some news."

Bryce sheepishly wandered back to his office. He had a horrible suspicion that even after his appointment as future CEO was officially announced, these women wouldn't treat him any differently. He would get respect, but it would come with a side serving of sass.

Just as long as they do their jobs. And save my neck.

Twenty minutes later Mia and Sheila appeared in the doorway of Bryce's office. He could have sworn that if he looked up the phrase 'cat who got the cream' online, he would find a picture of the two women wearing the exact same expressions as they did right now. Sheila closed the door behind her, while Mia crossed the floor and picked up Bryce's cell.

To his surprise, she easily unlocked it, tapped a few things into it, then handed it to him. "Vivian is on assignment in Texas, staying at the recently refurbished Silver Havens resort in Galveston."

He picked up the phone. "So you put her number in here? That's fantastic, thank you."

"Hold back the gratitude for the moment, Bryce. I've given you the number for the resort. If you want Vivian's personal cell number, you will have to get that from her yourself."

The sisterhood was closing ranks. Protecting one another. It was annoying, but he couldn't fault it. Mia clearly cared about Vivian. Just because he was a senior executive at her employer didn't mean she was going to simply give him direct access to her friend.

Sheila stepped forward. "I messaged your driver, and he will be here in fifteen minutes to take you to the helipad. The Royal Resorts jet is being fueled for the flight to Galveston." Her gaze landed on the travel bag, which Bryce kept permanently packed and ready by his desk. "Don't forget your luggage."

Bryce rose from his desk, cell still in hand. He held it out to Mia. "How on earth did you know how to unlock my phone?"

Mia and Sheila softly chuckled in unison. "We assistants are regularly called upon to use our bosses cellphones. Matthew and Jordan both have the same code, so we figured you would stay true to Royal family form, and you did. I dread the day that one of you finally figures out how to use the face recognition function, because that's when I might need to start looking for another job," said Sheila.

"You two would have to be the most skilled and devious people in this office. I'm sure you'll both go far. And thank you."

Swearing a silent vow to change his phone's code, Bryce picked up his travel bag and started for the door. As he passed Mia, she reached out. "Good luck Bryce. Whatever you did to Vivian, you need to sort it out. She is an amazing girl who worked her ass off to get that job. I've read her review, and it while it wasn't a pretty read, I would say it was accurate. As for the sex part, I don't want to even think about it."

In his anger, Bryce had shot the messenger. Vivian hadn't done anything to deserve his ire, and he was completely at fault in this situation.

"I'm going to go to Galveston, find Vivian, and apologize.

many New Yorkers, Vivian wasn't a regular driver, so this trip was a good opportunity to get some practice in behind the wheel.

She stopped on the sand and turned to gaze at the sea. It was strange to find herself staring out over the wide blue waters of the Gulf of Mexico, so far away from her last resort assignment in California.

Laguna Beach, what a trip that had been. From wonderful to nightmare in the blink of an eye. "Stop thinking about him," she whispered to the sea breeze.

No matter how hard she tried, Bryce popped into her mind at least a half dozen times a day. Bryce, the man who had given her the most amazing night of her life. Bryce, whose smile lit up her world. Bryce, the billionaire. Bryce, the bully. Bryce, the liar. She struggled to reconcile all the different versions of him that she knew. The last one hurt the most.

The sun was slowly sinking into the sea, its red fire stirring memories of the night she had first met him. That sexy smile of his as he stood close to her on the beach. How he'd charmed her over breakfast the following morning. The afternoon by the poolside. Dinner. And then that night in his hotel suite.

Vivian shook her head. If only she could let it all go. But men like Bryce Royal were impossible to forget.

He had struck out at her. Taken aim at her weakest spot, then fired. The fact that only a handful of people knew what Bryce had done didn't help. Her humiliation, while private, was still deep and painful. At least here in Texas she could spend some time alone and try to rebuild her self-esteem. This wasn't the first time a man had disappointed her, yet she was still unable to fully process why with him it had hurt so much.

Around her on the beach families were gathered, children

played at the water's edge. Other people were walking their dogs. She spotted a fellow guest stepping out from the resort path and making his way onto the sand. Several of the large cruise ships which sailed from the port of Galveston were visible on the horizon. The sea breeze was warm and gentle. It was a perfect evening.

I wonder if Lionel would ever consider letting me review a Caribbean cruise.

Surely there had to be one or two which met the luxury threshold for featuring in LHRW magazine. Not all cruise ships were ocean going mega-buffets. The thought of food set her stomach rumbling its interest.

I could do some serious damage to a large plate of nachos right now. Extra guacamole, please.

She pulled her cell out from her cross body satchel and snapped off some pics, sliding one into her Instagram feed. #gorgeousingalaveston

"Shoot I misspelt Galveston, now no one will see it."

The next few minutes were spent editing the post and fixing her hashtags. Her two hundred and thirty three followers deserved some decent content, even if half of them were bots. Only Lionel and a couple of professional photographers were allowed to post to the magazine's official Instagram page. Vivian stuffed her phone back into her bag and turned to leave.

The man who had appeared on the beach a few minutes earlier was fast approaching. His long strides eating up the distance between them. He gave her a small wave.

It was hard to see his features clearly in the fading light. Vivian narrowed her eyes. *No. It couldn't be.* She was seeing things. Her fingers curled into tight fists as he drew closer and the truth of who he was settled heavily in her heart.

"Bryce."

Lying awake late at night staring up at the glow of the

New York street lights as they shone on her bedroom ceiling, Vivian had practiced all the clever lines she would use on Bryce Royal if their paths ever crossed again. None of them were polite. Most involved threats of bodily harm. Now as he stood before her in the flesh, all those cutting and clever remarks fled, leaving her to barely grind out his name.

No matter how much she hated him, Vivian couldn't stop herself from gazing up into his warm brown eyes. These were the deep pools of emotional longing which she saw every time she tried to close her own eyes and sleep.

"How did you find me?"

"I'm a billionaire, we have our ways."

Smarmy prick.

His gaze dropped to the sand, and he slowly shook his head. "Actually, I groveled to someone who knew someone, who then called someone who told me where you were."

All the swagger in his stride and posture had fled. Bryce looked for all the world like a teen who'd been caught reading smutty literature while smoking in the back of the school library. Bookish and dangerously sexy.

No. He doesn't look like that, he's an asshole. Stop fantasizing and get angry.

"Why are you here?" she demanded.

If he thought to come causing her more trouble, he was going to find himself on the receiving end of some instead. She might be struggling with her bruised heart, but she could stand up to a spoilt bully.

"Because the review I left you on that dating app was really spiteful and horrible. You confided something deeply personal to me, and I abused that trust. It was wrong of me, and I'm here to apologize. Unreservedly."

His last remark finally saw some of her wit returning. "Wow. How hard was that for you to say?"

He met her eyes. "Not as hard as knowing I probably hurt

you. I'm not someone used to putting a foot wrong, but I have to tell you, Vivian, I'm limping all over the place. You were spot on about the resort at Laguna Beach and all its failings. My business meeting in LA the morning you left was with our linen suppliers. My brother Jordan, who was supposed to be making the resort perfect for its opening, has been sent back to California to personally remedy the situation."

Vivian swallowed deep. She hadn't thought she would ever get the opportunity to tell Bryce how much his words had hurt. *I owe it to myself to let him know the truth.*

"You are right, you did hurt me with that review on the dating app. It was a personal attack and nasty. People mightn't have known my identity, but they made it clear what they thought of me on the site. They downgraded my profile to junk status."

Bryce nodded. "So that's why you deleted your account. If it's any comfort, I did try and take down my review, but you were already gone."

"You shouldn't have posted it in the first place," she bit back, her anger rising.

"I know. I know. I'm sorry. I assumed you knew who I was, and that you must have thought I knew who you were. When I read the three star review, I took it as a critique of our sexual encounter." He kicked at the sand, digging it away with the toe of his hand crafted loafer. "It all sounds so stupid now, but I assumed you'd played me. I was so angry and humiliated. Then I remembered the millionaire dating app and took my revenge."

A couple out walking their dog passed close by. Vivian offered them a tight smile. Anyone who bothered to take a look at her and Bryce would notice their stiff stances. They may as well have hung a large sign above their heads which read 'couple having a fight.'

She waited until the other beach goers had moved away. "What do you want Bryce? For me to accept your apology so you can get back on your private jet and return to Planet Billionaire? No. I don't accept it. You lied to me, and then you deliberately hurt me. Now please leave."

When he moved nearer, the wind brought the scent of his cologne to her nose. Vivian breathed in deep. The last time they had been this close, he had been making promises about them spending another night of passion together. She had been so full of hope that morning. Right up until the second she discovered who Bryce Jones really was, and that he had lied to her.

"I want another chance, Vivian. A chance for us to get to know one another. No more lies, or hidden identities. Just Bryce and Vivian."

Hot tears stung her eyes. Her trust issues with men flared hot in her veins. How many times had she played out this scene in all its horrid variations with Pete? Stuff up, followed by apology, followed by another stuff up, and then usually ending in a heart breaking lie.

Nope. Not happening.

She brushed past him. "Go back to your glittering New York palace, Bryce."

This was one billionaire who wasn't going to get another chance to hurt her.

CHAPTER THIRTY-SEVEN

Hunger got the better of her an hour later. Vivian ventured out from her hotel room, and down to the parking garage. The resort had plenty of fine dining options, but for her Galveston meant an evening at Gaido's Seafood Restaurant along the Seawall Boulevard.

Her little blue dress had stayed at home, tonight was a night for a short flippy skirt and sandals. A dark green floral top finished her outfit. Only a fool wore white to a place famous for its fried seafood platter.

Turning right out of the resort, she drove along the beach road. A belly full of delicious food beckoned. She had only gone a couple of hundred yards when she spotted a familiar figure sitting on a low bench facing out to sea. He was alone, and in the fading light it was only his pale blue linen suit jacket which made him stand out.

"Go home, Bryce," she whispered, as she passed by.

Another hundred yards further up the road, she glanced in the rear view mirror then slowed. After a quick check of the oncoming traffic, Vivian turned the car round.

He hadn't moved from his spot on the blue and yellow

painted sea box when Vivian drew up alongside a few minutes later. She turned off the Corolla and climbed out. Vivian marched across to the beach seat and with hands on hips faced Bryce.

"You know what I've just realized, Mister Bryce Royal? I almost let you get away with it. But I owe it to myself to make you feel the pain, like you did with me."

"Yes."

"If I could have left you my own review on the dating app it would go something like this." Vivian huffed. "Girls, avoid this guy at all costs if you value your heart. His lies will leave you and what's left of your pride in the gutter."

Her voice broke on that last word, as Vivian fought against the tears. Just seeing Bryce brought back all those wonderful memories of that night they had shared.

"Goodbye Bryce."

"Vivian."

"No."

She made it back to the car and slid into the driver's seat. The seatbelt was in her hand. Then she let it go. "Why did you have to come here Bryce? I was just starting to have moments when I stopped thinking about you."

Her fingers tapped the steering wheel, while her mind and heart fought over what she should do. The logical thing would be to start the car and leave. To put Bryce and this whole disaster in the past.

"Damn."

Car keys dangling from her fingers, she marched back to the beach seat and dropped down beside Bryce letting out a resigned sigh. "Why are you still here, Bryce? Can't get the private jet out of the hanger?"

He glanced over at her and gave her a weak smile. "Planet Billionaire is on the other side of the moon's orbit right now, so I am stuck here on earth."

Bryce pointed out to sea, to the cruise ship distant on the horizon. "I've never been to this city before, our nearest resort is in Dallas. According to my quick google search, Galveston is a big port for cruise ships. Have you ever been on a cruise?"

Vivian shook her head. This was a strange conversation, but just being here with him seemed the only place that was right. She hadn't been able to find the willpower to turn on the car's ignition and drive away.

"Me neither. We have a couple of cruise ships under one of the other leisure branches of the House of Royal, but they sail in the Mediterranean around the Greek isles. Of course I have been on the odd yacht or two. My planet has quite a few of them."

He was taking her to task for her earlier angry remark about him going back to Planet Billionaire. But his words rang true. He did come from a different planet. She couldn't begin to imagine what it must be like to hail from a family who had created a major international conglomerate with luxury businesses all over the world.

Men like Bryce Royal didn't fall for girls like her.

His gaze drifted over her bare legs, up to her short skirt, where it lingered. "No sexy blue dress tonight?"

Vivian gave him a side-eye. "This is Texas, and besides Gaido's isn't the sort of place where you take silk."

"Gaido's?"

"It's a local famous seafood restaurant, that's where I was headed when I spotted you."

"I'm really sorry Vivian. I mean it."

She still didn't trust him and hated what he had done to her. He'd come to an entirely wrong opinion of what their time together in California had meant to her.

"I can't believe you really thought I had used you just for

sex, and that my review was an attack on your skills as a lover. Bryce, we shared a wonderful night together."

She wasn't going to confess that she was sure if they had spent more time with one another that she would have fallen for him.

"That's why I flew here. To apologize in person. Anything less would not have been right. You deserve to know that I am truly, deeply, sorry."

It would be easy to accept his words, then let him go. What was done was done. But she couldn't do it.

"Have you eaten?"

Bryce shook his head. "Figured I'd see what the resort nachos look like. It pays to benchmark against your own in house offerings. Though I expect someone has put two and two together by now and figured out who has taken the presidential suite. I checked in under my real name, so I don't expect I will be getting the run of the house food and beverage service."

Vivian got to her feet. "Come on, you might be a billionaire asshole, but let's at least share a meal. Break bread and call a truce."

CHAPTER THIRTY-EIGHT

She was asking him out to dinner. This was more than Bryce had dared hoped for with Vivian. Of course he was going to take it. If the relationship gods of the internet were watching, he was sure they would be giving him two solid thumbs up.

He struggled up from the hard concrete bench. With early starts at the office and some unplanned cross country travel, his gym routine had fallen away. As soon as he got back to New York, he would have to do something about getting an exercise bike and tread installed in his apartment.

"I would love to join you for dinner, Vivian, my treat," said Bryce.

She shook her head. "I'm getting the check for tonight. And besides, you paid for our meals in California. I would like for us to part not feeling that either was owed anything."

Her words spoke of having been made to feel somewhat less than him.

I did that, and I will forever regret it.

Earlier today he had placed his trust in the hands of two strong willed women, and they had come through for him. It made sense not to jeopardize his current run of good fortune. Even now he could hear Mia and Sheila ordering him to squeeze himself into the compact car and do everything that Vivian instructed. The night was his to either lose or claim.

"Thank you. I promise to tell the leader of my planet that you were a gracious host."

She jangled the car keys at him. "Come on, it's not far."

A little further up the road, Vivian pulled into the open air parking lot of Gaido's Seafood Restaurant. Bryce raised an eyebrow at the figure of a large blue crab which sat on the roof above the front door. The owners had clearly understood the saying 'it pays to advertise', as no one passing on the road outside could ever be mistaken for thinking this place didn't serve seafood.

He followed her inside, and when the waitress attempted to show them to the table Vivian had apparently reserved at the front of the room, his dinner companion requested that they be moved to a table tucked away in a private corner of the restaurant, far away from other diners. Vivian's peace offering wasn't going to come without conditions. She didn't want to be seen with him.

Menus were placed in front of them. Bryce's eyes grew wide as he took in the extensive selection of amazing seafood offerings. As his mouth salivated, he made a mental note to have a word with Jordan and when things had settled in California, have him fly Tony out here to try the food. This was the sort of thing they should have on the menu at Laguna Beach, not just sixty five dollar ribeye. "I don't know where to start."

He glanced at Vivian, who sat with her menu resting on the table. She hadn't even picked it up. "How hungry are you?"

There was a definite note of challenge in her words. He'd had two or three coffees for breakfast, he couldn't remember exactly how many. Managed to steal half a sandwich from the office kitchen platter at Royal Resorts and then downed an apple on the plane. Added to that were the numerous other coffees he had mindlessly gulped down over the course of the rest of the day.

Bryce pondered the question. "I think if they tested my blood, they would find it close to ninety percent caffeine. So, in answer to your question, am I hungry? I'm starving."

For the first time since he had caught up with her on the beach, Vivian actually smiled. It set his heart dancing to a joyful beat of pitter patter. He wondered if she had a clue as to how far she had gotten under his skin. Of the elation he had felt the moment he'd set eyes on her on the beach.

He sat back in his seat listening intently as Vivian gave their order to the waitress. It was an impressive sounding amount of food for two people. When the woman went to step away, Bryce added, "Oh, and two bottles of Stella Artois, please."

If they were going to have charcoal grilled oysters and the famous fried platter, they were going to drink pilsner beer. Vivian might well know Galveston, but Bryce knew his seafood.

When they were alone again, he ventured some small talk. "So how long are you in town, Ms. Holte?"

The waitress returned and set their drinks on the table. After she left, they clinked bottles. "Cheers. Here's to you and interplanetary relations, Bryce Royal," said Vivian.

Bryce's cock twitched at the word relations. It so badly wanted intimate relations again with this young woman. To be sunk deep in her wet heat, and once again experience that moment of heady sexual release that being with her had brought.

Down boy. I know you had a wonderful time last time with

Vivian's pussy. But first let me see if I can dig myself out of this mess before you get your hopes up.

"I'm in town for a few days. Lionel wants me to update a couple of other entries for the global magazine site. The resort will of course get the main feature, but we like to have information about places for people to visit and experience in the surrounding area. Gaido's has been here since nineteen hundred and eleven, so they have always had a listing on our site. And their food is the best."

There was something about the way she spoke that had his deliberations shifting from those of what might just physically happen between them to wanting a deeper connection. Bryce was not giving up on something more than just a fling with Vivian. California had just been the beginning.

"I love the bond that food creates. Some of my most special memories are of times when I've shared a simple meal with family or friends. My therapist says I should dig deeper about this, but for me it's…I don't know."

Vivian met his gaze. "Do you see your therapist often? I went to one when I was in my teens. My birth father died in a car accident when I was small, and my mom felt I should talk to someone. It helped me to put some things into perspective."

Seeing a therapist wasn't something he normally talked about. For many people it was a deeply personal thing. Bryce had only started going after Jordan had come out of rehab and encouraged him to work through his own private issues.

"I've been having sessions with one for a few years. I have a habit of catastrophizing things. Which is what I did with the review you wrote. I immediately thought the worst and didn't stop to think it through before I acted. You could say I have some way to go in my personal development."

Vivian's raised eyebrow was enough to tell him she agreed with that last remark. Her words helped to soften the blow.

"Nothing in this world is perfect Bryce, though the food in this place comes close."

His thoughts moved to the enthusiasm she had for this restaurant. It was palpable. Captivating. Dare he say, infectious. He wanted the food to be as good as she claimed.

He leaned forward. "You really do love this job, don't you? I can hear it in your voice."

Vivian took a sip of her beer. "Yes. For me there is nothing better than finding a hotel or resort that makes their guests not only feel welcome, but special. You must have guests who return to your resorts year after year because of the wonderful memories they take home with them each time."

"Yes, we do. And when they go home and tell friends and family about their magical holiday, their recommendations are better than anything our army of marketing people could ever create."

This conversation went to the heart of all the things which the Laguna Beach resort had thus far failed to achieve. He could only hope that Jordan had taken his advice to heart, and was doing everything to make sure that by the time their father's billion dollar investment officially opened all the teething problems would have been sorted.

"What are you going to title the review for the Silver Havens? Just interested. Royal Resorts isn't in this part of the country, so we are not really their competition," asked Bryce, running the tip of his finger down the side of his cold bottle of beer.

Vivian's brow furrowed. "I had initially come up with, *She Sparkles by the Seashore*, but then again Lionel might find that a touch tacky. I have to come up with something that gives respect to the history of the place, but also tells prospective guests that the resort has invested in all the right things in order to meet their twenty first century travel needs."

Bryce's ears pricked up at that last remark. He was always keen to hear what other people thought a resort should deliver. While coming from a life of luxury and privilege had its obvious advantages, there were times when he found it tended to leave him at a distance from what the ordinary guest might consider as being important for their holiday stay.

"What sort of needs do you think the twenty first century traveler has? I mean, what do you look for in a resort such as ours?" He was enjoying this conversation. Getting a different perspective from another professional in the industry was gold.

The waitress arrived with their oysters and set the platter down in front of them. Two small hand plates along with oyster forks were laid out. Bryce's stomach growled as he inhaled the smoky aroma. He and Vivian exchanged excited grins, before Bryce turned to the waitress. "These look amazing, where do you source your oysters from?" he said.

"Fresh from the market earlier this morning, please enjoy," she replied.

Forks at the ready, they both gleefully dug in. As the first taste of butter and garlic hit his tastebuds, Bryce let out a hum of appreciation. They tasted as good as they looked. Delicious. His gaze settled on the next oyster which was about to be speared onto his fork.

It was Vivian who was the first to set down her fork. She had downed her half dozen oysters in what had to be world record time, then chased them with a sip of her beer.

"They were even better that what I remembered."

I like this girl. She doesn't need validation, she lets herself feel the joy of life.

When Vivian dabbed at her lips with her napkin, Bryce had to look away. His mind and manhood were determined to keep skirting the edges of lustful desire. And while he ached to have her naked and beneath him once more, he also wanted to find out everything he could about the real Vivian. With no lies now separating them, here was the perfect opportunity for him to gain an understanding of this fun, sexy girl. She might have plans to be rid of him after tonight, but Bryce Royal was determined...he wasn't going anywhere.

"You were asking about what I wanted from a resort. Well apart from the obvious, such as making sure I have enough linen..." Bryce winched at that. "Sorry, I had to get that dig in on behalf of all the other guests who have gone without towels by the poolside. And those who have been forced to beg at reception for their bedding."

Bryce nodded. "A huge order of linen arrived the day after you left. I swear that no guest will ever go without fresh towels or duvets again in any of our US resorts."

He wanted to add *especially not on my watch as CEO,* but the time didn't feel right. Tonight was about them reforging their connection, not bragging about his career.

Vivian held up her hand, displaying three fingers. "My top three things are as follows. Firstly food. Not just great restaurants but a variety of places that serve the needs of guests throughout the day. Some places do a great breakfast, but then fail at lunch. Then others seem to put all their effort into the evening menu. For me its finding the right balance. I might want tacos by the pool during the day, but I also want the option of fine dining at night."

He could heartily agree with her sentiment. One of his worst hotel experiences had been at a rival company's new hotel in France where the main restaurant was closed for most of the working week. The in room dining options had been a scant toasted sandwiches and a terrible pasta that Bryce could have sworn was only cooked once a week and then reheated when ordered.

"I've stayed at places where I have had to resort to ordering in McDonalds."

Her mouth opened on an 'o'. "Wow. I didn't think they had McDonalds outside of earth. Tell me Bryce, what sort of dipping sauces do you have on Planet Billionaire?"

She clapped her hands together, and her shoulders shook as she laughed at her own joke. Much as he wanted to take her to task over her Planet Billionaire jibe, Bryce couldn't hold back his grin —and his relief. He was sitting sharing dinner with Vivian, at one of her favorite restaurants. And they were smiling at one another. This was more than he had dared hope he might find when he stepped off the jet earlier this afternoon.

"Aioli is my favorite sauce to have with my nuggets or fries. I'm guessing that yours would be barbecue."

Vivian leaned in close and whispered conspiratorially. "Don't tell a soul but its mustard. And my least favorite is apparently the most popular one, which is sweet and sour."

Bryce held out his hand for shaking, relieved for a second time when Vivian took it. "I wholeheartedly agree. Sweet and sour is terrible. My brother Matthew loves sweet and sour pork whereas I would rather stick this oyster fork in my leg than eat it."

She released his hand, and he sat back. Bryce was having the time of his life. "So food is number one, what's next on your guest list, Vivian?"

Vivian held up her three fingers once more, twerking the middle one. "Toiletries. I need good quality ones and for my room to be restocked every day."

That made sense. His resorts only ever provided the top shelf hotel-sized toiletries. They were the little treats which many guests took home with them. And while providing the toiletries cost more than a pretty penny, Bryce had learned long ago that they were often the deciding factor when it came to people choosing to return to Royal Resorts rather than go elsewhere.

"I would bet five bucks that you have a basket full of hotel toiletries in your bathroom at home in New York. You do, don't you?"

"Darn right I do. And I also collect the snack packs and mini bottles from the hotels which provide them for free."

She had him beat on that one. Royal Resorts made good money out of their mini bars. Then again in his experience, he had found that the so-called groovy hotels which did give away those little extras often cribbed their money back in over charging for other services. It was give and take, as his father often said.

Food and freebies. Bryce racked his brains, trying to think what the final thing on Vivian's list would be. She didn't strike him as someone who would put too much weight on things like gyms or car parking. "Is Wi-Fi your last thing? I mean complimentary and high speed."

"Close. Yes, a good internet connection is super important, but the other thing that always gets a big tick are the power outlets. I have lost count of the number of times I've had to unplug the alarm clock just in order to have somewhere to charge my cell. The best hotels provide plenty of outlets and in sensible places." She let her hand drop.

Bryce cast his gaze to his remaining oysters, not daring to explain that he carried a power strip with him at all times, so he didn't have to go looking for places to plug his electronics in to recharge.

"Those things do cost money and have to be considered early on when building resort rooms. So has the Silver Havens got all those things, right?"

He might not currently be in direct competition with the Galveston resort, but who was to say that in the future he wouldn't be opening a Royal Resort somewhere along the Texan coast.

"They have the toiletries part sorted, I've already got some in my bag. Since the hotel is old, an electrical refit is probably well out of their current budget, so they fail on that point. And as for the freebies, that's not really their brand. I wouldn't mark them down for those things, but they are a nice to have."

Vivian seemed to have a solid understanding of the hotel and resort industry. Branding was a big part of it. Guests responded to strong brands.

Maybe I should offer her a job.

He was about to give voice to that notion, when his manhood sent an emergency signal racing to his brain.

If you give her a job, she will be permanently off limits to me. Come on Bryce, I am begging. Remember how good that night was in California. I can't live on memories.

His lips joined in the protest. They pressed together in hurried support of his now throbbing cock.

Royal Resorts had written policies about office romances between staff and executives. And while they were not expressly forbidden, they were not exactly encouraged.

What if he and Vivian could find a way to forge a relationship, one which saw them both step out of their respective corporate roles when they were away from the office? No doubt it would be complicated at times. Even awkward. But not impossible. Bryce found himself wanting to try.

His manhood might well be wanting to repeat that night of sexual pleasure with Vivian, lust its formidable master. Tonight, Bryce's brain was calling the shots. It had other ideas.

If I am smart and take things slow, this could be more than a one or two night steamy affair.

Good things came to those who played the careful, long

game. Seated across the table from him, he was coming to view Vivian Holte in a whole new light.

If she wanted to know what Planet Billionaire really looked like, he would be more than happy to be her personal guide.

CHAPTER THIRTY-NINE

That last piece of fried fish had almost done Vivian in, her stomach was full, and she found it hard to breathe. From where she sat, Bryce seemed to be in much the same predicament. She could have sworn he whimpered when the waitress placed the dessert menu on the table and cheerfully suggested they take a look.

The moment the woman was out of earshot, Vivian tapped her finger on the table, catching Bryce's attention. "If you ever find yourself here again, I suggest ordering a smaller main course to leave room for the pecan crunch."

"The only thing I could fit in right now would be a long walk on the beach. That food was amazing, I couldn't stop eating. Thank you for bringing me here."

An hour or so ago, she'd been ready to write this man off. Push him out of her life and hope to never again hear the name Bryce Royal. Yet here she was, having shared a laughter-filled meal with him, and suddenly wishing she had eaten her food more slowly. Time was slipping away.

She should call for the check and then after taking Bryce back to the resort, bid him a fond farewell. Her rational head said this, but her heart...and over full stomach pleaded for her to take Bryce up on the offer of a stroll on the beach. It was growing dark, but there were plenty of lights along the sea wall. "We could go for a walk. Let our food get down. Then I could drive you back to the resort."

I am not going to do anything foolish like sleep with him. Tonight was about mending fences. Parting as polite friends. Nothing else.

Deep down Vivian was yet to forgive Bryce for his review. He was clearly disgusted with his own behavior, and she respected him for being man enough to admit his mistake and then come all this way to apologize to her. Sorry, however, didn't fix things. That was a hard lesson she had learned from her time with Pete. Her ex had been the king of sweet apologies, and repeated transgressions. Once bitten, twice shy.

"That would be nice," replied Bryce.

His hand was up in an instant, beckoning over the waitress. Before Vivian had the chance to speak, Bryce had politely declined a dessert order and asked for the check. The look he shot Vivian's way was clear. She needn't bother trying to pay.

Let him apologize properly. It will be a win-win situation if he leaves here tomorrow, and you both feel better about how things ended.

Vivian could admit to this evening having done a power of good for her self-worth. When the bill came, she made a small protest, insisting she should pay for their meal, but when Bryce furrowed his brow, she quickly let it go. This whole making amends thing reminded her of a Texan line dance. Everyone knew the steps, you just had to take your cues from the music, and not stand on anyone's toes.

The sun had set by the time they finally left the restaurant. They crossed the busy road and walked onto the beach. Vivian stopped and slipped off her sandals. Bryce who was wearing a pair of tan leather loafers followed suit. She forced herself not to say anything when she snuck a glimpse of the brand on the inside of the sole. *Ferragamo*. Grace's father wore the same Italian handmade shoes and Vivian had a pretty good idea how much they cost. The moment didn't however seem right to once more remind Bryce that he and she were from different worlds.

Vivian pointed toward the pier which sat a mile or so away in the distance. "That's the Pleasure Pier. I've taken some great sunset photos from the top of the Ferris wheel. You should go for a ride on it if you get the chance."

There was something special about the Galveston evening light. It was different to California. Texas sunsets had a deep golden fire to them, and they took up the entire sky. Like the state itself, everything here was bigger.

They walked slowly along the sand with no stated direction or destination. Just two people comfortable in one another's company. Vivian played a little game with herself, imagining that this was her real life. That Bryce Royal was a permanent part of it. When she glanced over at him, taking in his finely tailored clothes and expensive watch, a little voice in the back of her mind reminded her once more that men like Bryce didn't create futures with women like her.

Every girl dreams of marrying a rockstar but you know those men always go for the supermodel or a famous actress. And billionaires marry the daughters of other billionaires.

She had seen enough pictures in the papers and in the entertainment news sites. It was just how the world worked.

"So, how long are you back in the states, Bryce? I read in *Leisure Line* that you are normally in charge of the European side of the family business."

"Family business? You make us sound like the mafia," chuckled Bryce.

"I didn't mean it to sound like that, I just meant the House of Royal. From what I've read your family has connections all over the world. I'm sorry if I caused you offence."

He offered her a soft smile. "None taken. But you are right, my extended family is involved in everything from resorts to fashion to luxury private goods, right across the globe. America is where my part of the Royal family is focused. The assignment in Europe was only meant to be for a year or two, but we had some major acquisitions during that time, so I stayed on to make sure we brought them in properly under the Royal brand. The latest one has been transforming a castle to a high end hotel in Scotland."

The way he talked about running a luxury resort empire had goosebumps forming on her skin. Some women had a thing for shoes and fashion, her weakness was hotels. If Bryce had the slightest idea as to how this supposed mundane conversation was affecting her, he wasn't showing it.

How could she ever find a way to explain what high thread-count bed sheets did to her heart rate the second she brushed up against them? Vivian had saved for a whole year to be able to afford a set of percale weave sheets for her bed at home. Every time she slid naked between them, her nipples hardened.

I bet Bryce sleeps in all his glory on gorgeous high thread count... for heaven's sake stop thinking about him being naked.

Memories of that night in California had her mouth running dry. This was dangerous. With Bryce no longer her worst enemy, she couldn't trust herself around him. Every time she looked into those brown eyes of his, her mind went to mush. She didn't want to think about the state of her panties.

Asking more personal questions about him only served to make matters worse. It was time to cut her losses. And then go take a hot shower.

"I think I might head back to the hotel now, Bryce, if

that's alright with you. I had an early start and need to catch up on my sleep."

It was a flat out lie. She had slept perfectly the previous night and would be staying up late tonight in order to get ahead on her review. This long, tall drink of temptation was the problem. She had to get away from him. If she didn't there was a good chance that she was going to end up in his bed tonight. Come tomorrow, she would struggle to hate herself for it.

The pending lack of regret was a warning. When he had been Bryce Jones, the homewares distributor from San Diego, he'd been a safe enough bet. Bryce the billionaire bore all the signs of turning into yet another cautionary tale in her life. Something to be ignored at her peril.

An odd expression of disappointment followed by relief crossed his face. "Of course." He motioned in the direction of where Vivian's car was parked on the other side of the road. "I shouldn't keep you from your bed. You are on a working trip."

Don't be a gentleman Bryce, throw me over your shoulder, take me to bed, and have your wicked way with me.

Thank god she was wearing a loose top. If she had been in her little blue dress, it would've been impossible to hide her hardened nipples. The night air was cool, but it had nothing to do with why her headlights suddenly switched to high beam. Heated lust rippled through her body.

Bryce's gaze settled on her breasts, and Vivian was certain he could read her filthy, smut filled mind. She did her best to push away the heady sensual memories of what his lips, teeth, and tongue had done to her that night. Of the bites and small bruises he had left. Their short lived affair might have ended badly but he was the devil of a lover. Vivian would sell her soul to hear Bryce offer to thrust his cock deep into her heat and bring her to a screaming orgasm one more time.

And they wonder why sane women do such mad things for bad boys.

Vivian's heart hammered in her chest as Bryce drew closer. He bent and for a moment she thought he was about to kiss her. "Thank you for tonight, Vivian, it was wonderful."

The warmth of his words against her skin went straight to her sex. She reached for him, but Bryce turned away. The stab of disappointment in Vivian's heart had her gasping with pain. She tracked quietly in his wake as they made their way across the sand toward the road.

He came here to apologize. Nothing more. He doesn't want me. Of course he doesn't. He's a billionaire.

Reaching the sidewalk, Vivian stopped and put her sandals back on. Her approach to driving was tentative at best, she didn't need to try attempting it in bare feet. They crossed the road back to the restaurant parking lot.

Before climbing into the car, she took in a deep calming breath, doing her best to clear her mind. Driving a motor vehicle while being torn as to what to say to Bryce wasn't the wisest of combinations.

The mercifully short trip back to the resort quickly became a polite exercise in Vivian pointing out places of interest. At the hotel a parking valet took her keys, and Vivian and Bryce moved away from the car and came to stand alongside one another, outside the hotel's main reception area.

With her nerves rapidly fraying, Vivian offered Bryce a brief, micro hug. "Thanks for coming all this way to say sorry, Bryce. That was big of you. I really appreciate the gesture, when I know you could have so easily just sent an email."

Gripping what was left of her self-esteem by the fingertips she turned to leave. It was clear in her mind that to him, California had been a one-time thing.

Bryce caught her by the arm drawing her gently back to

him. "Don't go, Vivian. Please don't let things end like this. At least come and have a night cap with me. We can sit at the poolside bar and talk. Just friends. No strings attached. I promise."

She reluctantly met his gaze. Why did he have to choose this evening to behave as a gentleman? Did he suspect that if he asked her to come back to his suite, she would say yes? And that to his way of thinking, it would be a mistake for both of them? Something they would regret.

Her heart and mind continued to battle it out with one another. While Bryce seemed content to offer a no-strings late night drink, Vivian's heart was demanding that he buy her the whole stringed section of an orchestra. She would gladly take a room full of violins. Anything to keep the two of them together. And if he asked, she was more than willing to make him a devil's pact.

No. You are reading this all wrong. That is not what he is offering. One drink. A polite chat, then you both go back to your respective lives.

There would be no messing about. No more hot and sweaty sex on soft sheets. A glass of wine, and a final farewell. They would share one friendly parting drink. After that Bryce Royal would be out of her life. She painted a smile to her lips. "Alright, but I really can only stay for one drink."

Vivian couldn't find the strength to pull away when Bryce slipped his hand about her waist and led her into the poolside bar. When it came to this man, she struggled to say no. And after he was gone, and she was alone once more, she promised herself she would take a long steaming hot shower and have a bloody good cry.

CHAPTER FORTY

"To you, Vivian. And once again, thank you for giving me the opportunity to apologize for my terrible behavior." Bryce raised his glass in salute.

Vivian didn't know where to look as heat settled to burn on her face and neck. Her body thrummed with the need to have him touch her, to trace his fingers over her naked body. He'd said he wasn't finished with her when they parted in California. *I just wish we could go back to that night and do it all over again.*

She'd been comfortable in his company over dinner, but ever since they had left the beach, Vivian had been struggling with being this close to Bryce. The girl at Laguna Beach, and the hurt one in New York, were not the same version of herself who now sat next to him in the well-lit bar.

As tears threatened, she forced herself into reviewer mode. To a place where she could be detached from her emotions. Her gaze took in the bar and its odd décor.

If there was one thing the hotel had made a slip-up with in its big revamp it was with the brightly painted supposedly Caribbean themed *Winds of Change* cocktail lounge. The sad mish mash of tiki and pirate nick-nacks really ought to be tossed in the trash and started over.

The disaster of a bar didn't help with Vivian's growing discomfort. She caught several odd glances from the other guests and could just imagine what they were thinking. What was the smartly dressed and obviously wealthy man doing in the company of that young woman? Anyone with good taste could see she was batting well out of her league. His immaculately cut suit spoke fluent Italian hand tailoring, while hers whispered last season's value buy from ASOS.

The difference in our circumstances is yet another reason he'd be keen to leave our fling in the past.

Vivian shivered as he reached out and brushed the back of his hand down her right cheek. "And now I made you blush." His gaze darted to the couple a few seats further along the bar. They turned away, but before then they hadn't made much of an effort to pretend they weren't eavesdropping on Bryce and Vivian's private conversation.

"Would you prefer if we took our drinks and sat somewhere a little more secluded? I spotted an empty table when we arrived."

"Yes, please. I don't particularly like being stared at, or having strangers pry into my private business," she replied.

Away from the other patrons, Vivian's face returned to its normal temperature. She could handle the truth that Bryce didn't want her, but the last thing she needed was for other people to pick up on the dynamics of their relationship. Self-doubt was her constant companion.

He set their glasses on the table, then made room for her. "Where would you like to sit?"

Vivian immediately chose the chair where she could be seated with her back toward the bar. She sensed eyes were still focused on her, and in her current frame of mind she didn't want to meet anyone else's gaze but Bryce's. From the moment the two of them had stepped through the door, they had been an object of interest for the other patrons.

Fingers wrapped around the stem of her cocktail, she tried to think of safe topics for small talk. Silence would only serve to hold other people's attention.

"Did you fly directly into Galveston itself? I mean, did you come by way of private plane?" A number of famous people reportedly had homes in the area, and she doubted any of them ever flew commercial.

The main airports at Houston were some way of a distance from Galveston Island. The land link via the interstate was fast, but it was still a long drive. She couldn't imagine Bryce being keen to make the seventy odd miles trip from the main airport.

He picked up his glass of red wine and took a drink. "Don't judge me, but yes, I did bring the jet. It's sitting at the local airport a couple of miles from here."

Her question might have been posed as bit of an ice breaker, a way to try and calm her nerves, but she had always wondered what it must be like to travel on a jet. To experience that sheer level of luxury. The nearest she had ever got to First Class on a commercial plane was walking past the closed curtain as she boarded. Actually having your own private plane on standby to take you wherever you wished blew her mind.

"You are who you are, Bryce. I myself flew in to Houston Hobby, that's the smaller one of the two main airports. Only a few airlines service it, but its less of a drive. And they have a drive through Starbucks not far from the hire car depot."

He reached across the small table and lay his hand over hers. The warm comfort of his touch had her heart making more silent wishes.

If only he wanted more with me. If only we came from the same world. If only.

Vivian's gaze remained locked on where their fingers met. It would be so easy to turn her hand over and place it fully in his, so easy to let him know she was open to things happening. But she didn't want to risk him pulling away again. A public rejection would crush her.

"What is the attraction of the Frappuccino ? I just don't get it. The thought of even putting sugar in my coffee makes me shudder." There was a laugh in his voice, a sexy tease. It sent Vivian's mind racing back to Laguna Beach, and how Bryce's warm smile had made her throw all caution to the wind and spend the night with him.

But his thoughts were clearly elsewhere.

Tuck your hopes away and just be nice.

"A girl loves her sweet treats, what more can I say?"

The brush of his thumb over her skin promised a world of wicked things. This simple touch had the nerve endings in her body lighting up like fireworks. She wasn't sure if her heart and mind could handle much more of these mixed signals.

"Promise me something, Vivian. Never let anyone try to tell you what you should love. People might say I'm a coffee snob, but I love my strong espresso. If a Frappuccino is your passion, then defend it, with all your heart."

Coffee, he wants to talk coffee. Just let it go.

A moment of silence followed. Vivian sensed they had reached not just a natural pause in the conversation, but a fork in the road.

He said he was sorry, and you promised yourself you wouldn't let things go any further tonight.

The sensible thing, the honorable thing would be to say goodnight and goodbye. She could walk away with her self-respect intact, and her heart mostly still in one piece.

If only Bryce wasn't so damn handsome. So lovely.

An hour or two ago she could have easily channeled her

inner Elizabeth Bennet and informed Bryce that he was the last man on earth she could ever be prevailed upon to marry. Now she would have happily stood in the freezing cold of dawn and waited while he marched toward her through the early morning mist to declare his undying love.

"I'm probably heading back to New York sometime tomorrow morning, but I was wondering if perhaps before then, we could meet for breakfast."

Vivian's private fantasy of being a windswept character out of Pride and Prejudice snapped and fizzled into the humid Texan night air. The sweeping musical score overtaken by the canned reggae music which pumped through the bar's sound system.

Gathering what remained of her wits, she asked. "What time?" At least Bryce wanted to part as friends. He mightn't want her anymore, but friends was a good deal better than where they had been only a few hours ago.

She'd made a joke of the fact that they lived in different worlds, but the truth was they did. She would never get the chance to visit Planet Billionaire.

"How does around eight work for you? I plan to hit the gym just before seven." Bryce patted his stomach. "Need to work off some of tonight's food, plus I find it helps to center my thoughts. The combination of sweat and a bit of workout pain are a stress reducing drug for me."

Vivian nodded. Being a New Yorker, she well understood the sweat and pain of pounding the streets or being crushed into the morning hour on the subway. "I walk a lot. That's my way of trying to burn off the cortisol. And yoga, though I must confess I am not very supple at the moment. I've been doing a bit too much couch lounging, and not enough exercise."

Bryce leaned closer. "I would beg to differ. My memories

of you are of a woman more than capable of bending and stretching."

The heat returned to Vivian's face. Why did he have to go and remind her of their passionate encounter? And of the hurt it had later caused her.

"Yes well, it took days for the knots in my muscles to unwind."

He sucked in an audible breath. "I will never forget that day I spent with you, Vivian. You showed me a side of connecting with another person I hadn't seen before. And when you gave yourself to me, I truly felt humbled."

They were suddenly standing on the edge of a precipice. Temptation hung heavy in the air. On the table, her cellphone buzzed. The universe must have been listening. Grace's name shone enticingly bright on the screen.

Bryce moved his hand away and sat back. "Did you want to get that?"

Vivian was about to hit decline and send the call to voicemail. "I can call her back."

"It's fine, answer it."

She put the phone to her ear. "Hi, Grace."

"Hey babe, how's it going? Did you get to Gaido's?"

"We did. The food was really good."

"We? Who are you with. Tell me it's a nice guy."

Vivian's gaze settled on Bryce. Grace was loud enough that there was every chance he could her what was being said. "It's Bryce. He flew here to apologize. We went to dinner together."

"That rat bastard! He thinks he can sweet talk you. Oh! Put him on. Put him on. I'll give him the word."

"I don't think that's a good idea. We have just got things sorted."

"Put. Him. On. The. Phone."

Vivian winced but did as Grace demanded. A bemused

looking Bryce took the cell and held it to his ear. "Hello, Grace. This is Bryce."

She sat and listened as World War Three was declared at the other end of the line. To Bryce's credit he sat and took the tirade of abuse, with great calm. "Yes. No. I am sorry. Agreed, totally my fault. And no, I wouldn't ever want anyone to do that to me either."

Thank god they had moved out of earshot of the other guests.

"Yes, I will, and thank you, Grace. You are a true friend of Vivian's."

He handed her back the phone. "Grace said to say feel free to call her back when you are done with me."

If he hadn't brought this on himself, she would have felt a sense of pity for Bryce. Grace was a strong, opinionated woman. She had also been Vivian's rock over the past few months. If anyone deserved to give Bryce Royal a piece of her mind, it was Grace.

Her friend's call had finally broken the spell. Clutching her cell and purse, Vivian downed the last of her drink and got to her feet. "Thank you for this evening, Bryce. And as for your apology, it means a lot. If you will excuse me, I think it's time I went upstairs to my room. If you are still wishing to catch up tomorrow, I can meet you in the buffet line at eight."

He rose from his chair. "Let me walk with you." It was a request, but it was delivered with a definite tone of *I'm not taking no for an answer*. "We shouldn't give the other guests at the bar any more reason to talk about us." He offered her his arm, and she took it.

They crossed the lobby of the hotel and headed for the bank of elevators. Vivian slipped her arm from Bryce's. "What floor are you on?" she asked, pressing the call button.

He had the good grace to look embarrassed as he pointed

back in the direction from where they had just come. "I'm in one of the beach front presidential suites."

Of course he was... someone like Bryce Royal didn't lower himself to actually staying in a standard hotel room. While she woke to the sound of the TV from the room next door, Bryce would be hearing the gentle waves lapping at the shore.

"We could go back to my place and have another drink. Watch the sea." The offer was there but it lacked any real heat or conviction. There was a further awkward moment. Silence lingered, broken only when the elevator doors opened, and the automated voice announced it was going up.

"Good night, Bryce. Thank you for tonight, I had a wonderful time."

Vivian took one step into the car and reached for the button. A large male body followed her into the elevator, taking hold of her hand before she could press for her floor.

Bryce swept her up into his arms, and their lips crashed together. The kiss quickly turned tender. Their tongues danced in time and Vivian's heart was aflutter. Through the haze of their embrace, the elevator buzzer made its demands. *Choose a floor.*

Bryce kept his foot against the door, holding it open. When he finally drew back from the kiss, they were both panting hard. Lust and desire coursed through her veins. Sense and reason had fled. All she wanted to do was to go with him to his room and get naked.

But as he had done a little earlier on the beach, Bryce moved away. He took a distinct backward step. And then another. "Good night, Vivian. May your dreams be sweet and creamy. I will see you in the morning."

The elevator doors closed, and she was left alone. Bryce hadn't taken her up on her obvious offer of a night of passion. He had drawn the line at one kiss. She combed her fingers through her hair. "He really doesn't want me."

Heart heavy with disappointment she pressed the elevator button for the eleventh floor. Tomorrow morning she would give Bryce once last chance to make a move. If he decided to part as friends, she would graciously accept his decision.

And she would vow to never again fall for a billionaire.

CHAPTER FORTY-ONE

He really had to get back into a solid gym routine. The past few weeks of traveling had seen Bryce miss out on his daily workout. And he was feeling it.

His sluggishness was further compounded by the fact he hadn't been racking up the miles he normally did while running around after guests and senior hotel staff. Working in Europe and the UK, the pedometer in his phone regularly showed him clocking up over thirty thousand steps a day.

The pinch of the waistband in his pants was also a reflection of how quickly the American diet was catching up with his sedentary lifestyle. After leaving Vivian last night he had firmly resolved, no more platters or large plates of food. Meeting Vivian's friend Grace in the flesh was also high on his list of things never to do.

Bryce pushed himself hard in the resort's well-appointed gym, which meant that by the time he stepped off the treadmill, he was a sweaty mess. Wiping his face with his workout towel he pondered the relief that punishing his body had brought. Working out was one thing, but he would much rather have spent last night getting hot and sticky with Vivian.

You resisted the temptation of taking her to bed. Well done.

It had been a close thing. After that amazing kiss, his hardened cock had been ready to step up and take control of things. Vivian had given him all the right signals. She was more than willing to take another tour of orgasm city. He couldn't decide who was the more disappointed when he stepped away and bid her a pleasant goodnight.

Vivian had looked ready to claw at him, while his dick throbbed all the way back to his hotel suite in sex staved protest. Back in his room, Bryce had taken himself firmly in hand and jerked off. Anything to be able to get the blood flowing back to his brain. Hopefully his tortured manhood would soon be enjoying the benefits that came from Bryce being in a long term relationship with the cute travel reviewer.

He wanted more than just a hotel fling. He wanted Vivian in his life, and in his bed. And in order for that to happen, he was going to have to take things slowly. The woman he planned to share his heart with had to know what he felt for her was more than just simple lust.

Once I've explained things properly to her over breakfast, she will understand where I am coming from. Hopefully after that, there won't be anything stopping us from being together.

After a quick shower, Bryce slipped into a black short sleeved polo shirt, and tugged on a pair of chinos. He completed the look with a casual dark blue tailor made jacket. Anyone giving him a quick glance would likely think him no different from any other hotel guest, it was only those with a discerning eye who could spot the tell-tale signs of him having serious money. The understated Vacheron Constantin watch which sat on his left wrist was worth more than what most people spent on a new car. His shoes made from soft leather had been hand-crafted in England using a personalized template. They fitted his feet to perfection.

Bryce wore his wealth with graceful ease. He wasn't one for grand displays. The watch had been a twenty first birthday gift from his parents, and the artisan shoes had come from a company bonus he'd received after successfully launching a new resort in Portugal some three years earlier.

Even the jet wasn't something Bryce considered a luxury. Time was money and if he was able to work while on the plane and then land somewhere fresh and ready to do business, it was worth the cost to the company. His younger brother Matthew had a differing opinion on the subject and had been quietly pushing for the members of House Royal to find a greener way to travel.

Dressed and ready to meet Vivian for breakfast, Bryce picked up his cell. He stuffed the phone into his pocket, determined not to check his messages. He was on personal leave. Vivian was probably already downstairs at the buffet waiting impatiently for him and her first sip of sweet coffee.

Mustn't keep her and our future waiting.

Reaching the door of his hotel room, his gaze landed on an envelope which had been pushed under it. He picked it up, noting the resort name which was printed on the front.

He hadn't bothered to check in under an assumed name, so the management of Silver Havens had more than likely realized who Mister Bryce Royal was and had organized to send him a complimentary spa voucher or a free cocktail as a gesture of their goodwill.

"Thanks, but I don't think I will have time to visit the day spa."

He was about to toss it onto the nearby table and go catch up with Vivian when something told him it would be wise to stop and open it.

"Who knows, it might be important."

Pulling the single piece of paper from out of the envelope Bryce took in the contents of the letter. The blood in his veins quickly turned to ice.

You can take your apology and shove it where the sun doesn't shine. I should have figured you were up to something when you suddenly appeared on the beach, all smiles, and promises. Grace was right, you are a rat bastard.

What kind of an asshole kisses a girl while at the same time setting his wolfpack of company lawyers on the magazine she works for?

<u>*A Bryce Royal kind of asshole!!!*</u>

To think I wasted one of my favorite restaurants on you.

Don't try to contact me ever again. If you do, I will take out a restraining order, and publish its details in the New York Times.

"What the devil? Who is suing...what?" He stared at the paper, reading it several times over while the words sank in. No one had said anything about suing Luxury Hotels and Resorts Worldwide. Edward had actually agreed that Vivian's review was fair and balanced.

But she had to have got it from somewhere. Vivian wouldn't make that sort of accusation up on her own. She had no reason.

He spun quickly on his heel and raced over to the table where his laptop sat. As soon as it fired up, Bryce clicked through to the one place he guessed might be able to give him some answers. The whisper column of *Leisure Line*.

As soon as the site loaded, his gaze immediately landed on the article which was pinned to the top of the column.

Royal Resorts threatens to silence LHRW
Lawyers for Royal Resorts USA demand apology and full retraction

He skimmed the rest of the article, swearing as he read.

"Fuck. Fuck." His heart was racing. "Ok, ok. Calm down." This had to be a misunderstanding. A simple case of crossed wires that would take only a phone call or two to rectify. He pulled his cell out of his pocket, then glanced at the door. Did he call his father, or go find Vivian?

The urge to reassure her that it was all a mistake won out. Bryce ran from the villa, through the gardens, and to the breakfast buffet. Vivian was nowhere to be seen.

Of course she isn't here. You don't think she would be sitting sipping a bloody Frappuccino waiting for you to come and find her.

He made for the bank of elevators. Fists clenched, he mentally urged the next one to arrive. When the doors finally opened, he stepped aside waiting with gritted teeth while a group of other guests leisurely ambled out. They were busy chatting about breakfast and their plans for the day.

Bryce's plans had gone out the window. All he could think about was finding Vivian. It was only when his finger hovered over the row of elevator buttons, that he came to a sudden stop.

Shit. I don't know which floor or room she is in.

The elevator door beeped in warning. With a resigned sigh Bryce stepped out and back into the lobby. How was he going to find Vivian?

He was tempted to call the New York office and beg Mia to give him Vivian's number. But in doing so, he would be forced to admit he had yet again screwed up when it came to her friend. That was not the sort of thing he wanted to have his team knowing about, especially not when he was about to become their boss. There had to be another way.

Think. Reception won't tell me, they are paid to protect the privacy of their guests. And so they should.

Desperation threatened to cloud his judgement. He had to know if Vivian was still at the resort. His feet ate up the distance from the lobby to the hotel's entrance in a matter of seconds.

Reaching the entrance to the resort parking garage, Bryce shoved his hand into his pants pocket and retrieved his bill fold. Valets were not the most well-paid of staff, they relied heavily on tips. He pulled out a fifty dollar note, looked at it, then grabbed a hold of a one hundred dollar bill. "Come on Ben Franklin, I need you to buy me some information."

To his relief, the valet from last night was on the morning shift. The man recognized him and gave Bryce a friendly wave. "Good morning, sir."

Having grown up around the hotel and resort business Bryce had learned early the value of a welcoming smile, and a warm hand shake. "Good morning to you, too. I was wondering if you could help me. Do you remember the lady I was with last night? You parked her rental car when she and I came back from dinner. I meant to catch up with her this morning, but we seem to have missed one another. Could you maybe look and see if her car is still here?"

He held out his hand, the corner of the note poking out between his fingers. The valet glanced around, then came close and they shook hands. "Ms. Holte left about fifteen minutes ago, I think she was headed for the airport."

"Oh. That's a pity. Not to worry, I will send her an email. She and I can catch up later. Thank you."

Racing back to his room, Bryce quickly snatched up a few things and threw them into a bag. He didn't have time to pack everything or bother with check out. The airport and Vivian were his priority. If he could catch her before her flight left, he might just be able to salvage things between them.

The second his ass hit the seat of a cab, he dialed Patrick's number. The flight attendant picked up on the second ring. "Hi, Patrick. This is a bit of an emergency. Could you go to the front desk of the Silver Havens resort and ask for a key card to my room. Pack the rest of my belongings and take them to the plane. I'm..." He paused for a moment, unsure as to what he was actually doing.

He met the gaze of the cab driver in the rear vision mirror. Vivian had come in at Houston Hobby, so she must be headed there. "Houston Hobby airport please."

As the cab pulled out of the resort driveway, he went back to his call. "I am trying to catch a friend at the airport before her flight takes off. Just tell our pilot to be ready to leave once I know what is happening. I think. Yeah. Um. Thanks, Patrick."

Bryce hung up the call. His brain was as scrambled as his words. All his plans for a leisurely breakfast with Vivian, including a long conversation, and hopefully a repeat of their day at Laguna Beach, had flown out the window. She thought him a duplicitous bastard. Again. And now she was on her way home, determined to have nothing to do with him.

That damn article in *Leisure Line*. Someone had to have tipped them off about a pending law suit. If it wasn't Edward, then who else would have done such a stupid thing?

It might be super early in Los Angeles, but Bryce didn't care. The voice on the other end of the line was less than cheery in its greeting. "Do you have any fucking idea what fucking time it is? We had a wedding here last night, I didn't get to bed until almost three," growled Jordan.

"Yes, I am well aware of the time. And good morning to you, too. I trust you were overseeing the celebrations, not partying with the guests." That was a spiteful thing to say, but Bryce was currently running out of patience with the world. "Do you happen to know anything about a lawsuit and LHRW?"

Jordan's deep resigned sigh crossed the fifteen hundred miles which separated them. "Yeah. But I didn't instruct them to go ahead. I just rattled the chains. You said I needed to do something to let Dad know I was in control."

Bryce's gaze drifted to the window. The beach view was quickly turning into one of trucks and cars on either side. A road sign read Gulf Freeway, three miles. He took a deep breath as he struggled to keep his temper under control.

I meant talk to Dad, and convince him to give you another chance, not blow up my world.

"What did you actually say? And please be specific. Your future at Royal Resorts could well depend on what you said to our lawyers."

"Seriously? I took the initiative, like you suggested. So, I went and spoke to our legal eagles. They suggested I could do a few things, legal wise but then cautioned against it. Besides, anything legal has to go via Dad."

It quickly became apparent that Jordan hadn't thought his little chain rattling would go any further than the conversation he'd had with the company lawyers. But someone in the New York office had leaked the confidential discussion to *Leisure Line*. Once he was back in the office, Bryce was going to pay a visit to the in house legal team and find the source of the leak.

"But, um. There is something else I might have done...did do."

Bryce closed his eyes. "What did you do?"

"Everyone was so angry after the meeting where the reviews were read out, I figured it was worth letting the people at LHRW know that we were not just some mom and pop trailer park that they could dump on. The next time they thought to write a bad review of one of our properties, they might think twice about it."

Bryce slowly opened his eyes. The sea came into view out the window, and the cab changed lanes as it moved toward the highway which crossed over onto the Texan mainland.

The bright sun had Bryce regretting his oversight of leaving his sunglasses behind in his hotel suite.

"Jordan. What did you do? I need it in plain English."

"It was nothing really. Once I got out here to California, I sent a polite email to the magazine's editor. Some guy named Lionel. But all I did was ask him to come back to Laguna Beach in a few months and give his readers an update on how the resort was going."

"Ok, thanks, Jordan." He hung up the phone and moaned. "Why. Why." He couldn't bear to think what Jordan had put in that email. Whatever his brother had said, combined with the suspected leak from the New York office, had led Vivian's boss to believe legal action was pending against his magazine.

He rubbed at his temples. A dull headache had begun to throb at the back of his head. Lack of morning coffee was quickly taking its toll.

Jordan. Jordan. What have you done?

Two years ago Bryce been so full of confidence in his brother's abilities that he hadn't hesitated to back Jordan for the California project. And from what Edward had told him earlier in the year, things were going well at Laguna Beach.

It all left Bryce at a loss to understand what had happened with his brother. Why Jordan's management of the resort had failed so badly over the past few months. It was clear he was going to have to confront Jordan and somehow get the truth.

I don't know what I am going to do about him.

Bryce feared that if Jordan didn't bring the Laguna Beach Resort up to scratch by the time it officially opened, he might be compelled by the board to reassess his brother's position within the company.

I can't imagine having to fire my own brother.

CHAPTER FORTY-TWO

Her beloved Frappuccino in hand, Vivian lowered herself into one of the hard plastic seats in the departure lounge. The food offerings at the airport were surprisingly good but this morning she couldn't face them. Only the prospect of a long dehydrating plane flight had seen her shove her misery aside and join the long queue for a drink. While she waited, she silently chastised herself.

Why am I so surprised that Bryce turned out to be a dick? Am I that stupid? Desperate for a guy to like me for me? And I was ready to sleep with him. I should have let Grace go full throttle and rip him a new one.

Right up until the moment she had opened the *Leisure Line* site this morning, Vivian had been holding onto the hope that Bryce had simply decided to behave as a gentleman last night. He hadn't rejected her, he was biding his time.

If her fevered hopes held true, then this morning after breakfast, he would take her back to his ocean front presidential villa and make good on the promise that had been in that kiss last night.

As she'd read the article about Royal Resorts threatening

to sue her employer, nausea had knocked her both sideways and down. Her tears had come so fast she couldn't hold them back.

It was horrible to admit it, but Bryce Royal had broken her heart. She'd been tempted to call Grace back last night and ask for her friend's advice as to what she should do this morning. Thank god she hadn't.

When had she become so anxious for Bryce to like her? Answer…after the night they had shared in California. A night of unbridled passion which had completely thrown her life into a tail spin. With the news of the pending lawsuit, she couldn't find an emotional lever to pull in order to right herself.

The only good thing in her life right now was the cold, sugary heaven of a hazelnut Frappuccino. At least she could rely on her daily Frappuccino to see her through. Starbucks was a girl's loyal friend.

Another life lesson learned. On the drive from the resort, Vivian had come to a decision. She would set love and all its shitty complications to one side and concentrate on her career. If Lionel made good on his promise to send her to Italy, it would help lift her profile at the magazine. She would then be one step closer to her dream job of working as a travel columnist for Condé Nast. There was more to the hotel and leisure industry than just reviewing room-service menus and day spas.

Though I could have done with a session at a day spa. Damn you, Bryce Royal.

Her plans for today had included a lovely breakfast with a nice gentleman, who may or may not have just been playing a long game of seduction. And if it turned out he wasn't, Vivian's back up plan was a relaxing hour in the spa and getting her toe nails painted. She'd checked out the resort's day spa with its gorgeous collection of nail polishes. But instead of that pretty shade with the clever name *the grass is always greener* adorning her toes, she was about to board a hastily booked flight out of Galveston.

A group of businessmen bustled their way past where Vivian sat. One bore a slight resemblance to Bryce. Her chest tightened at the sight.

Royal Resorts was threatening to sue her magazine. It didn't make sense. Even Bryce had agreed that she hadn't written anything in her review which wasn't true. And if the rest of the executives at Royal Resorts didn't appreciate the three star rating, then they should be doing something about fixing the situation at the Laguna Beach resort rather than taking cheap shots at the messenger.

And while she didn't agree with the threat of legal action, she could at least understand why an organization would think that might be the way to go. What she couldn't however get her head around was Bryce. Why had he come all this way to smooth talk her into accepting his apology, spend an evening charming her, while at the same time knowing his company was about to do the dirty on her magazine?

And that single stunning kiss.

Did he honestly think he could keep his business and personal life separate? On one hand sue the company she worked for, while on the other tempt her into his bed. Billionaires. One rule for them, one rule for the rest of humanity.

But he hadn't invited her to his hotel suite. Perhaps billionaire assholes had their moral limits.

Oh, stop thinking about him.

When the last of her Frappuccino slurped up the straw, Vivian was tempted to go and order another one. The first boarding call for her flight put paid to that idea.

The sooner I am out of Texas, the better. Farewell lone star state.

The flight would hopefully give her enough time to come up with the right words to say to Grace. To explain that her private life had now reached the point where it had been officially designated a fustercluck.

She planned to get a t-shirt made with that misspelt word printed in bold letters on the front. If Royal Resorts went public with their law suit, she may as well get her fifteen minutes of fame out of it. Vivian could just imagine the look on Bryce Royal's face when she turned up to court sporting her new look. There would be no more sexy blue dresses for him. *Bastard.*

Vivian dropped her empty cup into the trash as she made her way to the gate. As she did, a thought struck her. She really ought to drink a beverage which used recyclable cups or find a way to bring her own reusable drink cup.

Maybe that's something we should start including in our rating of hotels and resorts. Their efforts to go green.

It was all well and good to ask guests to reuse bath towels, but what other things could they be doing? Should they be doing?

"Now that's the sort of thing Bryce Royal should be focusing on, not going after people like me."

She filed the idea under other things to talk to Lionel about when the time was right. With a lawsuit looming, presenting her boss with a fleshed out plan would be better than just offering up an idle thought.

Standing in the queue waiting to board, she googled *things that the hotel industry are doing to go green*. Tucking her cell into her bag, she glanced at the plane through the window of the gate, then added *get our advertisers to buy carbon offsets* and *avoid Bryce Royal for the rest of my life* to her mental list.

CHAPTER FORTY-THREE

Bryce dashed through the doors of the departure area at Houston Hobby Airport, narrowly avoiding tumbling head first over a suitcase which had suddenly stopped in his path. The owner of the luggage glared at him. The disapproving expression on the gentleman's face spoke of someone who always got to the airport with a good three hours to spare.

It had been a long time since Bryce had taken a domestic commercial flight. He couldn't recall airports having ever been this busy. Everywhere he looked, there were long lines of people and bags. Somewhere in this vast army of travelers was Vivian.

"Where are you?" he muttered.

If he could find her before her flight departed, he might be able to convince her that Jordan hadn't been serious about instigating legal action against LHRW magazine. *Leisure Line* had been given the wrong information. He hadn't come all the way to Galveston just to play some devious trick on her.

She has to believe me. I am not that guy.

Unfortunately in his world, there were plenty of other men who were *that guy*. They were the ones who never hesitated to screw people over both in business and their private relationships. New York's elite society was littered with the carcasses of failed deals and dead marriages. Bryce was unwavering in his resolve. His would never be that story.

Tell yourself all the lies you want, but no one else wrote that spiteful review of Vivian.

After his lies and now the rumored legal maneuvers, she had every reason to believe he *was* that guy. He'd really shot himself in the foot with that review.

Bryce came to a halt in front of the departures board, running his gaze down the list of flights which were scheduled for the morning. The only direct flight to New York was due to leave in thirty minutes. Vivian had to be on that one, and it would be boarding soon.

Worst case, he didn't get a chance to talk to her before the flight left. Best case, he got on the plane, found her, and hope prevailed. It's not as if she could get away from him mid-flight. And if things went his way, which he was determined they would, by the time they did land in New York, Vivian would be walking off the plane with him. Hand in hand to a waiting limousine.

Shoot, I need a ticket.

There were apps for those things, but in signing up they wanted registrations and email addresses. He didn't have time to opt in for notifications or agree to privacy policies.

I just want a bloody plane ticket.

Bryce raced over to the bank of desks bearing the logo of the airline which had the next New York flight. There wasn't a queue at the ticket counter, and he stepped straight up to the front. "Good morning. I need to get on the flight to New York. The one which is leaving shortly. Please."

The middle aged ticketing agent slowly looked him up and down. "On the run from the feds, or an angry husband?"

He slid his black credit card across the counter. "Neither.

I'm trying to catch up with a young lady. We had a misunderstanding. I have to find her."

The woman tapped away at her keyboard for a minute, all the while a sly knowing grin sat on her lips. Bryce could just imagine what she was thinking. *'I've seen that movie too.'*

"Do you have any bags to check in? Anything to declare?"

Bryce quickly shook his head. The only thing he had to declare was that he had been a fool to assume Jordan would go quietly out to California and not continue to mess up Bryce's life.

"No, I just have a small inflight bag, and me. I would appreciate an aisle seat in First Class if you can accommodate my request. Actually make that two seats together in First Class, please."

If he was going to have any hope of sorting things out with Vivian, he couldn't do it if he was up the front of the plane, and she was somewhere down the back.

The agent checked his ID, processed his credit card, then handed him his ticket. "I'm sorry Mister Royal, but there aren't any first or business class seats, available on this flight. You got the very last ticket, and it's in coach." She glanced at the clock on the nearby wall. "You had better hurry and make your way through security. Your flight leaves from Gate twenty two, and considering the time, you might want to run."

Flying around the world via private jet had many advantages but avoiding the lines at security had to be close to the top. When Bryce normally travelled in the US, he had use of private arrival gates, and even internationally he breezed through the VIP section of customs. The thought of having to wait to go through screening had him checking his watch. This was going to be touch and go.

Twenty minutes later, boarding pass in hand, he stepped onto the New York bound flight. He'd gotten his second piece of luck this morning, with Houston Hobby having recently upgraded its body scan security. The line had moved quickly. And whoever had come up with the idea of a TSA pre check was a certifiable genius.

He hadn't spotted Vivian at the departure gate, but he'd arrived after boarding had commenced.

She must already be on the plane.

Making his way down the tightly packed flight, Bryce scanned the passengers. There was no sign of Vivian. It was slow going moving down the plane as people in front of him stopped to stuff their luggage into the overhead lockers, before taking their respective seats. Bryce checked his boarding pass, which read row 24.

Vivian could be in any seat beyond that all the way to the back of the plane. People were still banked behind him when Bryce finally reached his seat. With only minutes before takeoff he didn't have time to go and check the rest of the passengers. The hard edge of a small wheel-on suitcase digging into his right calf muscle informed Bryce as to how eager the passenger behind him was to get to their own assigned seat.

He ignored his ill-mannered fellow traveler, and shuffled across to the middle seat, where he sat down. Some people weren't good flyers, while others were just rude asses. Starting a fight on a packed airplane was not on Bryce's bucket list, nor was meeting an air marshal and leaving the plane in handcuffs.

His thoughts were focused on Vivian. Had she possibly seen him get onboard? And if so, then perhaps when the flight finally took off and they levelled out, she might be intrigued enough to come and speak to him. To give him the opportunity to explain the misunderstanding which Jordan's actions had caused.

Who knows, the way my luck is running, she may just decide to come and tear shreds off me while the whole plane watches.

He pulled Vivian's note out of his jacket, read it, then stuffed it into the seat pocket in front of him. It might be better that she hadn't seen him. He could just picture the headline in *Leisure Line* tomorrow.

Resort reviewer rips Royal a new one on packed budget airline flight.

Scratch that, he would stay in his seat until after they landed in New York, then wait at the arrivals gate for Vivian to leave the flight. A public slanging match wouldn't be the best way for him to cement his future appointment as CEO of Royal Resorts USA.

A small boy suddenly appeared at the end of the row, accompanied by a flight attendant. There was a red lanyard around the boy's neck, and a tag which read 'Unaccompanied Minor.' He didn't meet Bryce's eyes as he took the empty aisle seat next to him.

"Now Jonathan, I just want to check that you know how to put your seatbelt on," said the flight attendant.

Bryce bit down on his bottom lip as he caught sight of Jonathan's eye roll.

"Yes, thank you I can manage." The boy stuffed an iPad into his seat pocket, then proceeded to make a grand display of his seatbelt wrangling abilities.

"That's terrific. I will be back to check on you after we have taken off."

The attendant's gaze settled on Bryce. He did a similar thing to what the ticket agent had done. A brief looking up and down, checking and clearly deciding if Bryce was trust worthy enough to be seated next to the young boy.

It was an odd experience. He might be from a world

where strangers judged each other based on appearance, but that was always about the cut of their clothing or the quality of their shoes. This was about him as a person.

Bryce dipped a hand inside his jacket, which he'd forgotten to take off, and pulled out his business card. He handed it to the flight attendant, whose name tag read *William*.

"My contact details if you need them."

William looked at the card, then back to Bryce. He was about to open his mouth, when Bryce answered the obvious question. "Last minute change of plans. My jet is on the tarmac at Galveston, and this was the first flight I could find which would get me back to New York in a hurry."

A pair of bright blue eyes appeared in his line of vision. "Do you really have your own plane?"

"I do, Jonathan, and it's a beauty," replied Bryce.

His card and easy manner with the boy, seemed to finally settle things for the flight attendant. Bryce tugged his jacket off and settled it on his lap. William gave a *tsk* of disapproval and held out his hand. "That looks Italian and superbly hand crafted. It would be an honor to hang it up for you, Mister Royal."

"Thank you."

Vivian clicked her seatbelt closed, then snuggled down in her seat. The second the safety demonstration ended, her headphones went over her ears and her thumb hit play. She had a long list of downloaded podcasts to get through.

Food was her refuge. Food porn podcasts had got her through the early days following Pete's final betrayal. She sensed her battered ego and wounded heart would need a lot more in order to get over Bryce, but at least a hearty serve of recipes would help see her through this flight. "The pasta and cheese podcast, here I come."

Bryce unclipped his seatbelt and squeezed out of the row. Food service was yet to commence, and the aisle was clear. Now was the perfect time to do a quick trip to the back of the plane and look for Vivian. Anyone who happened to see him would naturally assume he was headed for the bathrooms.

He took his time, slowly checking the seated passengers, searching from side to side.

Where are you?

Reaching the last row of seats, he stopped, then turned around. Had he missed her? She hadn't been in any of the forward rows, he'd made a point of checking as he boarded. The only way she could be on this flight and for him to have missed her was if Vivian had somehow boarded after him and taken up an empty seat he hadn't spotted. A sinking feeling formed in the pit of his stomach.

The flight attendant who was standing putting cups onto a cart met his gaze. "Can I help you sir?"

"Ah, no thank you. I just need to stretch my legs. I've been traveling for a day or two and don't want to get blood clots."

Bryce turned and headed back toward the front of the plane. He got as far as the curtain which separated the business class seats from the rest of the passengers. His fingers reached for the edge of the closure, before he drew his hand back. He'd checked those seats when he had first come on board, they were all fully occupied.

By the time he eventually made his way back to his row, Bryce had come to a horrid realization. Vivian wasn't on the flight. He had no idea where she was, but he now suspected she had taken a plane out of the other airport, Houston International.

If she had, then she could be in-bound to any one of the major airports which serviced New York and its surrounds. She might even be flying into New Jersey. And here he was, stuck on a non-stop no frills flight home without a clue as to where the woman he was falling for was, or how to get in touch with her. His day was going from bad to worse.

Retrieving his leather planner from his carry-on bag Bryce shuffled over to his seat. There were three remaining hours of flight time, and he didn't plan to waste a minute. It was time to figure out his next move. The one where he confessed to Vivian that she meant a lot more to him than merely a one night stand.

But what if the damage I've caused is already too great, and I've lost her?

CHAPTER FORTY-FOUR

It turned out that Jonathan wasn't as young a boy as Bryce had first thought. He was in fact a slightly built eleven year old, who had just spent a month with his grandparents in Houston.

"Did you enjoy Houston? I haven't visited before," asked Bryce.

Edward Royal had long had Houston down on his list of places for future Royal Resorts expansion, and Bryce planned to travel back to Texas as soon as he got settled into his new role as CEO. The US board would be looking to him for a detailed review of his father's growth plans, and to put a formal proposal together.

"It was ok. I didn't want to go, but my mom and dad made me."

Bryce frowned. As a kid he had loved visiting his grandparents in both upstate New York and the English countryside. Why wouldn't a boy want to travel to go and see them?

"Are your grandparents evil, is that it? Did they make you eat peas at supper?"

He was half teasing. Bryce loathed peas. In his book,

anyone who forced a child to eat them was nothing short of a villain.

Jonathan shifted in his seat, then with a sigh, hung his head. "No. They're nice. It's me whose horrible." The tone of self-reproach in Jonathan's voice spoke of someone who might have done something awful and come to deeply regret it.

"I don't think you are capable of being bad, let alone horrible. Would you like to talk about it?"

He didn't want to pry, but Bryce sensed his traveling companion was still carrying a good deal of guilt over something.

It must have been something bad if his parents sent him away for a few weeks.

"I took my little brother's Pokémon cards and sold them at school."

Pokémon, was that still a thing? Bryce could recall the craze when the mobile app had launched. Some of the Royal Resorts had been designated game stops and guests were running around catching creatures. At first, they had looked to have the stops removed from near the hotels, but his forward thinking brother Matthew had convinced their father that the game actually helped attract paying guests. People were checking into Royal Resorts just to play Pokémon.

"When you say took, do you mean you stole them?" His own experience with younger brothers meant Bryce was uniquely equipped to understand the complex language of siblings. Jordan's wild days had also taught him the subtle art of semantics. 'Took' could mean many things.

Jonathan nodded. "Yeah, I stole them. And I feel bad. I made him cry. He said he hated me. We had a big fight and I —" Tears rolled down the boy's face.

"But you regret it. I know brothers can be a pain. They can also be your best friend."

His own words hit Bryce like a punch to the gut. Jordan had made a mess of things, but had Bryce made much of an effort to stay in touch with him while he'd been in Europe and the UK? *Rarely.* If he'd reached out more often, he might have noticed the warning signs and Laguna Beach might not have gotten so bad. And as for Matthew, he hadn't even picked up the phone to ask how he was doing since their late night chat.

He might not have taken his brothers' trading cards, but he wasn't exactly being the best version of a big brother. Being protective of his siblings was something which came with the territory. *I have to do better.*

Jonathan wiped his face with the back of his hand. Bryce fished inside his pants pocket and produced a clean cotton handkerchief. It was monogrammed and had cost him more than his last-minute plane ticket. "Here, use this."

"Thank you." Jonathan blew his nose then offered it back to Bryce, who politely declined, saying, "You keep it. Ask your mom to wash it when you get home. You can say the B is for brother."

Bryce shifted in his seat and turned to his young friend. "I know it's hard being a big brother at times. I have two brothers. But you did something wrong and now you have to make it up to your brother. Tell him you're sorry. Tell him you know you hurt him. But that you love him and hope you can be friends again."

I haven't actually said a proper sorry to Jordan for going behind his back at Laguna Beach. I can't put all the blame on Dad. And when was the last time I told either of my brothers that I loved them?

He made a mental note to call his brother once he got back to New York. Make that both of them. And neither call would involve discussing business. Matthew and he were in grave danger of becoming strangers. Time spent away working in Europe meant Bryce was losing that precious connection with his siblings. Their relationship had to be based on more than just the Royal family business. He'd jokingly taken Vivian to task over that same phrase, yet that was the exact outcome his current behavior was risking would happen.

Chasing one possible future, the one he was considering with Vivian, shouldn't come at the cost of him putting the rest of his family to one side. She might not wish to be a part of his life if she thought his relationships with his brothers were dysfunctional.

The plane began to rattle, then dipped into a deep drop which took Bryce's stomach a second or two to catch up. Overhead the seatbelt sign came on, following by the head flight attendant announcing. "Ladies and gentlemen, we are experiencing some turbulence. Please return to your seats and fasten your safety belts. Cabin service will be suspended for the time being."

Out of the corner of his eye, Bryce caught sight of Jonathan's white knuckled hand gripping firmly to the arm rest. "It's alright, this is a big plane, and the pilots will take care of us."

He got a tight, thinly whispered, "I hope so, I hate flying," in response.

Bryce took a deep calming breath. Years spent travelling the globe had given him a thick skin when it came to rough flights.

The plane dropped once more, and a gasp rolled around the cabin. Somewhere up the back, a baby started crying. It was soon joined by a chorus of other small children whimpering. Bryce offered Jonathan another smile, but his young friend didn't see it. His eyes were screwed shut and his face had turned a horrid shade of gray.

"Cabin crew secure all lockers and take your seats," announced the pilot. Things then escalated quickly, the plane was shimmying and shaking. The man on the other side of Bryce started saying his prayers.

He had been through a few rough plane flights in his life, but this one was moving fast into Bryce's top ten list of horrible trips. It rocketed to the top of the charts with a loud BANG. A shudder heaved through the plane. Bryce reached out and took a hold of Jonathan's sweaty hand, gripping it gently. He started counting slowly backward from one hundred.

An agonizing ten minutes later, the pilot came back on the air and announced they were diverting the plane to Jackson, Mississippi. Bryce Royal was about to add an emergency landing to his already drama filled day.

CHAPTER FORTY-FIVE

Thursday afternoon
  Palm Beach, Florida

Vivian's flight landed in Palm Beach, Florida without incident. Having smashed her way through three hours of foodie podcasts, she was in a far better mood than the one she had been in when she'd left Galveston. Thoughts of a bully billionaire were squashed underneath images of thick pasta sauce and creamy blue cheese. It gave her a temporary respite from the ache in her heart.

She even resisted the temptation to call Lionel. As editor of the magazine it was his task to deal with the lawyers. Her role was to focus on her job as a travel reviewer and deliver him a well-considered but enticing review.

After a short cab ride, she was soon standing at the check-in desk of the luxurious White Foam Breakers Palm Beach resort. Reviewers were not meant to play favorites, but Vivian could secretly admit to being thrilled at having scored this particular assignment. Few hotels could compare to the stunning renaissance revival hotel which dated back close to one hundred years. An earlier version of the main building had been the playground for some of America's uber elite such as the Astor and Vanderbilt families during the roaring twenties. The new hotel was nothing short of luxurious.

An hour before they landed, Vivian had slipped into the cramped bathroom on board the plane and changed. Her comfy travel sweats and long sleeve top were now in her hand luggage. She wore a long sundress, patterned with simple yellow, white, and blue stripes. Her trusty plain sandals adorned her feet. As always, blending in was all part of a reviewer's job.

Since she was travelling in the off season, between holidays, the magazine's budget had been able to stretch just a little bit to afford her a two night stay. In the high season the room rates for this resort were several thousand dollars a day.

This was a much better option than having to go home to New York and lick her wounds. Or face her housemate. Grace was a great one for permitting Vivian a scant five minutes of comfort and pity, before she turned badass.

If her friend knew what was happening, she would be in the first cab down to Hudson Yards and on arrival would demand to see the head of Royal Resorts. One or more of Grace's top-shelf lawyer friends would be trailing close behind.

Nope. Not happening. Much as she would privately enjoy Bryce being torn to pieces by a feral legal team, Vivian wasn't going to lower herself to his level.

I am an adult, and I can fight my own battles. Lionel and the magazine lawyers will have to deal with Royal Resorts. Meanwhile I am going to go and dig my toes into the Florida sand. Anything to take my mind off Bryce.

"Good afternoon. Welcome to the White Foam Breakers Palm Beach resort."

The front desk attendants were immaculately dressed and wonderfully efficient. She could swear there was not a single hair out of place on the head of the woman who had processed her corporate credit card. This was peak tropical Florida, home of the frizz—she had to ask. "How do you manage to keep your hairstyle so fabulous?"

A soft smile threatened at the corner of the woman's mouth. "You are in suite 418. The elevators are over to your right. I will summon a valet to deliver your suitcase." She leaned forward and whispered, "There is so much product in my hair, a hurricane wouldn't wrinkle it."

The bellboy who showed her to her room gave Vivian a quick pointer on the amenities, and she handed him a tip. Whatever information he had imparted had gone straight in one ear and out the other. She barely noticed him closing the door. Her total focus was on the stunning view which greeted her out the expansive windows of her suite. The resort didn't lower itself to having such basic accommodation as guest rooms.

The blue of the Atlantic Ocean. Miles of golden, sandy beaches. Vivian stood blinking at the sight. Her suite could have had its own Instagram account and millions would follow it.

As she crossed the floor to the window, her sandals didn't make a sound on the plush cream carpet. Most hotels went with practical colors for their flooring, the White Foam Breakers didn't give a damn about being sensible. The sort of guest who could afford to stay here wasn't the kind to have a speck of dirt on the soles of their shoes. When she'd arrived there had been a long line of Maseratis and Bugattis parked outside on the concourse. If Planet Billionaire had a home, this was it.

"Don't think of billionaires. They couldn't give a damn about people like you."

Her cell buzzed. Vivian waved the message away, refusing to acknowledge the real world.

For just a minute she wanted to pretend she was Vivian, the millionaire fashion heiress who had checked into the hotel under a false name in order to rendezvous with her secret lover. He was her former bodyguard. A forbidden romance, frowned upon by her wealthy parents. They had sent him away. But true love couldn't be denied.

When her cell buzzed a second time, she snapped out of her fairytale. The real world could, and did, deny people like her their happily ever after. A message from Grace popped up.

> Where are you?

> Florida. Why?

> ???

After she'd lit into Bryce the previous evening, Grace would no doubt be keen to know how the night had ended up. It was with a good deal of reluctance that Vivian hit the video call button. Grace's warm smile instantly appeared.

"Galveston was ok. I left this morning. I'm at the resort in Florida." She didn't have the emotional energy to add much more detail.

Grace sighed. Her dark brown eyes held the glint of concern. "I don't know what happened after I spoke to Bryce, but something must have, because a friend of a friend called me a little while ago. You remember Mia, the girl with flawless legs that I swear went all the way to her…"

Vivian stifled a laugh. Her friend had a way with words. "You mean Mia, who used to work at LHRW. How did she get your number?"

Her friend's eyebrows rose and fell. Grace Collins seemed

to know everyone in NYC. And if she didn't know someone, she knew someone who did. "We were at school together. Mia had a full scholarship, that's how smart she is, the rest of us dumbasses had to rely on our parent's bank accounts."

Grace laughed at her own joke, and it occurred to Vivian that only the rich could possibly think themselves hard done by when they had to pay for tuition fees at one of New York's most exclusive academies for girls. Her friend was one of the sharpest people Vivian knew, which only served to show how clever Mia was, and why she had been selected for the management program at Royal Resorts.

"Anyhoo. Mia called me earlier this morning and wanted to know how your trip to Texas had gone. Considering that she now works for Royal Resorts, I thought it a little strange for her to get in touch. But when I remembered that it was her billionaire boss who you had dinner with last night..." Grace waved her hand about the air. "Oh, and don't think I haven't forgotten about that dating app. I'm going to talk to my dad's attorney and see what she can do to get your thousand bucks back."

Oh great. Now Mister Collins will know about my billionaire humiliation.

"My credit card says thanks but let me have a think before you do that, ok."

At least she now knew who had given Bryce the details of where to find her in Galveston. The second her boss asked her, uber efficient Mia would have been on the phone to someone at the magazine and schmoozed her way into getting them to reveal Vivian's whereabouts.

She was not going to be allowed to end the call before she gave Grace the details of what had transpired earlier this morning. But her heart wasn't in a sharing mood.

"We said our farewells not long after you spoke to Bryce. I flew here this morning. Alone."

Grace's dirty chuckle carried to her over the ether. "So that's the story you are going to go with, is it? Did he bow and beg to take his leave, like a duke? Mia tells me Bryce's great granddaddy was a real live English duke."

There was no easy way of getting out of this, only the truth would work. "Things have gone from awful to just plain terrible. His company is threatening to sue the magazine. They think I was too harsh with the review on their Laguna Beach resort. Bryce was all nice as pie last night, he even kissed me. Then early this morning I read about the pending lawsuit. I checked out the hotel and changed my flight and booking to come here a day early."

Grace said several words that were more Brooklyn than Manhattan in their origin. "That dirty, filthy...oh, I can't believe it. He flew all the way to Texas just to mess with you. What kind of guy does that? And he was all 'yes ma'am' on the phone to me. Fuck. I seriously underestimated how much of an ass this Bryce Royal guy is. Wow, just fucking wow!"

"I can really pick them, can't I? But seriously, just forget about it. I'm going to do my best not to think about him." Vivian turned the camera around on her phone and pointed it at the window. "See that gorgeous vista. That's what I am here for. And their day spa. Apparently, they have a deep sea pedicure. I have no idea what that is, but I am booking myself in for one. Lionel still owes me two hundred dollars of spa treatments from my ill-fated California trip, and I am going to use every cent. I'm all about self-love from now on." She pointed the camera back to herself. "If Mia calls again, tell her..."

Words failed her. What should she say? 'Mia, your boss is a complete ass and tell him to call off his attack dogs'. Her former work colleague had clearly kept on her stellar career trajectory. Mia was a girl determined to make it to the top. To break through both gender and racial glass ceilings. It wouldn't be fair to drag her into any of this, no matter her intentions. And if Vivian's memories of Mia still held true, her intentions would be good ones.

"Just tell Mia, thank you for thinking of me, and I wish her all the best."

"Ok, sweetheart. Are you sure you are alright?"

Vivian nodded. "Yeah. I will survive. I'm going to look into doing a day trip tomorrow. I'm here for two nights, so if all goes according to plan, I should be on a flight into New York sometime on Saturday."

She had been keeping a close eye on the weather reports for Florida. Fortunately this time of the year was nearing the end of hurricane season, and there was nothing currently on the forecast.

"Alright, I'll let you go. But if you want to talk, call me. I'm here for you. You know that."

"Thanks hon. And yes, I know you're here for me. Say hi to Marlon for me. See you in a few days." She hit end, then tossed the cell at the bed. It missed, falling onto the floor. In any other hotel room, it would have made it but the suites at White Foam Breakers were just that big. Even the enormous bed with its blue and aqua marine striped duvet seemed tiny in the generous space.

Vivian bent and picked up her phone. She grinned at the bed. Tonight she would be sleeping in it.

With the curtains fully open, and dreaming of anything other than tall, heartbreaking billionaires.

CHAPTER FORTY-SIX

The plane touched down on the tarmac at Jackson, Mississippi, in a text book emergency landing. Bryce gripped the armrest as he was pinned to his seat by the rapidly applied brakes. Out the window he caught a glimpse of the fire and airport service vehicles all lining the runway, ready to go into action if the landing hadn't been clean.

When the Boeing 737 slowed to a halt well away from the main terminal, a large sigh rose from the passengers. They broke out in a round of loud whoops and applause. Even Bryce applauded. A great performance should always be acknowledged.

"Welcome to Jackson, Mississippi, folks. We will be asking you to disembark here and collect your luggage. The airline is already working to get you all on other flights as quickly as possible, but I am advised some of you may have to stay here tonight. Hotels will be arranged for you. On behalf of the airline I sincerely apologize for the inconvenience, but your safety comes first," announced the pilot.

The flight attendant, William, arrived at Jonathan's seat. "Hey buddy, how are you?"

Jonathan smiled. "I'm ok." He turned to Bryce. "Bryce was with me the whole time and he helped me to not feel so scared. But I would like to get off the plane please. My stomach is sore."

The plane was eventually given clearance to taxi to the terminal, but all passengers were instructed to remain in their seats. Families with small children were shown to the front. William came for Jonathan. "You and I are going to catch the next flight to New York. The airline has called your parents and they know that you are alright."

Jonathan packed up his things and went to leave. He made it a couple of steps, then returned. "Thank you, Bryce, it was great to have a big brother on the plane. And I promise I will go home and say I am sorry to my brother."

Bryce swallowed a lump of emotion and nodded. "I'm glad I met you, Jonathan. You have a safe journey home."

Jackson Mississippi was yet another place Bryce Royal had never visited before. Courtesy of his cross country odyssey to find Vivian, he was getting to see a number of new places. He planned to visit them again when he had more time.

Next time I would prefer to arrive in a less white knuckled and sweaty state. That had to be the worst flight of my life.

He had kept his brave face on for the benefit of Jonathan, but Bryce's heart had been racing at a fast clip from the moment one of the plane's engines made a loud bang. According to the flight crew, the engine had completely shut down.

Once he made it into the terminal building, Bryce called Patrick. "Hi Patrick. Did you manage to get all my things from the resort?"

"Yes, Mister Royal. All packed and the jet is on standby. The pilot just needs your instructions to head back to New York."

Bryce moved to one side, out of the way of the other passengers who were hastily departing the interrupted flight. "Actually I am going to need you to come to Jackson, Mississippi and pick me up. We encountered some problems with the plane and had to make an unexpected landing here."

"Right. Let me go and talk to the pilot and see how soon he can get a flight plan approved. I'll message you back with details of where to go to meet us."

"Thanks Patrick. Oh, and in the meantime could you please call your mom and let her know that while I appreciate the respectful gesture, I'd rather you just call me Bryce."

He had barely pressed end on the call when his cell buzzed. *Chelsea F.C.* lit up the screen.

Security training taught all Royal children not to have their parents phone numbers listed under dad or mom in their phones in case they were kidnapped. Anyone who was mad enough to attempt to steal a member of the family would find that if they called the number marked *DAD*, they would be dealing directly with the global CEO of Royal Security Services. The House of Royal employed a small, well trained army of security personnel, most of whom were battle hardened ex-military.

Edward Royal was a passionate fan of the English soccer club Chelsea. "Hi Dad," said Bryce, trying to keep his voice on an even keel. He'd already had the morning to end all mornings and didn't want to have to deal with any more drama.

"Oh, you are alive. That's good news. I've been trying to call you for several hours, but your cell kept going to voicemail. I know I said to take some time off, but I didn't think you would take a vow of silence."

There were many people milling around the gate area, all talking. Many wondering aloud how they were going to locate their bags, and whether they would be on another flight or having to stay overnight. It made conducting any sort of phone conversation nearly impossible.

"Hang on a minute, let me find somewhere more private to talk. I'll call you back."

After stopping a passing airport official and asking for directions to any of the airline private lounges, Bryce was disappointed to discover there were none. His next best solution was a nearby café. He made his way to a booth in a far back corner. When a waitress came over, he ordered coffee. "Oh, and whatever fresh sandwich you might have, please."

Settling into the padded seat, he hit dial on his father's number.

"Where the devil are you?" demanded Edward.

"Would you believe the airport at Jackson, Mississippi? Our plane was diverted for an emergency landing."

"You broke my jet?!"

Bryce lowered his head and softly laughed. It was a strangled chuckle born of both the relief at having survived the flight and acknowledging his father's strange English sense of humor.

"No Dad, I didn't break your jet. It's in Galveston, Texas. Hopefully on route to pick me up in the next few hours."

He was trying to picture his father's face as he absorbed the details of their conversation. Jackson, like Galveston was not on Edward's map for Royal Resorts expansion. This not so minor detail would surely have his father fiddling with the end of his handmade silk tie. Either that or pulling on the cuffs of his expensive Savile Row shirt.

"Leave your suit alone," murmured Bryce.

There was silence on the other end of the line for a minute, then the click of a door being closed. Bryce checked his watch. It was mid-afternoon in New York, Edward would still be in his office. It was clear his father didn't want anyone else to overhear the next part of their conversation.

"It's a girl, isn't it? Please tell me this is about a girl."

The hopeful pleading in Edward's voice spoke of a man eager to see at least one of his adult sons settled with a partner. Of course the second Alice Royal got wind of this discussion, Bryce's mother would be checking her social calendar and picking out mother of the groom evening gowns. He could just imagine the cream of New York's society event planners hotly contesting the ultimate prize of being asked to arrange a House of Royal wedding and reception.

His parents romance had been love at first sight. Across a crowded, but elegant ballroom in London gazes had met, and hearts secured. Legend further had it that Edward Royal had asked to speak to his future father in law the very next morning. Thirty six years, three sons, and the marriage was still going strong. If only everyone's love story ran that smoothly.

I wonder if I will get the chance to share a similar story with Vivian.

A cup of steaming hot coffee was placed in front of Bryce, along with what appeared to be a chicken and coleslaw sandwich on white bread. He mouthed a silent 'thank you' to the waitress.

"Yes, Dad it is about a girl."

He held the phone away from his ear, while Edward let out a very refined English cheer. "Huzzah!" It was then backed up with an unrestrained, "Yes!"

Bryce picked up his sandwich and took a bite. It was delicious. The chicken tasted like it had been roasted in buttermilk. The coleslaw finely chopped by the hands of an artisan.

This sandwich alone was worth coming all the way to Jackson, Mississippi. He washed the mouthful down with the dark, bitter coffee. His tastebuds were still doing a happy dance when his father finally added a gushing. "So, tell me more. Who is she?"

God, we sound like a pair of school girls, gossiping over some cute boy.

There was no point in attempting to lie to his father. Janice, no doubt, would have spoken to her son Patrick, and news of Bryce's mystery expedition to Texas would have already gotten back to New York.

He sat back in the booth and composed himself. "Do you remember Vivian Holte, the writer from Luxury Hotels and Resorts Worldwide? She was the one who gave us a three star review for Laguna Beach."

"Yes, I know who she is, I've read that article several dozen times. Go on."

How did he phrase this without it sounding sleazy? "Well…Vivian and I met the first night I was in California. Neither of us knew who the other one was. We caught up again at breakfast. One thing led to another. Let me cut to the chase. To cut a long story short. Ah…"

He really didn't want to be having this conversation. Not in the middle of a small café in an out of the way airport. His father's silence was all the confirmation Bryce needed for him to know he wouldn't be getting away with not sharing the rest of the story.

"We shared a special night together, then she checked out of the resort and basically ghosted me. I was hurt. Ok, I was humiliated. When the review came out and I discovered who she was, and what she had been doing at Laguna Beach, I was furious. I then did something that was stupid and spiteful. I flew to Galveston to apologize to her."

"That doesn't explain why you are in Jackson, or why my plane is in Texas. Or what is happening with Vivian Holte."

His phone buzzed and Bryce pulled it away from his ear. The brief text from Patrick noted a time of arrival and a link to where he should go in order to meet the Royal Resorts jet.

"I've just got a message from Patrick. The jet will be here

in a few hours, and I will be back in New York tonight. I will tell you everything when I get home. I promise."

Edward mumbled something inaudible, but his message was clear. He was none too pleased with being made to wait. Bryce suspected the only thing which would satisfy his father was if he arrived home on the Royal Resorts jet with a brand new fiancée in tow.

Bryce ended the call. With no clue as to where Vivian was, the chances of him even beginning to solve the problem of their spluttering romance were remote at best. Wherever she was, he was certain she hated his guts. All the ground he had gained last night was now gone.

He could try and blame Jordan for some of this mess, but the truth was he had been the one to break her trust. He'd lashed out with his own review, and it had hit home.

What was he to do? Any message he attempted to leave with the receptionist at LHRW would likely be tossed in the trash. Or they would simply hang up on him thinking it a prank.

The only way he could think of getting Vivian to hear the truth was if he did what he had done in Galveston. Find her. Talk to her.

And this time for heaven's sake tell her how you feel. That you love her.

The first thing he was going to do once he did make it back to New York was to call on the match making services of Mia and Sheila. A smart businessman always relied upon the experts. He might be a well-connected billionaire, but he could admit to being a clueless male. When it came to securing his happily ever after, Bryce Royal wasn't leaving anything to chance.

CHAPTER FORTY-SEVEN

Vivian floated back to her suite. The massage had been that good. Over the years she'd found hotel massage therapists fitted into two neat categories. There was the one where they spent an hour just rubbing various lotions and creams onto her skin without actually untying any knots or kinks in her muscles. These tended to be the ones where the hard sell of beauty products came at the front counter as she made her way out.

The other type of massage, the kind she preferred, was the one which Vivian had just experienced. The therapist had known all the ways to get into tight muscles and release tension, without causing Vivian pain. They'd shared a little bit of harmless chat, but not too much, and the woman knew when to work in silence and let her client simply be. The rainforest background music hadn't intruded on Vivian's thoughts.

At the end of the session Vivian had been handed a hand written personalized card which noted the massage lotions which had been used on her body. At no time was she made to feel obligated to buy any of it.

With a paper tote bag containing a complimentary body brush for herself and some oils for Grace and Marlon, Vivian drifted back to her room. The resort's spa policy was that guests were requested to leave their cell phones either switched off or not bring them at all. A phone detox for a whole blessed hour added to the benefit of the spa experience.

The first thing Vivian did when she stepped through the door of her suite was to check her phone. Old habits die hard. She smiled at the message from Grace.

> Hope u r ok, call me if u need me.

> Thanks. All good. Heading to beach for some insta worthy pics. xxx

The spa treatment had not only relieved her tired muscles, but it had also given Vivian time to put the past weeks behind her. She had accepted the truth about Bryce Royal. He had been a foolish mistake and she was determined to put him firmly in the past.

The company jet touched down in New York later that night. As Bryce set foot on the tarmac, he made a vow to never again take the private jet for granted. Facing the possibility of his own demise while being crammed into a flying tin can with several hundred other people wasn't something he ever wished to repeat.

It was close to eleven thirty by the time he finally reached the offices of Royal Resorts in Lower Manhattan. Bryce wasn't the least bit surprised to discover Edward was waiting for him when he stepped through the door which lead into the executive suite.

"There you are, come and have a drink."

At the end of a long day which had seen him spend far too many hours seated on a plane and dashing through airports, all Bryce really wanted to do was drop his bag in his office, and head to his serviced apartment. A long hot shower was in order. And then sleep.

Seeing the inviting but slightly worried look on Edward's face had him nodding and following him into his office. Bryce's bed would have to wait. Time with his father was more important. And precious.

A thought struck Bryce on the way through the door.

I wonder what will happen when I take over as CEO? Will I get this office, or stay where I am? Hmm.

His father was far too young to retire, he must have plans for his own future. "I meant to ask what you are going to do when the time comes for me to take over. That's of course if the board agrees to the succession proposal."

It was a really two questions posed as one. Bryce's intention was to create an opening for Edward to explain what had come out of the board meeting. If Bryce was indeed going to be appointed CEO. He was also genuinely interested to hear his father's plans for the future.

Edward picked up an already opened bottle of shiraz and poured them both a generous glass. He handed a drink to Bryce. "Here's to you, the next CEO of the US branch of Royal Resorts. And its first American born CEO. The board unanimously approved your appointment. And while it's up to you and me to decide when exactly you take over, I should warn you that your mother has booked us on a cruise to Australia and New Zealand early in the new year. I'm still considering my next career move, but I won't get under your feet."

"Thanks, Dad." This was a big moment for Bryce, but his enthusiasm fell flat. His heart wasn't in the mood for celebration.

They touched glasses, and Bryce couldn't help but smile as he caught the expression of immense pride on his father's face.

"Congratulations Bryce. When I vacate this office, I know I will handing things over to a capable and visionary new CEO. I'm humbled to be able to call you my son."

"Just don't let Matthew or Jordan hear you say that."

"They know how I feel about them. Your brothers bring their own set of skills and strengths to the family business. Even Jordan. He will find his way back."

Bryce let the subject of the middle Royal sibling go. This was the moment he had worked hard and long for over the past years, and as much as his heart was torn up over Vivian, he wanted to savor it.

He'd been bloodied and battle hardened during his time in Europe, all with the intention of eventually taking on the US operations. Europe was a mature travel market, he was under no illusion that the growing American one would test him to his fullest.

I can't wait. I was born to take Royal Resorts to the top of our home market. To give the American traveler an entirely new level of luxury, one they deserve.

His pride in having the appointment confirmed was tempered by the events of the past few days. Of how badly things had gone wrong with Vivian.

Over dinner in Galveston, he'd felt the pieces of his life's puzzle finally dropping into place. For a brief wonderful moment Bryce had imagined what a future with Vivian might look like. Of the joy of being able to come home knowing he would find her there, waiting for him, and ready to step into his loving embrace. Now all he had was a terse letter and a promise to sue if he ever came near her again.

"I note a lack of cheer in your disposition. What happened with the girl from the magazine?" asked Edward.

Bryce explained it all. From the dating app disaster after California, to his hurried trip to Texas. All the way to how he had ended up talking to his father from a café in Jackson, Mississippi. Edward flinched at the mention of Jordan making veiled threats to LHRW.

"That's a tangled mess. I can't say I approve of what you did with the millionaire dating app. Whether you agreed with Ms. Holtes review or not, it was unprofessional of you to have reacted to it. A review is just someone else's opinion," observed Edward.

It hadn't been one of Bryce's finest moments. He would regret having hurt Vivian in such a callous way to the day he died.

She even accepted my apology, until the lawyer thing came up.

"What are you going to do about her? I mean you aren't going to let this...her... go, are you? I know you well enough, Bryce, that if this was just a fling, you wouldn't be running all over the country in pursuit of this young lady."

Bryce shrugged. He was tired, and at a bit of a loss as to what to do. His father had just informed him that he was shortly going to be taking control of the Royal Resorts US operations. This part of the family business had an annual turnover of close to half a billion dollars. The board was trusting him to grow the company. It was a huge step in his career.

And yet I can't manage my own private life.

"I don't honestly know what to do. Vivian isn't exactly about to send me a Christmas card." He let out a weary sigh. "The only thing I am certain of at the moment is that I need to finish this wine, then go have a shower and get some sleep."

Hopefully tomorrow morning would see him wake with a clearer mind. He would need to be at the top of his game to broach the subject of Vivian with Mia and Sheila. If he came to them asking for help and they sensed any sort of hesitation on his part, he would be in trouble.

Edward patted him gently on the shoulder. "Have a good night's sleep. I will talk to our legal team and make doubly certain Jordan hasn't put anything in motion."

His brother had said it was just an inquiry, but from where Bryce stood, Jordan had developed a horrible habit of taking things and making them worse than they had been at the outset. He could understand why their father was keen to check the legal situation. A good CEO always checked that the '*i*'s had been dotted and the '*t*'s crossed.

Bryce sipped his wine, then set the half empty glass on the coffee table. Exhaustion was fast catching up. "If it's alright with you Dad, I think I might just head back to my apartment. Thanks for the drink. And for your support. I will talk to you in the morning."

Edward held out his hand, and Bryce went to take it, expecting a handshake. His father huffed and pulled him into a hug. "My boys are never too big or old for a hug. Never forget that no matter what happens. Congratulations, you deserve the appointment."

"Thanks. It's a big step, and if it's alright I will come to you for advice when I need it. I'll see you tomorrow. Give Mom my love."

He left the office tired but determined. Bright and early tomorrow he was going to call on every person and resource under his command. He wouldn't rest until he had found Vivian, told her how he truly felt, and finally claimed her heart.

Come the morning, *Operation Win Over Vivian* was a go.

CHAPTER FORTY-EIGHT

Royal Resorts Offices
 Friday Morning

There were three people sitting in his office early the following morning when Bryce arrived at work. Two of them he recognized. Mia and Sheila. The third, was a well-dressed young Black woman he hadn't seen before, but from the way she shot a hard glare at him, he gathered she wasn't a Royal Resorts employee.

For a long, awkward minute Bryce and the mystery woman slowly looked one another up and down. She was clearly taking in his Italian wool suit and pale blue shirt, while he in turn noted the expensive watch on her wrist and her Prince of Wales checked pant suit. If he wasn't mistaken her outfit was straight out of this season's Gucci runway collection. He'd been in the audience with one of his European cousins during Milan Fashion Week, and she had praised the look.

"Hi, I'm Bryce, and you would be?"

The pant suit clad visitor rose from her chair and offered him her hand. "Grace Collins, we spoke on the phone when you were in Galveston with my friend Vivian." In between his heart missing a beat, Bryce caught the polished accent of someone who likely spent her summers in the Hamptons.

Bryce shook hands. "So... you are... that, Grace. It's a pleasure to meet you in person." *I think.*

When she gifted him with a deadly smile, Bryce was left in two minds. She was either here to help or murder him.

After Grace resumed her seat, reclining in her chair and crossing her legs in the way that people who didn't take no for an answer did, Bryce decided it would be smarter to turn his attention to his two employees. They were on the payroll and less likely to give him grief. The well-dressed Grace Collins had to be in his office at their behest. "May I ask what this meeting is in aid of?"

His plans had been to hide away in his office while making phone calls and doing what he could to locate Vivian, all with the expectation that he would inevitably go pleading to Mia and Sheila for help with his love life.

A stern faced Mia nodded at Grace. "Grace is here on behalf of her friend's broken heart."

Bryce took up a spot perching on the end of his desk. His office wasn't big enough for the four of them to gather around the small meeting table. Under any other circumstances he would have had them adjourn to a conference room, but those spaces were in the common areas. At this early hour there were few people around the office, even Janice was yet to appear, but Bryce was keen for there to be as few as possible number of witnesses to this conversation.

He cleared his throat, eager to get the first words in. "I have a horrible feeling I am being portrayed as the villain in this story, but before any of you decide to tear into me—

again." He nodded at Grace. "Let me make it clear, I haven't done anything wrong." *This time.* "If Vivian is upset, it's because she has been misled."

The second the words came out of his mouth Bryce regretted them. Three faces all turned to him, and judgment sat on every one of them. Great. There went his morning.

Grace crossed her arms and leaned farther back in her chair. "After lying about your identity in California, and then dragging her name through the mud on that dating app, I would say you were most definitely the villain of the piece. You hurt Vivian. And you made her cry. But like all good stories there is usually a moment where the asshole gets a chance to redeem himself. This is yours."

His gaze went to Sheila, catching the moment when she whispered to Mia. "What dating app?" Mia shook her head.

Shit. Now they will want to know about the dating app. Or does Mia already know?

Bryce held his breath. He could just imagine what would happen if his dirty little secret got out. He knew Mia well enough that she might even try to hold it over his head, to use it as a form of leverage.

Grace examined her immaculate finger nails. "The details of Bryce's crimes will remain, for the time being a private matter between Vivian and Bryce. And of course me. And my boyfriend."

Anyone else?

Whoever Grace Collins was, she was damn good. He would hate to come up against her in any form of contractual negotiations. She would be extracting concessions out of him by the handful.

I wonder if I should offer her a job. She looks the sort to have majored in something I could use around here. Then again, she probably owns half of the city.

"The private incident was a moment of misjudgment on my part, and I did apologize to Vivian," he offered.

Grace raised one of her dark eyebrows. "I would suggest it was more like a brain fart. Call it what you like, a duck is still a duck."

Sheila lowered her head and covered her face with her right hand. At least someone was finding this situation amusing. He wasn't.

Bryce held up his hand. "Ms. Collins, you know I went to Galveston to make amends. Vivian and I had a lovely evening. We went out to dinner, ate, and talked. Not long after you and I spoke on the phone, Vivian and I parted for the night. We were on good terms and planned to catch up for breakfast. Did she tell you that?"

"No. When I last spoke to her, she was doing her utmost to forget you ever existed. I have left her a few text messages, but from what I gather she is still licking her wounds. I've been trying to give her some breathing space, and not calling, but that doesn't mean I am letting this matter go. What sort of man kisses a girl while threatening to sue her employer?"

Bryce ignored the barb about the lawsuit. He was more interested in the fact that Grace was sending Vivian's texts. That didn't make sense. "I thought you were her housemate. Didn't Vivian come home last night?"

Grace shook her head. "No. She's at a resort in Florida."

Vivian hadn't said anything about going to Florida.

"So, you're telling me that Vivian is still on assignment, that she wasn't coming back to New York yesterday?" He speared his fingers through his hair. All that running after her at the airport and then flying all over the eastern states had been in vain. He'd been chasing after someone who was headed in a completely different direction.

"Yes, she isn't due back until the weekend. Which is why I am here," replied Grace.

To slay the dragon before she returns.

Sheila rose from her chair. "Alright girls, while I enjoy torturing a Royal male just as much as the next woman, I think it's time we put poor Bryce out of his misery."

A slow, wicked smile crept over her face. "I spoke to Jordan late last night. Then your father called Mia and me in for an early morning meeting at six o'clock. Apparently, Edward was on the phone to the in house legal team at some unholy hour, after which they drafted a statement. It's going to be issued later today." She pointed in the direction of Bryce's desk. He turned and spotted a piece of paper with Royal Resorts letter head on the top. Leaning over he picked it up.

Royal Resorts CEO denies any pending legal action against Luxury Hotels and Resorts Worldwide magazine.

Bryce skimmed the rest of the words which refuted any and all claims of litigation. At the bottom it mentioned something about who to contact for further information. The usual legalese etc. "Thank god," he muttered, then set the paper down. Now Vivian would know the truth. He hadn't gone to Texas just to be an asshole. She might even decide to accept his apology for a second time.

The letter at least explained the presence of the two Royal Resort employees in his office, but not Vivian's friend. "I'm sorry Ms. Collins. I still don't understand why you are here."

Grace pushed back her chair and rose. She sauntered her way over to Bryce and handed him a piece of paper. "This is the address of the resort, the White Foam Breakers, where Vivian is staying in Palm Beach. I did break my self-imposed rule of silence, and actually tried to talk to her just before you arrived, but she wasn't answering. She planned to do a day trip, whilst she was there, so she might well have gone on that this morning and be out of cell range."

Hope flared in Bryce's heart. These women weren't here to denounce him, they were here to help. Granted Grace didn't exactly appear to like him; he couldn't blame her for that, he'd done a dirty rotten thing with the dating app. And if as he suspected, Vivian had shared her pain over his villainy, then Grace was well within her rights to think poorly of him.

But she was here, and Grace had just handed him the golden ticket to finding Vivian. Relief flooded through his now warm veins.

"Is there any chance you could give me Vivian's cell number? I would really like to talk to her or at the worst send a text, so she knows what's going on."

If he was going to undertake yet another long plane flight, he would much rather it was with the knowledge that Vivian was prepared to speak to him.

Mia now got to her feet. She might have been the last one to stand, but from the expression on her face, Bryce dreaded her words. "Grace says you haven't earned Vivian's number. And while Sheila and I don't know exactly what transpired after California, if she says you don't deserve it, then we have to agree. Besides, that decision really rests with Vivian, not us. What I can however offer is the suggestion that you go back to your apartment, pack some Florida suitable clothes, and return here within the hour. Patrick and the jet are waiting for you at Teterboro Airport."

His heart raced at a fast clip. From the depths of hopeless despair another chance had now risen. Once Vivian saw the press release that Royal Resorts were not suing her employer, she had to give him the benefit of the doubt.

I don't know what I will do if she doesn't.

Giving up wasn't an option. He was going to go to Florida and see if he could salvage things with Vivian. To see if he could win back her trust and this time hold it, forever.

Mia stepped forward and offered him an encouraging smile. "Call me when you arrive at the resort. After you inform us as to what suite you are staying in, Grace will then get in touch with Vivian and let her know you're there. What happens after that is entirely in Vivian's hands."

Bryce picked up his briefcase and stuffed the press release into it. "Thank you, ladies. I really do appreciate your help." He held out his hand to Grace. "I'm glad Vivian has someone like you in her life. I promise if things go well in Florida, she won't ever have to deal with guys like Pete ever again. I will keep her heart safe."

"What about us, where's our heartfelt thank you?" said Sheila, holding out her hand. Bryce glanced at it. He was grinning as he shook his head. "You and Mia get paid to sort out Royal problems. Consider this as part of your job description."

Mia and Sheila's cries of mock outrage were still ringing in his ears as he headed out the door. Come quarterly bonus time, he wouldn't forget what they had done for him this morning. And it would be money well spent.

The thought of money had Bryce stopping and turning back. "Grace, could I have a quick word with you in private before you leave?" Mia and Sheila took their cues and promptly left the room.

As soon as they had gone, Bryce met Grace's questioning gaze. "I wanted to ask you about what Pete had done to Vivian's credit card."

For the first time since they had met, Grace offered him a tentative smile. "Yes, let's talk."

A few minutes later, Bryce had just farewelled Grace and

stepped back as the doors of the elevator closed, when Edward hurried over. "I'm glad I caught you before you left. Could you spare me a minute?"

The jet might already be on standby for him, and he was eager to get to Florida, but Bryce always had time for his father. "Sure, what can I do for you, Dad?"

"We are releasing a press statement on the rumors of the legal action against Luxury Hotels and Resorts Worldwide. I asked Janice to leave a copy on your desk. Did you get it?"

Bryce patted his briefcase. "I have it with me, and thank you for getting this sorted. Hopefully *Leisure Line* will publish our press release the minute it hits the media pipeline."

The sooner news of Royal Resorts official position was made public, the better. If Vivian had a clearer understanding of the truth of things, she might finally see that he wasn't a complete douche and would give him another chance.

"Yes, yes, the legal mess is sorted, but I didn't stay up all night in order to soothe the nerves of a magazine editor. Your mother and I want to know if you are going to go and find the girl. Sweep her off her feet and claim her heart. Alice said she is hoping for a *When Harry met Sally* ending." He dropped his head and gruffly laughed. "Actually she said *Pretty Woman*, but when I explained to her that in the movie, Vivian ended up with Edward, she had a sudden change of mind."

Bryce chuckled at hearing his mother's mistake. "How about you tell Mom that I would never rely on Hollywood to write the ending scene to my own love story." He'd already done the grand romantic dash through an airport only to discover his heroine wasn't on the same flight. "I'm going to find Vivian. I'm heading to the airport. I will be stealing your jet again but considering the fact that it's in the pursuit of love, I'm sure you won't mind."

"Whoever is the first of you three boys to bring home a

wife will be getting the jet as a wedding gift. I'll even throw in the annual airport fees and the aviation fuel as an extra bonus."

Bryce reached out and touched his father's arm. "No. Please, don't do that. It's not fair. You go offering a seventy million dollar jet as a wedding gift, one of us is going to hurry to the altar and possibly make a major life impacting mistake. You have to stop pitting us against one another."

The smile disappeared from Edward's face. "Is that how you boys see it?"

"Yes. The three of us discussed it the other night, and we all agreed it has to end. We are brothers, not rivals. There is no prize for besting family."

A pensive Edward nodded. "Then you have mastered one of life's major lessons. Something it would appear I am yet to learn. I'm glad you are taking over the US operations, you have a good heart, Bryce."

"Thanks, Dad. I have to go."

"So, the offer of the jet is off the table, but your mother still wants a brood of grandchildren within the next five years. That is one lesson I have taken to heart. She has summer activities for all your children already penned in her planner."

He could just picture his mother posting little washi tape images of babies in her journal. "Let me go and get the girl first. Just tell Mom I'm making no promises on the timeline for weddings or babies. Those decisions are not entirely mine to make." He wasn't going to put that sort of pressure on his and Vivian's relationship.

First, they had to actually be in a romantic relationship. As far as he was concerned, everyone else was getting well ahead of themselves. "I'll call you from Florida."

As Bryce moved away, Edward gave him a small farewell wave. "Take your time. And I really mean that; don't go rushing back here. If you have to spend a week or two in Florida to win Vivian's heart, then do it. I can tell from the way your face softens when you speak her name, that she has already got yours."

"She has, Dad. And I promise. If I don't come home with her, it won't be from lack of trying."

CHAPTER FORTY-NINE

Vivian flopped onto her bed. She lay with her arms spread out and stared up at the ceiling. Whoever had fitted out the resort with linen certainly knew their way around a luxurious duvet and soft as a cloud mattress. It was pity they couldn't change the weather.

Her day hadn't gone according to plan. The day trip out to Grand Bahama had been undertaken in choppy, rough seas. They were two hours out from port when the captain of the boat made the decision to turn around and head back to harbor. Vivian's stomach and hastily downed breakfast had barely survived the journey.

"At least I'm now back on dry land. No more boat trips."

Her hopes for a sunny day visiting one of the islands of the Bahamas and wandering through the local markets, taking in the sights, had been dashed. The sky was still an odd inky blue, but through the enormous windows of her hotel suite she caught the occasional glimpse of scattered patches of pale aqua. The weather was slowly improving.

Dinner at the resort's beach restaurant wasn't entirely out

of the question. It was early afternoon, so she and the sky still had time to come good once more.

Her eyelids grew heavy. When they fluttered closed for the fifth time, they stayed closed. A little cat nap was exactly what she needed. *I'll just grab a half hour of shuteye.*

Ten minutes later, her cell buzzed. It went to voicemail.

Patrick greeted Bryce on the tarmac at Teterboro Airport a little before nine o'clock. "Good morning, Bryce." The soft grin on his face spoke of someone who was in the know about the reason for the sudden turnaround trip this morning. Bryce pretended not to notice as they headed for the jet. He'd specifically asked Mia and Sheila to stay quiet, but Patrick wasn't stupid, he'd obviously been able to put two and two together.

Bryce handed Patrick his travel bag. It was full of freshly laundered and pressed clothes. He'd checked, no one had mistakenly given him a popstar tour t-shirt.

Jordan was acting really weird about that shirt. Hmm.

"I have checked the weather in Florida, Mister Royal. Sorry, Bryce. There was a little bit of cloud earlier in the day and a few spots of rain, but it has all cleared. The pilot informs me that we should have good weather all the way down the Eastern Seaboard, and he says he hopes to be touching down in Palm Beach a little after one o'clock local time."

"Thank you, that sounds perfect. Could you please let the pilot know I am not sure how long I will be in Florida? I expect it might be close to a week. I hope you have packed for a lengthy stay, Patrick. I trust that won't be too much of an inconvenience."

Patrick's grin transformed into a broad smile. "A week in Florida. Sun and sand. I think I will be able to muddle through."

Bryce boarded the jet. The sooner they had wheels up, the quicker he could be in Florida.

And the sooner I can see Vivian.

CHAPTER FIFTY

Vivian slowly opened her eyes. She stared up at the golden light which bathed the ceiling, taking in the various hues of bright oranges, and yellow. "You can't beat the wonder of a sunset," she murmured.

A golden sunset.

She sat bolt upright, pausing for a second while her head caught up. Staring out the window, her gaze settled on the waters and the reflection of the sun's last dying rays.

"Shit, I was meant to be taking photos of the resort!"

Her fingers roamed over the duvet searching for her phone, but they came up empty. Rising up on her knees, she patted the bed clothes. Nothing. "It has to be here somewhere."

It was only when she finally spotted the black rectangle on the floor beside the bed that Vivian remembered having left it on the edge of the mattress. "Ah, there you are."

Scrambling off the bed, she picked up her cell. The front screen happily noted fourteen messages and five missed calls. "What?!" With a racing heart, she swiped the phone open. Every app seemed to have at least ten notifications. While she had peacefully slept the afternoon away, the rest of the world had apparently been busily trying to reach her.

Grace was the first person Vivian called. It went straight to voicemail. She glanced at the time, it was close to seven o'clock. Then she remembered what day it was. "Oh shoot, it's Friday." Grace would be at her weekly physical therapy session until sometime after eight.

The next missed call was from an unknown number. She considered ignoring it, but the number had called three times while she had been asleep. It had to be important, even telemarketers were not normally that insistent.

Vivian hit call. The phone barely had time to make its first ring before a female voice gushed down the line. "About freakin time, Vivian Holte. We've been trying to get hold of you all afternoon. Where have you been?"

"I'm sorry, who is this?" she stammered. The voice sounded familiar, but she couldn't quite place it.

"Mia! Don't tell me you have already forgotten me."

Mia. Oh, of course. Mia.

"Hi, Mia. No, my lovely, of course I hadn't forgotten you. It's just that the number you are calling from is not the one I have in my contacts." Vivian moved closer to the window in order to catch the last light from the day.

"Oh yeah. Sorry. They gave me a corporate cellphone and a new number when I started travelling a lot. This baby has global roaming which has to be the best thing since sliced bread," replied Mia.

Staff at LHRW were always complaining about having to buy international sim cards. Lionel was too tight fisted to pay for an international corporate phone plan.

Mia, her former work colleague from the magazine had moved on and taken a job at the House of Royal. *Shit. She works for Royal Resorts.*

Vivian's mouth went dry. Was Mia's phone call designed to

give Vivian the heads up on the news of her employer launching legal action against the magazine? To sue Lionel and his people into submission. If it was, she was a day too late.

"Are you still working at Royal Resorts, is that why you are calling?"

She and Mia had been close friends at one time. Work and travel commitments had seen them drift apart. Vivian hadn't seen Mia in almost two years.

"Yes, but it's not about what you might be thinking. Scratch that, yes, it is— but it's not bad news." Mia sighed down the line. "Have you seen *Leisure Line* this afternoon?"

"No, I haven't, what's happening now?"

"Could you please log on and take a look. I think it's better if you read the article first."

"Ok, hang on." Vivian's eyes took a minute to focus as the screen on the laptop came to life. Setting the phone down, she wiped the crusts of sleep from her face. *Urgh, I need a shower*. The odd need for a strong coffee stirred in her blood.

After hitting the link for *Leisure Line*, Vivian dropped into the chair. Her gaze took in the header line. **Royal Resorts backs down on legal action.**

She picked up her cell. "So, what happened?"

"There was never going to be any lawsuit against LHRW. The executive team here in New York is trying to figure out how and where the rumor started. It's the closest thing to a full scale witch-hunt I've ever seen."

There hadn't ever been a lawsuit. Shock at the realization of how that now sounded in light of the way things had ended between her and Bryce in Texas had Vivian's hands trembling. She read the official press release letter which had been signed by Royal Resorts CEO, Edward Royal. Bryce's father made it clear that at no time had the company threatened to sue.

"Thank god," she whispered. At least Lionel and the magazine were going to be spared the wrath of the House of Royal, there was that much to be grateful for, but at the same time she sensed any hope of her and Bryce salvaging what was left of their friendship was now long gone.

I threatened to take out a court order if he ever came near me again.

"Hello Vivian, are you still there?"

Vivian wiped at the tears which rolled down her cheeks. "Yes, I am. Thank you for letting me know. I really appreciate it."

"Vivian. That's not the main reason why I am calling. It's about Bryce. He wants to see you."

A snort of disbelief escaped her lips. After standing him up at breakfast, and then leaving him that nasty note, she couldn't imagine Bryce would have anything pleasant to say.

"I don't think that is a good idea. Could you please let him know I'm sorry about everything? And when I'm back in New York, I'll try to come by the office."

The coward's way seemed the best. If she did make time to visit the offices of Royal Resorts, she would make doubly sure Bryce was out of town when she did.

"Vivian sweetheart, please write this down. Beach front villa number twelve. Apparently, it's at the end of the row in a private area of the resort. There will be a security guard at the gate, but he has your name."

Vivian roughly scrawled the address. "What's this in aid of?" Her voice cracked as she struggled to hold back the tears. Her composure was rapidly coming undone.

"That's where Bryce is staying. He doesn't have your room number or your cell. When I spoke to him a little while ago, he said to tell you this, and I quote. 'The local Starbucks delivers in under ten minutes, and I have them on speed dial. I'm ready to set aside all my self-respect and share with you whatever sort of caramel, white chocolate, or mocha mess you think best.'"

Her hand went to her heart. Bryce was in Florida, and not only did he want to see her, but he was offering the sweetest of peace deals.

I need time to think.

"Mia. I'm going to go and have a shower and change. Would you please let Bryce know you and I have spoken, and that I will get in touch?"

"Ok. But before I go, can I just say this, Vivian. From the little that Bryce has told me I gather he's done some stupid things. But it's clear he deeply regrets each and every one of them. Bryce Royal is a good man. Please give him another chance."

Vivian set down her phone. Her heart hurt from all the painful lessons she had learned when men had failed her in the past. Could she trust Bryce? Or would she be forever waiting for the next heartbreak?

I just don't know.

CHAPTER FIFTY-ONE

Bryce paced the floor of his ocean front villa like a tiger in a cage. He'd arrived at the White Foam Breakers almost five hours ago and since then he'd been waiting. Patience was not something he had much to spare today. On the three hour flight from Teterboro to Palm Beach, he had sat and struggled to put pen to paper.

Words were not normally a problem for him, he was used to writing and giving speeches. To sending clear instructions to his team throughout Europe and the UK. But nothing in his previous experience came close to the torture of trying to find the right words to express his emotions. To setting what was in his heart down on paper.

Things had gone wrong between them during the two previous occasions that he and Vivian had been together. He wasn't going to risk an unlucky third. He had to get this right.

I can't bear the thought of losing her. I just can't.

He picked up his cell phone and hit recent. At the top of the list was a number he had already called four times.

You only called her a few minutes ago, give Mia time to find Vivian.

Bryce put the phone down. If things between them weren't in such a precarious state, he wouldn't have hesitated to go up to reception and ask for the phone number of Vivian's room. He wasn't going to do that, the risk was too great.

Mia, Grace, and even Sheila had made it clear any action on his part like that or of a similar nature would be seen as crossing the line they had drawn firmly in the sand. They were calling the shots, and he was going to have to do what he was told.

They would be the ones to inform Vivian of the situation in New York, as well as letting her know that Bryce had checked into the resort in Palm Beach. If Vivian wanted to see him, it was her decision.

If he attempted any form of stalking, their words not his, they would cease to assist. The cupid collective, as Bryce had privately dubbed them, would pack up their bows and arrows and he would be left on his own. Bryce, who was used to being the one in charge, found himself struggling with this arrangement.

He could understand their desire to protect their friend, and quietly respected them for it, but he couldn't also stop thinking that there was a degree of punishment involved in their actions. Grace might not have told the other two what he had done with the millionaire love app, but it seemed to Bryce she was determined to extract her pound of his flesh in revenge.

His gaze went to the open door of his ocean front villa. The soft golden sand beckoned him to remove his socks and shoes and go dig his toes. He fought the temptation. The minute he heard from Vivian he would be heading up to the main resort building and knocking on her door.

For the twentieth time this hour, Bryce checked his

watch. It was getting late. The sun had begun its slow descent into the Atlantic. Soon it would be dark.

Where are you? Come on, Vivian. Don't give up on me.

Vivian had accepted his apology when they were in Galveston. They had parted with that brief, tender kiss.

Her note to him demanding that he leave her alone had been full of anger and pain. Trust wasn't something she was able to easily give, he understood that now.

She's not doing this to punish me. Hurt makes you wary.

"The girls said she was supposed to be doing a cruise out to the Bahamas today. Vivian might not even be back in the good old USA yet." He gripped the ends of his hair in frustration. "Come on Vivian, please. I won't ever fail you again."

His cell buzzed, and Bryce quickly snatched it up. "What's happening, Mia?"

"I have just spoken to Vivian. She's read the full press release from Royal Resorts on *Leisure Line*. Vivian also knows what number villa you are staying in. What happens now is entirely up to her. But if she gives you another chance, don't stuff it up."

Bryce wasn't used to other people telling him what to do, especially not his team members. Mia was treading the thin line between being Vivian's loyal friend and angering her boss.

"I'm sorry if this is a difficult situation for you, Bryce. Did Vivian happen to mention anything about her last boyfriend?"

Bryce gritted his teeth. He would dearly love five minutes alone with that piece of shit. "Pete?"

"Yes, that's him. Well according to Grace, he not only did a real number on Vivian's credit card, but when he left, he took a huge chunk of her self-respect with him. Vivian has been burned and bruised."

Don't let her be too burned and bruised to let me in.

"I'm not him. You have to know that is not the sort of

man I am." He hoped the time that Mia and he had worked together in Italy had left a favorable impression.

"I think I know you, Bryce. And as I have already told Vivian, you're a good man. But this isn't about you, or me. It's about Vivian. It's about consent. Her choice is what matters."

He couldn't argue with that logic. Everyone should have friends like Mia and Grace. People who had your back. The way these girls protected one another left him humbled.

"You're right, Mia. Vivian and what she wants is all that truly matters."

"Good, I'm glad you see it that way. Can I ask that you stay in your room for an hour or so longer? I expect this is frustrating, but we are all praying that this plays out as it should. If it doesn't, I hope you won't hold it against me."

Another hour. He could do that. For Vivian he could wait. "Thanks Mia. Rest assured we won't ever speak of the last few days again no matter what happens with Vivian and myself. When I get back to New York, we will all need to reset and go back to our respective work roles."

As he hung up the phone a soft grin sat on his lips. His words would give Mia plenty to think about. She had a bright future ahead of her, and if the way she had just played him was any indication, Mia Allen would eventually find herself seated at the executive board table. He was about to become CEO for the entire Royal Resorts US, so it made sense to let his team members know where the line between work and his private life began and ended.

"Damn. Maybe I should have said that *after* I've spoken to Vivian."

CHAPTER FIFTY-TWO

Dressed in a blue and white gingham sundress, Vivian slipped out of her hotel suite and headed for the beach. She wasn't entirely certain as to why Bryce was here. Mia had asked that she give him another chance, but a chance for what? Was it to finally end things on a positive note, to let her know that bygones were bygones? That by parting as friends, he could go home with a clear conscience?

And while her head told her this was a sensible enough reason for Bryce to have made the trip to Florida, her heart pleaded for more. For him to want her.

Am I enough?

The article in *Leisure Line* had come as a huge surprise. She'd spent the past day hating Bryce Royal, and his billionaire privileged lifestyle. For thinking that because he was uber rich, he could pick on a small travel magazine, and litigate it to its knees.

While on the phone to Mia, she had struggled to read the rest of the short press release, the words blurring through a sheen of tears. Bryce hadn't turned his pit bull lawyers against her and her employer. Lionel wouldn't be having to find the money to fight a legal battle. Vivian would still have a job when she got home.

The relief was so overwhelming, that after her phone call with Mia, Vivian had headed to the bathroom, and there she had sat on the floor of the shower sobbing while the hot water rained down on her head.

Bryce Royal had got under her skin. Reconciling her emotions for him, and the duplicitous man she had thought him to be, had been near impossible. In her mind she had branded him as an evil billionaire who enjoyed destroying the lives of those who dared to cross him. Then in Galveston he had been lovely. Discovering he was about to sue her employer had come as a huge shock. And now he had followed her all the way to Florida. Every time she thought she had him figured out, the world changed.

Bryce hadn't ever been going to sue. The truth of that left her now having to face her own insecurities. Yesterday morning at the hotel in Galveston, she'd not given Bryce the opportunity to defend himself. She had acted as judge and jury, relying purely on a rumor from a gossip blog.

And I found him guilty. I left him a note and then got on a plane. I didn't give him a chance.

The issue of the lawsuit was solved. The bigger problem was what she was going to do about the man waiting for her in beach villa number twelve.

What if he does want me, can I trust my heart again?

They had started out as a passionate affair, a moment of temptation that had burned bright, then flamed out. Galveston had seen them shift to slightly more solid ground, before fate had once more stepped in and torn them apart. One thing was certain. They were well past the point of this thing between them being just a California fling.

Reaching the gate of the beach front villas, the security guard greeted her with an expectant smile. "Good evening."

Nervous, she mustered a half-smile in response. "Hi, my name is Vivian and I understand a friend of mine is staying in villa number twelve."

He handed her an envelope, then opened the gate. Vivian walked a little way before stopping and slipping a thumb under the seal flap. Her heart was racing as she pulled the piece of paper out.

The only thing harder than building a business is finding true love.

"Oh Bryce," she whispered as she took in the short note. It was honest and it was perfect.

She let out a slow breath. He was ready to forgive her, now all she had to do was pull up her big girl panties and go knock on his door.

Passing by villa number eight, Vivian gave a wave in response to the cheery 'good evening' offered by the middle aged couple sitting on matching beach chairs out the front. The way they held hands reminded her of Steve and her mom. Still nuts about each other after many long years.

I wonder if that sort of love is in my future. If I can find it with Bryce.

Her fingers crushed the piece of paper in her hand. She didn't need to read it again, she understood what it meant. Her heart had spoken loudly in reply. She wanted a chance with Bryce.

The door to his villa was open. The sheer white drapes which hung either side of the entrance billowed out from within, their ends tossed around in the light sea breeze. It gave an ethereal look to the place. She could imagine any moment now a knight clad in shining armor would step out from between the curtains and come seeking a damsel in distress.

Vivian grinned at the unbidden thought. The fading sun and a long nap had clearly scrambled her brain. *He doesn't need to be my hero, he just has to be Bryce.*

Pushing the curtains aside, she stepped into the villa. "Wow," she whispered. It was like walking into the middle of a Saks Fifth Avenue catalogue. Everywhere she looked was gorgeousness upon gorgeousness. Cream and pale beige sofas with the hint of a gold stripe on the edges sat either side of the elegantly furnished entrance.

If her heart and mind hadn't been so focused on finding Bryce, she might have lingered and taken it all in. But she only wanted one thing. One person.

"Bryce?"

The breeze rippling through the curtains was the only reply. Moving further into the villa, Vivian checked the living room, then both bedrooms. Bryce was definitely staying here, his luggage was in the master bedroom. His laptop sat open on a table, the red and gold House of Royal insignia shone bright on the home screen.

Her teeth grazed over her bottom lip, as butterflies danced in her belly.

Where are you?

She turned and headed back to the entrance. She'd been too focused on the villa and what lay within to have checked the beach when she arrived.

Through the open door she glimpsed the silhouette of a man. He was framed by the orange of the sunset on the ocean. His back was to the villa, but she had no doubt as to who it was…

CHAPTER FIFTY-THREE

The soft hush of footsteps on the sand had Bryce turning from gazing out to sea. At the sight of Vivian, his heart leapt in near painful longing. Smiling, he held out his hand, relieved beyond measure when she took it. "You came."

"I did. I mean I would have to be crazy not to make the effort, especially since you flew all the way from New York just to see me. I understand you threw yourself on the mercy of my friends."

The fairy lights which hung from the trees overhead bathed Vivian's face in a pale shade of champagne. *Please let this be a champagne moment.*

Bryce gently squeezed her hand, just to reassure himself that he wasn't dreaming. She really was here.

"Friends." *More like the three witches from the opening scene of Macbeth.* "Yes, those three helped get me here."

Her brows furrowed. "Three? I thought Mia and Grace put you up to this, who is the third person?"

"Sheila. She is my brother Jordan's executive assistant. Though since he has been sent back to California, she will probably be working for me for the foreseeable future."

"I see."

"They are a protective bunch. I couldn't even get your phone number out of them."

Vivian let go of his hand and pulled her cell out of the pocket of her sundress. "Give me your number." Bryce recited his details and she tapped away at the screen. His own cell pinged in his pants pocket. "That's a contact message from me. Now you have my number. Don't lose it, Bryce Royal. I'm hoping you will use it for the purposes of good, not evil, in the future."

He was already planning to have the number tattooed on the inside of his wrist. Or at the very least a thousand business cards printed. God forbid he ever lost his phone.

When Vivian drew in a shaky breath, the lightness of the moment transformed into something more solemn. Bryce waited. His heart was thumping hard in his chest.

Please. Please god let her want me.

He was desperate to know Vivian's take on where this encounter might lead. She was here and it was more than he had dared hoped for over the past twenty four hours. But who was to stay she hadn't gone back to her *let's part as friends* mode? He would be gutted if she had.

"I'm really sorry about Galveston, Bryce. I truly am. Instead of giving you the chance to explain yourself I just fled. My trust issues are kinda heavy at the moment, but you shouldn't be the one to bear the weight of them." Her gaze dropped to the sand at her feet. "I'm surprised that a man like you would still want to have anything to do with me."

The sadness in her voice tore at Bryce's heart. Vivian had been hurt. "I have to confess I was completed blind-sided when you took off in Texas— but can we please put it all behind us? I'm sorry for what you have been through. Some of the NYC brotherhood have let you down, Vivian Holte.

I'm hoping you will give me the time and space to correct that oversight on behalf of all the males in the greater New York area— starting with your credit card."

"Huh?" said Vivian, her head lifting. She met his gaze.

Bryce curled his toes up in his Italian loafers. He'd been waiting hours for this exact moment, to tell her what he had done. "The charge for the dating app has been refunded, in full. And I paid off the rest of the balance."

Her eyes grew wide. "But...but how?"

He leaned in close and smiled. This was pure magic to his ego. "Don't you remember where I'm from? On Planet Billionaire we simply have to ask, and problems disappear." Vivian raised her eyebrows. "Ok, I asked Grace for the name of your bank. It just so happens that the CEO of that particular financial institution plays tennis with my dad every second Saturday."

She shook her head and laughed. "Planet Billionaire, of course. Oh, wow. I don't know what else to say other than, thank you. You've just saved me from a steady diet of cheap noodles and no social life for the rest of my entire existence. How can I ever repay you?"

Bryce had an answer for that question ready and waiting. "A thank you hug would be nice. I'm a sucker for them."

Vivian stepped into Bryce's embrace. As he wrapped his arms about her waist, she sent a plea to heaven. *Please don't let this just be a hug.* She smiled up at him. "I know it might be a small thing in your world but clearing that debt off my card makes such a huge difference. I really don't like two minute noodles."

Bryce probably couldn't imagine what instant noodles must taste like as she would bet her reclaimed credit limit that he'd never eaten them. The Royal family probably had an army of chefs permanently at their beck and call.

His lips brushed the top of her forehead, in a gentle benediction. A gesture which captured the perfect emotion of the moment. Loving and caring. "It sounds like I really saved you, Vivian. Perhaps I should have pressed for a kiss rather than a hug. I mean I did..."

She didn't let him finish what he was going to say. Vivian's hands were on the front of Bryce's shirt, and she was pulling him toward her. "I am going to kiss you. And then I'm going to do it again. In fact, I'm going to keep kissing you until you think you might pass out. because if you do, I promise to revive you using the kiss of life."

As his warm, tender lips touched hers, the tears came. These were tears of joy, so Vivian gladly let them fall. Her heart had been praying for this moment, when love would heal its wounds. When hope was reborn.

Even when she had to break the kiss to suck in a lungful of air, she came back. It was messy. Needy. And it was the best kiss in her entire life. From the way Bryce shook as he held her, she sensed he was also heavily invested in the embrace.

Bryce murmured. "I won't ever let anyone hurt you again. If you allow me into your life, I will stand with you against the world."

Vivian sniffled back her tears. "Bryce Royal, you are my forever hero. If it's alright with you I might just take a moment to make a dramatic swoon."

"My arms are ready and waiting to catch you when you fall." He wrapped his arms around her, and she rested her head against his chest.

"Can I ask you something?"

Bryce rubbed his hand up and down Vivian's back. "Ask away, sweetheart. If there is one lesson I've taken out of the past few weeks, it's that you and I need to establish clear paths of communication."

"Can I ask you about Galveston and why you didn't come up to my room that night?" If he hadn't been about to sue her employer, then why had he let their last encounter in the hotel elevator end at merely a kiss? He had to have known what she was offering, what she wanted. She could admit to feeling disappointed over him having taken his leave. Those emotions had certainly played a part in her reaction to the *Leisure Line* story. Her self-worth was still nursing its bruises.

"I wanted to, believe me. I wanted nothing more than to have you naked and beneath me. But I also wanted us to take things a little slower. We had repaired our friendship over a fantastic meal, and I was sorely tempted to ask you to spend the night with me. When we went for the walk on the beach later on, I watched you. That was when I knew you and I could be much more. Vivian, I want you in my life. The only way I can see you wanting a future with me is if I can have your trust."

She swallowed a lump of emotion. Bryce hadn't been looking to reject her in Galveston, he'd been trying to reset their connection. To show that the Bryce who had hurt her with the nasty review on the dating app was an aberration. A minor glitch. He wasn't that guy.

The pain of her ex still lurked somewhere in her thoughts, but the memory of Pete was slowly fading into the background. Her heart whispered its longing. For her to step up and take a chance with this man. To risk being hurt again.

Isn't that what love always demands? To claim the prize, you have to risk it all.

Taking his hand in hers, Vivian threaded their fingers together. She met his gaze through a sheen of unshed tears. "I am placing my trust and my heart in you Bryce. Promise me that I won't ever come to regret it."

Bryce lowered his lips to hers and they sealed their bond with a long lingering kiss.

CHAPTER FIFTY-FOUR

Bryce shut off the water and stepped out from the shower. He reached for one of the fluffy, luxurious towels which hung on the rail. He hadn't needed to wash, it was just something to help pass the time. In the past three hours he had ordered two strong espressos through room service, started watching then quit three different movies, all while pacing the floor of the villa.

Taking his second hot shower of the evening had been as a last resort. It was either that or go mad. "Hurry up woman, how long does it take to write a gushing review of a resort," he grumbled.

Bryce been about to strip Vivian naked and have his wicked way with her, when Lionel had called. He needed Vivian to file her story tonight. The only thing which had stopped Bryce from picking up his own phone and calling her boss was Vivian's sultry promise of what the two of them would do later tonight as soon as she had finished her review and returned once more to the villa.

And now he was left waiting. His hunger unsated. He didn't care about food, he wanted to feast on Vivian.

Another man might have slaked their thirst by simply jerking off to release the tension, but Bryce was not going to touch himself. A quick session of self-love wouldn't cut it, his manhood demanded more. His whole body craved Vivian.

I want her hands in my hair, as I delve my tongue deep into her wet heat.

The second she appeared at the door, he was going to sweep her up into his arms, toss her on the bed, and ravish every inch of her sweet, soon to be naked body. And when he got her to the point of being beyond aroused, and was begging for him to fuck her, he was going to give her what she wanted. His cock deep in the hot heaven of her sex. Bryce couldn't wait for the moment when Vivian screamed his name as she came.

He glanced down at his erection, not daring to brush a fingertip near it. "Patience boy. Vivian will be here soon."

She'd better be. "Where are you?" he muttered, tossing the towel on the floor. Then recalling the green energy program in place at the resort, he picked it up and hung it on the rail. The sea breeze coming in from outside would have it dry before they went to bed.

From the bathroom, he headed across the villa to where his suitcase lay open. A pair of dark green linen pants and a cream button up shirt sat waiting. A late night stroll around the resort grounds might be the only thing to keep him from going out of his mind with lust.

Catching a small movement out of the corner of his eye, Bryce halted. He let out a slow breath. Vivian stood a few feet inside the door. She didn't meet his eyes, rather her gaze was fixed firmly on something lower on his body. Sensing it had a favorable audience, his cock twitched. If it had arms, it would have waved.

Bryce was caught in two minds. Continue dressing and be

a presentable gentleman or throw caution to the wind and make a naked grab for her.

"I'm here about a rumor," she said, her eyes not moving from his erection.

"Oh no. What rumor? Don't tell me another drama has sprung up in the past couple of hours. I don't think I can keep up."

When Vivian let out a dirty chuckle, the remaining blood in Bryce's body all rushed to the one place. For a second he feared he might faint. She moved closer, her gaze finally shifting north of his hardened member. "The one doing the rounds is about a billionaire resort boss. Apparently, he's been flying all over the country in his company's private jet chasing after some resort reviewer he has fallen in love with."

Oh. That rumor. He hadn't heard that one. He was living it. "What a schmuck. The poor guy must be madly in love with her to do such a foolish and romantic thing. Perhaps you could come a little bit closer, and we could discuss the rumor in more detail."

"Are you in love, Bryce? Because if you are... well, that would make two of us who Cupid had shot with his little arrow."

"Yes, I am in love with you. Utterly head over heels," he replied, his voice gruff with emotion.

He took her hands in his, and they stood gazing into one another's eyes.

"I love you, Bryce. I wouldn't be here if I didn't think you were the man for me."

His whole world lit up at her words.

Vivian's gaze dropped from Bryce's face down to his naked torso. When she licked her lips, Bryce swallowed deep. In his current state, she had him at a clear disadvantage.

The muted sound of other guests talking outside stirred Bryce from his ponderings of conducting all future conversations with Vivian in a state of complete undress. He picked up a pair of pale blue silk boxer briefs and taking his cock in hand, somehow managed to put them on. A soft but clear mewl of disappointment escaped Vivian's lips.

If you are a good girl, I might let you take them off.

"Did you read that rumor about us on *Leisure Line?*"

A slyly grinning Vivian shook her head. "No, your father called my boss. I am led to believe they had quite an interesting conversation. Lionel called me after I submitted my review. What's this about an emergency plane landing in Jackson, Mississippi? You have some explaining to do, my love."

My love. It was amazing to hear her say those words.

CHAPTER FIFTY-FIVE

"From all reports Edward Royal is a little concerned, he might not see his eldest son or his seventy million dollar private jet ever again."

She grinned at Bryce, taking in the pleasurable view of him trying to dress. The bulge in his silk boxers had her licking her lips. When he slipped his arms into his linen shirt, he teasingly paused for a moment. The glint in his eye inviting her to take her time and make a thorough inspection of the goods she was about to sample.

She did. From the slight bump of his Adam's apple, her eager eye traced its gaze down and across the fine dark hair which covered his chest. He playfully toyed with one of the shirt buttons, but let his hands drop away when she gave a slight shake of her head. Her thorough study of Bryce then reached the top of his treasure trail, and she gently sighed.

"What was I saying? Oh, yes, your father is worried about his plane."

A dirty laugh reached her ears. It had her sex clenching with aching need. She could just imagine lying naked on his bed, legs spread open while Bryce blew hot kisses on her clit as he told her a wicked, filthy joke.

Bryce moved closer. "Is that why you came back here? To check on my billionaire papa's jet, or was it to tell me that since you have finished your homework, you are ready to come and play? Only good girls get to play."

I think I might spontaneously combust.

She swallowed deep and nodded. Words were starting to fail her already sex-scrambled brain. When Bryce brushed a fingertip down her right cheek, Vivian closed her eyes.

"I suppose it's a bit of both."

"My father is rather attached to the jet but that wasn't the biggest of his concerns. When I told him I was coming to find you, he said I had better not return to NYC on my own. There might have been something said about sweeping you up in my arms and convincing you of my love."

Love. That was a big word in her world. The last man who had said those words to Vivian had then gone on to cheat on her and ruin her credit rating.

He lowered his lips to hers, brushing the merest trace of a kiss on her skin. "It hasn't been all plain sailing since you abandoned me in Texas. The emergency landing in Mississippi isn't something I ever wish to repeat."

Vivian returned the kiss. "Really? How about you tell me, then I will decide what pity I will give."

Bryce sighed. "Well, I raced out of the resort trying to catch you, but I went to the wrong airport." He kissed her. "And then I had to take a commercial flight."

"Oh, you poor man." She kissed him more deeply, their tongues touching. "Then what?"

A strong arm wrapped about her waist, pulling her closer. "I don't how to say this other than…I flew coach. In the middle seat."

She kept dropping kisses on his lips, not just to let him

know she was with him, but to stop herself from laughing. "That must have been quite the ordeal."

He nodded. "Actually it was. In all seriousness it was the worst flight of my life. The plane lost an engine, and we had to make an emergency landing in Jackson, Mississippi. And then I had to wait hours for the jet to arrive from Galveston. It was traumatic. I may never recover."

"Oh, you poor little billionaire. I can't imagine what it must have been like for you." Vivian's hand shifted from where it had settled on the side of Bryce's waist, working its way to the front of his boxer briefs. She let it linger, listening to his breath as it grew shallow. "Let me make you feel better." Her fingers wrapped around his hardened length, and she gave it a gentle but firm squeeze.

Bryce gasped. "Minx. You had better make good on that promise."

"Don't move a muscle, I'll be right back," she commanded.

The door of the villa was swiftly locked, and the heavier drapes closed. This had the desired effect. The room was plunged into semi darkness. Vivian stopped and turned on a lamp creating the perfect mood lighting.

"Vivian?" came his voice, filled with lust and aching need.

His gentle plea had her seeking him out. "I wanted to do this to you in California, Bryce, but you were too busy doing other delicious and fabulous things to me."

The light bruises and marks might have slowly faded, but the memories wouldn't ever. Being held while taken by a man in such a commanding way had long been the stuff of Vivian's private fantasies. The notion that this might well be her future, had her licking her lips with anticipation.

She sunk to her knees, sending out a prayer of thanks to the heavens for the thick carpet which these sorts of fancy resorts fitted in their luxury villas. From the moment earlier this evening when she had decided to come and find him, this particular act had been set firm in Vivian's plans. Tonight she would show Bryce what being with him truly meant to her. How he made her feel.

Vivian began to toy with the band of Bryce's pale blue boxers. "These are rather nice. Expensive. I trust you have a whole collection of them at home. All waiting for my personal inspection."

"Yes," came the breathless reply.

He shuddered as she slipped her thumb into the top of them, running it gently across the light dusting of hair. He had no idea what this was doing to her, to the pulse that throbbed at Vivian's core. She was hoping that if she played her cards right, he would soon find out.

Her hands gripped the side of his boxers, and she peeled them down his body. The waistband had barely moved an inch before his erection popped free. A large, gorgeous piece of man flesh met her gaze. "You really are a well-endowed gentleman, Bryce Royal. I hardly know where to start."

He brushed his hand over the top of her hair. "Thank you. If you are looking for tips, your tongue dragged along the length of my cock would be greatly appreciated."

He gasped as she did just that, stroking her tongue over his sensitive flesh. All the way to his balls, then back to the head. Over and over again. When she was done, Vivian parted her lips and took the head of Bryce's cock into her mouth. She traced her tongue over and around the end. When she touched the underside, his grip on her hair tightened. He pulled, lighting up her nerve endings.

Her right hand held him fast, while she worked her mouth over his sensitive flesh. Her other hand gently cupped his balls, her thumb running little circles over and under them. Every time she hit the sweet spot between his balls and his ass, Bryce let out a groan of grateful pleasure. Doing this to him, giving him this moment of intimacy, was a heady experience. It thrilled her to reduce Bryce to such a desperate state.

"Tell me, Vivian. How wet is your pussy? I expect a woman with your sexual appetite would be dripping by now. How about you let me check to see the disgraceful state of your panties?"

Bryce Royal might well be an educated and refined man, but when it came to the art of talking dirty, he was down right as wicked as any other man. *And oh how I love it.*

A pop echoed in the quiet of the room as Bryce's cock escaped Vivian's sensual prison. She glanced up and offered him a grin. It was the smile of a woman who knew exactly what sort of power she held over her man.

He was her man. Tonight, she would ensure he knew where she stood in this relationship. If the glint in his eye was any indication, he felt the same.

Bryce held out his hand, pulling Vivian upright. Her dress fluttered around the bare skin on her legs. If every nerve ending wasn't already sensitive, this simple action sent them into overdrive.

Their lips met once more in a slow sultry kiss. When it ended, he whispered, "Have I mentioned that this beachfront villa is booked for the rest of the week?"

"That's a shame because I am booked on a flight back to New York on Saturday afternoon. You are going to be lonely all week."

His fingers grasped the hem of her sundress. "Something tells me the airline is going to be missing a passenger on that flight. In fact, I can guarantee it. Because when you do return home, it will be with me."

"On your daddy's private jet?" she purred.

Bryce let out a huff, and scooped Vivian up in his arms. "I can see I am going to have to take a firm hand to you this evening, teach you how to be a good girl." He tossed her onto the plush duvet of the enormous California king bed, then followed. Giggling, Vivian tried to escape his grasping fingers, but quickly gave up the fight.

As Bryce rose over her, tugging on the bodice of her sundress, her merriment softened. Vivian took in the warmth of his brown eyes, and she whispered, "No more missteps between us. Open communication and above all else, honesty."

"Agreed. Now the first thing I want to be clear about is the need for this sexy little bra and pantie set to be off. And then for me to fuck you senseless."

His fingers pulled on the front of her bra, freeing her breasts. Vivian didn't have time to protest before her nipple was in Bryce's mouth. She lay back and closed her eyes as he sucked hard. Her legs opened as his skilled fingers peeled back her underwear and went to work. "I knew you would be wet and ready for me," he murmured.

"Always."

CHAPTER FIFTY-SIX

The White Foam Breakers Resort
Two nights later

Vivian woke to the gentle caress of the sea breeze. And an empty bed. Her fingers searched the sheets, but Bryce was gone. A horrid memory of the last time she had woken alone in his bed sent a chill down her spine.

This is not the same. There are no more secrets or lies between us.

Climbing out of the tangled sheets, she slipped a light dressing gown on and headed for the open door of the villa. Tiki lights either side of the entrance revealed Bryce's whereabouts. He was sitting outside on a wooden beach chair, clad in a hotel robe, his gaze was on the dark night ocean. From where she stood, Vivian could just make out the white caps of the waves as they reached the shore. "Bryce?"

He turned and smiled at her. She came to him, and he pulled her into his lap. "I thought you were asleep."

She shook her head. "I was, but somewhere in my dreams

I sensed you were gone. Why are you out here, alone? Is there something wrong?"

"No, in fact everything is perfect. For the first time ever, I feel that the pieces of my life are falling into place. You are a big part of that, Vivian."

To hear him speak of her in that way had Vivian blinking back a tear. She hadn't encountered many men like Bryce before, men who were comfortable in sharing their feelings. Of accepting and acknowledging their emotions. It was wonderful.

"Thank you." She lay her head against his shoulder and gave a happy sigh. "The only thing missing from this perfect picture is a salted caramel mocha."

The rumble of his chest as he laughed had her wishing she could frame this moment. The uncertain, regretful version of Bryce she had encountered on the beach in Texas had transformed into this confident, happy one. He found humor in her sugary cravings, something she couldn't have imagined only a matter of days ago.

"It's two in the morning, and I am sure all the little Starbuckers are tucked up fast asleep in their beds. And if they aren't then they should be," he replied.

Vivian let her fingers roam over the fine dark dusting of hair on Bryce's chest. She had a thing for chest hair. "Have you ever tried a frappé?"

He shuddered. "No. I consider life too precious to waste on such things. Now an espresso, that's something I could walk a mile for. In fact I have. There is a particular coffee shop in central Rome, hidden in a laneway out of sight of the tourists. I've been known to rise before the dawn just in order to be at their door when they open. I will take you there one day."

Bryce Royal was a man prepared to travel far and wide in search of the things he loved. He had clocked up a few air miles in finding her. And in the days since their mind-blowing reunion, the only time he had let her out of his sight was when she went to get a haircut at the resort spa. He'd even offered to come with her.

Here in his arms, Vivian felt comfortable to say the words. "I love you, Bryce. I want you to know that, and for you to never have any doubts."

"I love you, too. I knew you were special that first night I saw you standing on the beach in California."

If someone had told him a few months ago he was about to fall hard and fast for a woman he'd just met, Bryce would have given them a dismissive snort and denied it. Only fools and love struck teens behaved that way. He was thirty four years old and about to become CEO of a major corporation, his heart had never made life altering decisions for him.

And yet here he was, and he couldn't fight what he felt for Vivian. It was too strong. The only thing he wanted to take on in battle was any lingering doubt about their future. To slay it once and for all and secure a life with her. Which was why he had come out here to sit in the dark and think. To plan.

"When you call your boss later this morning, I want you to offer your resignation."

Vivian stirred in his lap. As she went to pull away, he placed his arm behind her back, and held it there.

"I know we're planning on being together, Bryce, but asking me to give up my dream job is probably not something I can do, not right now."

He had anticipated her answer. If he was being asked to

walk away from his career, he would also refuse. Not unless he had a better offer.

To his way of thinking he had a brilliant offer.

"I want you to move in with me when we get back to New York. I know it seems like we are moving fast, but with work and commitments I don't want us to end up passing each other like ships in the night. I did that once before long ago, and it was a mistake."

"Is it because I go away for work? Is that why you want me to leave my job, because to be honest that's not really fair. Won't you also have to make business trips?"

Bryce reached for the iPad he had tucked into the side of the chair and touched the screen. He handed it to Vivian. "This is why I want you to resign."

The glow from the screen lit up the expression of bewilderment which appeared on her face. Vivian pursed her lips, then asked, "Are you serious about this, Bryce? I mean it's amazing, but won't people think you are just trying to find a job for your new girlfriend? And your father, have you thought that he might not agree? And the salary, wow."

This was why he had fallen for Vivian. She wasn't just thinking of herself or the fantastic career opportunity he had placed in front of her. Her concerns ran to what others would think of it, of her and how she had come by such a sweet gig.

He had spent the past hour coming up with all the reasons why she should quit her job and come to work for Royal Resorts. And while there were many, most of them boiled down to the simple truth that he wanted her name to be on the list of employees. For her to have skin in the House of Royal game.

"If you and I are together, I can't have you working for the travel magazine. If you stay with them, conflict of interest will mean you won't be able to review any of our resorts or hotels here in the US. And anyone who reads your reviews of our competition will wonder if your words are truly objective. They wouldn't be, because I would make sure your review told them that the offerings from other resorts were substandard to ours. Ouch."

She had pinched his nipple. Hard. Later, when this serious conversation was done and dusted, he would make Vivian pay for her tweak. His cock twitched its approval of his post discussion plans.

Her gaze went back to the iPad. "It's a great offer Bryce. I would be lying if I said it's not something I have considered doing, amongst a few things."

Bryce gently prized the tablet out of Vivian's fingers and placed it on the side table which sat on the other side of the chair. Taking hold of her now unencumbered hand, he raised it to his lips, placing a soft kiss in the middle of her palm. When her breath caught, it sent blood rushing to his loins.

"Then do it. One of the things that came out of the Laguna Beach report was that we not only need more mystery reviewers at our properties, but that we need...I need...someone who can take recommendations and implement changes. And it's not just for the existing resorts. I am trusting you with the secret that we have grand expansion plans for the US. If you agree to come on board as the new head of guest amenity development, and sign the usual non-disclosure agreement, we can sit and discuss those plans in more detail before we head home."

"So I would be reporting to your father?"

Bryce shook his head. "No. You would be reporting to the new CEO for Royal Resorts USA. That would be me."

CHAPTER FIFTY-SEVEN

Bryce was going to be appointed as CEO for the US operations. Vivian hadn't seen that coming. She wasn't sure what was more of a shock, the news of his new role or the job offer.

Be brave and take a chance.

Grace's personal mantra sat itself firmly in the forefront of her thoughts. Moving in with Bryce and coming to work for him would be taking a huge risk. If it failed, she would be left not only without a job, but possibly homeless.

"Alright, I accept the job offer. The salary is insane, but I will do my best to live up to it." She bit down on her bottom lip, suddenly unsure of her next words, and how Bryce might take them. "But there are two conditions. One, I want to wait a little before we move in together. Maybe just a few months."

He growled his impatience at her request. She could understand how he might feel about having his grand plans questioned, or even slightly undermined. Bitter experience had taught her the wisdom of putting space between major life changes.

"Can we pencil in say three months? That gives you time to leave the magazine and get settled into your new role, and also to decide if you want to move in with me. How does that sound?"

"It sounds like I am hooking up with a man who knows how to push a bargain and win." Vivian nodded. "Three months should be long enough."

Bryce gave her a look which spoke volumes. He would be champing at the bit for every one of those three months. Vivian had a sneaking suspicion she wouldn't make it to two months, but she wasn't going to tell him.

"What's the second condition, my love?"

You make me feel so amazing when you say 'my love'.

"Lionel promised me a review of one of the classic hotels at Lake Como in Italy. I still want to do that next summer. If it's a problem I can use a different name for the piece."

She was about to give up her resort reviewer career, but this final review of the resort in Italy meant a great deal to Vivian.

I hope he understands.

Bryce sucked in a deep breath and sighed. "Como. Such a beautiful place, especially in summer. Insanely crowded with tourists, but still gorgeous. I will be waiting with bated breath to read the last great Vivian Holte review."

She whispered in his ear. "Will you promise to teach me some Italian before then? I mean I want you to talk dirty to me in Italian while we fuck."

"It would be my pleasure to service you in any language you wish. But to be serious for a moment. Your new job will involve being enrolled in the management training program. Learning a second language is part of that. I can see you becoming a valuable member of the New York team."

He slipped his hand inside her robe and gave her hardened nipple a tweak. Vivian whimpered with need.

"Speaking of the team in New York. You and I will need to keep our phones and access codes secure. I don't want anyone being able to read our messages if we are going to conduct a secret steamy office romance, Ms. Holte."

An office romance. It sounded all too illicit. Too naughty. For a foolish second Vivian was tempted to set some clear and firm boundaries over their conduct at work, imaging that HR might have something to say if someone walked in on her and Bryce as he bent her over the board room table.

A throb began to pulse at the apex of her thighs. She was going to indulge in that fantasy and deal with the consequences.

I might need to keep a spare collection of clean underwear in the bottom drawer of my desk. Just looking at him sets my blood on fire.

"But people will know we are boyfriend and girlfriend, how is it possibly going to be a secret?"

Bryce's other hand traced its way up the inside of Vivian's thigh, only stopping when it reached the thatch of hair at the opening of her sex. She gasped as his thumb slipped inside.

"Lay back and come for me, I want to hear your sweet sobs as you climax," he murmured. Vivian spread her legs, which allowed Bryce room to stroke her sex deep and hard. Just how she loved it. Each time he drew close to pulling all the way out, he ran the tip of his pointer finger around her clit sending spears of pleasure through her body.

"It will be a secret affair because no one will know the filthy things I am going to do to you when we are at work. I know all the places where we can play in private." A wicked chuckle tickled her ear. "The bathroom in the CEO's office is soundproof. No one will hear you scream."

Vivian gasped as Bryce pushed two fingers into her wet clasp. He was working her hard, any moment now her world would explode.

"You and I should set up our own group chat so we can

talk privately on social media. Something secure, just for us. I have many filthy things I will need to say to you, Vivian." His teeth nipped at her earlobe. "And in return I expect you to send me lots of pics. Photos of you lying naked on a bed with your legs spread open for me, sliding a vibrator over your clit. I will need to have something to beat off to while you are on assignment at one of our resorts."

As a thick thumb replaced his fingers in her sex, the strokes slowed. He wasn't going to let her climax any time soon. He was going to torture her first before she came. She knew this game and loved it. Bryce was going to make her beg.

Dirty pics. Vivian swallowed. They were going to have to become experts at hiding, or they were going to get caught. She could just imagine the scandal if their sexual antics got leaked to *Leisure Line*.

"If we are going to play that sort of game, I'm warning you now, it runs both ways. I will be expecting to receive artistically curated dick pics from you on a regular basis." She tapped her finger against his crotch. "We'll have to be careful. Those images are going to have to be kept so secure that even foreign agents wouldn't be able to hack them. All hell would break loose if a video of me riding a dildo meant for your private pleasure only suddenly found its way online."

He groaned. "That's a hell of a picture you have just put in my mind, but ok, I agree we need to be White House level secure with our communications. Speaking of riding things, how about you and I park that sex toy fantasy for a minute, and you come and slide your luscious legs either side of my hips. I have something hard that you can mount." Bryce's fingers moved free of Vivian, leaving her heated and desperately aroused.

They were outside, where a random late night wanderer

on the beach might see, but she didn't care. She shifted off the chair. "Condom?"

Bryce dipped a hand into his robe. "A gentleman always comes prepared." His cock was sheathed and ready to party in under ten seconds. Throwing aside any thoughts of modesty or good behavior, Vivian climbed back on to the chair. Legs spread wide, she sunk down, taking the full length of Bryce inside her. She sighed as he thrust up burying his cock in the heat of her sex. "Oh, Bryce. Oh god."

"Now be a good girl and rest your head on my shoulder, while I screw you just the way you like it. Hard, deep, and without mercy."

Vivian did as told, and together they began the long slow climb to paradise.

CHAPTER FIFTY-EIGHT

Six bliss filled days in Florida had Vivian wishing she never had to go home. But at least she wouldn't have a large laundry basket of clothes which needed washing when she walked in the front door of her and Grace's apartment. Her wickedly indulgent new boyfriend had bought her an embarrassing amount of designer clothes, and more skimpy panties than a girl could possibly wear in an entire lifetime. To her surprise, Bryce wasn't a thong man, he liked a bikini bottom, and even a boyleg.

Not that she had got much use of them over the past few days. During their time at the villa, she and Bryce had worked together fleshing out Vivian's new role in greater detail. Her sexy man had been happy to talk business, but he had also made it clear that while they were alone, they were both to wear the bare minimum of clothing, and she had to be ready to meet his sexual demands whenever they arose. Vivian was tired, sore, and the happiest she had ever been in her life.

Dinner in the sumptuous and elegant restaurant at the resort was one of the few times she had been allowed to fully dress. In the spirit of equality, Bryce had spent most of his days naked, only throwing on a pair of swim trunks when their breakfast arrived each morning or they took an impromptu stroll on the beach.

The week had been magical, made even more special by the arrangement that '*I love spoiling my girl rotten*' Bryce had made with the local Starbucks. At eight am every morning, a steaming hot espresso would be delivered to their villa, accompanied by either a Frappuccino or a frappé. While her lover stuck to the same beverage without fail, Vivian was left guessing as to which one would be her treat on any particular day.

If she hadn't already fallen hopelessly in love with Bryce, the frappé vs. Frappuccino daily challenge would have sealed things.

Standing at the end of their bed, she stared at her brand new suitcase and considered whether she should souvenir the toiletries or not. It was a tradition. And according to her parents, traditions should be observed and upheld.

The door of the villa opened, and a handsome man dressed in a dark gray Saville Row suit stepped into the room. She was from New York, had seen hundreds if not thousands of men walking the streets dressed in three piece suits. None of them came close to how Bryce Royal looked in his expensive tailor made clothes.

"You are so hot," she whispered.

He caught her eye and grinned. "Actually, it's not too bad outside. There is a cool breeze. Or were you perhaps referring to the cut of my suit rather the weather?"

"I was actually talking about the way you fill that suit but thank you for the weather channel update."

While Bryce had gone to talk to the resort manager and offer his personal praise for the staff and amenities, Vivian had finally hit *SEND* on her letter of resignation. Lionel would no doubt be disappointed, but she hoped he would also be happy for her.

She had submitted her last official review. It was a sparklingly good one; the White Foam Breakers had earned itself a full five stars, along with a highly recommended status. Even Bryce, when she caved and let him read the review, had reluctantly agreed with Vivian's sentiments. Though she suspected some of his views may have been swayed by the amount of sex he'd had during his stay at the resort.

"You look a little perplexed, what's wrong? Didn't you like your morning cold, sweet thing," he offered.

Vivian reached for a nearby pillow. This was one argument she couldn't ever win. She could just imagine Bryce having 'he never let a chilled coffee beverage touch his pure espresso lips' as his final epitaph.

"My Frappuccino was perfect. It's just that I usually take the complimentary guest toiletries from the resort or hotel. They are one of the little perks of my job. Soon to be ex job," she corrected herself.

"And you are wondering if I will judge you for lifting the ones from the bathroom in our villa?"

"Hmm."

"I will judge you, but they are L'Occitane so definitely worth taking. Come to think of it, that could be one of your first tasks when you come on board, check our personal grooming range against those of other resorts. Speaking of coming on board, did you email your resignation to Lionel?"

Emotion suddenly welled up inside her. She had fought tooth and nail to get the job at the magazine, it had been one of her proudest moments the day she first started at Luxury Hotels and Resorts Worldwide and now she was walking away. It all felt a little too surreal.

Italy next summer. Then I am done.

Strong arms wrapped around her, holding her close. "I

know this is the start of a whole new life, but sometimes it's good to be a little afraid. It means you really want that thing you are chasing."

Vivian rested her head against Bryce's solid chest. The notion that fate had somehow conspired to make certain that the two of them found one another had her closing her eyes and offering a prayer of gratitude. There were so many little things that had happened to ensure that she was standing on the beach that night in California, so many signs from the universe that she and Bryce were meant to be together. Signs she was no longer ignoring.

"Grab the toiletries, sweetheart, and let's get out of here. The car is waiting for us out the front of reception. And the jet has a departure slot locked and loaded."

She scurried into the bathroom and snatched up the goodies, stuffing them into her travel bag. No sooner had she stepped back into the main living area, than a porter arrived at the door and took their luggage away.

Outside Vivian paused, lingering to take in the final precious moments of her stay. The girl who was leaving Florida was not the same one who had arrived a week ago. A smile sat on her lips as she turned to see Bryce. He held out his hand.

"Ready to take that next step with me, Vivian? To Planet Billionaire."

He was never going to let her forget that remark. And while it was now a private joke between them, it was also her new reality.

The truth of that finally sunk in as their town car swept through the gates and onto the tarmac at Palm Beach County Airport a short while later. Vivian sucked in a deep breath as she caught her first glimpse of the Royal Resorts jet. Bryce turned to her and smiled. It hadn't escaped her notice that whenever their gazes met, he broke into a happy grin.

Love looks good on him.

The steps of the jet were lowered. There were people standing alongside a wide strip of carpet, waiting. All waiting for them. This was another world she was stepping into, one a million miles away from long check-in queues and baggage claim tussles.

The car drew up next to the carpet, the door perfectly in line so that when it opened the passengers could disembark without their feet having to touch the asphalt. A suited attendant moved forward and opened the door. Bryce climbed out first, and Vivian followed. He took hold of her hand. "Vivian, this is Patrick our flight attendant. He will take care of any of your needs on the trip home."

Vivian and Patrick stared at one another for a second. She cleared her throat. "How was it?" She ignored the *huh* of surprise which escaped Bryce's lips.

"I chose the caramel, like you suggested. It was delicious," replied Patrick.

"Oh no," huffed Bryce. "You haven't turned Patrick to the dark side. Hang on, how do you two know each other?"

"I'll go and check the plane," said Patrick, his feet moving quickly toward the jet.

"Janice called me a few days ago and gave me Patrick's number. He and I chatted while you were at the gym earlier this morning. Turns out he is also a sweet tooth when it comes to his beverages. And in answer to your next question, Mia gave Janice my number."

Bryce growled his clear annoyance at this development, but it held no heat. He pulled Vivian into his arms and kissed her. "You might be in good with Janice, but don't you go getting any ideas. I get first dibs on the jet when I need to travel."

Vivian laughed. "Oh, you poor deluded man. I already have Patrick and the pilot on speed dial."

She slipped out of his embrace and headed with hurried purpose toward the plane. "And I know the best place to sit. It's on the right hand side, middle of the cabin. That's where my Frappuccino is already waiting." Her foot had barely touched the bottom step before a pair of strong male arms wrapped around her waist and drew her back.

"I see you are going to have to learn the rules of Planet Billionaire. The first one being you don't steal my favorite seat on the jet."

Vivian turned in his arms, rising up on her toes to plant a wicked, teasing kiss on his mouth. Their tongues danced over one another in a languid embrace.

When they finally drew apart, he leaned in and murmured in that deep rough voice which always went straight to her sex. "How's this for a compromise, Ms. Holte. I have the chair for takeoff and once the seatbelt sign clears, you come and snuggle onto my lap. I'm sure there is room enough for both of us."

She turned her head and whispered in his ear. "Only if you promise that on our next flight, we go without Patrick. What's the point of having a private jet if you can't join the mile high club?"

His groan of heated anticipation followed her all the way up the steps of the plane.

EPILOGUE

The offices of Royal Resorts, NYC
 Ten weeks later

Vivian caught a glimpse of Jordan Royal as she entered the executive floor of Royal Resorts. He was talking to his father's personal assistant, Janice. From the sound of things she was offering him some gentle words of advice.

"How about you go for a walk around Hudson Yards and burn off your nerves? Edward and Bryce have another private meeting scheduled ahead of yours." Vivian caught Janice's attention. She held up her hand signaling the five minutes she hoped to grab with Bryce. "And I think Vivian wishes to speak to Bryce before then," added Janice.

The middle Royal son looked nervous, his left hand was shoved stiffly into his jacket pocket. Since the debacle at Laguna Beach, which to his credit he had more than set to right, Jordan had barely set foot in the office. The sum total of her interactions with Bryce's brother was a few polite words they had exchanged at the recent Royal family New

Year's Eve dinner, some three weeks ago. Other than that, Jordan was a ghost in her life.

"Good morning, Vivian, lovely day," said Mia, striding into the executive reception space. One day Vivian hoped to be able to make such a confident entrance. Two months into the job and her mouth still went dry whenever she stopped in front of the glass doors which were etched with the words Royal Resorts along with the family crown insignia.

Mia took in the gorgeous dark blue suit, which Vivian privately acknowledged she seriously rocked. The pussy bow on her pure white silk blouse was the perfect blend of office and sexual tease attire. When Mia's gaze dropped to the strappy shoes on her feet, her friend let out a sigh. "Are those from Jimmy Choo?"

"Sophia Webster." Vivian turned her left foot to show off the silver butterfly motif which sat on the heel of the shoe. "Bryce has a thing for them. Boxes keep getting delivered to my office, and I'm not allowed to ask how he managed to get a hold of them, or heaven forbid how much they cost." From what Vivian had been able to find out online, they were the favorite shoe of many of Hollywood's hottest actresses and more than one international pop star.

Vivian's gaze shifted briefly to Jordan, and she moved a little closer to Mia. "Are you wishing to speak to Bryce? I'm hoping to catch him for five minutes, but Sheila informed me earlier that his diary is back to back meetings all day."

"I was, but it's not a problem, I'll just send him an email. The list of things Matthew needs Bryce to look at for the Colorado project can go in it as an attachment."

The two women fell silent as Jordan turned and moved away from Janice's desk. On his way to the door, he passed them, giving them both a brief nod in greeting before continuing on his way out to the elevator.

Mia shook her head. "Poor Jordan, he looks like he is

about to go to the executioners. They couldn't fire him, could they?"

"I don't know what they have planned. Bryce and I have a firm policy that we don't discuss business outside of the office, and in here... well let's just say the state of the careers of Royal executives is a level or two above my current pay grade."

It took a light, careful touch to conduct a romance with the recently appointed CEO for the US. Bryce wasn't just Vivian's boyfriend, he was her boss. In the first weeks after their return from Florida, they had worked hard to establish the right sort of boundaries between work and their private relationship.

The lines did however tend to blur whenever she visited Bryce in his office late at night. No one had been foolish enough to raise the subject of why the new CEO had deemed it necessary to install smart glass in his office not long after he took it over. Glass which went from clear to solid white at the touch of a button.

Vivian would never forget the night she had to suddenly take a naked dive under Bryce's desk in order to avoid an embarrassing encounter with an office cleaner. Nor would she forget what her boss had made her do to him while she knelt between his legs, and he fisted her hair in his hands.

She stirred from her lustful daydream as Edward Royal strode out of Bryce's office and made his way over to Janice. Vivian saw her opportunity. "I'll talk to you soon, Mia." She hurried into Bryce's office and quickly closed the door behind her.

He rose from behind his desk and greeted her with a tender kiss. "Hello my love. I wasn't expecting to see you this morning."

"I just wanted to touch base and let you know that the

new couch, along with the bed for the main bedroom have arrived in your new apartment."

Bryce had recently dropped a cool twenty five million on a five thousand square foot apartment in the building. Vivian had been forced to bite her bottom lip when he explained it was a *bargain starter* home for them, and they would upsize when the time came.

"That was nice of you to come and tell me." His eyes narrowed in suspicion. "Was that the only reason why you came here? Well, apart from showing off your gorgeous business suit and those '*I am going to let you fuck me in these later tonight, butterfly sandals*'".

She patted his chest. "Shh, Janice might hear. No, that wasn't the only reason why I am here. I came to tell you that I'm bringing forward the timeline on moving in with you."

A broad grin instantly lit up his face. He looked for all the world like a little boy on Christmas morning. "When?"

"The courier is bringing my boxes over this morning. I figured since you are now officially moving in, it would make sense that I did the same. I can oversee the furnishings and other details."

One of the few fights they'd had so far in their relationship was about Bryce's choice of furnishings. What he had apparently seen as being practical and unobtrusive, Vivian had viewed as dull, boring, and akin to living in a hotel suite. She appreciated the creams and beige the interior decorator had chosen, but she had stood her ground in her refusal to let it be the design palette for their home. Like it or not, Bryce needed color and a little drama in his world.

"You will upset the designer. She'll complain."

"Trust me, it will all work out for the best. I'm more than happy to work with her and create the perfect home for us. My training at Royal Resorts has instilled in me the golden rule of never settling for anything that was merely adequate.

Need I remind you that I was the one who wrote that insightful and thoroughly accurate review of the Laguna Beach resort." She batted her eyelashes at him. "What was the title of that article? I can't remember. I must still be mentally scarred by the lack of towels and duvets."

His deep chuckle reverberated between them. It went straight to Vivian's heart. Bryce trusted her instincts. It was one of the many reasons why she loved him. And why she held such hope for them sharing a bright future together.

"Cheeky minx. How about we meet at our new home at seven thirty for a bout of naked wrestling? You can point out any areas of my technique where you see room for improvement."

Vivian snorted. "I see what you did there. 'Room for Improvement.' Never let it be said I would settle for anything less than the best. And you Bryce Royal are an exceptional man. I love you. I don't think there is a thing in the world I wouldn't do for you."

He dropped a kiss on her forehead. "I love you too. So does that mean I can have the Royal Resorts private jet back?"

"Not a chance."

Bonus VIP members story.
When Vivian travels to Italy to file her last review for her old magazine, a wicked billionaire can't resist the urge to secretly follow her...

For your free copy of **An Italian Villa Escape** join the VIP Suite at **Planet Billionaire.**

BONUS EPILOGUE

These men might be his father and his elder brother, but they still had the power to fire him. To push him out of Royal Resorts, and into the cold. Jordan couldn't begin to conceive of a life outside the family firm. He was Jordan Royal. All Royal family members worked in some capacity at the House of Royal.

When Camille started up her own fashion label her father kicked her out the house. Don't forget about her.

Camille might be doing well, but she had talent. Jordan had long feared his skills began and ended in the bedroom.

And even then, they hadn't been enough to secure the heart of the woman he had loved and lost. In the months following their bitter, secret split, he had blundered through his job at the unfinished resort lost in a regret-filled haze.

The Laguna Beach resort project, the one he had fought so hard to win, had turned into his worst nightmare. He'd stuffed up with his father's pet project. With the Platinum Collection resort that was meant to see the first US located Royal Resorts feature in the top one hundred resorts in the world.

What he had delivered had become the laughing stock of the hotel and resort industry. Who doesn't order enough linen for a fucking hotel? Answer. Jordan Royal. He could just see that as being a question on some nightmarish game show.

He hadn't slept. The email from Bryce asking him to come to his office for a meeting this morning had seen Jordan leave his luxurious apartment last night and take a long ride on the New York subway. Unlike the rest of his siblings, he actually owned a metro card. Travelling around the city in an old brown overcoat and baggy sweat pants gave him the sort of anonymity that a Lincoln town car and a sharp cut suit couldn't deliver.

She had taught him that trick. It was her way to escape from the limelight. From the paparazzi and the blinding flash of cameras.

He'd arrived early for the meeting, hoping to get whatever was about to happen over and done with then made a hasty exit. The family hideaway three hours out of New York was where he would go to lick his wounds.

But he'd been forced to wait. To pace back and forth across the executive reception area. Janice's kind attempts hadn't had the desired effect. He was too old, too jaded for her motherly advice to reach him.

He'd gone downstairs hoping to take a walk around the block, but the chilly sleet falling outside had quickly put paid to that notion. Late January in New York had become Jordan's private bitterly cold version of hell.

I wish I was back in California. At least the sun shines there. And it's on the other side of the country. Far away from everyone.

"The Laguna Beach resort is in good hands," he muttered, then swore under his breath.

He shouldn't start with that line. It was Bryce who had sourced and hired the new resort manager for California. His older brother had shortlisted the three best candidates, interviewed them all via Zoom, then flown out to the West Coast to make the final decision. Bryce had even been the one to decide that Austin Brown was actually a decent assistant manager and should stay on.

But under a capable resort manager.

The instant the door of his brother's office opened, Jordan made a beeline for it. Red-headed Sheila, barely had time to get out of his way as he stormed past. He would find her later and apologize. His former executive assistant had been one of the many team members based in New York working demanding hours to get Laguna Beach back in line, ready for its official, long delayed, opening in the Spring. If by some miracle he survived today, there was a long list of people he intended to seek out and personally thank.

Bryce and Edward were stacking papers and chatting as Jordan strode into the room. His heart sank as he took in the layout of the meeting space. The table had been arranged with them seated on one side, and their visitor on the other.

"Close the door will you please, Jordan," asked Edward.

Keep your temper. No matter what happens do not start shouting.

Another long ride on the New York subway beckoned. This time he might endeavor to see just how long it took to get all the way out to Coney Island.

Bryce rose from the table and made his way round to where Jordan stood. He glanced back at their father. "I'm going to go get a coffee and leave the two of you to talk." He patted Jordan on the shoulder, then added a reassuring squeeze. "Good luck, I hope you find your feet in your future career." Bryce then left the room.

Oh fuck. I am getting fired. Bryce doesn't want to be here when the sword falls.

With his brother having only recently been appointed as CEO, it was clear that their father was going to take responsibility for what had happened in California. The disaster had happened on his watch, so it made sense that Edward be the one to deal with the problem of Jordan.

The problem of Jordan. How many times had he heard those words in his younger, wilder days?

Edward rose from his chair, and as he came to Jordan's side, motioned for his middle son to take a seat on the long brown sofa which sat under the window. "Let's talk."

Jordan's gaze flittered to the expansive view of New York city which the floor to ceiling glass afforded. The view from the Eighty Fifth floor took in much of the city and parts of the Hudson River. No matter how many times he had taken in the sight, it was still breathtaking. He lowered himself onto the soft leather couch. If the ax was about to fall on his Royal Resorts career, he couldn't think of a better or more private place for it to happen.

Edward sat next to him, his hands gently clasped together. "Firstly I want to say how pleased the board and I have been with the uplift in the Laguna Beach resort ratings. I haven't seen anything less than a four in the past month. Our average rating on most travel sites is heading toward that number. I feel quietly confident that we are over the worst of things."

It would take time to undo the initial damage that Jordan's poor management had inflicted. The resort was still a long way from nearing the magical five that Edward was aiming for, but hopefully in time the more recent excellent reviews would dull the bad ones.

"That's encouraging news, Dad." Jordan had made it his mission to check all the review sites every morning since he had been sent out to fix the California resort. Every review was read, analyzed, and then acted upon. Truth was sorted from fiction. Staff retrained. New staff hired. His assistant manager Austin Brown had turned out to be a solid hire, eager to learn. Just as importantly, he was willing to admit and deal with his mistakes.

It had taken two and a half months of solid grind, but by the time he had officially returned to NYC, Jordan was confident he had handed the new resort manager a six star luxury resort.

"Yes, I am pleased that you have turned things around, son. Bryce said he wants you to know he appreciates your efforts."

Edward paused and Jordan's heart sank. This conversation sounded very much like a shit sandwich. His father had started off with the nice bit, but from the expression on his face, he was now handing Jordan the rest.

"I will resign if that makes things easier for you and Bryce."

New York business whispers would soon have it that the middle Royal son had been fired from the company. He had done enough damage, so falling on his sword would be the right thing to do. The honorable way out for everyone.

"That won't be necessary. Admirable, but not required."

Edward Royal had spent the better part of thirty six years in the States, but he still spoke the King's English in his private school clipped accent. Jordan found it oddly soothing. Those carefully crafted words held less fire than if they had come from Bryce. They were still powerful. The sense of fatherly disappointment in them burned deep into his soul.

His father and brother had gone into bat for him with the US board. Put their reputations on the line. They had convinced the other executives that he was up to the task of launching Laguna Beach. Of handling a billion dollar resort.

And I failed.

"We discussed your next career move at the monthly board meeting the week before Christmas. The majority of the board wanted to move you to another resort, a well-run one where you could learn under a solid manager. I fought against that, as did Bryce. Aside from the fact that it would be humiliating for you, I don't think you could actually learn much from someone else."

Thank god the board hadn't gone ahead with that idea. His fragile ego couldn't ever allow him to agree to that sort of shameful demotion. Bryce and Edward would know he'd refuse.

"So what is to be my fate, an overseas posting?"

Out of sight out of mind. Then eventually come home when everyone has forgotten about my billion dollar fuck up. Not that they ever will.

Edward gave a fatherly pat on Jordan's knee. "Cheer up, old chap. It's not all bad. Bryce and I have come up with a role that we think will suit. Everyone deserves a second chance, and while you may have had more than a couple of second chances in your time, we still want you to succeed."

I will never outlive my past. Never truly fit in.

In his younger years he had been Wild Boy Jordan Royal. That's what the party scene and gossip columns of Manhattan's elite had dubbed him. He had lived hard and fast on a steady diet of parties, cocaine, and gorgeous trust fund debutantes. He'd gained a well-deserved reputation as an uber rich bad boy. Written off a couple of expensive cars. Destroyed the side of a barn while driving a stolen tractor. Got arrested. And worst of all, reduced his mother to tears.

The night his mom had flown all the way to Iowa just to bail him out of a jail cell had been his lowest point. To this very day, Jordan still didn't know for certain if she had told Edward about that night. If she had, his father had never mentioned it to him.

The House of Royal might have its fair share of misfits and fuckups, but they were loyal.

There were moments, fortunately brief, when he resented

Bryce for never having put a foot wrong, but Jordan respected him and the sacrifices his brother had made to ensure that the European and UK operations were on solid ground. And now he was back here in New York, as the recently anointed CEO for the US.

While I am a disappointment.

He had lost count of the number of times he had heard the words 'second chance' being offered to him. With his track record, it was more along the lines of this being his three hundredth second chance.

Can we just get this over and done with. Let me take my punishment.

"We've decided to send you to Las Vegas for the next six months."

Oh no. Not Vegas. I'm being exiled to the desert. To the land of tourists and tacky themed hotels. My career is as good as dead.

Las Vegas was the last place Jordan wanted to go and spend his days. Vegas was fun for a wild weekend, but the prospect of actually living in the city filled him with a sense of…meh. There was a reason that what happened in Vegas stayed in Vegas, people could easily forget what might have happened over a drunken two or three day period.

How am I going to hide those missing six months?

In the bad old days he would have said he'd gone into rehab, but everyone in New York knew he had been clean and sober for over five years. He could pretend he had gone hiking in the Himalayas, but people would eventually find out. Even Nepal had reliable internet. There was nothing else to do but suck it up.

Six. Fucking. Months.

"How is the upgrade going?" asked Jordan, suddenly recalling that the main Las Vegas resort had been undergoing a major refurbishment program over the past year. Once the work was complete it was going to join the

Laguna Beach property as part of the new Platinum Collection.

"The finishing touches will be done by the end of this month. That's why we want you to go. The resort management team is solid. They've done everything they could with what they had in the past, but now we need people flowing through our doors. Money coming in. And that is where you have a part to play my lad."

Edward rose from the couch and headed to Bryce's desk. He returned carrying a thick folder, full of papers which he sat on the coffee table in front of Jordan. "Did you know that Elton John and Britney Spears made millions upon millions from their residences in Las Vegas?"

Jordan nodded. He had connections in the entertainment industry, and the sort of money an established artist with a solid fan base could make from featuring at a resort were well known. Vegas was no longer the place where old careers went to die, stars were falling over themselves to perform at the big casinos and resorts.

"The reason why those musical acts could ask and receive huge fees was that the resorts themselves made five times that money from having guests stay, play, and shop at their properties. People will spend freely while they are in town to see their favorite star. For the relaunch of the Las Vegas resort we need a major headline act. One which will fill the theatre every night they perform."

Jordan glanced at his father and scowled; Edward was bouncing up and down on the balls of his feet. Excitement crackled in the air. "Earlier this week I flew out to Los Angeles to meet with the new management team for a top artist. They called last night, and their client is going to sign a contract to do a six month residency with us."

Edward clapped his hands. Any moment now Jordan feared he was going to break into a happy dance.

Jeez Dad, what was in your tea this morning?

"So you want me to help manage the resort while this star is in the house?" It made sense. Having a major artist at the resort would bring millions of dollars flowing into the Royal Resorts coffers. Whatever he could do to support the venture would surely go a long way to getting back in good with the senior executives and the board. There had to be a way for him to make it out of Vegas.

"No. I don't want you to be involved in running the resort. To be honest I would say you have managed your last Royal Resorts property. Bryce and I agree that your talents lie elsewhere."

Honest. Brutal. But I can't blame them. My failures are my own.

"So what role do you wish me to play exactly?"

He didn't want to end up working the front desk or glad-handing the high rollers. His ego could only bend so far.

"I want you to handle the talent. Do everything for them. Anticipate whatever they might need, and above all—keep them happy. This is your golden opportunity to show the board and Bryce that California was a slip up. Do an outstanding job with this assignment, Jordan, and they will soon forget what happened at Laguna Beach. There are other places for you to shine within the House of Royal."

His father's words were clear. He wasn't going to be trusted with a resort ever again, but the company felt he was the perfect man to work his charm on a mega star and make sure the money flowed.

Vegas. Ok. I can do six months. I just have to manage the demands of an artist. How hard can that be? Peel a grape or two. Sort skittles into separate bowls and remove the yellow ones.

"So who have you signed?"

"About to sign. Their management has agreed to the terms of the contract, but I thought it would be nice for you to go out to Los Angeles and be the one to get our star's signature. Start the relationship with the personal touch."

Edward bent and flipped open the folder, talking out a piece of paper. He handed it to Jordan. "Here is the address. It's in Beverly Hills, Los Angeles."

Jordan's heart stopped beating. He knew that address. And who lived there. Just when he thought his life couldn't get any more complicated, fate had decided to throw him a monstrous curveball.

"Her name is Chloe." Edward waved his hand about absentmindedly. "Apparently, she doesn't use her surname. Vivian says she is a huge fan of this pop star, but you know me, if they weren't producing music in the first few years of the twenty first century, I haven't a clue."

His father kept talking, but Jordan's gaze remained locked on the piece of paper. He was torn between wishing the address would suddenly change, and the dark, bitter regret he had felt in the long months since he had last walked out of that particular house.

Talk about jumping out of the frying pan and into the fire.

"They will be expecting you and the contract to be at that address on Wednesday at three o'clock for the signing. We want you to be at the resort in Las Vegas when the big announcement is made at the end of next week. Tickets will go on sale to the public shortly afterwards. If you stay in Los Angeles with Chloe until then, that should give you ample time to get to know her. It would be nice if you could make an effort to find out the things she likes." He cleared his throat. "And the things she doesn't."

Jordan let out his breath as slow as he could. His heart still hadn't kicked back in. What the devil was he going to do?

Get to know her. You have no idea.

He knew Chloe. His fingers and tongue had traced their

way over every inch of her sweet, naked body. Jordan could write a whole book about the things the world's biggest pop star liked. And the things she hated.

His name was likely at the top of her hate list.

The next six months of his life was going to be utter torture.

Read A Suite Temptation.

A SUITE TEMPTATION

When your popstar ex writes a revenge song and it becomes the mega hit of the summer.

Reformed billionaire bad boy Jordan Royal has done his best to stick to the straight and narrow but the moment he and Chloe, the world's biggest popstar, meet in a Berlin nightclub the sparks of passion ignite.

Conducting a secret romance with the woman adored by millions comes with its own set of problems, and when the relentless pressure of money and egos begins to take its toll, Jordan walks away.

But in the months following his and Chloe's breakup, Jordan's career has spiraled down. He is given one last chance to prove himself or he is out. His job. Go to Las Vegas and cater to the demands of the megastar who Royal Resorts has just signed for an exclusive six month concert residency.

Chloe's management have taken her for everything and she's on the verge of bankruptcy. If the price for salvaging her career and keeping her gorgeous LA home is having to share a luxury hotel suite with her ex, Chloe will gladly pay it.

All she has to do is resist the temptation of a certain billionaire's steamy looks and his heated touch.

A Suite Temptation is a second chance rom-com. Be warned this is a wicked and super steamy book.

JOIN THE VIP SUITE AT PLANET BILLIONAIRE

Do you want to read all the steamy, romantic things which happen when Vivian finally gets the chance to go to Lake Como in Italy and write her review?

For your free copy of **An Italian Villa Escape** scan the QR Code to join the VIP Suite at **Planet Billionaire.**

SOUNDTRACK

I Made It (Cash Money Heroes)
Kevin Rudolf, Birdman, Jay Sean, Lil Wayne

Miracle
Calvin Harris (Ellie Goulding)

California King Bed
Rihanna

Our Song
Anne-Marie, Niall Horan

New Rules
Dua Lipa

Feel It Still
Portugal. The Man

Attention
Charlie Puth

Sorry
Justin Bieber

24K Magic
Bruno Mars

ALSO BY JESSICA GREGORY

House of Royal

Royal Resorts

Room for Improvement
A Suite Temptation
The Last Resort

An Italian Villa Escape

ACKNOWLEDGMENTS

A huge thank you to my editor Madeline Ash, your support and tough love helped to bring Bryce and Vivian to life.

To the design team at Qamber Designs & Media, especially Jennifer Silverwood. Creating the moodboards and images was a blast.

To my family. Thanks for your amazing support.

ABOUT THE AUTHOR

Jessica Gregory writes sassy steamy rom com. She loves strong heroines and making her heroes grovel. She hopes to one day live on Planet Billionaire.

Jessica is the romantic comedy pen name for USA Today bestselling author Sasha Cottman.

Visit
Jessica Gregory Books

"Ready to take that next step with me, Vivian? To Planet Billionaire."

Printed in Great Britain
by Amazon